Willful Parties

by

Liz Ellyn

Willful Parties

Contact Information: info@thewildrosepress.com

Cover Art by *Lisa Dawn MacDonald*

The Wild Rose Press, Inc.
PO Box 708
Adams Basin, NY 14410-0708
Visit us at www.thewildrosepress.com

Publishing History
First Edition, 2025
Trade Paperback ISBN: 978-1-5092-5850-5
Digital ISBN 978-1-5092-5851-2

Published in the United States of America

Dedication

To expanding the possibilities of love, where compersion is embraced and love flourishes.

Chapter 1

Seth

Seth slammed the car door harder than necessary. The impact reverberated in his head as his parents drove off into the bustling Chicago traffic without looking back at him. He stood abandoned on the sidewalk. Their refusal to celebrate his law school graduation with his friends at Lawson's Bar soured the triumph of his immense accomplishment.

Shaking his head, Seth turned away from the empty, prime parking spot on the street and faced the entrance of the pub. He steeled his shoulders, willed the negative feelings away, and focused on making the most of the important night.

Seth entered the traditional Irish bar, his home away from home, and grinned. Hundreds of balloons floated in the side room. The bright purple color shouted like an exuberant mob at a college football game in contrast to the low-key, subdued tones of the bar frequented by attorneys working in the Chicago loop.

The cheers and laughter of his former classmates rang out over the otherwise quiet Sunday crowd sitting in the central area. He caught some admiring looks and reflexively returned a delighted smile. As he strolled toward the smaller party room, he stopped and acknowledged every one he knew along his path. He hugged all his friends lightheartedly and awarded a congratulatory kiss on each person's cheek.

Once he found Kat standing by the temporary drink station, his smile turned mischievous. He lengthened his stride and closed in on her. Like everyone else, Seth kissed Kat on the cheek. But damn, those lips of hers beckoned him every time he saw her. Her bold red lipstick tempted him to cave into his desire and plant a kiss on her.

But Kat preferred to keep her private life quiet and he respected her concerns. Seth refrained from swooping in for a kiss in front of their friends and her father, who remained in the dark about their relationship. They had kept their romantic involvement on the down-low for the past three years of law school.

Despite her desire for discretion, Seth grasped each of Kat's hands, held out her arms flamboyantly, and checked her out from head to toe. Her little black dress clung to her thin frame. Her appearance defined natural beauty with her fair skin, dark hair, and minimal makeup. She looked like a modern-day version of the elegant movie star of the fifties. Seth fixated on her striking red lips and conjured images of those lush beauties wrapped around his cock. "Damn Kat. I had no idea you were wearing *that* under your graduation robe. You look stunning." His whole body gravitated toward her. He wanted to kiss those enticing lips.

Seth's gaze lingered. Normally, she wore jeans and a button-down or a basic long-sleeve t-shirt. Occasionally, during law school, he had seen her dressed in a business suit for court but then she appeared austere. In the little black dress, she was feminine and magnificently radiant. He fought back his carnal desires, gave her a friendly embrace, and whispered in her ear, "You are fucking ravishing."

Kat smiled, tucking her head off to the side. She never took compliments well.

Mr. Lawson, Kat's dad and owner of the bar, interrupted the intimate moment between them. "Congratulations." Mr. Lawson embraced Seth in a full-bodied bear hug. Seth welcomed the affection but angled his body away, hiding the evidence of how attracted he was to the man's daughter.

"It's a big day. I'm so happy for you. And I'm so proud of my little girl." Mr. Lawson sported a huge smile and thrust his chest outward like a proud papa.

Seth appreciated Mr. Lawson's enthusiasm for celebrating this momentous accomplishment. He had personal knowledge regarding the magnitude of the sacrifices Mr. Lawson endured financing Kat's law school tuition as he had assisted Mr. Lawson with his accounting over the past couple of years.

Kat plucked at the purple graduation hood hanging on her shoulders. "He's so proud, he insisted I keep wearing this."

"Now all the other attorneys here can see that *my* daughter is a law school graduate too." Mr. Lawson beamed.

"Purple suits you. Why not wear it? And, you match the balloons." Seth smiled while sexy images from the other night of Kat dressed in a purple bra and matching thong flashed in his mind.

"And look at you in blue. Your suit matches your smiling blue eyes. Of course, you do it knowingly." Kat teased with a lascivious smile. "The black graduation gown looked all kinds of wrong on you. The only blue was the small triangle of your necktie peeking through."

"I tried convincing the university to change color schemes to suit my eyes but I obviously failed to make a convincing argument." Seth elicited a laugh from both Mr. Lawson and Kat.

"Did your parents come with you, tonight?" Mr. Lawson asked.

Seth hid his disappointment. "No, they don't like to deviate from their normal routine. You know, boring accountants." Seth could see the sympathy in Kat's eyes, but he would have preferred a hug. She was lucky to have such a supportive father. He wished he did too.

Changing the topic, Seth asked Mr. Lawson, "Did my little surprise for Smirnova arrive?"

"What surprise?" Kat interrupted and glared at Seth and her dad.

"It's all ready when you are." Mr. Lawson ignored Kat and pointed behind the bar, reassuring Seth.

"Thanks, I appreciate it."

"*Hello*. What surprise?" Kat nudged her dad's shoulder.

"I love you, but you could never keep a secret." Mr. Lawson looked away.

"Dad, I'm not five years old anymore. I think I can keep a secret. You know I'm going to be liable for holding client information confidential." She leveled her dad with a fierce stare.

Seth knew Kat could keep a secret. The true reason for the secrecy of their relationship finally arrived at the bar. In walked Dylan, the other third in their throuple. No one besides the three of them knew about their threesome.

Dylan made quite the entrance as he stood at six feet

three inches with a million-dollar smile. Doctors of orthodontics everywhere should have studied his mouth to best customize teeth. His commanding presence made all parts of Seth take notice. Seth wanted to run his fingers through Dylan's perfectly jelled-back, dark hair and tousle it into a sexy mess.

As Seth and Kat remained stationary, Mr. Lawson welcomed Dylan with an extended hand. "Congratulations Mr. President-elect."

Dylan laughed. "Thank you. Mr. President? Heh. My parents would like the sound of that. They're currently at some political fundraiser in California."

Dylan leaned in and graced Kat's cheek with a demure kiss. "You're gorgeous, Kat." He gazed longer than necessary at Kat and tipped his head to the side like a confused dog. "Why are you still wearing the hood from the graduation ceremony?"

"Because I told her to keep it on," Mr. Lawson piped up. Dylan didn't question him, as Kat always followed anything her father told her to do. Seth's toes curled in his shoes at his pitiful envy of Kat's close relationship with her dad, which cemented following her mother's death. Seth forced himself to smile.

Staring up at Dylan's strikingly handsome face transformed Seth's small grin into a full-fledged smile from ear to ear. "Congrats to you, Mr. President." Seth hugged Dylan and kissed him on the cheek like everyone else. He continued with more than a bro hug, but stopped short of calling unnecessary attention to them. "You do look very presidential today in your suit."

"Thanks, but seeing as I'm getting on a plane tomorrow, let's avoid any unnerving comparisons to certain political families."

"You've got my vote." Kat grinned.

"I appreciate your show of support, Kat." Dylan turned his polished smile on Seth. "How might I win your vote?"

With a devilish smile, Seth said, "I'm sure I can come up with something." Many ideas came to his mind. Most of them involved them both being naked. The thought created a growing problem in his suit pants. However, at the top of Seth's list, Dylan would change his career plans, which included moving to California.

Mr. Lawson said, "If you move back here to Chicago, you've got my vote. We need more decent people like you to clean up the corrupt politics."

"Thanks, Mr. Lawson."

Thoughts of Dylan heading off to California made Seth's heart hurt, but it cured the problem in his pants. He needed to get his mind off Dylan's miserable impending departure. "It's time for a round."

"I'll be right back." Mr. Larson headed behind his bar and grabbed a few glasses. He didn't bother asking what everyone wanted to order. He had served them throughout law school and knew everyone's preferences.

Kat intently eye-fucked Seth and Dylan while her father busied himself behind the bar.

"If you keep looking at us with lust-filled eyes, we are going to have to leave this party immediately, even if your father isn't done celebrating your big day." Seth winked.

"Have some patience, you two," Dylan chastised as he stared at Seth's lips.

"It was easier to hide when we all were in the library focused on studying. Constitutional law sucked all the sexual energy out of me," said Seth.

"I thought I did that." Dylan raised a knowing eyebrow.

"The jury would like to see that evidence again," Seth flirted.

"Can I be the judge?" Kat's eyes lit up.

Mr. Lawson returned with three classic old-fashioned drinks. Seth took a sip. "Kat, your old-fashioned is great, but I think your dad still has an edge on you behind the bar."

"Soon, Kat will be too busy to mix drinks. She will be knocking people's socks off in court," said Mr. Lawson. Kat cast her gaze down at the floor.

Dylan took a sip and asked Mr. Lawson, "You're not drinking with us?"

"Not tonight," Mr. Lawson mumbled with a quirk on his face. His joyful expression returned as he raised his glass of water. "To my amazing daughter and her two great friends on making it through the past three years. May you have all the happiness and luck life can hold."

They all took a long sip. "I'm sure your parents are just as proud as I am."

Dylan rolled his eyes. "Their lack of appearance may suggest otherwise."

"You are on your way to clerking for a federal judge in California. That's incredibly impressive. Of course, they're proud. I'm sure they are telling everyone about it."

The flex of the small muscles in Dylan's cheek exposed his clenched jaw.

"And Seth, your parents, like myself, have been plotting and planning this educational feat for years. Now you're starting an entire legal group in their firm."

"We're just jealous we can't have a cool dad like

Kat." Seth buried his pain.

"I'm lucky to have the greatest dad." Kat gave her dad an extra hug.

Dylan said, "And we are extraordinarily lucky her dad taught her excellent bartending skills. She makes some great drinks." Mr. Lawson beamed.

Cole bounded over. "Code vodka! Code vodka! She's here."

Seth, Cole, and Dylan dashed around the corner of the bar and each grabbed several bottles and handed them out to their friends, except Kat.

Kat frowned and shook her head at Seth. She murmured, "I'm glad you didn't include me in your little conspiracy."

Seth smiled nonetheless, all too pleased with the idea.

When their friend entered the party area, everyone hoisted the bottles of vodka in the air. "Congrats Smirnov…" They all dropped the vowel at the end of Smirnova's name, imitating their first-year professor.

Cole reached Smirnova first, hoisted her in the air, and swung her around in a huge hug.

"Was this your idea, Cole?"

"Absolutely. Pun intended." Even Smirnova laughed.

"Thanks, Cole."

Seth bit his tongue and didn't correct Cole. The idea was initially Seth's, but Cole was the only one in the group who wouldn't think twice about dropping the money on the vodka solely for a joke.

Mr. Lawson approached her and gave her a one-armed hug as she was struggling to carry the bottles of vodka. "Congratulations to my favorite Smirnova."

"Thank you, Mr. Lawson."

"Would you like me to put all those bottles somewhere for you?" Mr. Lawson unloaded the bottles out of her arms.

"Thank you. You're always looking out for me. I told my dad back in Russia you are my American dad."

As soon as she had set down the bottles in her arms, Seth and Dylan popped up beside her, on opposite sides, kissed her on her cheek, and handed her two more bottles. Smirnova blushed. Either all the attention embarrassed her or the affections of two incredibly hot men had triggered some very naughty thoughts.

Kat approached with sympathy in her eyes. "I'm sorry. I had no idea these idiots were planning a vodka attack."

"You know we all love you, right?" Cole hugged her again.

Smirnova smiled and shook it off. "Looks like I'm set on vodka for the rest of my life."

Mr. Lawson put a hand on Cole's back. "Back in the day, your dad was quite the jokester."

"You mean he wasn't always a stodgy asshole?" Cole quirked the side of his mouth.

"I could tell you a story or two, but you know about that bartender-patron confidentiality agreement. I can't reveal any details." Mr. Lawson mimicked locking his mouth with a key and throwing it away.

"Really? That wasn't my ethics class?" Kat narrowed her eyes at her dad.

"That's because it's a business school thing, not law school."

Kellie and Carter came over and handed another bottle to Smirnova.

Seth cut them off before they could say anything. "Double congratulations!" Seth kissed Kellie on the cheek. "There's one kiss for you and another for the baby on its way."

A hand on Seth's arm restrained him. "Don't even think about kissing my wife again." Carter halted Seth.

Instead, Seth turned toward Carter and kissed him on the mouth. Addressing Kellie's enlarged baby-filled belly, Seth stage-whispered, "Your daddy seems to be jealous of not having all the attention. Careful when you get out of there."

"But seriously, congrats to both of you." Seth's warm tone radiated sincerity and concealed his envy for the love the couple shared. Seth marveled at Kellie and Carter's hands entwined together in everyone's view.

Carter patted Seth's back, forgiving Seth's joke. "Congrats to you too, man. Are we going to see you at the bar review classes?"

A collective groan rolled through all the graduates. Despite it being graduation day, the dreaded bar exam was at the forefront of everyone's mind. A law degree meant nothing unless they passed the bar exam in two months. Without passing the exam, they couldn't practice law. Several of their classmates had job offers, which would be rescinded if they didn't pass. Failure would financially cripple some, but it would humiliate all.

"I need to take the classes at night so I can help at my parents' accounting firm during the day. They helped pay for law school, so I need to work off the debt." Despite the exceptional inconvenience posed by his parents, Seth maintained his genuine smile.

"I can't imagine taking classes at night. This baby is

making me so tired; I can't keep my eyes open past eight o'clock." Kellie stifled a yawn.

"Well, you don't look tired. You are glowing." Seth opened his hands and fingers like a flower blooming.

"Thanks, Seth." Kellie patted her belly.

She asked Kat, "What about you? Will you be taking classes during the day?"

"Yeah. I'm going to be working here at night."

Carter poked at Dylan. "I suppose you aren't worried at all. Everyone knows you are a walking-talking treatise as editor-in-chief of the law review."

"You've got to be kidding," Dylan deflected, rubbing at his chin. "I have to take the California test. It's the most difficult bar exam in the country." Dylan presented himself in a poised manner but worked crazy hard behind closed doors. He worked like a synchronized swimmer, beautiful above water and hustling beneath the surface. Seth had witnessed the hours of extra work he put in to remain at the top of the class.

Dylan pointed to Cole. "He doesn't need to worry at all. After his clerkship, he will be working for Daddy." Dylan tossed back his drink.

"Fuck off, Dylan. If I don't pass, my father would personally castrate me for embarrassing him." Cole glowered at Dylan.

A few waitresses came by with trays full of tequila shots and offered them to all the graduates. One waitress pointed to a group of young attorneys who acknowledged the onlooking graduates by raising similar glasses. "The table of people over there sent these over here with a message." She pulled out a napkin with a scribbled note. "Congrats on graduating. Enjoy the moment. If you thought law school and studying for the bar were competitive, just wait until you start working." The graduates laughed and threw back the shots.

By 10:00 p.m., early by bar standards, Mr. Lawson excused himself from the party. Kat's eyebrows drew together as she watched him walk toward his apartment above the bar. Seth put an arm around Kat. "He's probably emotionally exhausted from today. He's been waiting for this for a long time."

Kat nodded. "You're right." She smiled and mouthed the words thank you.

Kellie leaned against Carter with her eyes drooping closed. She and Carter bailed on the party next.

Dylan excused himself and stepped away from the group. Seth shot Kat an apologetic look. "Be right back." Seth left Kat on her own and followed Dylan.

Seth didn't want to miss a single moment with Dylan. Time ticked until Dylan set off for California. Seth relished every minute.

He caught the swinging door of the bathroom before it closed behind Dylan. Dylan turned around and his eyes filled with rapture. Ignoring their surroundings, Dylan yanked Seth into an intense kiss. Their lips locked hard. Dylan held Seth's face between his firm hands and clung to Seth. Despite Dylan's strong façade, he leaned on Seth. Dylan sucked at Seth's mouth like Seth was his salvation.

A cough broke their moment. A guy stood in the open doorway. "Hey. Can I get past?"

Dylan growled. "Yeah, sorry man." He stepped aside and washed his hands in cold water.

Seth almost smiled in amusement at the situation as he never felt embarrassment. But the interruption irritated his straining hard-on.

Upon returning, Seth caught Smirnova chatting with Kat. Seth and Dylan refrained from intruding on her girl time, as Kat didn't have many close female friends. Seth stood within earshot behind Smirnova, eavesdropping.

Smirnova stood with her back to Seth and Dylan. "Oh. My. Fucking. God. I just saw the hottest fucking thing ever. Seth and Dylan were kissing in the bathroom as I passed by."

Seth froze. He didn't want Smirnova to out he and Dylan as a couple. Seth never corrected people's assumption that he was gay. And Dylan had admitted to dating men. In either case, none of the descriptions were entirely accurate, as Kat was sleeping with both Seth and Dylan.

Seth locked eyes with Kat as she responded, "I think Seth has kissed every single graduate at this party tonight." Kat shrugged her shoulders and waved away the impression.

Seth nodded affirmatively at Kat's logical response.

Smirnova grabbed Kat's shoulders and leaned closer. "No. It wasn't some quick peck on the cheek or even a friendly kiss on the mouth. They were *totally* going at it. They're both fucking hot. The two of them together…they were on fire."

Seth agreed wholeheartedly. He felt a burning need when he was with Dylan. Dylan inched toward the women, but Seth held him back. He saw the confidence in Kat's eyes, indicating she had their backs.

Kat cocked an eyebrow. "Damn, I wish I could have seen it too. But I don't think they would want us talking about it with anyone else." Seth sniggered quietly.

"Oh, I won't. But I had to tell you." Smirnova tittered.

Seth and Dylan intruded into Kat and Smirnova's space. Smirnova turned red. He hoped, she kept her mouth shut. At least she didn't bring it up again the rest of the night. The next day, everyone would be focused on studying for the bar and consumed in their own lives.

As Lawson's Bar neared closing time, Dylan peered at the group of his friends. "Do you guys remember our very first lecture on the first day of law school? The professor had warned us about attorneys falling victim to alcohol and drug addiction." Dylan nodded toward all the inebriated people. "I hope he was exaggerating."

Seth wanted to kiss Dylan as he respected his genuine concern for society.

"I'm not on closing duty tonight. You guys ready to get out of here?" Kat threw a smoldering glance at both Seth and Dylan.

"Hell yes." Seth quirked a smile.

"Let's go." Dylan's deep voice lit a fire within Seth.

The music on the radio filled the silence during their ten-minute drive from the Loop to Streeterville. The lack of conversation gave Seth exactly what he didn't want, time to think. Dylan heading to California was going to cause the collapse of their triad. A three-legged table couldn't remain standing after removing a leg. The impact of their crash was sure to result in internal injuries. With each passing moment, the weight of their impending future pressed down on him and cloaked him in a shroud of doom.

How long would it take for Kat and Dylan to finally realize that they would never find a relationship better than the one they already shared?

Chapter 2

Dylan

All of Dylan's muscles relaxed as he entered the lobby of the seventy-floor building. For him, his condo wasn't just a place to lay his head, it offered him the privacy to drop his perfectly manicured façade and be himself. No one dared look at anyone sideways in the building. The incredible piece of real estate even housed a larger-than-life talk show host. The property officially belonged to Dylan's grandparents, but Dylan made an informal agreement with them in exchange for the right to live in the lavish condo. Each month, Dylan joined his grandparents for dinner in the suburbs. As much as Dylan delighted in the comforts of the condo, he cherished the relationship with his grandparents even more.

He unlocked his dark, silent home. The only illumination came from the faint glimmer of city lights reflecting on the ripples in Lake Michigan thirty-one floors below. He turned on a small light on the foyer table, casting a warm glow on the beautiful people by his side. In the dim light, he hid from the stark reality he was about to be separated from two exceedingly important people in his life.

Kat stepped toward the floor-to-ceiling windows and paused as she gazed out into the darkness. "I'm going to miss this view."

"I can't believe you have been depriving us of this view for the past few years." Dylan caught Seth in his peripheral vision staring at Kat as well.

"Huh?" Kat turned back around and faced the two men.

"You look gorgeous in this sexy little dress." Dylan raked his eyes up and down her tiny body.

Kat fidgeted.

"Oh no you don't," Dylan said. He took a step closer. "Don't you dare shy away from our compliments."

"And don't you do that chick thing where you act self-conscious about your body." Kat glowered at Seth, as his remark hitting close to the mark.

She fiddled with her dress.

"I understand if you feel less comfortable dressed up, I felt the same way when my parents made me dress up for all of my dad's political events." She smiled back at Dylan, confirming his suspicions. "I adore you in your jeans and tees. But the woman before us is glamorous. You've been hiding *this* woman." Dylan's stare lingered as he loosened his tie.

She embodied conventional standards of beauty. While more thin than curvy, she exuded femininity. Dylan didn't claim an interest in a particular type of woman. No other woman had ever made him turn his head, but he got lost in explicit thoughts while admiring Kat.

Seth's breathing intensified. As a long-distance runner, his quickened heart rate and breathing signaled he was equally aroused as Dylan. "I want to see the woman under the dress. The sexy as fuck woman with the LBD on the floor beside her." The sound of desperation in Seth's voice made Dylan hard.

"Don't be ill-bred, Seth. We should place the nice dress across the chair, out of the way. It would be a shame getting cum all over it."

Kat laughed. "If I don't take the dress off soon, the cum running down my thigh is going to ruin my dress."

"Your panties will protect the dress," Seth countered.

"Damn! That's what I forgot." Kat winked.

With a glint in his eyes, Dylan smirked at Kat's playfulness. He continued to remove his tie, followed by his suit jacket. He reached inside his pants pocket and pulled out his phone. Turning on the night-mode option on his camera, he snapped a quick photo of Kat. "I might not get a chance to see you dressed up like this again. Soon, you'll be wearing conservative suits every day to court."

"Get a good photo?" Seth drew closer to Kat.

"Oh yeah."

"Excellent. Let's get you out of the dress." Seth twirled Kat around and unzipped her, exposing her pale skin inch by inch.

The hum of the tiny little plastic teeth separating left Dylan buzzing. He seized on the opportunity. While Seth busied himself with her zipper, Dylan flew in and kissed Kat soundly. He tasted appreciation in the kiss. It wasn't gentle, but assertive. It thrilled and stoked a fire inside him.

She stepped out of the dress and Seth set it aside.

"Commando." Dylan approved of her choice.

"And ready for action." Kat punctuated her corroboration with a searing kiss.

Dylan broke away first and turned to Seth. “As for you, you look stunning in a well-fitted suit, but I’ve seen it many times. It’s time to get you out of it.” Dylan loosened Seth’s tie as he kissed him. It started out slowly but quickly escalated. Dylan detected urgency in the way Seth ground his lips against his own.

Kat stepped behind Seth, sandwiching him between herself and Dylan. With her heels on, her lips reached the back of Seth’s neck. He shivered as she brushed her nose along the sensitive skin behind his ear. The vibration travel through Seth’s body. The shared sensation intensified Dylan’s desire.

He pulled on the two ends of Seth’s tie until their bodies aligned like matching puzzle pieces. He deepened the kiss. Dylan’s muscles tightened like he was working out at the gym. He gripped Seth like a vise around metal. Then Seth tangled his fingers into Dylan’s thick dark hair. “Oh God,” Dylan groaned. The attraction between them had their chests pinned together. Seth’s ribs heaved in and out against Dylan’s front. Dylan ached to hang on forever.

Dylan’s eyes popped open wide as Seth broke away from his embrace. He found Seth craning his neck and torso forward to reach him, but his arms extended backward. When Kat finished tearing off Seth’s jacket, Dylan yanked him back closer.

Between kisses, Dylan ordered Kat, “Shirts. Off. Now.”

Kat wiggled her fingers between the men, pried their chests apart, and started unbuttoning each of their shirts. She began at the top and worked her way down, button by button. Her thumbs fumbled between the collision of manly chests. Her hands danced at the top of their slacks.

Their pelvises grinding together. She slid her palms along each of their lengths until Seth and Dylan's moans filled the room.

"Fuck this." Seth yanked his shirttails from his pants, undid the buttons at his wrists, and threw the garment to the side.

Dylan mirrored Seth's frantic undressing. His cufflinks clinked on the marble floor as the platinum studs bounced away.

"In a hurry, boys?" Kat laughed.

"Yeah. My dick is like steel and I fucking want you both." Dylan's patience vanished.

"You need to work on your laid-back California attitude," Kat teased Dylan.

Seth took a step backward and the brightness in his blue eyes dimmed. Although Kat made the comment, Dylan cursed himself for causing Seth pain by moving to California. Dylan found himself powerless in altering the decision or influencing Seth's emotions, but he could take full advantage of the final night with Seth and Kat.

Kat lifted her palm to Seth's cheek. "Let's not rush tonight. Let's focus on now. The three of us."

Regardless of the looming despair, they had a few hours left. Dylan intended to make the most of it. He recognized the significance of the moment. The evening might mark the last time they would ever be together as a trio.

"Seth," Dylan whispered. Seth faced him. Dylan went mute. Instead, he ran his skilled fingers through Seth's blond waves. Dylan held back his feelings and remained silent. He stared into those pleading baby blues. He yearned to express his longing for Seth's company, yet hesitated, wary of adding to the already complicated situation.

Dylan didn't think trying to keep up a long-distance relationship would be productive for any of them. Extended distances required a lot of energy, which none of them would have an excess of while starting their new careers. Instead, Dylan hid his unease about moving to California.

Seth peered at Dylan, his Adam's apple bobbing. The wordless communication made Dylan's head and heart ache. Dylan kissed Seth passionately, attempting to convey all of his unsaid thoughts. The heat between Seth and Dylan surged.

Kat murmured, "Fuck. Smirnova was right. The two of you kissing is fucking hot." Her hand wandered over Dylan's shirtless body and down his abs.

Her knuckles rubbed against his cock as she stroked Seth. Hunger and lust took hold in Seth's eyes once again. Those eyes and his tousled blond hair made him sexy as sin.

Kat raked her fingernails down Dylan's side. A shiver went straight to his dick. Dylan refused to be a greedy asshole. Kat deserved attention. He broke the sexual tension by biting Seth's lip with the power to sting.

Seth adjusted his response. "Stand by the window, Kat." The glass facing the lake didn't afford possible voyeurs a glimpse inside the condo, but provided the sensual suggestion of being exposed. They never violated the rule of exposing their relationship, but dancing along the line provided a tantalizing thrill.

Kat's pale skin created a perfect, erotic silhouette against the darkness of the windows. "We need to capture this image." Seth's voice sounded strained and gravelly.

"Noooo," Kat breathed.

"No photo, no worries. I'll never forget this picture." Dylan committed the vision to memory.

Simultaneously, Dylan and Seth removed their slacks. Her pupils dilated as she gawked at the pair. "Damn. You two are fucking incredible. If you don't pass the bar, you should consider stripping for a living."

Time suspended as they each gazed in appreciation of each other.

Seth and Dylan stalked closer to Kat. The men first alternated kissing her. While Dylan engaged in a lip lock with Kat, Seth kissed Dylan on the neck. And when Seth was tongue-tied with Kat, Dylan began stroking Seth's length. Their hands, mouths, and tongues became a tangled web. Each reaching for more. Wanting more of each other. Taking and giving in equal measure. Moaning and gasping in pleasure.

While Seth and Dylan shared a deep kiss, Kat dropped to her knees, alternating orally satisfying each man. She stroked and sucked until one groaned and then switched her attention to the other. The mix of agony and ecstasy drove Dylan mad.

He bent down and lifted Kat to a standing position and spun her around, pressing her front up against the floor-to-ceiling window. She shrieked as the glass chilled her firm nipples. Seth held her hands above her head while Dylan inserted his fingers in her core and fondled her clit. Dylan abruptly stopped. "Feel the cold against the flame burning inside. That frustrating duality is what we experience when you alternate edging each of us."

"Fuuuuuck!" Kat screamed.

"Fuck is right, baby," Seth growled.

"Please. I need to come." Dylan delighted in her whimpering desire.

"We all need to come, baby. But we're going to come together tonight."

Dylan had a strong hunch about what Seth intended. This wasn't a night of exploration or improvisation. They all deserved the best sex. Dylan stepped aside and returned with a bottle of lube and condoms in one palm. His other hand fisted his cock, thoroughly lubricating it from base to tip. Seth and Kat watched as Dylan's powerful grip lathered his firm, lengthy shaft.

"Fuck." Seth and Kat sighed.

Dylan smirked. He enjoyed their rapt eyes focused on him. Then handed a foil packet to Seth.

While rolling on the condom, Seth directed Kat toward the couch. "Sit on the arm." Seth playfully pushed her backward so her shoulders rested on the seat but her legs remained draped over the arm. He tugged on her legs until they rested on his shoulders. "Damn, baby."

Dylan maneuvered himself behind Seth and yanked on his lush hair. "Hey, lean over." Dylan brushed his nose along the shell of Seth's ear. "Taste our girl." Seth lapped at Kat's opening and swirled his tongue around her clit. The sweet and spicy scent of Kat's arousal filled the air.

Dylan pressed his lube-coated finger into Seth's tight entrance.

"Mmmmm." Seth hummed and pushed back, begging for more.

Kat whined, "Please, please. I can't wait any longer."

Dylan gritted his teeth together. "I can't, either."

Seth lined himself up against Kat's entrance and plunged inside. "You are so warm and tight. Fuck."

"Deeper Seth," Dylan said. Seth leaned over Kat, pushing her legs backward.

Dylan slapped Seth's exposed ass as a signal to still himself. Dylan pressed inside Seth's well-prepared opening, pausing until Seth relaxed and his body accommodated his presence. A couple of deep breaths later, Seth began to thrust his hips. As Seth slid in and out of Kat, Dylan stroked in and out of Seth. The men moved like dancers, synching their rhythm.

"Harder," Kat begged. Dylan aimed to please by fucking Seth deeper, thrusting in long, quick motions.

Seth readjusted his angle and Dylan shoved Seth against Kat.

"Fuck." Kat and Seth groaned in harmony when Dylan rammed all the way into Seth.

Dylan repeated the slow deep penetration until the instinct to increase the pace took over. He stretched his arm around Seth and found Kat's clit with his fingertip.

"Yes! Yes! Yes!" Kat cried out.

"She's close Dylan. I can feel her core gripping me tighter." Seth let out a guttural cry.

"Come for us, Kat!" As if Dylan's intense deep voice had physically touched her, she flew apart.

"Oh God." Her body trembled.

As soon as the first wail escaped her mouth, Seth fucked her as hard and thoroughly as Dylan pounded into his ass. The sound of flesh slapping flesh blended with their moans and shouts.

"Fuck!"

"Fuck!"

"Fuck!"

"Ohhhhh." Sighs spluttered amidst their pounding hearts.

Dylan let all his weight rest on top of Seth. Dylan could feel Seth's gasping breaths against his own heaving chest. "Fuck. That was so good."

"Hell yes. I think we destroyed Seth." Kat strained beneath the weight of both Seth and Dylan.

Seth didn't respond.

Dylan kissed Seth's neck. "Seth, you okay?"

"Amazing," he murmured.

"Good. Who is joining me in the bathroom?" Dylan stood beside their collapsed bodies and offered a hand to Seth and Kat. Seth rolled over and Kat accepted Dylan's proffered hand.

Seth meandered over toward the massive windows, staring out onto the water. "I'll be there in a second."

Dylan and Kat took a quick shower and dried off. Kat yawned and set off toward the bedroom. Dylan found Seth still gazing out the window. "Come on Seth. Wash up and come to bed with us."

"Us," Seth whispered then closed his eyes.

Dylan placed a gentle kiss on Seth's cheek. The hint of salt clung to his lips. Was it Seth's perspiration or was it tears? Dylan cupped Seth's face. "Please." When pleading with his eyes failed, he tugged on Seth's hand until Seth acquiesced. At the entrance to the bathroom, Dylan kissed Seth once again. "Hurry up."

"Sure."

By the time Seth returned to the bedroom, Kat had already fallen asleep with her head resting on Dylan's chest. Seth eased into the bed and saddled up beside Dylan. Seth placed a gentle kiss on Dylan's lips.

"Goodnight." Dylan's heart constricted as soon as the word escaped his mouth. The sentiment felt too similar to goodbye. He pinched his eyes closed and willed away the tears.

He concentrated on Seth's leg wrapped around his own. His lean muscular leg hugged him. On his other side, Kat nuzzled her head on his chest like an affectionate cat showing love. Together, Kat and Seth pinned him down in the bed. Dylan's pulse quickened. The realization hit him with the force of a freight train. Their possessive touch epitomized their hold on his heart.

Dylan fought sleep and appreciated every last second in bed with Seth and Kat. Kat's rhythmic breathing sounded similar to a purring cat and eventually lulled him into unconsciousness.

The alarm screeched. The incessant annoyance forced them awake. Kat reached out and silenced the wretched device. She turned and snuggled closer.

"Don't get all cozy again. I need to get to the airport." Dylan attempted to sit up.

Seth pushed his chest back down, preventing him from sitting upright. "Don't get out of bed." Seth smiled and straddled Dylan.

Dylan grinned at the gorgeous man on top of him, tempting him to remain in Chicago. "I can't miss my flight. I must attend my parent's event tonight. They made it clear that skipping it isn't an option." Dylan tried sitting up again, but Kat kissed him until she broke his need to flee. His resolve weakened.

Seth shifted to the side and wrapped his fingers around Dylan's cock. "You didn't think we were going to let you leave without a proper goodbye?"

Before Dylan could object, Kat glided down toward the foot of the bed so her head was mere inches away from Dylan's already-stiffening length. Her warm breath blew across the crown.

Seth released his grip and grabbed the bedside bottle of lube. Kat and Seth pushed and pulled together until Dylan lay on his side. With Seth behind Dylan, Dylan moved his leg forward, providing Seth full access to his star-shaped entrance.

The expectation of Seth's expert touch made his cock grow long and thick. His eyes fell shut as the desire to come consumed his thoughts.

Kat's lush mouth encased his needy cock and his back arched as a sense of urgency surged up his spine.

"Oh fuck, yes." He relaxed into the merciless onslaught of Kat's tongue. The addition of Seth's expert fingers stroking his prostate heightened the experience. Urgency shifted to inevitability. The buzz of an orgasm took seed. A slow burn morphed into a tingling sensation. A flashback to all the incredible times he shared with Kat and Seth in bed sent him uncontrollably over the edge.

He didn't move. He shut his eyes and considered upending his plans. *Maybe he should stay in Chicago?*

Kat pulled him back to the present with a kiss. "Let's go, Mr. President. Your California constituents await." Dylan appreciated Kat's never-ending support as she repeated her father's previous praise.

Seth bent over Dylan's face. Their eyes locked they reaffirmed their unyielding connection, without needing to say anything. They may never have the chance to share in such a relationship again, but their friendship would last forever. Seth sealed the bond with a sincere kiss, but Dylan's heart sank.

After grabbing a quick shower, he stared out the window and enjoyed the view for the final time. In the daylight, he could see for miles. The blue sky and gray water matched their state of affairs. Brilliant careers awaited on the horizon for all three of them, but the end of their voyage together was deep and dreary.

Kat laced her fingers with Dylan's, reassuring him. "We have been incredibly lucky to have had this wonderful relationship. For that, I'm beyond grateful. With a little more luck, fortune will continue to be on our sides."

Dylan sought the support of their third.

Seth rubbed at his neck and bit his lip. He looked like he wanted to say something, but kept it inside.

Dylan reached for Seth's hand. "Okay, I'm packed and ready to go. Still willing to drive me out to the airport?"

Kat answered for Seth. "Of course. Seth's car is in the garage."

The quiet in the sedan nagged at Dylan's insides. Departing from the security of law school and his lovers rattled him. Over the years, his parents had proved to be devoid of emotional support.

Moving from Chicago to San Francisco meant putting a 2,000-mile divide between the three of them filled with barren plains and insurmountable mountains. With too many obligations, flying back and forth wasn't an option.

He tried to diffuse the bubble of nerves brewing inside him. "You guys should follow me to California. The weather is way better than here. No snow. No humidity. Hardly any rain." He knew Seth and Kat's family commitments were as important to them, and they couldn't leave. They too, faced the next steps in life all on their own.

"That would be nice. And we could continue as friends with benefits." Kat tossed in her positivity from the back seat of the car.

"Exactly! That movie was all wrong. Who says friends with benefits can only last a few months? We lasted nearly three years."

Seth remained quiet.

Dylan revealed one of his many vulnerabilities. "I'm truly going to miss studying with you guys this summer. I hope the Cali bar doesn't kick my ass."

"You made law review, we didn't. You don't need either of our help," said Kat.

"I might not need help making outlines, but I am going to miss you guys. Having two people I can trust." Dylan's voice trailed off, not finishing his thought.

"We will always be here for you."

Seth didn't corroborate Kat's offer.

Not only did Dylan fear venturing out on his own, but he also worried about being left out. "Well, you two can still study together and fuck like rabbits." He failed to mask his envy with his flippant comment.

"We have opposite schedules, so we won't be able to study together." Seth rubbed at his neck with one hand while he continued to drive.

Where was Seth's sense of humor?

"Kat, you could try wearing a strap-on."

Seth's head snapped toward Dylan. "Don't be a dick, Dylan!" Seth focused again on the road as his knuckles glowed white against the black steering wheel.

"Sorry." Dylan cringed. He overstepped and felt

sick to his stomach for mocking Seth's bisexuality. He slouched in the passenger seat and closed his eyes.

"You still don't get it. Being bisexual doesn't mean twice the fun. It's double the disapproval."

"It was a shitty thing to say. I'm really sorry." Dylan berated himself for sticking his foot in his mouth.

As the peacemaker, Kat, tried her best to smooth things over. "I don't want you to leave on a bitter note. We all have a lot of stress heading our way with commitments to our families and studying our asses off. Let's all be grateful for how lucky we were to find each other." After Kat lost her mom, she internalized the notion of celebrating memories of loved ones rather than crying over their loss.

"You're right." Dylan chastised himself for acting like an impertinent teenager. *What was wrong with him?* They stayed silent for the rest of the drive.

Seth stopped the car in the departures section of the airport and helped Dylan grab all his luggage from the trunk. Otherwise, he remained speechless. He gripped Dylan's face and kissed him firmly and possessively.

Dylan looked into Seth's moist eyes and a lump formed in his throat. Rather than saying something stupid again, Dylan pressed his lips against Seth's for one last taste.

Kat broke them apart and hugged Dylan. "I'm so proud of you. You're going to do great." Dylan gulped back his emotion. He pecked Kat on the mouth a single last time before picking up his luggage and heading inside the airport. He paused before entering the terminal and watched Seth and Kat drive off.

While waiting at the gate, Dylan shot Seth a text.

Dylan—*I'm sorry for being a dick—*

Dylan smiled when Seth replied.

Seth—*You are a dick (winky face)*—

The tension in Dylan's shoulders eased.

Seth—*But I happen to like you and your dick (kissing smiley face)*—

He let out a breath he hadn't realized he was holding.

Dylan—*Hopefully you and Kat can still maintain friends with benefits*—

Seth—*Nah. She shut it down during the car ride back home. She apologized for not being polyamorous and said she refused to "restrain my sexuality"*—

Dylan—*Fuck*—

Seth—*Completely cock blocked me*—

Dylan—*TBH I'm surprised by her response*—

Seth—*I'm not. Most girls can't handle me also dating men*—

Dylan considered what a pain in the ass it would be to date women. Women always seemed very high maintenance to him.

Dylan—*Kat isn't like any other woman I have ever met*—

Seth—*She's one of a kind and so are you*—

Dylan—*(heart) Time to board the plane (kissing smiley face)*—

He shut off his phone. His eyes closed.

The screech of the brakes reminded him of his surroundings. He had slept the entire flight. The emotional roller coaster of the previous day had zapped all his energy. His adrenaline surged while giving the graduation speech, but his parents' absence deflated his high. While the plane taxied to the gate, he yawned.

He turned off airplane mode on his phone and

checked his messages. Dylan smiled at the eggplant emoji from Seth. His smile faltered when he read the next message.

Mom—*I'm too busy to pick you up. Order a rideshare to the house. You need to be ready by 4 for photos. There's a new suit on your bed.*—

He sighed at the unaffectionate welcome home.

Dylan leaned back in his seat and closed his eyes. Kat and Seth hadn't shoved him into a car by himself. They made the trek all the way out to the airport. He could feel Seth's chest up against his as he hugged him goodbye. Recalling the entirety of his morning, the affectionate hug topped the list. The embrace even surpassed their sexy gift in bed.

His phone chimed with a message from Kat.

Kat—*XOXO (four-leaf clover and smiling hug)*—

The tightness in his heart eased.

Dylan—*Just landed. Thanks for the Cali welcome (kissing face)*—

Chapter 3

Kat

The large auditorium appeared unremarkable. Row after row of padded stadium seats with flip-up tabletops. Entering from the rear doors, Kat descended the steps and proceeded to the front, where her friends sat during their law school classes. She scanned the first few rows, but they were nowhere to be seen. All the unfamiliar faces left an unsettling feeling.

Her stomach roiled. She chewed on the inner part of her cheek. It was the only chewing she had done all morning. All the tension in her body prevented her from choking down a single bite. She threw her full bowl of cereal in the sink.

Now she reached into her backpack and grabbed her phone. A soft voice from behind pulled her from her panic. "Hi Kat, come sit with us." Kat turned around and found Kellie and Carter sitting in the rear row along the aisle.

She had breezed right past without noticing. "Oh hey, what are you guys doing way back here?"

Kellie patted her pregnant belly. "Easy access for a quick escape. I doubt my bladder can hold out for an entire lecture."

"Besides, there's no need for sucking up to professors anymore. The bar exam is anonymous."

Carter took Kellie's hand and diverted the attention away from her needs.

Kat crept past Kellie and Carter and sat down. She shot a text to Alex before getting out her computer.

Kat—*sitting in back row, saved you a seat*—

Alex—*(thumbs up) CU in 5*—

Carter reached out his hand and halted Cole from getting lost in the theater. "Cole? I didn't expect to see you here. I thought you were taking the New York bar."

"New York and Illinois have reciprocity. My dad wanted me to take the Illinois bar."

"Why are you doing a clerkship in New York instead of here?" Kellie asked.

"Strategic choice for my dad's firm. It's probably the same reason Dylan is out in California." Cole sat down in the row in front of Kat.

Kat closed her eyes at the mention of Dylan's name. The queasiness in her stomach returned.

Alex walked in next. Cole put his hands on each side of his mouth and theatrically shouted, "Smirnov…"

She folded her arms across her chest. "You call me that one more time this summer, then I'm going to refer to you as Mr. Kensington the Fourth."

Cole held up his hands in surrender. "I'll pass on that one. How's Alex?"

"Perfect." Alex made her way down the row and sat next to Kat.

Cole turned around and faced Kat. "Where's Seth?"

Kat remained quiet while Kellie explained he was attending classes at night. Kat's stomach did a complete somersault. A chilling shiver ran down her spine.

The professor took his spot at the lectern and pulled Kat from her misery. With all her attention on taking notes, her brain diverted her focus away from the pain in her heart. As long as she focused on the bar material, she safeguarded herself from the negativity clouding her mind.

Several hours later and Kellie's two trips to the restroom, the class concluded. Kat and her friends exited the auditorium. She stood by the front doors of the school and watched her friends ascend the main, oversized staircase leading to the cafeteria. They planned to grab food and claim a table in the library. They moved as a pack, determined to conquer the bar exam together.

But Kat remained alone. She bailed on her friends because her dad asked for her help during the lunch rush at Lawson's Bar.

She stepped out the door and released a cleansing breath. Instead of inhaling a big dose of calm, a strong breeze smacked her in the face. She turned away and curled her body protectively. A dark sky loomed above. She pulled out her umbrella from her back and readied herself. She picked up her pace.

Heavy, oversize raindrops plopped on Kat's head. She opened her umbrella, but a mighty wind whipped around and inverted it. While attempting to fix it, the metal supports broke. She tossed the useless device in a nearby trashcan.

The springtime sky grew darker. Despite her best attempt, Kat failed to reach Lawson's before the clouds unleashed a clothes-drenching amount of rain. The wind blew so hard the raindrops attacked her from above and from the side. She didn't bother sneaking into a café and waiting out the storm. Her dad needed her. Instead, Kat persevered. By the time she arrived at Lawson's, her hair looked like she had just stepped out of the bathroom shower and her soaked clothes clung to her body. Luckily, her excellent waterproof backpack kept her computer and notes for the law exam safeguarded.

Kat scurried inside the main door of the pub. She shivered from head to foot as the air conditioning assaulted her. Making a quick detour to the apartment above, changed into dry clothes and hurried back down.

She crossed paths with her dad, with three serving plates in his arms. Her dad only carried food when the bar was crowded. He slowed his steps as he passed her. "Thanks for coming in to help. Can you jump back there and fill orders?"

"Sure." Her dad continued walking away.

Kat tied an apron around her waist and joined the other bartender. "Hey Josie, how can I help?"

"I need two chardonnays, a bottle of the new IPA, one old-fashioned, and a vodka cranberry." Kat repeated the order for clarification and filled it.

Josie handed a credit card tablet to a couple sitting at the bar and then efficiently turned to another person with an empty plate. "Are you done?" Josie snatched away the dirty dishes.

Kat and Josie skirted a collision with one another. "Kat, can you take these?" She took the plates out of Josie's hands and dumped them in the kitchen. She returned behind the bar and cleaned until Josie stopped her. "I need a tray of fifteen shots of tequila."

Kat's jaw dropped open. "It's not even noon yet!" *Dylan was right to worry about our friends' drinking habits.* She lined up the glasses and poured the clear liquid. She loaded a bowl with slices of lime and placed it all on a serving tray.

A server picked up the tray. "Can I get four lemon

drops?" She walked off without an answer.

Kat's brow furrowed and tapped Josie on the shoulder. "Are those on the menu?"

"No, but people always order whatever they want. Don't worry. I got this one."

Her dad approached Kat. "*'Bout ye* bus the tables?"

Kat grabbed a tub and circled the bar, and cleared the tables.

By 2:30 p.m. only a handful of patrons remained, and the staff had everything under control. Kat took advantage of the lull.

She retreated to the unit above the pub where her father lived. She lacked any spare time to run back to the library and study with her friends. His apartment couldn't measure up to the gorgeous library at the law school, but at least its construction included excellent sound insulation. Her dad used to rent out the space to law school students. Maybe the ghosts of previous renters would serve as her study buddies instead of her friends.

Kat didn't bother knocking before sticking her key in the handle. Surprisingly, the door was unlocked. She found her dad in his reclining chair, leaning back, with his eyes shut. She narrowed her eyes. Normally, he never took a break and engaged in endless conversation with his patrons.

Despite her best efforts at locking the door quietly, the deadbolt squeaked.

"Kat?" Mr. Larson rubbed his eyes and blinked several times.

"Sorry. I thought I would study before the next rush downstairs."

"Great idea. I was just grabbing a power nap. I'll get

out of your way. I've got a long list of things to do." Her dad lumbered from his chair.

"Lunch was almost as crazy as happy hour."

"Yeah. It's good for the bottom line."

"I bet. I'll be down in a couple of hours." Kat cracked open her book at the kitchen table and grabbed a highlighter. She crammed as much legal information into her head as possible during her brief window of opportunity.

During happy hour, Kat predominantly worked behind the bar. She was quick and capable as long as customers ordered drinks listed on the menu. Kat poured bourbon and lemon juice into a shaker and lined up the other ingredients for a whiskey sour.

Her dad clapped his hand on the customer's shoulder who waited for his drink. "My daughter here is going to be a member of the Illinois Bar just like you."

Kat's stomach sank. *What if she didn't pass?* She placed the man's cocktail on a paper napkin.

He took a sip. "Congratulations. That's fantastic." She forced a smile on her face.

After the early evening rush, she headed back to her apartment. She opened her study materials and yawned. She read a few sentences but, her dry eyes begged for relief. Without any breaks since the early morning, she struggled to remain awake.

The red glowing numbers on her clock burned into her thoughts like a devilish distraction. Seth's bar review class had ended. Did he stay to study in the library? Did he go home? Was he hooking up with someone he met in the class? Although he was born in Chicago and lived his entire life in the Midwest, he sported a California look. His vibe attracted lots of attention, both men and women. And, he was single.

Kat moaned.

Memories of her, Dylan, and Seth fooling around after study sessions danced in her thoughts. Their fun ritual balanced out the stress of studying. Her musings aroused her as well as stung. The absence of both guys made her heart ache.

Kat's head dropped to the table with a thud. Why had she forced Seth away? *Of course, he's hooking up with some guy. Or girl.*

A groan escaped her lips.

She had no one to blame but herself. She'd told Seth she wasn't interested in continuing a relationship. Although she thought about reaching out, she didn't want to *interrupt* him.

Picking at her cuticles. she reached out to Dylan instead of wallowing alone.

Kat—*How's the Cali sun treating you?—*

Dylan—*Hey Kitty-Kat (smiley face with sunglasses)—*

Kat smirked at Dylan's new endearment. She wondered if it had to do with her name or the fact she was the only woman he had had an intimate relationship.

Kat—*Things going well?—*

Dylan's life appeared easy to most people, as his family had lots of money. But with the fortune came a great deal of responsibility and high expectations.

Dylan—*Weather's great. Not complaining—*

Kat—*Really?! Did you switch careers and become a meteorologist? What's up?—*

Kat refused to allow Dylan to slink away from their friendship because of the distance. Even if they weren't together anymore, they shared a serious bond.

Dylan—*My family isn't easy*—

Kat—*How so?*—

She might not be able to relate as she got along well with her dad, but Dylan needed a friend to confide.

Dylan—*They're frosty (snowman)*—

Kat—*How is that possible in the Cali heat? (melting smiley face)*—

Dylan—*That's SoCal, not NorCal. I'm their circus monkey. I only get fed if I perform*—

The way Dylan accepted his position made the hair on Kat's neck stand on end.

Dylan's sculpted body and chiseled face captured people's attention. Only the fortunate cracked him open and got access to the affectionate core. Kat counted herself lucky to be among the select few.

Kat—*You deserve better*—

Dylan—*(heart) How did your first day go?*—

Kat—*Not bad*—

Dylan—*???*—

Kat smiled. Neither she nor Dylan allowed one another to put on a fictitious front.

Kat—*Difficult studying all on my own*—

Dylan—*You CAN do this. You WILL pass!*—

She wanted to believe Dylan. If only she shared his confidence in her ability to pass the bar. The desire to please her dad and make him proud motivated her each day.

Kat—*(fingers crossed)*—

Dylan—*If you have questions, call me*—

Kat—*Thanks*—

She had lots of resources for studying. Knowing Dylan offered her support as a friend strengthened her self-assuredness. She released some of the tension in her muscles.

Dylan—It's late there—

Kat—*Yeah, I should get some sleep—*

Dylan—*(kissing face)—*

Kat paused and considered her response. Rather than fixating on the choice of emoji, she returned the same.

She missed Dylan's kisses. And Seth's kisses. And fooling around with them after they studied. It was easy. It was convenient. More than that, it was amazing. *Could she manage the insanely stressful process of studying for the bar without them?*

The next morning, Kat woke up somewhat refreshed. While brewing her coffee, she crossed off yesterday's square on her wall calendar. One step closer to the dreaded two-day bar exam, which she had marked with black frowny faces in late July.

By Father's Day weekend, her routine became a daily grind. Fears about the exam littered her dreams at night, leaving her fatigued each morning. When her morning coffee failed to invigorate her, she hopped in the shower and prayed the water jump-started her mind and body. She squirted a dollop of her apple-scented shampoo into her hand. It smelled like fall, which triggered looming thoughts of the fast-approaching test date. Massaging conditioner into her hair didn't calm her nerves. Instead, her mind raced. She rinsed and shut off the water. Evidence of her stress settled in her drain. If she failed to manage her anxiety better, she would be bald by the time of the exam.

Her busy schedule intensified her continuous anxiety about preparing sufficiently. Despite her frayed nerves, she didn't blame her dad. She preferred panic and pressure over disappointing her family. *How could she cram in more study hours into the next month and a half when working at the bar cut into her review time and wore her down?*

Saturday night brought in a busy and animated crowd to the bar. Most of her orders were simple like straight liquor or wine, which she filled swiftly. She spent her spare time listening in on conversations where the patrons discussed legal concerns. Kat tested her knowledge by deriving her own arguments as an additional form of studying for the bar exam.

Her dad caught her. "So, counselor, what's your take on the issue?"

Kat blushed but shared her opinion with her dad.

"I always knew you were going to be a smart attorney."

"Thanks, Dad. I remember when you used to ask me similar questions when I was younger."

"Where do you think I got the questions from? From eavesdropping, like you." Her dad winked and begged off toward his office.

Out of her peripheral vision, Kat noticed someone seated at the end of the bar. She wiped her hands on a dry towel and headed over to take their order.

Damn, he looked good. A smile exploded on her face and a warmth spread through her entire body. His artfully sculpted blond hair made him look like he stepped off of a modeling runway rather than walking around the Chicago loop. Those sparkling blue eyes lit up the bar. Seth was a sight for sore eyes.

She glided up to the end of the bar. "Hello there, my sexy stranger. It's good to see you."

"Making my weekly rounds."

Had the six out of the seven days of the week by herself blinded her from noticing and appreciating Seth's Saturday night ritual? "Can I get you the usual?"

"Thanks."

Kat filled a pint for Seth and walked the drink back over to him. He wore a shit-eating grin as he focused on his phone.

"Watching porn on your phone again?" Kat raised her eyebrow.

"Yeah, I was checking out those links you sent me. Damn, Kat. I didn't realize you had such a dark side."

Kat cackled. The customer beside Seth blanched, not appreciating their sarcastic joking. Seth appeared unphased and immune from embarrassment.

"I was looking at the pic Dylan posted this morning."

"I didn't see it." When did she have time to thumb through social media? "I need to chop up more garnishes. I'll be back in a bit."

Kat sliced the lemons and limes into wedges and wheels. The scent of fresh citrus reminded her of lemon trees growing in California. Kat continued cutting, but then yanked her hand away. The sting hurt like a bitch. She checked her fingers for a nick. No blood, thank goodness. She washed off the acidic juices under cool water. Never before had she been bothered by the routine task, even during the cold Chicago winters, when her hands were dry and cracked. Something else must have caused her unusual sensitivity.

Kat recognized the laugh coming from the end of the bar. She needed a laugh, deciding to join her best friend. "What's so funny?"

Still laughing, Alex caught her breath. "This hot guy

tells me he's your official Saturday night cock blocker. He's here to fend off all of the men from hitting on you."

Out of nowhere, Mr. Larson appeared and patted Seth firmly on the back. "Good job, Seth. Keep up the good work."

Mr. Lawson turned to Alex. "Are you coming tomorrow for Father's Day?"

"I wouldn't miss it."

"Great." Mr. Lawson turned back to Seth. "Is there any chance I could steal you away for a few minutes? I have a question in my office."

"Sure thing." Seth finished off his beer, set the empty glass down, and pointed to Alex. "Hold my seat and don't let any men approach Kat while I'm gone." He winked.

"No problem." Alex blushed.

"What can I get you to drink?" Kat asked Alex before needing to help another customer.

"White wine. Thanks." Kat appreciated Alex's simple order.

When Kat placed the glass in front of Alex, she turned her phone around to show Kat. "Did you see Dylan's post? He looks damn fine. It must have been golden-hour when he took it. The leaves are gleaming with a yellow glow and highlight his face."

Kat leaned in closer for a better view. "Yeah. You're right."

Alex leaned in across the bar and whispered, "I still haven't gotten over the sight of Dylan and Seth kissing."

A pain shot through Kat's fingers again. She clenched her hand into a fist.

"Yeah, I bet it was insanely hot." Kat flushed.

"Speaking of hot, why is Seth slaying away all the

good-looking guys like they are dragons? If he's gay, why would he care?"

Kat chewed on her lip instead of correcting Alex's incorrect assumption about Seth's sexuality. However, the question intrigued Kat. They weren't seeing each other. She had made it clear he was free to date anyone else. Why was he spending his Saturday nights at Lawson's? She hadn't seen him leave with somebody at closing time, neither man nor woman.

"It doesn't matter. I don't have the time or energy to hook up with a guy." Kat rolled her eyes.

"I hear ya. My vibrator and I are quite close these days." Alex sipped her wine.

Kat smiled wistfully. "Heh." She leered at the bar's office door.

"You okay Kat? It has to be tough studying, making nice with customers, and generally busting your ass."

She deflected from the uncomfortable topic. "We all need a party when this test is done."

"Definitely! With lots of available men. Maybe then we can both find ourselves a warm body to replace the electric devices."

One of the waitresses handed Kat a piece of paper. She glanced at the order and looked toward Alex. "Fruity duty calls." The waitresses overloaded Kat with drink orders until the bar closed. Most of the requests involved time-consuming mixed drinks, which didn't leave room for chatting with Seth or Alex.

During the brief lull before Kat needed to kick out all the customers, she grabbed three tequila-filled shot glasses, slices of lime, and salt. She set the small tray in front of Seth and Alex. "Okay, time to shoot and scoot."

While Alex poured the salt on her hand, Seth stared

heatedly at Kat with a saucy smile on his face. Kat cast her gaze to the side and fought the instinct to flirt back with Seth.

She snuck a peek at Seth under her eyelashes as he licked the salt off his hand. She closed her eyes, but the memory of Seth bending her backward over the couch played like a movie in her thoughts. A twinge of pleasure struck between her legs. The burn of the tequila did not remove the image.

Those blue eyes almost made her cave and change her mind. Her will weakened. Giving in to her needs guaranteed a fun, erotic night, but risked a broken heart. Knowing Seth enjoyed the company of men and women didn't bother Kat. It was hot! But sharing him with other men, other than Dylan, inflamed her Irish temper. Green was a great color on St. Patrick's Day, not as an emotional state.

Kat looked away and grabbed the empty shot glasses. "And now it is time for you two to scoot on out of here."

"Goodnight Kat. I'll see you tomorrow. I hope your dad likes what I got him for Father's Day."

"I'm sure he'll love it."

Seth kissed Kat on the cheek. The kiss lasted longer than a peck. She debated turning her head and kissing Seth on the mouth. By the time she swiveled her head in Seth's direction, the touch of his lips disappeared. Her stomach tightened. "Goodnight Kat."

"Thanks for stopping by."

Kat began cleaning up behind the bar. She placed the cut-up lemon slices in a container to store overnight.

A hand on her shoulder stopped her. "I've got this. Go home and get some rest. I know you have been burning the candle at both ends."

"You sure, Dad?"

"Get out of here! I'll see you tomorrow."

"Thanks."

Kat walked back to her apartment and collapsed onto her bed. "Yessss." Her body sunk into the mattress, but her brain continued to buzz. Seth's devilish smile had gotten under her skin.

She unlocked her social media app and mindlessly swiped through posts. Had she scrolled too quickly and missed the photo of Dylan? She opened his profile page, but the image was gone. "What the…?" Kat liked the photograph and planned on saving it. She texted him instead.

Kat—*What happened to the hot pic you posted earlier today?*—

Dylan—*My dad's PR team made me take it down because I wore the outfit in a commercial*—

Kat—*Damn, I wanted to save it*—

Dylan messaged her a copy.

She saved it to her phone. His cheerful expression offered her reassurance. People can smile even when things aren't perfect. And, well, he was fucking hot. His chiseled jaw defined manly perfection.

Kat—*(red heart) It's late, I need to crash*—

Dylan—*(smiley face with heart eyes)*—

Chapter 4

Seth

He entered his spotless apartment. The plumped pillows lay atop the bed with blankets smoothed to military precision. No dirty laundry interrupted the traffic flow on the wooden floor. The sink sparkled and the dishwasher was empty. Everything settled in its proper location.

Since graduation, Seth had spent many of his anxious moments organizing. Without Dylan and Kat filling him and his time, he needed to release his surplus nervous energy. Unfortunately, the tidiness didn't provide a sense of comfort. The immaculate state of the place projected lifelessness.

The faint aroma of cleaning supplies offended Seth's senses. He still craved Kat's scent, which he captured during his goodnight kiss with her. Hints of rugged earthliness mixed with wildflowers clung to her skin. The memory of her inviting fragrance clashed with his sterile apartment. She enveloped him in a sense of warmth and vitality, whereas his home reeked of loneliness.

Fatigue washed through Seth. All night he had itched to hurdle over the bar and kiss Kat's pouty red lips. For the past six Saturdays since graduation, he had planted himself in the same seat and analyzed how her mouth conveyed different expressions. Seth longed for the days when they engaged in a titillating dance of flirting while concealing feelings for each other in public. Kat's new summertime frosty manner challenged Seth's persistence.

Discouraged, he trudged toward the bathroom, washed up, and brushed his teeth. He stared in the mirror. "Hang in there. They'll come around." *Great. Talking to yourself?* His lack of sex threatened his sanity.

In bed, Seth pulled up the photo he had recently saved earlier that night. Dylan's sun-kissed skin looked scrumptious. The thought of licking his way up Dylan's neck made Seth's mouth water. Seth burned to claim Dylan's face between his hands and sear their lips together.

Scrolling back further, Seth found the picture of Kat on graduation night. Her statuesque pose captivated him. He considered printing out a copy, framing it, and placing it next to his bed. Kat had mentioned how lucky they were to have enjoyed an amazing relationship. Seth agreed with Kat about being fortunate, but she lacked the experience to appreciate the extent of their fortune. They shared a once-in-a-lifetime love, even though no one used *that* four-letter word. Seth fought the tears bubbling in his vision.

He tossed his phone to the side. He didn't need the visual images on the device The memory of Dylan and Kat's beauty, scent, and touch stayed with him, ingrained in his brain. Closing his eyes, he conjured the taste of their kiss, the erotic vision of Kat's lips wrapped around his cock, and the feel of the tight grip of Dylan's sheathed teeth sliding up and down his length. Fuck. Seth's cock hardened in his hand. The flashback of them both, together, tonguing his balls, pushed Seth to the brink of release. Streams of cum jettisoned onto his naked chest.

The warm cum turned cold and uncomfortable on his skin. Wiping it off with a nearby tissue rubbed him the wrong way. The frigid sensation remained because the chill lingered within his heart.

Seth considered calling Dylan in hopes his deep masculine voice would melt away the bitterness surrounding him. It wasn't an unreasonable time to call, as Dylan was two hours behind. Seth held the phone in his palm, debating. "Fuck it." Seth dialed.

Dylan answered, "Hey, handsome. What are you up to?"

"Jacking off."

"Mmm. Can I watch?"

"Already finished."

"Damn. Want to watch me?"

Seth hadn't expected the conversation to head in such a direction. He didn't know how to answer. Pounding on a solid wood door broke the momentary silence. Muffled words followed.

"Sorry, I need to go talk to my dad. Raincheck?"

Seth played it off as a rhetorical question.

After a silent beat, Dylan asked, "You okay, Seth?"

"Of course. It was good to hear your voice. Let's catch up another time."

"Sure thing." And Dylan was gone once again.

The next morning, Seth woke up in the middle of the bed with his arms and legs spread out like a starfish, his blankets tossed every which way. All his muscles ached as if he suffered from a hangover, but he fell asleep nearly sober. The coolness of the sheets surrounding him emphasized the absence of their warm bodies enveloping him.

Seth glanced at his calendar and rolled his eyes. His dad had bought him a ticket for the baseball game. Since it was Father's Day, Seth couldn't refuse. He enjoyed attending games, but his dad's habit of over sharing statistics annoyed the fuck out of him.

The silver lining of sitting at the ballpark with his dad included a fresh Chicago dog. Contemplating the high-caloric indulgence, Seth dragged his ass out of bed and readied himself for a well-paced ten-kilometer run.

Seth checked a weather app. No need for a shirt. In a hurry, he threw on some lightweight shorts and laced up his running shoes. He shuffled through several songs on the warm-up play-list he created during his cross-country days during college. As he strode toward the lakefront, he dodged people on the crowded sidewalk.

With the sandy shoreline in sight, Seth stopped and stretched his hamstrings. He shut off his music and soaked in the repetitive sound of the water crashing against the boulders along the water's edge. He set off northward on the wide concrete path. Seth pushed harder during the second half of his loop.

The architectural marvel where Dylan lived jutted out beside the curve along the waterfront. He increased his pace, putting the building and the reminder of his time with Dylan and Kat out of his line of sight.

With the fountain in view, he sprinted to his finish line.

Seth bent over. His chest heaved in and out, while he checked his stats and smiled. By forcing his body to stand straight and lacing his fingers behind his head, he opened up his ribcage for more air. He walked aimlessly for a couple of minutes until he regained a normal breathing rate.

His legs recovered during his walk back to his apartment. Unfortunately, the burn in his muscles only served as a temporary distraction from the ache in his heart.

Seth stepped into the shower. He tried washing away his loneliness. When that didn't work, he considered other soothing, more visceral, options. With his eyes closed and his head leaning backward, the water rained down his naked body. The pulsing drops massaged his scalp. His soapy hands caressed his face, his neck, his chest, and his lower abs.

His hand brushed against his stiff cock. The need for relief prodded him. He wrapped his fingers around his length with the same intensity as Dylan's grip. Seth mimicked the movement and embraced the memory of Dylan's deep, coaxing voice. *"You like this? Me stroking your cock? Slowing and speeding up? I'm not going to let you come until you beg me. Then I'm going to fuck you hard and deep and make you come as I fill you with my cock."*

Seth's moans echoed against the tile walls. He rested his forearm on the cool tile and leaned his head and weight against his supporting arm. With his eyes closed, he dreamed of Kat's kisses on his neck. The lightness of her touch contrasted with the firmness of Dylan's grip. Seth's control began to slip. His desire intensified.

His hand sped up as he neared orgasm. The ache began at the bottom of his spine and proceeded to his balls. His muscles flexed. His breath became quick and ragged. "Yes, yes, yes," he chanted. His release sprayed against the tile walls, and his body convulsed in aftershocks. "Fuck." He closed his eyes and took pleasure in the tingling bliss blanketing him.

Was this the only way he could keep Dylan and Kat close to him? Fortunately, for his sake, he stored lots of memories in his vault.

With a towel wrapped around his waist, Seth applied styling gel to his damp hair. He put extra effort into looking good, because the walk between the train station and the stadium went through in a vibrant neighborhood filled with rainbow flags fluttering in the breeze.

He admired the rest of his body in the mirror. He managed to keep himself lean by running and watching what he ate. He scrutinized his shoulders. The muscular delineation was clear, but when he compared himself to Dylan, he looked thin. He lacked Dylan's mass and strength. He needed to hit the gym, lift weights, and bulk up, but he didn't have the time between working and studying.

With sufficient manipulation, Seth stylized his hair to perfection. The blue shirt he chose for the day both highlighted his eyes and showed team spirit. He put on some khaki shorts and completed the outfit with a matching brown belt and shoes.

Having time to spare, he sat down with his review guides before he met up with his dad for the game. Father's Day or not, his mom's plan impinged on his study time. She didn't appreciate how a baseball game, lasting several hours, impacted him. On top of studying, he put in over forty hours a week at his parents' accounting firm. None of that stopped his mom. The power of her guilt knew no bounds.

He cracked open his bar review materials. The topic of the day was trusts and estates, a subject he knew well based on his accounting degree and years working at his parent's firm.

His phone rang. It was Kat. He assumed she needed help with the subject.

"Hey, sweetheart."

"Why the hell are you not coming today?"

He considered flippantly answering he just had. He frowned. He lost the right to tease her like that, anymore. At least he still maintained that level of friendliness with Dylan.

"My dad told me you aren't coming over for Father's Day. I didn't even think to ask you last night. You always stop by. What the hell?"

Seth smiled. Her tone made it clear she was ticked off. He didn't want her upset, but he liked knowing his absence made her Irish flare.

"Take a breath, Kat. I told your dad last night I wouldn't be able to make it. I'm going to the baseball game with my dad."

"Oh."

"Trust me, I would swing by if I could. Hanging out with your dad is a lot more fun than mine."

"True. At least you can get a Chicago dog at the game. I'm salivating at the thought." Kat moaned a little and Seth's dick reacted.

"I'm totally in it for the hot dog and beer. Are you working today?"

"Nah. We are expecting it to be quiet at the bar, which is great because I could really use the extra time to study. Alex is going to drop by and then we'll head to the library after brunch. You should stop by after the game. If you want. Or, if you aren't otherwise occupied after you walk your sexy-ass body through a crowd of

20,000."

Seth scowled and rubbed his forehead with his hand. Kat's insinuation that he picked up people everywhere he went bugged him. He realized that all the crap she saw at the bar had skewed her opinion of men. Particularly, seeing men hooking up all the time. But he hadn't. Why didn't she see that? He spent the past six Saturday nights in her pub, alone.

"Been keeping an eye on the state of my ass? Good to know. I don't have eyes in the back of my head." If she hadn't been thinking about his backside before, he placed it at the forefront of her mind.

"You don't need me to check out your ass. I'm sure you were admiring it in the mirror when you got dressed today."

"Touché." Kat knew him well. His vanity wasn't a secret.

"I'll text you after the game and see if you and Alex are still interested in studying." Seth set out to prove Kat wrong about him hooking up. Even if he didn't need to study today's particular topic, he would show up. He didn't want anyone besides Kat and Dylan.

"Have fun at the game."

"Thanks. Wish your dad a happy Father's Day for me. Talk later."

Seth hung up and banged his phone on the table. "Ahhh." He threw his hands in the air. He cursed her assumptions about him. *What was wrong with her?* Was there a different reason she didn't want to continue a relationship with him?

Without enough time to calm down after speaking with Kat, Seth met his parents at their home in Lincoln Park. His mother insisted on serving them breakfast before he and his dad set off for the game. She failed to understand the point of going to a game wasn't simply about watching nine innings of baseball. It was a total experience, which included the food, the crowd, and the comradery.

She claimed the food at the stadium was overpriced and unhealthy and therefore completely unnecessary. His dad agreed with his mom, but would sneak the good stuff behind her back. On the other hand, the money created a trickier situation. Having two accountants for parents meant every penny in the household was meticulously tracked. His mom would know if his dad, according to her perception, wasted money frivolously on food at the stadium. Thus, Seth and his father conspired together. Seth paid for the food, but they both kept their mouths shut about their indulgences.

Seth and his dad missed a lot of the intense traffic by taking the early L train. He slid on his shades as he and his dad stepped down the metal stairs from the train platform to the street. With his eyes concealed, Seth checked out all the attractive people along the ten-minute walk to the stadium. He flirtatiously smiled back at the men and women ogling him.

While waiting in line at the stadium entrance, his father leaned in close to Seth. "You do catch the eye of numerous young men. I think you get it from me."

Seth raised an eyebrow. Was his father about to come out of the closet?

"I mean, I used to attract a lot of women back in my day."

"Ahhh. Like father, like son." Seth smiled outwardly. Internally, he laughed his ass off at the true similarity. His father and mother had no idea he was bisexual. Seth counted himself lucky his parents supported him when he came out as gay during high school. They told him they loved him and they were there for him no matter what, whether he dated boys or girls.

After passing through security, Seth's dad directed them down toward their seats. They descended each concrete step until they reached the seats just behind the first base line.

"Wow, I can't believe mom sprung for such amazing seats." Seth appreciated the fantastic view.

His dad eased into the seat. "We're finally done paying for college and law school. Now, we can splurge on nicer things for ourselves." He turned back to the field.

Seth's brows pulled together, uncertain of the appropriate response. Was he supposed to be forever grateful his parents paid for his education? He had already repaid them with summers of work and years as an accountant. After he passed the bar, he would contribute even more to their firm.

Changing the subject, Seth asked, "Want me to go grab us some hot dogs before the game starts?"

"Yes. I pretended to eat your mom's brunch. I saved room for a true Chicago dog. Need an extra hand?" His dad maneuvered to reach for his wallet. Had he forgotten their arrangement?

Seth shook off his dad with his hand. "No worries. I got it. Beer?"

"Let's wait until after we finish eating."

Seth waited in the long line, drooling as the vendor filled others' orders. The aroma teased his tastebuds. Finally, he reached the counter. The checkout person handed him two fully loaded hot dogs. Before heading back to his seat, he set both of the overflowing, paper-serving boats down on a nearby bar table. Seth took a photo of the hot dogs with all the fixings: bright green relish, chopped onion, tomato wedges, pickle spear, sport peppers, yellow mustard, and topped with celery salt. He texted the photo to Dylan and captioned it, "Love a huge wiener."

He carefully shuffled back to his seat, making sure not a single sport pepper fell along the way. He sat beside his dad, and they ate in companionable silence. Seth's phone vibrated with a message. With a hot dog in hand, Seth ignored his phone.

After a mouthful, Seth said, "Why is it these hot dogs taste even better at the stadium?"

His dad swallowed. "Be it here or at any hot dog joint, they all taste good to me. With your mom micromanaging what I eat, I hardly ever get to have a hot dog. Thank you, again."

"Sure thing."

His dad narrowed his gaze on the pocket. "You aren't going to check the message you got on your phone?"

"It can wait until after I finish. I think your generation has a Pavlov dog response issue with running to answer phones."

"Maybe." His dad gazed at him.

Seth and his dad continued to savor the food.

His dad thumbed through the brochure and rattled off statistics. Seth tried to ignore it as much as possible. When it came to baseball, Seth kept it simple. Watch, cheer, eat, drink, and repeat.

He checked his phone.

Dylan—*Come on man. Teasing me with a Chicago dog is cruel*—

Seth—*You don't enjoy being teased? (smiling devil)*—

Dylan—*Only when I eventually get what I want*—

Seth—*What would you want right now?*—

Dylan—*To get teleported away so I don't have to attend another political event for my dad*—

Hoping for a fun, dirty response, he took it upon himself to cheer up his friend.

Seth—*Teleportation might be beyond what I can offer, but there is an international airport close by. I would be more than happy to give you door-to-door pick-up service. Anytime*—

Dylan—*Time to go kiss some babies*—

Who else was Dylan kissing? The image of Dylan with a California model didn't settle well.

Seth—*(Taking-off Airplane)*—

He added a praying hand emoji, but then erased it.

"Beer here! Beer here!" the vendor chanted.

Perfect timing. Seth needed to wash down the hot dog and purge away thoughts of Dylan with another man. He got up out of his seat and bought a couple of beers.

The home team started out strong in the first inning. They knocked in a few runs, which had the crowd up on their feet screaming. At the bottom of the third, the home team hit a foul ball in Seth's direction. The added netting prevented the ball from careening into the stands.

"Darn, that would have been fun to have caught a foul ball."

Seth turned in the direction of the feminine voice beside him. She must have snuck into the seat next to him when he was on his feet cheering along with the rest of the crowd. Immediately, the woman ticked off his boxes. She looked to be about thirty, well put together, designer clothes, and upscale sunglasses.

"If I caught it, I would have given it to you. At a price, of course." Seth winked.

"At what price?" She pursed her lips.

"A fresh beer to replace the one I would have dropped to catch the ball." His charm never failed.

"That seems like a fair deal."

A crack of wood smacking into cowhide grabbed Seth's attention. He turned toward the action on the field. The ball soared toward the wall in left field. The crowd roared. The announcer's voice boomed, "It's going. It's going. It's gone, baby. Home run!" Cheers filled the stadium.

"I'm glad lady luck is on our team today." The beautiful brunette snagged a piece of popcorn from the box in her hand.

"Maybe you'll get lucky at the game too."

Her jaw popped open.

Seth let the double entendre hang in the air for a moment. "And you'll get a fun prize in your box of caramel-coated popcorn and peanuts."

She laughed. "Actually, the company replaced the toys with QR codes. I don't care. There's something nostalgic about this treat. Makes me think of stories my grandpa would share about coming to games as a child."

"Are you a traditional girl? The mojito at your side says different."

"I may be sentimental, but it doesn't mean I can't go both ways." She took a long sip of her drink. "You know, modern and traditional."

"Nope, nothing wrong with going both ways." He

wholeheartedly agreed.

After she and her friend beside her finished their drinks, they set out in search of a restroom.

Seth's dad elbowed him. "It's impolite to hit on a woman when you have no interest in them. It's misleading."

The rebuke stung. Seth bit his tongue and didn't respond. He crossed his arms and ground his teeth. *What the hell?* He wanted to argue with his misguided father. *When did being friendly become rude?*

Seth ordered several more beers during the rest of the game.

At the conclusion, he stood up and wobbled. The beer hit him harder than expected.

He messaged Kat. He didn't want her pissed at him for blowing her off. But more than that, he didn't want her to assume he was hooking up with someone else. His stomach churned. He frowned. Those closest to him didn't understand him. His fingers fumbled on the keypad.

Seth—*Drunk. Sorry, can't study*—

Kat—*U okay? Getting drunk isn't your thing*—

Seth—*Neither is hooking up with random people*—

He let her read between the lines of his message. He awaited her response.

Kat—*I know*—

Seth—*Do you?!*—

Kat—*Yes*—

He snorted. He didn't believe her. She didn't get it. His heart felt heavy.

Kat—*I'm sorry if I hurt your feelings*—

Her crack about hooking up wasn't funny. If Smirnova had made a similar comment, he wouldn't be upset. He owned his flirtatious personality. Kat's sarcastic remark reiterated her perceived concern about him *needing* to date other men. Her crappy attempt at humor didn't hurt his feelings. It broke his heart. She used it as an excuse to pull away from him. Friendship was nice, but he wanted more. He missed their intimacy and not just the sexual kind.

Kat—*XOXO (three red hearts)*—

Unfortunately, Seth understood her position. He had heard similar concerns from other women in his past. Kat was unique, as she could share with Dylan. She drew the line at accepting a metamour in her life. She opposed the idea of Seth having another partner. *How could he prove he didn't want to look for anyone else?* Seth loved Kat for what she could offer. While he grasped her unwillingness, it left him wounded.

Seth—*(kissing heart eyes)*—

Chapter 5

Dylan

He opened an email from his father. It wasn't actually from his father, but rather from his father's assistant. The email contained a schedule for the entire weekend, with details of all the times and dress code that Dylan was expected to follow.

"Fuck!" Dylan had constructed an entire strategy for getting ahead in his studies. In a single email, his dad shot his plan to hell. He leaned forward with his elbows on the desk and rested his head in his hands. He massaged his temples as he tried to find an alternate time to get his work done. Heat emanated from his cheeks. "Fuck." He grunted and his head thudded onto the desk.

A couple of days later, his alarm blared before the sun rose. He groaned. Did he get to sleep in on Saturday morning like a normal human? No. Even the birds weren't singing yet. Opening his eyes at such an ungodly hour was a struggle for him. He groaned again, wiping the sleep from his eyes and his hands over his stubbled chin. He forced his feet to the floor and slid out of bed. With not enough time to shower and shave, he brushed his teeth and threw on some casual clothes.

He arrived promptly at his 4:00 a.m. call time. After hair and make-up, one of the many assistants handed him a pair of beige tactical pants, brand new brown boots, a neutral-colored, button-down shirt, and a dark green vest. Was he supposed to blend into the scenery in these clothes? Probably. His opinions were also largely overshadowed. Dylan donned the clothes set out for him like a dutiful son.

He kept his mouth shut and didn't complain. He behaved like a well-trained circus lion. His father served as the ringmaster and his mother held the whip. Through the years, he learned senseless disrespect gained him nothing but a headache.

He climbed into the oversized SUV with his parents. His mom clicked away on her phone. His dad recited a revised version of his stump speech. Why wasn't this downtime marked on Dylan's schedule for the day? He wished he had his bar review materials with him.

"If we aren't leaving immediately, can I go run back up to my room and grab my backpack?" Dylan looked back and forth between his parents, awaiting their answer.

Abigail, his dad's assistant, entered the car and closed the door. "We're leaving now."

"It will *literally* only take a minute."

"You will ruin your hair and make-up by running and studying." She opened her tablet, dismissing Dylan.

Dylan looked at her like she was crazy. His hand reached toward his hair, but he fisted his fingers before pulling at his hair and proving the damn assistant correct.

They drove for about forty-five minutes and arrived at a plateau situated in the mountains. The small open area with green grass could have been a peaceful location if there weren't also four other trucks, a full photo crew, huge light-reflecting screens, and other photo paraphernalia.

He and his parents exited the car. The director didn't waste any time introducing himself and explaining his intent for the commercial. His vision included the picturesque view of a family at the break of dawn, as if they were getting ready for a morning hunt. The night sky started fading. The squawk of birds filled the silent gaps between Dylan and his parents.

An assistant handed a rifle to both Dylan and his father. Dylan handled the gun gingerly, like he was holding a newborn baby. He stared at the gun. Was it loaded? Despite the cool breeze, a sheen of perspiration formed on Dylan's forehead.

The director placed Dylan and his father on their marks. "Aim at the bullseye on the sign out in the distance."

An assistant clanged the clapperboard. "Action."

Dylan wobbled as he attempted to aim at the sign as he was told.

Five seconds hadn't even passed and the director shouted, "Cut!" The director marched toward Dylan and his dad until he was inches away from their faces. "Have either of you ever shot a gun?"

Fuck no. No one in his family was a gamesman or hunter. They didn't even own a gun.

Dylan's dad glowered at the director. "I hired you to create an image for a commercial. You're the director. Direct."

"We can't keep shooting like this. Training is necessary for you all to make this appear believable." The director turned to the rest of his crew. "Does anyone here know how to shoot?"

"Photos, sure. A gun, no way." An assistant holding a light reflector chuckled.

The director pointed to another assistant with his lips pressed into a strained line. "Get me someone that can train them on how to shoot. ASAP." He pointed to the assistant who mocked him. "I don't joke about wasting time. You're fired."

Dylan agreed. The shoot was a joke. Politics were a joke. His father's representation as a man with conservative values and a liberal heart teetered between the aisles. If his father's plot backfired, he would look like a joke.

Dylan didn't outright object to his father's new political position. His father had dedicated his life to helping the public. His lack of authenticity bothered Dylan. Nonetheless, he maintained his pristine smile and bit his tongue. He played the role his father expected of him without protest.

While figuring out the shoot, the sun emerged into the sky. The rays shot down at a glorious angle. Dylan took advantage of the time and lighting, snapped a few selfies, and posted the best photos on his social media.

Numerous likes on his post rolled in. His phone pinged with a message.

Seth—*Hey handsome. Love the gold-kissed look (fire) Even hotter than the last photo you posted—*

His fake smile turned genuine. Seth always made him smile.

Dylan—*Thanks man—*

Seth—*Would have been a better shot with fewer clothes—*

Dylan—*I'm not alone—*

Seth—*Hot date spent the night?—*

Dylan—*(genie and a bottle) Shooting a commercial for my dad at the ass crack of dawn (angry face with swear over the mouth)—*

Seth—*Professional naked pics! (smiling devil)—*

Dylan—*The political scandal (open mouth)—*

Seth—*Is that open mouth an offer?—*

He laughed.

Dylan—*Sorry, no time. Need to go practice not shooting a gun—*

Seth—*WTF?—*

Dylan—*Long story (peace fingers)—*

Seth—*(blow fish)—*

Damn Seth. All Dylan could think about was getting a good blow job. It had been weeks since he had been with Seth and Kat. Sure, the opportunities had presented itself. California men were more forward than Chicago men.

Earlier in the week, Dylan had been running along the palm tree-lined streets of the university campus when he encountered a stunning blond running toward him. The guy looked fit and ran at a fast clip. Dylan grinned, remembering how easily Seth could outrun him. As the man neared Dylan, the stranger slowed his stride and shamelessly checked out Dylan.

****

The blue eyes looked back at him and stopped Dylan in his tracks. The resemblance made his heart skip a beat. Was Seth in California?

Dylan spun his neck as the man passed him and grabbed a double-take. His mystery runner turned his head at the same time. Their gazes locked on one another. An instant mutual attraction flashed between them. They both stopped.

A tongue-tied Dylan stumbled on his words. The quintessential California-looking man introduced himself. “Hi, I’m Asher. Are you a grad student? I thought I knew all the cute runners here, but you are hella fine.”

The word “hella” woke Dylan out of his fog. Before he’d left Chicago, Seth had joked that Dylan would start using the term after moving to the Bay area. Dylan also noticed how Asher’s skin was several shades darker than Seth’s.

Dylan slipped on his political smile. The flirtatious tone faded. “Hey Asher, I’m Dylan. I did my undergrad here, but I’m studying for the bar.”

Asher’s eyes dimmed. “I did my undergrad here as well. Now I’m working in the administration offices. I need to run. Sorry for the terrible pun. Maybe our paths will cross again. Nice to meet you, Dylan.”

Dylan walked away. When Asher mentioned crossing paths, Dylan imagined crossing swords with Seth. He intended to jog, but encountered a problem. Thoughts of Seth had aroused him.

Like Highway 80, all roads led back to Chicago.

****

A high-pitched squeal pulled Dylan from his musings. “Let’s go, Dylan.” Abigail stood over Dylan with her tablet in hand. She peered at him with anticipation in her eyes. “We’re shooting footage without guns. The senator wants you and Mrs. Levine in the background.” She looked him up and down. “This outfit is wrong. You need to change and touch up your make-up before we lose the advantage of the morning sun.”

Dylan stood up and followed Abigail. “You know taking the video without the guns is a better idea. My father doesn’t have a permit for a gun. People would be up in arms about a fictitious photo stunt. He would be better off standing behind people who own guns and support people's choice to own."

Abigail turned back and faced Dylan. She mumbled something and then darted toward his dad's circle of advisors. She leaned in to speak to his dad's communication manager, who then hurried to speak to his dad. A flurry of conversations transpired amongst his father's team.

Dylan meandered toward the small trailer, entered, and closed the door behind him.

The door whooshed open. Dylan spun his head and the sunbeams shot him in the eyes. Abigail gasped, "Skip outfit B and put on outfit C." Again, he obeyed without question.

After Dylan changed and the make-up artist touched up his face, he sat around waiting. He regretted not bringing his bar review materials to study. He cracked his knuckles by his side.

"Dylan, please." His mother's condescending tone made his jaw clench. He shamefully stopped and resumed his required pose like a dog ordered to sit in place. No fidgeting. No distracting movements of any sort.

The director finally pulled him into the video and placed him on his mark like a mannequin. In every shot, the director placed Dylan leaning in the back so he would appear shorter than his dad. He served to promote his dad, not outshine his father in the scene.

While filming, Dylan paid attention to his dad's speech. He had softened his position on guns but drew a line with the need for gun safety. His dad floated his stance closer to the middle of the aisle in contrast to how

Dylan jumped full in on taking sides in legal arguments. Dylan let out a sigh of relief when his father nailed the speech in three takes. He hoped they wrapped up and returned home.

Abigail approached Dylan once again. "You need to return your clothes to the wardrobe trailer." She crossed her arms over her chest and narrowed her eyes at Dylan. "I saw the photos you posted this morning. As I told you before, you can't post personal shots in the same clothes as the senator's videos."

Dylan took her about as seriously as he would a yappy pomsky and smirked. "The outfit I was wearing earlier won't be in any of my father's promotions." Dylan didn't bother containing his contentious smile. He didn't have any respect for people who kissed his father's ass and tried to assert power over him. "I'm glad we don't have a problem." He sauntered toward his father's SUV.

His mother didn't acknowledge him when he got in the car. Luckily, he didn't have to endure her frigid silence for long, as his father joined them soon after.

His father finished up his call and set down his phone. "Good catch about checking for a gun license. My team is going to correct that ASAP. You've got a great mind for details."

"A chip off the old block."

"Be kind with the word old. I prefer seasoned." Dylan and his dad laughed, but his mother's lips remained in a straight line. "You are going to have a brilliant career in politics. After your clerkship, you can work on my staff."

And, get paid to be on your staff? Unlike today. Dylan nodded in agreement and kept his skepticism to himself.

His father planned out his entire future, but Dylan focused on the present. He needed to study for the bar exam. His parents didn't understand. Neither of them had gone to law school, let alone passed the bar.

After returning home, Dylan hit the books. He maximized his time he had, the following day was packed with Fourth of July activities alongside his family.

The next morning, Dylan returned from an early morning run and yanked off his sweaty shirt. He smiled at Kat's name on the caller ID. "Well good morning, Kitty-Kat."

"Hey, handsome. How's our California hunk?" Kat's use of the word *our* confused Dylan. He brushed her use of the possessive pronoun to the side.

"It's a bit of an adjustment." Dylan downplayed his uneasiness.

"Having fun on the campaign trail?"

"I went from writing argumentative articles on law review to being cast aside to the children's table," Dylan snarled in the privacy of his room.

"Working in the family business is never simple." Kat sniffled.

Kat's dad propped her up and put her on a pedestal, whereas his dad pushed him into the background. Dylan winced. He knew better. Comparing his situation to others was wrong. He grew up in a lavish lifestyle.

Dylan cleared his throat. "How's your studying coming along?" Her father had a much better appreciation for studying than his parents. A twinge of envy nagged at him.

Kat swallowed. "I'm fucking stressed. I feel like I

have to cram my studying into little bits of time because I'm working at the bar every day. It was easier when I was studying with you and Seth. I miss you." Kat whimpered.

Dylan's heart clenched. He hated hearing her distress. "Kat, you got this. I know you do. You never needed us. It was great, especially when we finished studying and had time to fool around." Dylan hoped to hear a giggle. Instead, Kat drew in a sharp breath.

"You are smart and completely capable of doing this. Maybe you just need to flick the bean. A good orgasm and some oxytocin should erase this negative energy." Dylan considered his own advice and thought he should take it in hand.

"Maybe you're right." Kat's breathing calmed.

"Of course. I'm always right." Her laugh eased Dylan's tension. "And get out and go study someplace different today. Give Seth a call. Take a beat and have some fun. And don't fucking tell me you don't have time. A little fun and you'll feel much better."

Mentioning Seth, had Dylan thinking about him. He wished he could simply call up Seth and see him. The 2,000 miles separating them felt like an insurmountable distance. He didn't have room in his schedule for a four-and-a-half-hour flight.

"Thanks. And Happy Fourth of July. Go enjoy one of those crazy burgers with avocado on top."

"Don't knock it until you try it."

"A hot dog is more my thing. With a pickle, not avocado."

"Mmmm. I can imagine you trying to stretch your mouth around a huge hot dog. Well fuck, now I'm hard. I better go do something about this. I need to head out soon for another one of my father's events. There's no way I'll make it through with blue balls."

"Sorry, not sorry."

"Never apologize for being our sexy little pixie."

Chapter 6

Seth

He slipped on his dark navy joggers when his phone beeped with a message.

Dylan—*Our pixie is falling apart—*

Seth grabbed his cell and dialed Dylan. "Hey, what's going on?"

"Catch your breath, Seth. Kat will be fine, but she needs a little of your smile-infused spirit."

Seth forced himself to take two deep breaths. *How did Dylan know, and he didn't?* "Did she call you?"

"I just got off the phone with her."

Why hadn't she called him? "Did she call you, or did you call her?"

"What? Why?"

Did it matter? Did Seth expect her to depend primarily on him for advice? Maybe she hadn't talked to Dylan and was just catching up with him. Seth ignored Dylan's questions. "What did she say?"

"She's overwhelmed with studying and work. I think she needs a break."

Seth understood needing a break. He needed a break from their breakup. "Like sex?" He hadn't intended to say it aloud.

"Don't be a selfish prick. She doesn't need the pressure of trying to satisfy anyone else but herself today. I'm sure she has enough sex toys to take care of herself. She needs a friend." The harsh tone in Dylan's voice snapped some clarity into Seth.

Their separation affected all three of them, not just himself. "I appreciate the heads up. You doing, okay?"

Dylan evaded answering the question. "Let's catch up some other time. I have a full day of events to get ready for."

Seth didn't want to let down both of the people who were most important in his life. These little missed opportunities for conversation over long distances were how relationships crumbled. "Dylan, what's going on?"

The other man sighed. "It is becoming clear my father has a much longer game plan for my career than I had expected." *You and me, both.*

"What's the plan?"

"He has high political aspirations for me in politics."

Seth could envision Dylan in politics. He had the height, the look, the wit, and the heart. "I'm sure you would do amazingly well. Kat's dad called it when he referred to you as Mr. President."

"Speaking of Kat, reach out to her."

"Yeah. I'll text you with an update. And Dylan, you will kick ass at whatever you do."

"Thanks." Dylan hung up.

Seth closed his eyes, wishing Dylan the best.

Still shirtless, Seth phoned Kat. Her phone rang several times before she answered. "H-hi."

He heard a quiver in her voice, as if she had been crying. "Hey. I'm not working at the firm today and was wondering if you wanted to study together?"

After a beat, Kat said, "Did Dylan call you?"

Shit. He should have played off the introduction

better and asked her if she had been working. He should have laid a better foundation. His criminal procedure professor had taught him better.

"No." Seth's voice wavered.

"Did Dylan text you?" Seth enjoyed hearing the sass in Kat's tone over her sadness.

"He texts often." He tried to sound nonchalant, but he knew where Kat was going with her line of questioning and played along.

"Okay Seth, did you and Dylan communicate recently where he suggested you call me?" Seth smiled, enjoying the argumentative banter.

"He may have mentioned you might be available and willing to save me from the boredom of studying on my own."

"Really now?"

Seth ignored her question and sarcasm. "Would you? Study with me today? And get some lunch with me first? You know I can't concentrate on an empty stomach." Seth attempted to guilt her with his most pitiful voice.

She remained silent. He upped his game. "I know you don't need to study with me. It's been weeks of working on my own. I miss studying with you and Dylan. We are both free today, let's take advantage of the situation."

"What makes you think I'm not busy?" *Shit.* Kat had caught him, again, admitting to knowing too much.

"Come on. Don't make me beg."

"Just studying? Nothing else?"

"And lunch. That's all, unless you want something else. I wouldn't object to something else…like dessert." He cringed at his miserable double entendre.

“Studying and lunch. Nothing else. Got it?”

“Deal. But it is a woman’s prerogative to change her mind. In case you are hungry later.” He hoped she reconsidered.

“Don’t push it.”

“Okay. Okay. Twenty minutes from now, good?”

“Sure. See you soon.”

He thew on some clothes, not wanting to be late. He picked from his array of blue shirts that fit snugly and showed off his well-defined biceps and pectoral muscles.

Seth arrived on time. Kat opened the door and her jaw dropped open and her eyes lit up. “Damn.”

He beamed, achieving the exact reaction he had intended. Seth leaned in closer and kissed her on the cheek. His body stood within a hair’s distance of brushing up against her chest. Similar to two magnets on the precipice of pulling each other together, Seth and Kat hovered on the verge of connecting. There wasn’t a two-foot-wide wooden bar separating them like their last kiss at Lawson’s. His heart raced.

Seth deepened his voice. “Ready to change your mind about dessert?”

She froze. Seth stared into her eyes and observed the gears turning in her head. What was preventing her from moving ahead? The heat between them should have melted all her reservations.

He didn’t want to push too hard and create more stress. He stepped back and created a gap between them. A breeze swept between them and chilled the immediate fire.

Seth reached for her hand. “Let’s grab some food. I’m starving. We can go sit in Grant Park and eat before studying.”

"Do you not get it? I don't have time for a picnic, Seth." She let go of his hand, crossed her arms, and scowled.

"Kat, you need to step outside and catch some rays. Vitamin D is good for you. We can be back in an hour. Don't waste time fighting me." Seth put on a saucy grin and pried her arms and hands loose. After a deep sigh, Kat agreed.

He held her hand as they walked the streets of Chicago. The sun perched high in the sky, flooding all the spaces between the skyscrapers with light. Kat squinted and blocked the sunlight with her hand. Her comfort was Seth's priority for the day. He snatched his sunglasses off his eyes and handed them to Kat. "Here."

They paused on the concrete sidewalk and avoided the foreboding grating beside their feet so his expensive shades didn't fall into the abyss below. Kat placed the steel-rimmed frames on her face and grinned at Seth. "Thank you." She gave Seth a quick peck on the mouth. "Damn. Your blue eyes are gorgeous."

Seth cocked his head to the side and smirked as he ran his hand through his blond hair. "I'm never wearing sunglasses again around you."

They walked a few blocks further and Seth stopped at the entrance of a crowded café. Kat yanked on his hand as he reached for the door. "We can't stop here. The service is too slow. I don't have time for this. Let's grab a slice of pizza somewhere. Something quick." Her brow furrowed.

"Sure, pizza is fast, but the food here is great and much healthier. It will help energize our bodies and not put us in a food coma. Plus, I ordered ahead. It's ready for pickup." Seth punctuated his impressiveness with a kiss on her cheek.

Kat smiled and mouthed the words, “Thank you.” Her smile made his planning worthwhile.

They brought their order to the park and got lucky. A couple vacated a bench under the shade of a maple tree, leaving it available. They claimed it. Seth welcomed the reprieve from the unnatural air conditioning in his office. Children played and laughed in the nearby fountain.

Kat unwrapped her turkey sandwich and took a bite. She giggled as she chewed.

“What’s so funny?”

She covered her mouth with her hand, still laughing. “Avocado.”

Seth’s eyes drew together in confusion. “I’m sorry. Do you not like avocado? I thought you ordered this same sandwich the last time we picked up food here.” *Did he remember incorrectly?*

She swallowed. “No. It’s great. Thank you. I was teasing Dylan about eating hamburgers with avocado.”

He scrunched up his face. “Ewe. That’s all kinds of wrong.”

“I know, right?”

They laughed together. “I teased him a few weeks ago about eating a Chicago dog.”

“Ha. Me too.”

“Maybe we can tempt him with food to move back here?” His joke fell flat.

She narrowed her eyes. “Seth.”

He rolled his eyes. “Yeah. Yeah.” He inhaled deeply, but it didn’t ease the pain in his chest.

“I think he deals with even more family pressure than me and you.” She took another bite of her sandwich.

Seth stabbed a cube of melon with his fork and stuffed it in his mouth. He chewed instead of arguing with Kat. They finished their lunch in silence and watched the children splash in the water.

Kat leaned her head back and closed her eyes. She looked beautiful, wearing a contented expression on her face. Seth's cock thickened, recalling a similar look after she orgasmed. Her smile broadened when she gazed at Seth. He wanted to kiss those upturned lips.

He tossed away their trash in a nearby bin. "Ready to go study?"

"Mmm hmm."

Was she considering the option for dessert?

They walked several blocks to Seth's apartment. Keeping his promise of lunch and studying only, he refrained from making any suggestive passes toward Kat while they worked. But that didn't stop his mind from contemplating other delicious options. His devilish thoughts distracted him many times throughout the day. Despite the underlying temptations, they focused on their studies until the fireworks broke their concentration.

"I think I'm going to head home now before the crowds block up the streets. Thank you for today." Kat tossed her materials into her backpack.

Seth hoped the day's productivity boosted her confidence. "I've missed studying with you."

They stood beside the table where they had been working. Kat turned and kissed Seth briefly on the lips. Her eyes widened as if she had surprised herself. "Goodnight Seth." She spun around and darted toward the door.

She fumbled with the deadbolt. Seth placed a calm

hand on top of hers. He assisted with the locks and opened the door for her. "Goodnight."

She dashed down the steps. The main door to the building below squeaked open and closed with a bang.

Seth shut his apartment door and leaned against the solid wood frame. He took a deep breath and grinned. His apartment no longer smelled like cleaning solution. Kat's perfume hung in the air.

Wanting to keep Dylan in the loop, Seth texted him.

—Spent the day with Kat. Lunch in the park and studying the rest of the night. Thanks for letting me know—

Dylan*—OFC—*

The quick reply surprised him. He assumed that Dylan would be caught up in some political event.

Seth*—No fireworks show tonight?—*

Dylan*—Not dark yet—*

Seth forgot about the two-hour time difference between Chicago and California.

Dylan*—I'm at this damn function. My dad's campaign claims to be pro-environment, but we're sitting awaiting a huge fireworks show in an area prone to wildfires. The hypocrisy is disgusting—*

Seth*—They should have done a drone display instead—*

Dylan*—It's all about costs, expectations, and tradition. Not what is appropriate—*

Seth*—You have an incredible mind to look at all the sides. It's what made you a great editor-in-chief of law review—*

Dylan*—Politics is a different animal than the law—*

Seth*—You have almost a year and a half until completing your clerkship—*

Dylan—*True. Gtg and pose in another photo*—

Seth—*(fingers forming a peace sign)*—

****

The final weeks flew by. Like during finals, it was a race to cram as much information into his head.

Tuesday morning, day one of the exam finally arrived. Seth popped out of bed. When he turned off the alarm on his phone, he found a text message.

Dylan—*Stop thinking about getting fucked and focus on kicking ass on the test today. Good luck!!! XOXO*—

Seth smiled. It didn't matter what Dylan wrote. The fact he was in his thoughts felt like a hug.

Seth—*(heart)*—

He blared rap music during his shower. With the swagger of a multi-platinum rapper, he danced while he dressed. He looked himself up and down in his full-length mirror. "You got this."

Seth pressed the start button on his coffee machine. The hissing and bubbling of percolating java reminded him of Kat serving drinks.

Seth—*Morning Einstein. See you soon. (kissing smiley face)*—

She responded with a thumbs-up tapback. *Maybe she didn't have time to text back.*

Upon arriving at the theater, law grads scrambled about the lobby, lining up at the check-in desks. Seth found Kat standing in line, gnawing on her finger.

He approached her from behind and whispered in her ear, "Morning, future chief justice." She gasped and spun around.

With wide eyes, she snarled, "Shit. You scared me. You're lucky I didn't smack you."

"Sorry, you must have been deep in thought." Seth gave her a hug and felt the tension in her shoulders ease. "Quickie in the bathroom before this exam starts?" Seth waggled his eyebrows. She laughed. Those smiling lips called to him.

"I don't think we have time for both of us to get off. Shall we flip a coin?"

Seth knew she was kidding, but loved her cheekiness. And, well, part of him liked that she hadn't ruled out the thought of having sex with him.

The mention of sex reminded Seth of Dylan's earlier message. "Ready to kick some ass?"

Kat pulled her shoulders back and took a deep breath. "Let's do this!" Seth loved hearing the confidence in her voice.

Hours later, they ate some lunch together before the second half. When the day's exam ended in the late afternoon, most everyone shuffled out of the building. But some engaged in debates over their answers. Seth rolled his eyes at their fruitless behavior. Their second-guessing was a surefire way to undermine their confidence for the next day of testing.

Seth pulled Kat's attention away from the nonsense. "Want to grab some dinner?"

Kat looked uncertain. "I'm exhausted. My brain is worn out. Too tired to talk. I just want to stuff some food in my face and get to bed."

"I can do no talking and no foreplay and skip to the good stuff." Seth shot her one of his sinful smiles. She grinned but didn't offer a smartass comeback. She looked lifeless. Seth upped the ante. "We can get your favorite double fudge milkshake."

Kat's eyes lit up. "Okay."

Seth ate with Kat in amicable silence. He gazed at her as she took a long pull on her straw and then licked the drop of chocolate remaining on her lip. His jaw dropped open. *Ohhhh.* He shoved a French fry in his mouth, silencing his moan. *Did she realize how much she was turning him on?* "How's the shake?"

"Good." Her grin didn't meet her eyes.

He knew the perfect way to make her smile. A few minutes with his head between her legs would do the trick. But by the end of the meal, his adrenaline plummeted. He, too, was mentally exhausted from the extensive testing.

Twenty-four hours later, Seth and Kat finished the entire exam. Did they pass or fail? They remained in the dark until the results would arrive in October.

Seth hung out in the lobby, waiting for her. She had raced along with Kellie to the restroom. Kellie looked comical trying to run with her round, pregnant belly. Seth gave her kudos for completing the exhausting exam with a baby growing inside her.

He joined Carter, who stood near the bathroom. "I'm glad that's fucking over."

"No kidding. Between reasoning out answers and worrying about my pregnant wife, I'm drained."

"Well, get used to it. A newborn means months of sleep deprivation." Seth smiled, happy not to be in Carter's shoes. He was not ready for such an enormous responsibility.

The women exited the restroom and joined the rest of their friends. Smirnova piped up over the chit-chat. "Enough of talking about the damn exam. Who's up for drinks at Lawson's Bar?"

"Hell yes. Let's go." Cole stretched his long arms

above everyone and gestured in the direction of the exit.

"I'm out. All I want is my bed and a pillow." Kellie massaged her round tummy.

Seth shook his head from side to side with a frown. "Sorry Carter, no celebratory sex for you tonight." Carter rolled his eyes.

Kat ducked her head toward her shoulder and sniffed. She scrunched her nose. "I'm in, but I need to go home and change first. Meet up in about an hour?" Everyone agreed and headed out.

"Perfect," said Smirnova.

Kat got a few steps ahead of Seth. He tugged on her shirt, finding it soaked with perspiration, despite the testing room being ridiculously chilly. "Do you need a ride? I drove here this morning."

"Sure, thanks."

Seth parked his car on the street, in a safe location, around the corner from Kat's building. He had no intentions of driving after hanging out with his friends at the bar. He followed Kat up to her apartment.

As she strode toward her bedroom, Seth opened her refrigerator. "Mind if I grab a beer?"

Kat shouted back, "No. Go ahead. I'm going to hop in the shower."

He popped the top off the beer and took a long gulp. His body relaxed as he swallowed the cool liquid. He took another sip. He gazed longingly at Kat's open bedroom door. She darted across the hall into her bathroom, wrapped in only a towel. He blinked several times. The image nagged at him. *One swift tug on the towel and she would be naked.* He wanted her.

The shower sprang to life. And so did his cock. She stood naked only a few dozen feet away.

Should he make a move? Would it put too much stress on her? How intent was she on only being friends? He finished his beer as the water turned off in the bathroom. Well, shower sex went down the drain.

He kept an eye out for her reappearance. Once again, she crossed the hallway wearing only a towel. Seth closed his eyes and enjoyed repeating the image in his head.

"Can you help me pick out something to wear?" she called out from her bedroom.

He lunged forward, taking a couple of steps, then stopped himself. Was she teasing him? Preying on his fashion-focused interests? Or was she flirting with him?

He entered her room. She stood in front of her closet, still wearing the towel. "What do you think?"

"Huh?" How was he supposed to think when all of his blood had gone south? "You're beautiful, no matter what clothes you choose." His voice came out rougher and deeper than he intended. Perspiration beaded on his neck.

"Come on. Pick something please." She looked at Seth and her expression changed. Her eyes darkened and filled with desire.

He fought against the urge to pounce on her. He stepped toward the closet. His side brushed against her shoulder. Electricity shot through him. Absorbed in his ache for her, he blindly reached into the closet and grabbed a hanger.

"That's my trench coat." Her sultry laugh ignited every nerve in his body.

"Mmm hmm." *What did she say?*

"Okay, then." She pulled the hanger from his hand and tossed it to the floor. Kat closed the distance between them. Her plump lips parted and her minty breath escaped as she panted. “I need this, Seth.” She dropped the towel.

Seth needed her. He wanted her. Damn the consequences. She extended her arm in his direction and her hand landed on his waist. He clutched her face between his hands. They fell into each other and their lips collided in a blazing kiss.

Their mouths remained locked as they shuffled towards the bed. He kicked off his shoes and unfastened his belt. He reached into his pocket, out of habit. *Shit.* “I don’t have any condoms.”

While she grabbed a silver wrapper from her nightstand, Seth removed the rest of his clothes. Shoving down his boxer briefs, his fully erect length sprung to life.

He snatched the condom from her and rolled it on his weeping cock.

Worries about the bar exam disappeared. His sadness over the dissolution of their threesome vanished. Kat was naked. And he wanted her.

“Hurry up.” Kat pulled him on top of her. He neared his mark, finding her slick entrance. Her heat beckoned him, and he drove his cock into her inviting channel.

“Of fuck yes, Kat.”

She moaned, “Yes, Seth. Yes.” The urgency in her voice made his balls draw up tighter. He teetered on the precipice of coming.

She wrapped her legs around his waist, constricting his movements. At the same time, she lifted her hips and rocked her pelvis against him.

He wanted to give her the best release. An explosion of bliss where all her stress disappeared. He longed to give her everything she needed and desired. He let her lead, finding the perfect angle and sending herself flying.

"I'm so close, Seth." Her breathing hastened. She dug her nails into his back and her legs gripped him like a python. "Yes, Seth."

"Oh, hell yes." His heart beat hard. He had so much love to show her. He wanted to blanket her in his love. Seth pounded into her harder.

"Oh god!" she wailed. Her guttural roar triggered his primal urges, and he came deep inside her. He fell on top of her, pinning her to her mattress.

After weeks of resistance, Kat finally returned his affection. Relief spread through his body like a calm wave following a riptide, which had assaulted him since graduation. The surge of adrenaline he experienced while concentrating on the bar exam plummeted. Fatigue gripped him like an invisible force bearing down on him and immobilizing him. His mind drifted into unconsciousness.

But then Kat ruined the peaceful moment and began wiggling away. She pried her body out from under him.

He hadn't intended to trap her, but her escape concerned him. What was she thinking? Why was she racing away? "Hey…Kat?"

She remained mute as she hurried around the room and threw on the same clothes she had discarded before her shower. Kat zipped up her jeans. "We promised to meet everyone at the bar."

He moaned into the bedding. "A nap sounds better."

Kat smacked him on his leg. "Get up. Time to go."

Ugh. She killed his bliss. He didn't move an inch. He rested on his stomach and peered at Kat with her hands on her hip. "Let's just call it a night."

She threw his clothes on top of him. His belt almost grazed a delicate part of his body between his parted legs. Her direct manner of conveying her desire for him to get up and out seemed out of sorts for her.

He narrowed his eyes at her as he sat up and righted his inside-out shirt and pants. "Are you angry?" Seth worried he might irritate her further.

"No. We promised we would be there. I don't want to be late and tick off Alex." Kat finger-brushed her short dark hair. Seth preferred her messed-up, I-just-got-fucked hair.

As Seth stood and pulled up his boxers and pants, Kat busied herself in the room. She focused on everything in the room, except for him. He rested his hand on her shoulder. "What's going on? Did I do something wrong?"

Kat's mouth drew into a tight line. "No, Seth. This was fun. But I want to go meet up with everyone else."

Seth's stomach sank and looked sideways at Kat. "Did you just use me for a quickie?"

"It's not like I asked you to go down on me and didn't return the favor. You got off." Kat raised an eyebrow.

"Wow," Seth mumbled. Being with Kat meant something completely different to him than it did to her. "I thought maybe you had changed your mind about wanting to be more than friends."

He sat down on the bed and yanked too hard on the laces of his shoes. His toes went numb. "Are we fuck buddies, now?" That wasn't his preference. Sure, sex was better than no sex, but he wanted more. He loved her.

"I don't know what we are. All I know is I don't

want to end up getting hurt." She chewed on her lip. Honesty showed in her glistening eyes.

"I have no intention of ever hurting you, Kat." Seth reached out to hold her hand. He craved the connection.

She refused to take his hand and folded her arms. "I don't think that."

"Is this because you still think I have some insatiable need to always be with a man and a woman? Kat, I haven't been with anyone since graduation night. I'm bisexual, not a fuckboy."

Kat rolled her head and took a deep breath. "I know you aren't. I'm sorry if my comment the other day about you picking up people at the baseball game insinuated that."

Seth bit back the urge to interrupt her. He needed clarity.

"It's not that I'm afraid of you wanting to date men as well as me. The problem is you are too lovable. What if you are dating a man and he decides he wants to be exclusive with you? What if he is better for you than me? And I get left heartbroken?"

"That's a lot of what-ifs."

"I don't have an issue with polyamory. Things were great with you and Dylan. But I can't do it with you and some other guy. I can't handle being your other lover's metamour." She wiped at her eyes. "Listen, I would never ask you to be someone you aren't, please don't ask me to be. I know I am enough as a person, but I also know I'm just not enough for you."

"You're amazing." He loved her. Seth reassured her with a kiss on the top of her head. He refrained from pushing her further because fighting over a hypothetical didn't benefit them.

"Thank you." Kat reached for Seth's hand and pulled him closer. She graced him with soft loving eyes. "Like I said before, we had an amazing threesome and we were lucky for what we had."

They shared a once-in-a-lifetime relationship. Seth knew it in his bones. The three of them belonged together. He wanted to gain a better understanding of the full picture in Kat's mind. "Do you miss Dylan?"

"I support him. I understand trying to meet your parent's career aspirations. As I'm sure you can relate. But he had to move to an entirely new state. He's alone."

"But do you *miss* him?" he pressed as she evaded answering the heart of the question.

"I'm grateful for the relationship I get to continue to have with him. It's not like I lost him."

Kat's phone rang. She glanced at the screen. "Speak of the devil." She accepted the video call.

"Hey, Dylan."

"You did it Kitty-Kat! The exam is done. I knew you could do it." Seth heard Dylan's praise through the speaker. *Since when did he call her Kitty-Kat?*

"I hope it *is* over. Time to wait and see if I passed." Kat sighed.

"Are you going out to celebrate? Wish I could join."

"We can celebrate later after you take the exam."

"Definitely. Seth, too. I need to call and congratulate him."

Seth stepped into the view of the camera beside Kat. "Hey, man."

"Nice hair, Seth." He ran his hand through his disheveled blond locks. "Pairs well with your shirtless chest." Dylan threw his head back in laughter. Kat scowled at Seth. "You two already celebrate or did I interrupt? Can I watch?" Dylan waggled his eyebrows.

"We were about to head over to Lawson's for drinks." Kat crooked her mouth.

"Damn. I missed the good part. Glad to see you guys found a way to make the friends-with-benefits thing work."

Seth shook his head back and forth, hoping Dylan would notice and drop the subject.

"Nah. It was a onetime slip." Kat dumped a bucket of water on Seth's feelings.

"As in Seth accidentally slipped his cock—"

"Let it go, Dylan," Seth cut him off. If Dylan kept up the jokes, Kat would reinforce the wall she constructed between them. He reached for his shirt and slipped it on.

Dylan's lighthearted tone shifted. "Well, congrats again."

"You okay Dylan?" Kat asked.

"Yeah. I'll be through with the test soon enough." Seth doubted Dylan was telling the whole story. Something must have been bothering him because he was too bright to be upset about the exam.

"Let's all plan on celebrating together when you're done," Kat reiterated.

Seth's lips turned up at Dylan's irresistible smile.

If they all gathered in one city, maybe they all could enjoy an intentional slip?

Chapter 7

Dylan

Using his tracking app, Dylan refreshed his screen repeatedly until Seth's plane touched down on the runway. His leg bounced as he sat in the airport, waiting for Seth to deplane. His phone beeped.

Seth—*Landed*—

His heart raced. Seth was in California.

Dylan—*(smiley heart-eyed face) Meet you at the luggage carousel*—

He got on his feet. His height gave him a significant advantage for seeing over people's heads and seeking Seth in the crowd. Without seeing his face, Dylan recognized his hand-crafted signature-looking hair peeking out above the barrage of people. Seth's carefree blond hair appeared immaculate even after hours on a plane.

He emerged from the throng. Dylan smiled from ear to ear. The image of Seth's blue eyes and matching shirt rippled through the screen of Dylan's watering eyes. He swallowed the lump in his throat. Dylan found himself caught off guard with an unexpected surge of emotion.

"Hello sexy." Seth rushed into Dylan's arms.

Too choked up, Dylan remained speechless and clung to Seth, holding him tight. It didn't matter. Dylan zeroed in on what he wanted and kissed Seth. His hands trembled as he held Seth's face. Dylan cut off the kiss before it morphed into something inappropriate for a family-friendly environment.

He hugged Seth firmly, refusing to let go. Appreciating Seth's presence in California hit home. "What a sight for sore eyes. I'm so fucking glad you are here. Damn, you look good." He released Seth from his hold and intertwined his fingers with Seth's.

"Thanks for the personal airport pickup."

Dylan understood the significance of such gestures and prioritized Seth over the items on his list that needed attending. He still resented his family for not taking the time to greet him after graduation.

He kissed Seth again and Seth flashed him a huge grin. "Your lack of concern about PDA is hella sexy."

"We aren't in the Midwest. It's one perk of the west coast." Dylan placed another chaste kiss on Seth's smiling lips. "Since when do you use the word hella?"

"When in Rome." Seth winked and Dylan laughed. Last spring, Seth had given Dylan a lot of grief about using that expression.

"Let's grab your luggage and get out of here."

After pulling the black rolling bag from the carousel, Seth and Dylan hurried through the circular parking garage. Dylan popped open the back of the white, upscale SUV.

"Nice ride."

Placing Seth's luggage inside the vehicle, Dylan shrugged. "The rents' car."

Before Dylan started the car, Seth leaned over and kissed Dylan again. In the confines of the car, Dylan didn't rein in his feelings. He surrendered to his lustful desires, which caused his cock to grow in his slacks. "I am so fucking glad you flew out here."

"Me too." Seth adjusted his pants before buckling his seatbelt.

Dylan exited the parking garage and merged onto the highway, letting go of Seth's hand. "Drivers out here are nuts. People in Chicago will cut you off in gridlock, but cutting people off going seventy miles per hour is insanity." Another car swerved in front of them and Seth swore under his breath.

Dylan answered a call through the speaker system of the car. "How are my handsome men?"

"Hey, Kat. It would be better with you here too." Dylan kept his eyes glued to the road.

"I wish I could have joined in the fun, but I had to help my dad train the two new bartenders and waitress taking over for me."

Dylan said, "Of course, he needed to hire three people to do the job you were doing."

"You could run the entire bar with one hand tied behind your back." Seth doused her with praise.

"It's time to hang up my bar towel and start my law job in a few days."

"You're going to kick ass at the law firm too. I bet you'll make partner before any of us." Dylan respected the hell out of Kat and reminded her often because she lacked confidence in her legal skills.

"Ha!" Kat chortled. "I should return to work, but I wanted to wish you both a great weekend. Miss you both."

"We'll send photos," said Seth.

"Take care." Dylan ended the call.

He drove through the gated entrance of his parent's neighborhood and onto the circle driveway. Dylan frowned. Several cars were parked on the brick path. His parents were most likely home. He wished he had the place to himself with Seth. He wanted privacy.

Dylan grabbed Seth's luggage from the back of the car. "I apologize in advance for my mom's behavior." He took a deep breath and hoped for the best with his parents.

Seth paused in the foyer. His head panned around the open-air entrance. "Nice digs."

"Dylan, is that you?" His mom emerged from the corner, holding a glass of white wine. "Oh hello. You must be Seth. Dylan mentioned he had a friend arriving today."

"Lovely to meet you, Mrs. Levine." Seth kissed Dylan's mom on the cheek. Dylan should have warned Seth not to bother warming up to the ice queen. "You have a beautiful home."

"Thank you, Seth. Such a polite young man." Dylan noticed his mom fixing her gaze on Seth. "You do plan on joining us tonight at the gala?"

He wasn't aware of any formal function. His mom withheld the information from him until she met Seth in person and had determined whether he met her standards. Seth looked at Dylan with questioning eyes.

"You must join us tonight. I insist." Dylan didn't bother suggesting otherwise. He knew better.

"I appreciate the invitation, but I don't think I brought anything appropriate to wear to a fancy event." He narrowed his eyes at Dylan.

His mom made a scoffing motion with her hand. "Oh, don't worry. We have people for that. Dylan will take care of it."

Seth's eyes lit up. "Sounds fantastic. And thank

you."

"I have a lot to get done this afternoon. Dylan, I hope you can manage to make Seth comfortable. Take his luggage and help get him settled. But you must take him to get fitted immediately. We are leaving at 7:30 tonight." His mom shot him a stern expression.

In a saccharine voice said to Seth, "I look forward to getting to know you better."

"It was a pleasure to meet you." Seth reached for his luggage.

She coughed. "Dylan." She pointed her beady eyes at Seth's suitcase. She hadn't even given Dylan a moment to take the luggage from Seth.

"I got it." Dylan took the bag from Seth's grasp. His mom left them standing in the foyer by themselves. Seth raised an eyebrow at Dylan.

He said nothing, but cocked his head toward his bedroom. Seth followed him up the stairs. Dylan pointed out the guest room, where his mom intended for Seth to stay, but he continued on, taking Seth to his own.

Dropping Seth's luggage unceremoniously inside, he pushed Seth up against the wall and kissed him with the passion of a wildfire, consuming everything in its path. The need to strip Seth of all his clothes surged through him. His fingers tingled. Dylan wanted to get lost in Seth for hours with Seth's hands all over him and Seth's lips wrapped around his length.

Dylan pried his lips off of Seth. His breath came in heavy gasps. Dylan pinched his eyes closed as he feared seeing Seth would break his will to stop. "We need to put a pin in this."

"Why?" Seth whined.

"We have to get you fitted for a tux."

"Seriously? Now? Should be interesting having my inseam measured with a hard-on." Seth rolled out his shoulders.

Dylan laughed. "I think the stylist will enjoy it. My guess is you are just his type."

"You know you could help me out here." Seth dragged his thumb over Dylan's lip. "I don't care about embarrassing anyone, but I would prefer…"

Dylan knew what he preferred and he dropped to his knees. Seth didn't waste time, unzipped his slacks, and pushed his pants and boxers down to the floor. Dylan held his thick length in his hand, stroking as his tongue circled the head.

"Oh hell yes. Watching you suck my cock is so fucking hot."

The thought of teasing Seth had its appeal. But Dylan needed to get him to the stylist, which meant he needed to get Seth to orgasm quickly. He tongued Seth's balls and stroked his steely shaft.

"Dylan, I'm about to come."

He opened his mouth wide as Seth plunged inside. He held Seth's hips, swallowing every drop.

Seth repeated the sensuous motion of wiping his thumb over Dylan's lip. In its wake, Seth kissed Dylan. "It's good to be in Cali with you."

Dylan enjoyed the satisfied look on Seth's face. "Let's go before I throw you down on the bed."

"I bet we could be a few minutes late." Seth ran his finger along the bulge in Dylan's pants. "And take care of you."

"You know what they say, anticipation makes everything better."

Seth cupped Dylan's balls and his cock threatened

to burst from his khakis. Dylan gasped. “Let’s get this over with.”

“I’m sure your mom won’t be upset if we are a bit late.”

At the mere mention of his mother, Dylan went flaccid. He sighed and rolled his eyes. “Well, you cured the problem of hiding my hard-on.”

Seth placed a gentle palm on his shoulder. “What is with you and your mom?”

“That discussion would certainly make us late.” Dylan took Seth by the hand. “Time to get you sized up for a monkey suit.” Seth’s eyes lit up a little. He was a clothes whore and loved getting dressed up. Dylan found it to be more of a necessary chore, like eating vegetables.

He pulled Seth into a room dedicated to wardrobe. Asa was busy labeling clothes racks separated by events. Dylan knocked on the door. Asa spun in Dylan’s direction, looking startled. Asa reached his hand to his ear and pulled out a pair of earbuds. “Oh, hello. So glad you both are here. I have your tux all ready for this evening.”

Dylan clenched his jaw, realizing Asa knew before he did about the gala and his obligation to attend. He didn’t blame the other man. “Thanks, Asa.”

Asa shamelessly looked Seth up and down. “Aren’t you gorgeous? And I think the navy tuxedo I chose for you will be amazing with those pretty blue eyes of yours.” Asa’s friendly nature amused Dylan. “Your eyes are even better looking in person. The photo didn’t capture those gleaming beauties.”

What the fuck? His mother had planned this all out ahead of time and hadn’t communicated a damn word with Dylan. She could have at least spared him the courtesy of a heads-up. Would copying him in the email she sent to Asa have been too much of a burden for her?

Seth's lips curled into an arrogant smile. With enthusiasm, he rubbed his hands together.

Dylan forced a grin on his face. He didn't want to rain on Seth's fashion fun. "Thank you, Asa. Let's see what you have in store."

He held up the suit next to Seth. "Oh yes, you are going to look fabulous. I think I estimated the size correctly, but I'll need to make some fine-tuned adjustments." Asa pointed to the opaque room divider in the corner. "Go slip it on."

Seth walked out from behind the screen. "Oh, hell yes, I look good." He beamed from ear to ear. He was suited for high-end garments. "You have great taste, Asa."

Dylan agreed, liking the view in front of him.

"Come here." Asa twirled his finger around and Seth spun in a slow circle. "A few tweaks here and there and you will look perfect." Asa pinned up the tux.

As Asa worked on the cuffs, Dylan mouthed to Seth, "You look hot." He didn't like his mother's subterfuge, but seeing Seth happy and looking stunning in the tux made it worth it.

Seth undressed and handed the suit back to Asa.

"When I'm done altering this, I'll have it sent up to the guest room."

"You can place it in my room." Dylan stopped in the doorway. "Actually, never mind, leave it in the guest room. I'm not in the mood for any interruptions."

"Is there anything else I can bring you?" Asa cheekily pursed his lips and raised his eyebrows.

"Seth is all I need." Dylan took Seth's hand.

“Thank you, Asa.” Seth flirted and Asa blushed.

After an entire afternoon together with Seth, Dylan emerged a much more cheerful man. The Seth-induced oxytocin served as a balm for the pain caused by his mother.

They showered and dressed on time. Arriving first in the limo, Dylan poured Seth a glass of wine, wary his previous bliss might not be strong enough to combat his mother’s toxic nature.

His mom joined them in the car. “Well, don’t you two look stunning?” She wore a thin smile, which may have been muted by her recent Botox or simply her resting cool demeanor. Dylan questioned his mom’s choice of words. She had orchestrated the coordinating tuxedos and the final approval of their actual invite. And as soon as she opened her mouth, she commented on their appearance.

Dylan returned her supposed compliment with a furtive smile. On the other hand, Seth lathered on the charm. “You look lovely as well.” The fact he had climaxed three times earlier in the afternoon probably aided in his amenable conversational skills.

“Thank you, Seth, such a gentleman.” She turned to Dylan. “Perhaps you could use your manners and offer me a glass too.”

Dylan bit his tongue and handed her one.

Dylan’s father joined them in the limo. The driver closed the door. “I’m sorry for keeping you all waiting.” He extended a hand to Seth. “You must be Seth. I’m thrilled you are joining us tonight.”

“The pleasure is all mine, senator.” Seth took an extra sip of wine.

“Ever been to a political gala, Seth?”

"No, sir."

"My one suggestion is to drink just enough to smile the entire night, but not too much, so you remain the most quick-witted person in the conversation."

"Unlike the other notable political giants who have a reputation for slurring their words?" said Seth.

Everyone laughed. Dylan's eyes widened, taken aback by the ease at which Seth handled himself around his parents.

"I have a feeling you are going to do just fine tonight." His dad bobbed his head affirmatively. His father wasn't easily impressed. The fact his dad had approved of Seth made Dylan happy. His reaction surprised Dylan, as he had never cared about his father's approval of a date.

"Thanks for the advice." Seth emptied his glass and set it down.

"I hear you are starting a new legal section at your parents' accounting firm. We could use someone with your skills on my team. Far too much of what I do entails financing and not enough about brainstorming how to help others."

Dylan maintained a poker face and avoided fidgeting in his seat. He hadn't expected his father to approach Seth for a position on his staff.

Seth crossed his legs. "I'm sure being a part of your team would be an amazing experience. Much more exciting than working in an accounting firm. But I owe it to my parents." Seth gestured between Dylan and his dad. "I'm certain you can relate to raising your kids to follow in your path."

"Dylan is going to make a fine politician someday." His dad's eyes sparkled with confidence.

His mom smiled at Seth. "You seem to have a healthy, heart-centered balance and understand the importance of family." She took another sip of wine and glared over the rim of the glass at Dylan.

"Perhaps one day, I'll get you to switch to my team. I've learned things can change. Nothing is set in concrete." The senator's confidence never faltered.

After arriving at the venue, Dylan and Seth separated themselves from Dylan's parents. Seth glanced around and whispered, "What is the deal with your mom? She's all warm and fuzzy with me and she's stone cold to you?"

Seth's recognition wasn't news to Dylan. "She's been like that my whole life. I don't expect anything different from her." The topic of his mom bored him. "Damn, you look good in the tux. Asa was right, the deeper shade of blue brings out a richness in your eyes."

"Thanks. You're looking mighty fine. I love the black jacket on you, although I prefer you naked." Seth winked and leaned in a tad closer. "Am I allowed to kiss you here, or is it against the rules?"

Dylan didn't hesitate and planted one on Seth. He liked the freeness. A flash of light distracted Dylan. He opened his eyes and pulled away from Seth to see a photographer lower his camera lens. "Dylan, are you willing to tell us who the man at your side is tonight?"

From out of nowhere, his mother stepped in to answer. "Dylan is attending with Seth Soloman tonight. Seth and Dylan attended law school together and graduated this past May."

The photog turned his camera around, showing the screen to his mom. "Thank you. Do you approve of the photograph, Mrs. Levine?"

"Yes, you can print it." His mother and the photographer strutted off in separate directions.

Dylan fought the urge to wipe the frustration off his face with his hands. Instead, he laced his fingers in with Seth's. His stomach felt queasy. "I'm so sorry."

Looking gorgeous, but clueless, Seth asked, "For what?"

Dylan reminded himself that Seth was new to the political environment. Nothing occurred by happenstance. The arrangement of the invitation, the tux in Seth's size and color, and his father's knowledge of Seth's resume were part of a plan. His mother's proximity following the photo was yet another giveaway.

Dylan inhaled through his nose and let it out slowly. "I didn't mean to invite you to California to serve as a prop. I don't want you to feel like I somehow tricked you out here to take advantage of you."

"And here I was thinking you asked me out here to use me for sex. I was counting on it." Seth's sexy grin made it difficult to resist kissing him again. Knowing his mother had an eye out, Dylan replied with a devilish smile.

"Let's put a pin in those thoughts while we are here. Are you hungry?" He spotted a server.

Seth's eyes widened as a waiter approached. "Fillet with horseradish?" He snatched the napkin and tiny plate. Seth popped it into his mouth.

The server faced Dylan. "Sir, do you care for one as well?"

He accepted the offering, but the uncertain state of his stomach made him hesitate. Seth eyed the steak. "You aren't going to eat that?" Dylan handed it to Seth, who devoured it.

"Aren't you hungry? We didn't eat all day." Seth started looking around. "I'm starving. Let's go hunt down some more food."

"I guess I forgot to feed you. I'm a horrible host." Dylan's stomach settled as he continued to banter back and forth with Seth.

The creamy avocado bruschetta looked tempting. With only a few left on the tray, Dylan stopped the server. Before stuffing the food in his mouth, Dylan teased Seth, "When in Cali you need to learn to embrace the avocado."

"I like avocados. I just like Chicago hot dogs a lot more." Seth bit off half of the appetizer.

"I can't argue." Dylan's craving for a hot dog had him thinking. "You know, I should come to town when you and Kat get your bar results next month. We can all celebrate together."

Seth choked on the food in his mouth. "Hell yes, that would be amazing. I can't think of a better way to celebrate. Well, except if you had your passing results as well. But I know it takes a lot longer to get the California scores."

Dylan's father came by and placed an affectionate hand on Seth's back. "Are you guys enjoying yourselves this evening?" His father's practiced smile was plastered on his face. "I bet the food at these events tops the meals at an accounting firm. There's another reason for you to consider transferring out here." His father did the thumb-emphasis thing politicians always do. "Something to keep in mind."

"Thank you again, senator, for the invitation tonight. Everything has been outstanding." Seth winked at Dylan.

"Excellent. I need to move on to another event. Seth, if I don't get another chance to see you before you leave, it's been great to meet you. And don't forget about my offer." His dad patted him on the back again.

When his father was out of earshot, Seth questioned, "Is your dad serious about a job offer?"

"Most likely." Dylan knew his father's ability to plan and manipulate. *What was he up to?*

"He doesn't even know me." Seth's lips morphed into a dazed smile.

"I'm fairly sure he already had you completely vetted before you stepped into our home." Dylan's lips flattened into an emotionless line.

"Ahhh. That explains the tuxedo and the resume details in the limo." Dylan nodded in agreement.

"What do you say? We grab another drink here and head out?" Dylan caught sight of a tray of champagne and snagged a couple of flutes. They finished the glasses and headed home.

In the car, Seth weaved his fingers between Dylan's and then lifted their joined hands to his mouth. He kissed the back of Dylan's hand and then the seam where their skin united. "Can I ask you a question?"

Dylan braced himself as something pleasant never followed that phrase. "Sure."

"Do you think you only dated men because of your mother's frosty nature turned you off of women?"

Dylan laughed out loud, but Seth wasn't smiling. "You're serious?"

"Yeah." Seth placed his other hand on Dylan's.

"I don't know. I never considered it. There is just something special about Kat." Dylan rubbed at his chin.

"I agree. She's incredible."

“She’s loving and caring, but not in a girly way. When I’m with her, I don’t think about her being a girl. Maybe I had too much to drink. I’m not making any sense.” He relaxed as memories of Kat came to mind.

“I understand. When it comes to sex, I don’t think about everything in terms of who has what parts. I simply focus on pleasure. Speaking of which, I fucking can’t wait to get you out of this tuxedo.”

All seriousness concluded. Dylan wanted Seth. Now.

Chapter 8

Seth

A buzz of anticipation hummed in the pub. A rumor swirled that the Illinois bar exam results were about to be posted. Seth and many of his friends hovered over their phones and repeatedly refreshed the app. No one spoke. How could they engage in small talk when all of their careers were on the line?

Dylan sat beside Seth at Lawson's Bar. While Dylan attempted to distract Seth with light conversation, Seth preferred Dylan hold his shaking hand for support. But to keep their affair under wraps, Seth kept both of his hands on his phone. He didn't need a bunch of gossip about the status of their relationship. Too many complications.

Mr. Lawson brought over a couple of old-fashioned cocktails he had made himself and set one in front of Seth and Dylan. Seth accepted the glass and took a lengthy sip. His nerves needed it.

"Good to have the two of you back. It's been too long."

"I've missed your old-fashioneds. No bartender out West compares to you."

Seth half-listened as he refreshed the website on his phone.

"Are you in town to observe Yom Kippur with your

grandparents?"

"Yeah. It's also great to be here in Chicago and celebrate Seth and Kat passing the bar." Dylan patted Seth on the back.

Seth glanced upward. Mr. Lawson crossed himself with his hand. Seth counted his blessings Mr. Lawson didn't seem to notice Dylan only mentioning Seth and Kat and none of their other friends. Seth didn't need any more stress. If Mr. Lawson discovered his daughter's involvement in a threesome, the shock might kill such a religious Catholic.

Mr. Lawson's eyes drew together as if confused. Seth tensed. Did he just pick up on Dylan's misspeak? "Dylan, you don't seem concerned. Did you already pass?"

"No, California takes longer to return the results. I won't hear for about another month." Seth exhaled in relief.

Mr. Lawson fidgeted and looked toward the door. "Have either of you heard from Kat? Is she on her way?"

Seth pulled his head from his phone. "I just got a text. She'll be here any minute. Her boss understood her need to leave early when she said she wanted to open the results with her dad." A warm smile replaced the otherwise tired expression on Mr. Lawson's face.

"I bet she'll be happy to have you two with her."

Dylan laughed. "She doesn't even know I'm in town."

Seth added, "I thought it would be a fun surprise."

He refreshed the website one more time. A glitch occurred. The site wouldn't load. Seth pressed the icon again. He tried again. And again.

"Yes!" someone yelled from behind him.

He tapped on the arrow in the tiny circle. The loading button spun. It stopped again. *Dammit.*

Another person exclaimed, "YES!" and then another.

"Dylan! You're here!" Seth knew the voice well. Kat hugged Dylan. "I can't believe you are here!"

"I wanted to be with you when you both pass."

Kat stood beside Seth, seated in a chair, and grabbed his hand. He looked up at Kat. "Let's do this together." She nodded enthusiastically. They clutched their phones next to each other. The loading bar completed its progress. He held his breath. The page finally opened. The word "PASSED" appeared on both screens.

Seth jumped out of the chair, grabbed Kat, and lifted her into the air in an enormous hug. "Yes!" Seth kissed her. "Congratulations."

Tears ran down Kat's smiling face.

Dylan pulled Kat from Seth's embrace and kissed her. "I had no doubts you could do it!" Dylan then turned to kiss Seth soundly on the mouth. "Fucking congratulations."

Seth broke apart from Dylan and found Kat's dad beside her. "You did it! My lass is now a real attorney!"

Shit. Mr. Lawson witnessed Seth, Dylan, and Kat embrace one another. Seth stared wide-eyed as Kat's dad hugged her. His stomach plummeted. He didn't have butterflies. There was a cave full of bats in his belly.

"This calls for shots!" Mr. Lawson stepped back around the bar and grabbed four shot glasses and filled them with vodka. Seth paid close attention, looking for any signs of anger, disgust, or anything negative. Nothing. The only thing Seth saw was a very proud father.

Mr. Lawson held up a tiny glass. “Two down and one to go. Here’s to all three of you.” They all tossed back the shots.

Kat glared at her dad. “I thought you weren’t supposed to drink?”

“It’s small. I’ll be fine. Besides, if there was ever an occasion to celebrate with a shot, it is you becoming an attorney in my bar.”

“Cheers to that!” Dylan took another sip from his old-fashioned.

Mr. Lawson scanned the room. “Speaking of shots of vodka, where is my sweet Smirnova?”

Kat checked her phone and smiled. “She passed. She sends you her best wishes. Her boss won’t let her leave the office to celebrate.”

“Tell her I say congrats. Lots of orders are coming in. I need to help.” He returned behind the bar.

Kat wiped away the tear stains on her face. Her minimal makeup remained intact. She wasn’t the only one weeping with joyful relief. Seth took hold of her shaking hand. She grinned in return. “Did you know Dylan was going to be in town?”

Seth smiled conspiratorially. “Of course, he’s staying at my place.”

“I can’t believe you didn’t tell me.” She playfully smacked Dylan’s arm. “But I’m thrilled you are here.”

Dylan lifted his chin toward the opposite end of the bar. “Let’s go over and celebrate with everyone else.”

Seth led the way to the other side of the room. The smile on Cole’s face stretched from ear to ear. “I take it you passed?”

“Hell yeah, I did!” Cole shouted. “Drinks are on me!” Cole looked around for a waitress.

"The bar is slammed. I'll take care of the order. What can I get you?" said Kat.

"Shots! Shots! And more shots," Cole howled.

Seth placed a gentle hand on Kat's arm. "I thought your waitressing days were behind you?"

"It's no big deal." Kat stepped away.

Dylan asked, "Where are Kellie and Carter?"

Cole chuckled. "She shot out a little girl last week. She messaged they both passed the bar and were about to pass out from exhaustion."

Kat returned with a tray full of shots of vodka and placed it on a table for everyone to grab. "Here you all go." She grabbed one for herself. "Anyone hear from Connor?"

"He bombed it." Cole laughed.

Dylan shook his head back and forth with a smirk on his face. "You mean cheating his way through school didn't turn out well for him? Shame." He put on a dramatic, sad face.

Seth snagged another shot off the tray. He had lost track of the number he had tossed back.

One by one, their friends called it a night and left the bar. Cole was the last man standing among their classmates. "Kat, I don't know how you can weigh so little and still drink me under the table!"

"Practice."

"I'm out." Cole offered a one-arm bro-hug with Dylan. "It's good to see you, man. You should come back to town when you pass, and we can celebrate again." Dylan knuckle-bumped him.

He asked, "When do you move to New York?"

"After the holidays. I'm sure I'll be seeing you guys around. I'm working at my dad's firm until then."

Seth and Kat waved goodbye.

"Want to get out of here?" Seth finished the last of his drink.

Mr. Lawson stopped by the table. "Well, it looks like you three outlasted the rest of them."

"Do you need any help tonight, Dad?"

"I got this, Kat. Head on out before I have to fire you."

"You wouldn't?" Kat feigned horror.

"Of course not. This is always your home. Congrats again, boys. Take care of Kat for me."

Seth had a sneaking suspicion Mr. Lawson knew more about their relationship than he let on.

"Thank you for everything, Dad. I couldn't have passed without your help and encouragement." She hugged her father and kissed him on the cheek.

As the three were walking out, Dylan turned around to face Kat, who was following behind the men. "You're coming with us."

Seth didn't react to Dylan's double entendre. He waited for Kat's response. After their last time together after the bar exam, he made no assumptions about Kat's interest in sex.

"Is that a promise?" Kat raised her eyebrows.

Dylan took her hand. "Hurry up. It's my only night in town, free of my family."

"Hope you don't plan on rushing everything." The return of Kat's cheekiness made Seth smile. God, he had missed it. Seth wanted to bite her bottom lip.

He opened the rear door of the car for Dylan. Kat followed and Seth sat beside Kat in the back seat. "Where are we going?"

"My place." Seth worried anything he said would

make her change her mind. A lot was riding on the night. The negativity from when they were together after the bar exam needed to be undone. If the three of them shared an amazing time together, it could spark a new commitment between them. At least, Seth hoped.

"Not your palace on the lake?" Her crooked grin concerned Seth. Was she worried about being in Seth's apartment?

"My grandparents are doing some renovations. I'm crashing at Seth's."

"Are you cool with that?" Seth checked her temperature.

"No lake view, but the eye candy is still delicious." She winked. Seth smiled and the tightness in his chest eased. Thankfully, previous fears were alleviated.

Dylan squeezed her thigh, launching Kat forward in her seat, laughing. "Eye candy? Mmmm. Want to lick my lollipop?"

"Let's find out how many licks it takes to make you explode." Kat turned to Seth. "And I know where I want your king-size treat."

"Best Halloween ever!" Seth supported the idea of celebrating the fun holiday a few weeks early.

"I'm game for some trick or treating." Dylan kissed Kat. "It's good to be back in Chicago."

"If you stayed until the end of the month, we could all dress up like in an angel and devil trio. I could be the angel and you two could be a red and black devil." Kat's eyes lit up.

"I can imagine you strutting around in white lingerie with large feathery wings. Perfection." Seth unbuckled his seatbelt and attempted to adjust his pants.

"Seth and I will be your devils tonight."

The car stopped in front of Seth's apartment. "Take me to the dark side, boys."

Seth yanked on the door handle and stumbled out of the car, encumbered by his erection. Kat wiggled her sexy little self across the seat. He offered her a hand to exit the car and did the same for Dylan.

Seth unlocked his place and held the door open for his guests. Kat sauntered into his place, but Dylan blocked him from entering with an imposing frame and kissed him. While loving the feel of Dylan's lips, Seth kept a watchful eye on Kat.

Standing at the entrance of his bedroom, Kat gestured in their direction with her index finger and a diabolical grin. "Come here, my devils."

Dylan paused their kiss and turned to face Kat. "You can smile like you are the devil in this threesome, but you will always be our little angel."

Seth kicked the door shut behind him. "Time to fill our angel with a double dose of the devil." He strode toward Kat, unbuttoning his shirt along the way.

Dylan stripped down the quickest and assisted Kat with the zipper on her suit skirt. They gave her space to remove her stockings carefully. *Too bad she wasn't wearing a pair of thigh-highs.* Left in her bra and panties, Seth steered Kat into his bed.

"Screw the sugary wrapped packages of chocolate. This is my kind of candy." Seth eye-fucked Kat and Dylan.

Seth sidestepped to the nightstand near the headboard. He reached inside the drawer.

The bed jostled beside Seth. "I want your lollipop." He swiveled his head, hearing Dylan moan as Kat licked the crown of his cock.

Watching her stretch and strain her lips around Dylan made Seth's dick grow hard. He grabbed his firm length, stroking in tempo with Kat's ministrations. The scent of sex filled the atmosphere. Seth paused and acknowledged his gratitude for the presence of all three of them lying together in his bedroom.

"Hurry up with the lube." Dylan reached toward Seth.

Seth took the lube and condoms from the drawer and dropped them in the middle of the mattress. Dylan's legs remained hanging over the end of the bed.

"Baby, hop on up and straddle Dylan." Seth offered her a hand while Dylan rolled a condom down his length.

She twisted around and kissed him. "I think I know where you are going with this, and I can't wait."

Kat placed her knees on the bed beside Dylan's hips. Seth held Kat's waist as she descended and Dylan's cock disappeared into her wet folds. A mix of struggling moans rang out. Kat moved up and down. She increased her pace. "Slow down there, Kat. Let me catch up." Seth coated his finger with lube. "Dylan, keep our pixie amused while I get her ready."

"Ohhh." Kat panted. Seth hadn't even touched her yet. Dylan must have had his fingers on her clit. Seth found her opening between her firm ass cheeks and eased into her entrance. "Oh god, yes."

"Kat, lean forward a little." Seth stood behind Kat and between Dylan's legs as he pushed his dick into Kat's star-shaped hole. The overwhelming sensation made his head spin. He steadied himself by placing a hand on Kat's shoulder.

Amazing wasn't the right word. Seth had been dreaming of this moment for months. A state of euphoria flooded his body. Could he extend this forever?

"Dude, you need to move." Dylan's rasping plea spurred Seth into action.

He moved his hips with precise motion, rejoicing in the exquisite sensation created by Kat tightening around both men. The simultaneous rubbing, gripping, and sliding pushed Seth to the brink.

Dylan held still as Kat and Seth set the pace. "Holy shit. It feels so damn amazing," said Dylan.

"Baby, you good?" Seth couldn't see her face and read her expression.

A sob burst from Kat. "Oh my god." She whimpered. Seth choked up on hearing the emotion in her voice.

"Fuck, she's coming. Seth, faster!" Dylan cried out. Seth obliged and moved earnestly. Relishing every stroke, in and out. Dylan's cock massaged his length through Kat's thin wall.

"Fucking hell," Dylan bellowed.

"Fuck!" Seth wailed as he came like a volcanic eruption after years of dormancy.

He fell onto his back in a pool of exhaustion. Kat lie in between them. All three breathing hard and not talking. Seth stared at the ceiling. Kat's arm brushed past his own. A tiny sniffle cut through the heavy breathing.

"Are you crying?" Dylan whispered.

"Sorry, I must be hormonal."

"Passing the bar is an emotional milestone. Kat, it's okay." Dylan kissed her forehead.

"You sure it wasn't the sex?" Seth teased. She intertwined her fingers with Seth's. The last bit of tension in his muscles eased. Unlike their previous time together, she held him rather than pushing him away.

"You brought Kat to tears and I'm about to pass out. Seth, you're killing us both."

"Death by great sex, now that's the way to go." Seth laughed.

"Kill me now." Kat kissed Seth.

"Raincheck on round two? I'm beat." Dylan dragged himself to the bathroom first.

Kat rested on his bed, smiling with her eyes closed. His eyes teared up with joy. What an incredible end to an intense day.

After they each took a few minutes to clean up, they all curled into bed, yawning.

Everything was perfect. Both Kat and Dylan were in his bed. Sure, he reached sexual ecstasy, but the connection between all three hit a new pinnacle.

The fact that Dylan flew in to celebrate with him and Kat said a lot, even if Dylan claimed the purpose of the trip was to spend the Jewish high holidays with his grandparents. His reasoning seemed all too convenient, as his family wasn't religious. While Dylan had exceptional verbal skills, this time, his actions spoke louder still.

While no one proclaimed love, their night together affirmed their perfection as a threesome. They reveled in each other's joy. Their support for one another manifested in their acts of appreciation. Subtle gestures revealed their respect for each other.

Seth found himself in a state of complete bliss after their previous night together. After a contented night's sleep, Seth awoke in bed, sandwiched between Kat and Dylan. He skipped his daily early-morning run in favor of savoring more time entwined with his trueloves and dozed back to sleep.

Kat jostled Seth's arm. "Did you hear something?"

Seth kept his eyes closed and moaned. His apartment front door slammed shut.

"What the fuck?"

Kat's fingernails dug into his biceps. Dylan sat up, wiping his eyes.

"Congratulations on passing the bar. Look what I brought you. I drove all the way out to your favorite bakery in the suburbs." The clank of high heels on the wood floor approached the bedroom.

"Shit." Too late to run and hide. Seth's pulse throbbed in his ears.

"I'm so proud of you." His mother halted in his doorway. Her eyes grew into large, angry saucers. The sheet cake slipped from her hands and splattered on the ground. "Seth!" Her nasally shrill sent chills down his spine. "What in god's name is going on in here?"

Kat yanked the linen up and covered her naked breasts. Seth tried to answer, but a golf-ball-sized knot stuck in his throat.

Dylan coughed. "I'm sorry you caught us in a state of disarray. We weren't expecting you this morning. Can you give us a minute to get dressed?"

"That won't be necessary. I'm leaving." She scoffed.

"I'm sorry," Seth murmured.

"You're sorry? For hiding the fact you apparently are just as happy to be with a woman as with a man? I was supportive of you when you came out as gay. Your father and I never once made you feel lesser. We accepted a path in life which meant I most likely would never have grandchildren. But we were okay with it because we *loved* you. But now I know it was all a lie.

You do, *obviously,* enjoy the company of women, and have *purposely* chosen not to find one."

"Mom, it's not like that."

"I'm not blind, Seth, and I am not stupid. Are you blaming me for stopping by and finding you in this unsavory situation? Can't a mother stop by to congratulate her son?"

"Please, just give us a minute, so we can all talk." Dylan finger-combed his hair.

His mom sneered at Kat. "And you, if your mother knew about this, she would be unbelievably disappointed in you."

"Go to hell. My mom died of cancer years ago."

"Lucky for her. She didn't find you like this, in some depraved and pornographic heap." She closed her eyes and shook her head back and forth quickly while shaking her hands.

Seth stood up, placing a pillow in front of his private parts. "That's enough!" He stomped toward his mother. She took a step backward. His foot accidentally kicked the cake on the floor. "I will not let you speak to Kat like that."

Dylan got up from the bed and shielded himself with a pillow as well. "I believe it's time for you to leave. You and Seth can talk about this later." He stepped behind Seth and placed a supportive hand on Seth's shoulder.

Kat rose from the bed, wrapping herself in the sheet. She got right into his mom's face. "Maybe with a minute to think about things, you will come to realize that being a good mother has less to do with baked goods and more about accepting him for who he is. And by the way, Seth prefers vanilla frosting and white cake to chocolate. He spared hurting your feelings when you couldn't be bothered remembering his preference."

His mother harrumphed and walked out.

The front door shut with a bang and pain slammed into Seth's chest. He reached for his heart with both hands. The pillow dropped. He leaned against the nearby wall and slowly sunk to the floor. Was he going into cardiac arrest, or was this what it felt like when the world fell apart?

With no will to lift his head, he stared at the ground where the crumbled cake lay. "I'm so sorry Kat. That was a horrible thing my mother said to you."

"Don't worry about me. Words from people who are batshit crazy roll right off me. It's the words from those who are close that have the power to penetrate." Kat crouched in front of Seth.

"You are amazing, Seth, and don't you forget it." She kissed the top of his head.

Dylan sat beside Seth and put his arm around his shoulders. "I bet after the shock of catching you in bed wears off, she'll come to her senses." Dylan squeezed him close.

Seth closed his eyes, recollecting all the times his parents had made small heterosexist comments. They were subtle digs, not necessarily directed at Seth. Little tiny slices at his self-esteem like stinging paper cuts. At some point, the cuts healed, but the memory of the sting lingered. "I doubt she's going to get over this or accept the fact I'm bisexual. She probably faked being okay with me being gay. I think she pretended she accepted me to make her look good. That way, her friends would be less likely to judge her or me."

"You mean like if you keep repeating a lie, you eventually believe it yourself?" Kat placed her head on

Seth's knees, leaning their heads against one another.

Dylan rested his head on Seth's shoulders. "We're here whether she comes around today, tomorrow, or whenever."

Seth anticipated whenever meant never. He exhaled. "You won't even be here. Aren't you heading back to California in a few days?"

"I think I'll stay a little longer."

Chapter 9

Dylan

A couple of days later, he woke up alone in bed. The smoky scent of bacon tempted him. He threw on a pair of boxers. His stomach growled as he stepped into the kitchen. His cock reacted to the sight of Seth standing in front of the stove with nothing on but gray sweatpants hanging on his slim hips. Dylan cleared his throat, hoping not to startle Seth. "Morning." He closed in behind Seth and kissed him on the neck while he stirred the skillet full of scrambled eggs.

"Morning to you too." A timer rang. Seth pushed Dylan out of the way of the oven door. He pulled out a tray of cooked bacon. "Can you transfer the slices from the trays to the plate?" He pointed to the nearby dish covered in paper towels.

"This is a treat. A sexy man and good food. Don't get me wrong, I'm not complaining, but aren't you going to be late to work?" Dylan focused on his assigned task, avoiding burning himself with the hot grease.

"The firm is closed for Yom Kippur today." Seth turned off the burner and started assembling a couple of croissant sandwiches. He garnished the plate with grapes and set it in front of the chairs at his kitchen island.

Dylan devoured a huge bite out of the sandwich. "Mmmm." He finished chewing. "This is good. Thank you for cooking breakfast." Dylan paused before he took another mouthful of the flakey delight. "Aren't you fasting today for Yom Kippur?"

Seth answered by taking a large bite and overemphasizing the chewing motion. Dylan wasn't criticizing. Despite not being raised practicing Jewish traditions, Dylan learned about the culture from his paternal grandmother. "Going all in with the combination of eggs, cheese, and bacon? Throw in a little lobster with the eggs and you can really crush the holiday," Dylan said.

"I don't keep kosher." Seth twisted his face as if Dylan's ignorance confused him.

"I'm just giving you shit, man. I don't care if and how you observe the holiday." Dylan worried he had offended Seth.

Seth set the sandwich back down on his plate.

Shit. Dylan feared he made Seth lose his appetite.

Seth stared down at his plate. "Today is the day of atonement?"

Where was Seth going with this? Dylan kept his mouth shut, avoiding sticking his foot in his mouth again.

"Neither my mom nor dad has contacted me since the other morning. It's been forty-eight hours. I was hoping, given that they are religious, they would apologize for my mom's behavior. I think my father's silence means he disapproves of me as well."

Dylan wanted to scream. He was furious and disgusted by Seth's mom's conduct. Despite her strictness with manners and social graces, his mother fully accepted his homosexuality. "Are your parents at temple today for services?"

"Most likely." Seth looked up from his dish.

"Well, then they won't call before the breaking of the fast this evening." Dylan didn't want Seth waiting around all day for his parents.

"Maybe I should call to atone."

"What the fuck do *you* have to atone for?" Dylan understood Seth was upset and disappointed in his parents' actions, but there was no chance he would allow Seth to take any of the blame. Seth hung his head, laced his fingers together, and covered the back of his neck like he was prepared for a tornado. The image concerned Dylan.

He growled, "Nothing. You have nothing to apologize for." Dylan knew better than to spew words without knowing the other person's primary concerns. It was rule number one in political negotiations. Dylan tamped back his ire to a simmer as he waited for Seth's explanation.

Seth bit his lip. "Maybe I should have come out sooner? Maybe the fact that I lied to them hurt them the most?" He started fidgeting with his hands. Dylan had never seen Seth behave like this. Normally, he was carefree.

"Maybe if I apologize, I can open the door to a discussion. What do you think?"

What a crap idea! Dylan observed too many shitty politicians over the years and their bullshit exteriors. He knew there was something wrong with Seth's mom, but he didn't want to be the one to extinguish Seth's hope. "Do you plan on calling them?"

"If I call now, I can just leave a message."

Dylan urged Seth to consider this before exposing himself to further pain. "Why don't you finish your food while it is warm? It is amazing, by the way." Dylan kissed Seth on the lips. "Thank you again. It's delicious."

When they finished eating, Dylan cleaned up. As a guest, it was the least he could do in return for Seth's cooking. While drying the dishes with a dish towel, Dylan watched as Seth paced back and forth across the living room floor. "I think I'll call now," Seth said. Dylan put down the dish towel and held Seth's hand as he dialed.

"Hi. It's Seth. *Shana Tova.* I wanted to say sorry for the awkwardness the other morning. I hope we can share in a good upcoming year together." Seth ended the call and let out a long breath.

"I'm proud of you." Dylan hugged Seth until the other man pulled away. "I think you said it just right."

"I won't apologize for being bisexual if that's what you were worried about."

Dylan blushed sheepishly. He kissed Seth again. "It isn't easy to be the bigger person and make amends."

Seth looked a little lost, but Dylan had a plan to distract him for the day. "Care to continue on your antireligious kick today? Let's go fuck in the shower."

"Gay sex isn't antireligious."

"All sex is forbidden on Yom Kippur."

"Hell yes, to some good old debauchery."

They fooled around several times throughout the entire day. Although Dylan wasn't going to complain, he couldn't help but feel something was missing. Dylan texted Kat.

—Are you coming by Seth's tonight?—

Kat—*Can't. Firm is having a party for all the new hires who passed the bar—*

Dylan—*K (kissing face)—*

Later that night, the city lights cast a glow on Seth's face as he looked out onto the dark and empty streets. "It's 1:20 a.m. My parents' breaking of the fast must have ended hours ago. They didn't call me."

Dylan came up behind him, placing his hand on his shoulders. "Hopefully, things will look up in the morning." Dylan prayed for Seth.

They called it a night and got into bed. Seth cuddled into Dylan's protective hold.

The following day, Dylan kissed Seth as he set off for the office in his redefined role as an attorney at his parent's accounting firm. Seth didn't seem nervous as he walked out, but maybe he was hiding his nerves too.

After Seth left for work, Dylan sought to burn off some tense energy. He plugged in his earbuds, searched for a suitable playlist for his walk, but got caught up in social media and ended up watching several videos instead.

Without warning, the front entrance burst open, which was followed by a slamming door and the windows vibrating. Seth stood in the entryway, holding a cardboard office box. *What the fuck?* Dylan checked his watch. Only forty minutes had passed since Seth had left. He almost didn't have sufficient time to get to his job and back.

Seth dropped the carton. "They fucking fired me. My own parents fired me."

"What the hell?" Dylan jumped to his feet.

Seth held up his hand, stopping Dylan. "And they're suing me. I showed up at work and there was a process server in my cubicle. He served me notice. My shit was packed up and a security guard escorted me out of the damn building." Seth's breathing came in ragged beats.

Dylan listened, trying to contain his anger. He didn't want to inflame the situation and make Seth feel like he needed to console him. Dylan grabbed at the back of his neck, which was slick with perspiration.

There was a lot to unpack. First, Seth's feelings of betrayal, and second, the legal implications. In reality, the two were very closely intertwined. Dylan wanted to grab the summons and prepare a defense.

Instead, he took Seth into his arms as the other man sobbed. Dylan gripped him tighter while Seth's chest convulsed and the devastation ripped through his body.

Dylan's mom was uncompromising, but she was never cruel to this degree. Seth had done nothing at work justifying being fired. This was an assault on Seth, personally. They weren't just berating him. As if firing him wasn't a sufficient form of cruelty, they were fucking suing their own son for being bisexual.

"I've got you," Dylan murmured. Seth's head felt like lead resting on Dylan's shoulder. "You don't deserve this shit."

He guided Seth to the couch before he toppled over. Dylan sat down and Seth lay down with his head on Dylan's thigh. He stroked Seth's hair, running his fingers through his soft golden locks. Seth drifted off to sleep. Dylan tossed his head backward, relieved. Seth deserved a moment of peace.

As time passed, Seth fell into a deeper slumber and began snoring. His eyes moved underneath his eyelids. Dylan hoped he had pleasant dreams and not nightmares. He slinked out from under Seth, replacing his thigh with a pillow, and draped a blanket over Seth.

Dylan sat down with the summons at the kitchen island, where he wouldn't disturb Seth. He read through the document and took notes about what type of defenses could be made on Seth's behalf. As irate as Dylan became and as much as he wanted to help Seth, he couldn't represent Seth because he hadn't passed the bar yet.

He texted Kat.

—*You need to get to Seth's* ASAP—

She called about a half hour later. "What's going on? I just got your message. I was inside a prison with a client. There wasn't any cell phone reception."

Dylan gritted his teeth. He disliked the thought of Kat working on criminal cases, but he had other priorities at the moment. He conveyed all the details about what had happened to Seth.

"What the fucking hell? That's fucking bullshit. Fuck them and their fucking idiocy." Hearing Kat vent thoughts similar to his own acted like a valve release on a pressure cooker.

"My sentiments exactly. I would scream too, but Seth is asleep."

"What a relief."

"Precisely, but he can't sleep forever. Can you come over now? He's going to need you when he wakes up."

"I'm heading back to the city. I was at the state prison, which means I'm going to hit rush-hour traffic. The reverse commute sucks."

"Okay. While you are driving, think about who would be best to represent Seth."

"Yeah, I'll give it some thought. I can't believe this is happening. If Seth wakes up before I get there, please let him know I'm on my way."

Dylan got out his computer and started doing some research on firms appropriate for Seth's case. The research took time. When the hell did Seth's parents find time to hire attorneys and have this written up? Perhaps there was still room to negotiate with his parents. He hoped so. Otherwise, things were about to get ugly.

A soft knock on the door sent relief through his bones. He rose, opened the door, and scooped Kat into a hug. While the situation didn't have a direct impact on Dylan, it cut to his core. "Thank you so much for coming here."

"Of course, I would come here for Seth."

"I need you here too." Dylan surprised himself with his admission. Kat stood open-mouthed.

A moan came from the couch. Seth rose to a sitting position.

"What the hell time is it?" He stretched his arms and yawned. "Kat?"

She strutted over to Seth's side and hugged him. "I'm so sorry, Seth."

"Thanks for coming over."

"Don't be ridiculous. Dylan and I will always be here for you." She begged for support with her eyes.

"We are going to be with you every step of the way," said Dylan.

"See." Kat kissed Seth.

"Before we jump into this shit. You haven't eaten all day. Let's order something," added Dylan.

"Sure," Seth muttered. Dylan didn't expect enthusiasm from Seth, but the weakness in his voice concerned Dylan. He burned with a fire to fight in Seth's defense.

Kat held Seth's hand. "Can I make you a drink while we wait?"

Seth nodded with a bit more energy. "I think I could

use one." Kat meandered through the kitchen.

"Me too. Good thing we have our bartender here. Otherwise, we would be stuck doing shots of vodka!" Dylan kissed Kat on the head. "Thank you."

They continued to chat as Seth remained silent. The pizza arrived shortly thereafter. Dylan's lips curled into a relieved smile as he watched Seth eat a few slices.

He remained silent, so Dylan took it upon himself to just jump right into the meat of the issue. "I reviewed the summons. Besides firing you for breach, based on their morality clause, they are suing you for the money spent on law school."

"That's total crap!" Kat snarled. Dylan glowered at her. Hysteria wasn't helpful. Seth closed his eyes and took a deep breath.

"I know it isn't easy, but we can tackle this together. As Kat put it, their claims are crap. They are muddling personal and contractual issues. As far as firing you, while you have an at-will employment contract, they can't fire you for being bisexual. Because they dismissed you immediately after finding out about your sexuality, *they* are in a massive amount of trouble."

Seth sighed. "I can't think logically right now."

"That's why people hire attorneys for this kind of shit. It's too difficult to parse out feelings and logic." Kat put an arm around Seth.

"I've given it some thought about who I think you should hire. Kat's firm only does criminal work, so that's out. Cole's firm would be a great option." Kat winced, and Seth frowned.

"I know Kensington is expensive, but let's reach out and talk to him."

"I guess an initial consultation can't hurt." Seth

finished his cocktail. Kat stood and made him another.

"I have some savings but I didn't expect unemployment before I even started. Maybe I should take your dad up on the job offer."

Kat's jaw dropped open.

"You're going to move to California?" She threw back a shot of vodka.

"I would love for you to join me in Cali," Dylan said. Kat poured another shot and pounded it. "I don't think accepting his offer would be your best option. His favors tend to come with a lot of strings."

"With your work experience, you are a hot commodity in the job market. You'll have plenty of offers coming to you." Kat handed Seth a fresh drink.

"Hah. Can you imagine when they call up and verify my previous employment?" He took a sip.

"If they disparage your name, they worsen their situation when you file your counterclaims," said Kat.

"Want me to reach out to Cole?" Dylan needed to be helpful.

"Sure."

Dylan shot off a text to Cole, which he had composed earlier with all the details.

Kat and Dylan cleaned up the kitchen and disposed of the pizza boxes. Dylan's phone buzzed.

Cole—*That's incomprehensible for a parent to do. Let me discuss this with my dad and I will get back to you—*

Dylan—*Thanks—*

They piled in the bed and watched a mindless action movie, per Seth's request. Dylan knew things were truly upsetting for Seth when he didn't make any sexual advances.

His phone chimed again.

Cole—*My dad wants to meet tomorrow, himself. This must be important to him. He rarely takes on a case anymore. Can Seth come in at 9:00?*—

Seth read the message over Dylan's shoulder and agreed to the meeting.

Dylan—*Yes. Thank you!*—

The next morning, the three of them sat down in Mr. Kensington's office. The grandiose lavish workspace sported high ceilings and a crystal chandelier resting above a casual seating area with a fireplace focal point. Mr. Kensington didn't hide behind the desk. Instead, he sat beside Seth.

Dylan spoke up, "Thank you for agreeing to meet with us, Mr. Kensington. When Cole mentioned it, we were thrilled. Will he be sitting in today?"

Mr. Kensington said, "No, Colton will not be joining us as he is not technically an employee of the firm and could impair the client-confidentiality agreement if you so choose to retain our services." Seth nodded. Dylan noted Mr. Kensington's use of Cole's full name.

"Do Dylan and Kat need to step out for us to discuss matters?" Seth darted his gaze between everyone, with a hint of unease in his expression.

"No, not exactly. They can be qualified as essential third parties. I would like the three of you to sign a document specifying as much as to indicate you have requested their assistance in the case, as they have close ties to the initial incident, and you wish to maintain the expectation of confidentiality. Okay with all of you?" Seth nodded in the affirmative. Mr. Kensington pushed the nondisclosure papers in front of the three of them to sign.

"Colton shared Dylan's text message about what occurred last Saturday morning when Mrs. Levine stopped by Seth's apartment," Mr. Kensington said. "I have also reviewed the summons you received from Mr. and Mrs. Solomon's attorney."

"What do you think about my parent's case?"

"First, I know it sounds harsh, but you must start referring to them as Mr. and Mrs. Solomon. It will make this process easier for you to handle."

"Okay."

"Listen. I'm going to cut to the quick of things here. The Supreme Court has ruled that an employer cannot fire someone based on their sexual orientation. The timing of the incidents makes it clear the knowledge of your bisexuality prompted your termination. Their claim that you violated their morality clause fails on several levels. It violates federal law. The fact they knew you were gay for years and allowed all other employees to engage in male-female relationships nullifies the enforceability of their moral standards."

Seth's shoulders curled inward, making him appear smaller. "I obviously don't want to work there again."

"Of course. You can sue for damages for wrongful termination. In addition, you may claim sexual harassment and a hostile work environment.

"Regarding tuition reimbursement, companies often require repayment if you don't remain in employment for a minimum of two years. Did you sign a contract for tuition repayment?"

"No. My parents…I mean Mr. and Mrs. Solomon paid it from personal accounts for tax purposes." Seth twisted his mouth.

"Great. Then there's even less justification for the

claim. Even if they claimed a verbal agreement, you did not leave the firm of your own accord."

Kat held Seth's hand. "Do you think Seth should countersue?"

"This is a messy entanglement of family and money. Seth, if you want, we can start by trying to negotiate amicably to get them to drop the suit. Or, I have an excellent contact at the ACLU who would like to go nuclear on Solomon Accounting. There is plenty of middle ground too. It comes down to how you wish to proceed."

All eyes turned to Seth, waiting for his reply. "I tried leaving a message the other day, but I didn't get a reply. I guess it wouldn't hurt trying to reach out to dissuade them from continuing with the lawsuit."

"That's fine. Are you interested in hiring my firm to represent you?"

Seth gnawed on his lip.

Dylan said, "I think you should hire him, Seth. You need a big gun attorney for this. I can loan you some money for the retainer fees."

Seth frowned.

"Don't worry about some large upfront deposit. I'm interested in your case. Your situation enrages me. But let me be clear, I'm not doing this pro bono. I don't mean to alarm you, but I believe this case will escalate and there will be a significant payout. I will take a percentage in the end."

"You don't deserve anything they are throwing at you. What do you think about this plan? Seth?" Kat placed another hand on Seth's.

"Let's go ahead." Seth hung his head.

Mr. Kensington stood up. Dylan offered Seth a hand

out of his seat. Kat followed as well.

"My assistant has all the necessary paperwork to fill out. I will be in touch as soon as I contact their attorney." Mr. Kensington put out his hand. Dylan returned the handshake with an equally firm, confident grip. "I can't promise I can fix your family, but I can assure you will be compensated fairly."

"Thank you." Seth shook Mr. Kensington's hand and the three of them stepped outside the office.

While signing the forms, Cole greeted them. "Did everything go alright in there?"

"Thanks, Cole, for whatever you said and did to get your dad involved." Seth shook Cole's hand.

Kat tugged on Cole's suit jacket. "Can we talk over here a second?" Cole followed her off to the side. "Is there any way we can keep this under wraps? We never intended to come out like this, to our friends or our parents."

Unlike his usual demeanor, Cole lowered his voice to a murmur. "I might usually be a loudmouth, but I also know when to stay quiet. Your relationship is your own business. I am a little jealous." Cole winked. *Was he kidding?*

They exited the office and paused on the sidewalk, away from traffic. Dylan welcomed the fresh air outside after enduring the heaviness inside the office.

Kat took Seth's hand in hers. "Are you going to be alright, Seth? I need to get back to the office."

Seth hugged Kat. "Yeah. Thanks for coming with me today."

"Of course. I'll come by tonight?"

"That would be great," Dylan said, hugging Kat.

"Take care of our Seth." Kat marched down the

sidewalk toward the elevated train with a stop located a couple of blocks away from her office building.

Dylan turned to Seth. “Let’s get back to your place. I need a damn shower. I think I sweat through my shirt.” Seth smiled. It was the first honest smile Dylan had seen in days.

Back at Seth’s place, Dylan wished Seth could relax. He knew he was asking for too much. Seth was unusually quiet. It put Dylan on edge.

After Seth showered, he threw on some sweats. “Are you sure I shouldn’t reach out to your dad for a job?”

“I’m a little scared Kat could kick my ass if I convinced you to go to Cali with me. She’s petite, but seriously she might be able to take me.” Seth laughed. Dylan happily emasculated himself when it put a smile on Seth’s face.

“What about working at another accounting firm? Any of the big four would hire you in a second with your resume. And you could shove it in Mr. and Mrs. Solomon’s faces when you’re working at a top company. Stick it to them.” Dylan made a stabbing motion with his hand. “Or would you rather do corporate work?”

“Fuck. It’s a big decision. I don’t think I can decide today.”

“You don’t need to. I’ve got an idea. Let’s go for a run.” Seth followed Dylan to the bedroom and changed into running gear. As they walked out of Seth’s apartment, Dylan stopped Seth with a hand on his shoulder. “Try not to leave me in the dust.”

Seth kissed Dylan. “You can check out my ass as you try and keep up.” Dylan let out a sigh of relief, hearing the laughter in Seth’s voice.

After a five-mile run, attempting to keep pace with

Seth and failing, Dylan's muscles ached as he walked up two flights of stairs to Seth's place. Seth laughed at him as he unlocked his door. *Damn him and his endurance.*

"Care to join me in the shower?" Dylan enjoyed hearing Seth talk more like himself.

"Hell yes."

After a long, satisfying, stress-releasing session of screwing, Seth padded around the apartment with only a towel wrapped around his waist. Damn, he was sexy, with water dripping from his blond hair onto his lean frame.

Dylan, also only wearing a towel, answered the unexpected knock.

"Well hello there, handsome and handsome. You two are looking mighty fine, nearly naked." Kat kissed Dylan.

"What are you doing here?" Seth met Kat at the door and gave her a warm kiss.

"I talked to my boss and he agreed to let me work remotely for the rest of the day. I wanted to see how you are doing. I can tell by your flushed cheeks some things must be looking up." Kat raised an eyebrow. Seth flashed her a mercurial smile. She fanned her face with her hand. "Okay, you guys need to get dressed. If not, I won't be able to get some work done."

Kat typed away at her computer when Dylan returned from the bedroom with clothes. He opened his laptop beside her and started researching jobs for tax attorneys. Seth sat on the couch, remaining quiet and absorbed on his phone.

Seth's phone rang. Dylan and Kat jumped and their heads spun toward Seth. "It's Mr. Kensington." Seth swiped to answer. "Hello." He stood up and started pacing around the coffee table. "Okay…Yes, I agree. Let's go ahead. And, thank you." He hung up.

"Well? What did he say?" Dylan fired the questions at Seth.

"There is absolutely no room for negotiation. We are filing a countersuit." Seth set his phone down.

"Are you going nuclear on their asses?" Kat leaned in expectantly.

"Not yet, but I've decided to apply for a job at a top accounting firm."

"I think my grandpa has some connections. You start on your resume and I'll give him a call. Time to stick it to your procreators."

Chapter 10

Kat

By the end of the week, Dylan's parents insisted he return to California for an event. He asked both Kat and Seth to join him. Unfortunately, her job rendered it impossible. She yearned for more time with Dylan and also itched to get a glimpse of his life on the West Coast.

And Seth, while he made a lot of progress, he wasn't up for meeting a bunch of people.

Despite some slight hesitations about spending quality time with Seth without Dylan, Kat planned on going over to Seth's after work like she had been doing each evening. Her previous concerns about being with Seth hadn't faded. But, the one thing she did know, she would never cause Seth any extra pain. She didn't pity Seth, but felt a great desire to protect him.

She lifted her fist to tap on Seth's door. After a week of spending every night with Seth, did she need to knock? Probably not. Nonetheless, she rapped her knuckles against the wood panel, preserving a virtual line in their relationship. She wasn't *living* with Seth. She remained a guest.

Seth opened the door and greeted Kat with a soft peck. The sweet, warm kiss tempted Kat. As they stepped apart, their chemistry pulled her toward him. Seth's saucy smile baited her for more.

"How was work, honey?"

Kat laughed at Seth's trite greeting.

She kicked off her heels and put down her satchel with her computer. Her toes sighed in relief. She preferred wearing casual shoes like when she worked at the bar. "Exhausting. Everything is new. There's a lot to learn."

Wanting to get out of her business suit, she wandered to the bedroom. Kat opened up one of Seth's drawers and pulled out a pair of sweatpants. "Cool?"

"Of course." He leaned against the doorframe while Kat shed her work attire. "I got an email from Dylan's grandpa. He spoke with some people at the big accounting firms and shared my resume. Supposedly, they are all interested in hiring me.

Kat finished pulling on a t-shirt and hugged Seth. "That's great news! Next comes the bidding war."

"Knock on wood." Seth slouched and looked at the ground.

She reassured Seth with another hug. "You're amazing and going to land a terrific job. I know it." Seth's smile stirred the butterflies in her belly.

"You hungry? I cooked a lasagna today." The mere mention of Italian food made Kat salivate.

"Yeah, please." She followed Seth to the kitchen and gazed at the way his hips moved as he fixed a plate for her. She dug in and took a bite of the cheesy goodness sans meat. With her fork in mouth, she moaned. "It's so good you could almost convince me to go vegetarian."

"I'm saving the meat for later." Kat laughed at the terrible joke, relieved Seth's mood had brightened.

He sat beside her and they both enjoyed the dinner he had taken the time to prepare. She savored each bite.

Since she started work, she hadn't prepared a proper meal for herself. Take-out food never offered the same satisfaction as a home-cooked dinner. Between bites, she kissed Seth on the cheek. "Thank you again for a delicious meal."

A discomfort eased into the kitchen like a drifting fog. The silence sent a chill through her. After a few moments, she recognized the problem. "It's really quiet here without Dylan."

"Yeah. He fills a room." Seth sighed.

Kat hesitated, then asked, "You miss him?"

Seth spun his head and furrowed his brows. "Of course. Don't you?"

"Yes." The intensity of his reaction shot up red flags again. Did he always need both?

"I can see the wheels spinning. What are you thinking?" Seth leaned forward, resting his elbows on the counter.

"I pray I am enough for you."

"I hope you aren't staying here out of pity…although, even if you were, I don't think I would kick you out." He elbowed her in the side.

Kat gave him a peck. "If you keep feeding me, a girl could get used to the hospitality." She took another bite, smiling around the fork.

"Thank you for being here. Not just tonight, but all week. I couldn't have gotten through these past few days without you and Dylan."

"Seth, I'm not here out of pity. I'm here because I care about you very much. I wish I could perform some kind of magic to make this all better." She waved her arm in the air like she was casting a spell.

"Let's hope Kensington brings the magic. And I'll

get a job sooner than later."

"I'm sure you will. Want to watch a movie and chill?"

Seth picked up Kat's empty plate and his own and placed them in the sink. "Go find a show while I rinse these off." Seth turned on the water and Kat made herself comfortable in his bedroom with the remote.

She continued to scroll down the list of movies as Seth entered the room. He jumped on the bed. The vibration of the bouncing mattress jostled her hand, causing her to press the button on the controller. "Hey, this movie sucks."

Seth straddled Kat's legs. "Who cares? I want to suck—"

"Don't even think about ending that sentence with toes." The thought disgusted her.

He leaned over and tugged on her lip with his teeth. His moans echoed between kissing and nipping. She melted into his affection. Wrapping her arms around him, she never wanted to leave him.

He slipped his tongue between her lips, making love to her mouth as intimately as anything else. "Oh god, yes." His touch transported her to paradise. Her concerns disappeared as he breathed life into her. She held back a long-winded proclamation of her pleasure, not wanting to interrupt his actions.

Seth sat up, breaking their connection. She gasped for breath as he threw off his shirt, messing up his perfectly coiffed hair in the process. His toned chest made her sex ache.

"Baby, you need to get those clothes off." Seth tugged her t-shirt up and over her head, exposing her free breasts. He tugged on her erect nipple with his teeth. The desire between her legs intensified.

Kat shoved the sweatpants down while Seth stripped off his own. He dove in, face first, kissing just below Kat's belly button. A giggle bubbled out. The ticklish sensation morphed into heat as he slid off her thong in a slow, tortuous glide. "Grab a condom," he commanded.

She yanked open the nightstand drawer. He pulled back the covers as she opened the foil packet. She rolled it down his length. "Kat." His voice strained. A sparkle glinted off his shiny blues. He murmured, "I need you."

She kissed him, not knowing how to respond and avoiding saying the wrong thing. She embraced him in a tender hug. "Seth." Needing him as well, with her hand she directed him between her legs.

He pushed into Kat's core until he was deep inside her. Unlike his usual dizzying pace, he maintained a slow tempo. In an unhurried manner and with long strokes, he moved in and out. The intimacy captured her full attention.

"Baby, you feel so good. You're perfect."

Kat's heart clenched. She glanced at his closed-lidded eyes, contentment showing in his upturned grin.

He kissed her with one of his soul-owning lip locks as he continued to slowly stroke in and out. Kat's heart felt like it was growing beyond the confines of her chest. The sensation overwhelmed her, as she had never experienced something so dynamic. Her body trembled. Heat exploded in her core. Had they both just climaxed together? The intimacy was transcendent. It wasn't merely a fuck session. Her body tingled all over. She settled there in complete bliss, with Seth's weight on top of her. Pure happiness.

"Kat?" His breath brushed over her heart.

"Yeah." Her eyes remained shut.

"Was it as good for you as it was for me?"

"Yeah," she whispered, scared to admit it aloud. Neither said anything else.

His phone rang. He didn't move. It rang again.

"You should see who's calling."

"No one can make this moment any better." Despite his words, he reached for the phone and answered the video call.

He remained lying down. "Hey, Dylan."

"Are you in bed already? I didn't wake you, did I? It was the first chance I had to check-in."

"No, we're not asleep." Seth utilized his expert linguistic skills and pulled Kat into the conversation.

She leaned into the camera frame, placing her head on Seth's shoulder and exposing her bare shoulders.

"If you weren't sleeping, did I interrupt something else? Can I watch?" Kat's cheeks heated. She didn't want to share the moment with Dylan. First, it felt very private and personal between just her and Seth. And second, she hadn't had a chance to process it in her own head.

"Sorry, you already missed the money shot," Seth teased. Perhaps the sex didn't hold as much significance for Seth as she had just assumed.

"Speaking of missing things, I already miss the two of you. It was really great being able to spend the entire week together. Well, aside from the shit show."

"We miss you too." Speaking from her heart, Kat answered for both of them.

"Hopefully, we'll get to see you soon," said Seth.

"You two look awfully cozy. Will there be space for me in the bed when I come to town for Thanksgiving next month?"

"Absolutely!" Kat and Seth exclaimed. Their exuberant answer didn't minimize their intimate moment but revealed a common appreciation for their threesome.

"Good to know." Dylan smiled. His genuine smile, not the political one.

"We could send photos the next time."

Kat smacked Seth's arm and glared at him.

"Thanks, but I'll pass. In politics, unwanted photos tend to surface when you least desire."

"But video is okay?" Seth questioned.

"Eh." Dylan shrugged his shoulder. "Listen, I'm tired from the travel and dealing with my parents. I should go. I can't wait to see you both. Fingers-crossed, we can celebrate I passed the bar like you two."

"We should celebrate at Lawson's. My dad will want to congratulate you in person."

"Sounds like a plan," Dylan agreed.

Seth ended the call and put his phone back on the nightstand.

She turned on her preferred sleeping side. Seth draped his arm over her body and tugged her close to his chest. She sighed and began processing her feelings.

"Kat? What we shared earlier was something special between the two of us," he whispered. Kat nodded in agreement. "It's still okay if you miss Dylan. I do. The bond between you and me strengthens the connections between the three of us. It's all interconnected."

"Yeah." She started understanding Seth's perspective.

"I'm glad you're here Kat."

"Me too." They fell asleep together.

A few weeks later, Kat clung to a half dozen balloons, emblazoned with "Congrats," in the back of

Seth's car as he circled around the airport. Due to Dylan's concern about a decreasing amount of helium in the world, she opted for regular balloons. She didn't want to offend his position on environmental issues.

She spied Dylan up ahead. "Pull over by vestibule D."

The car came to a halt and Kat jumped out with the balloons in tow. She hurled herself into Dylan's arm. "Congratulations!" His suitcase crashed to the ground and his arms enveloped her in a tight embrace.

Seth joined them on the sidewalk and blew into a loud noise maker. "You did it!" Seth gave Dylan a huge kiss, which got interrupted by the blaring horn of a Chicago cop.

Kat turned toward the red and blue lights beside Seth's sedan. The officer glared at them. "Move it along!"

Seth shuffled back to the car and Dylan and Kat shoved the luggage and balloons inside. They escaped without getting an expensive ticket from the crazed airport cop.

"Thank you for the warm welcome." Dylan beamed with a genuine smile. Kat favored it to his practiced one.

Seth faced Dylan while he paused at a light before merging onto the highway. "It's our pleasure. We're really happy you are here." Seth snuck in another kiss before the signal turned green.

Then he continued, "Alex, Cole, Kellie, and Carter are meeting us at Lawson's to celebrate with you. With Thanksgiving tomorrow, everyone can leave work at a reasonable time. And Kellie and Carter have family in town to watch the baby. I think Kellie is super excited about getting out of the house."

"Cool. It will be great to see them." Dylan's voice didn't sound appreciative, but Kat chalked it up to being tired from the plane.

"We have just enough time to swing by my place and drop off your stuff."

Seth searched for a parking spot on the street while Kat and Dylan took his stuff up to Seth's apartment. Kat waited by the door while Dylan put his suitcase in the bedroom. As he walked out of the room, he raised an eyebrow. "When did Seth start wearing business skirts?"

"Huh?"

"You left the closet door open."

"Oh." What was Kat supposed to say? Why was he making a big deal out of her keeping a few suits at Seth's apartment? He knew she had been staying with Seth most nights since the last time Dylan was in town.

Dylan grabbed her elbow. "Are you and Seth a couple now? Am I even welcome here?" Kat felt a chill go down her spine.

She had never seen or heard Dylan show such insecurity. She kissed him and looked him directly in the eyes. "We're beyond happy you're here. It's the only thing we have been talking about for the past week."

Dylan crossed his arms. "I'm getting the sense we are no longer a threesome, but rather the two of you *and* me." His Adam's apple bobbed.

What the hell? Where was his attitude coming from?

"I'm sorry if I did something that led you to think that. Distance complicates things, but nothing has changed about how I feel about you."

"Something feels different."

"After the party, I plan to make you feel a whole lot of wonderful." She winked wickedly.

"Kat…" He leaned in and kissed her. The kiss started off tentatively, then intensified. Kat could feel his length harden against her belly as he pressed himself into her.

The door opened, but Kat didn't stop kissing Dylan. His firm grip prevented her from pulling away. She had no intention of stepping away.

Seth coughed loudly. "You two couldn't wait for me? I was stuck parking the car while you guys were fooling around. You're greedy." He laughed.

"You're here now." Dylan tilted his head toward the bedroom.

Kat put up her splayed hands in a stopping motion. "Okay. That's enough. Our friends are waiting for us. Let's not all be rude." She moved closer to the foyer. She turned back to them, but rather than following, they pouted. "Let's go." Kat circled her hand and pointed in the direction of the exit, signaling them to move it.

She watched her blond and brunette gorgeous duo descend the stairs. "Don't frown, we have all night." The view, as she pulled up the rear, made her look forward to the after-party with her men.

"Thank fuck."

"Yessss."

Anticipating there would be a considerable amount of drinking involved, they ordered a ride on an app. While waiting on the chilly sidewalk, Kat wrapped an arm around Dylan's waist and looked up at him. "I am *very* glad you are here." She stepped up on her tippy-toes and meowed in his ear.

"Don't tease me, Kitty-Kat, unless you want me to pick you up and drag you back upstairs."

"A little extra anticipation will make it even better

later." Seth winked.

"You two are acting odd." Dylan narrowed his eyes at them.

Seth ignored Dylan's comment, glanced down the street, and verified the approaching car. "Our ride is here. Let's go." Just in time.

At the entrance of Lawson's Bar, Kat opened the door for her men to enter. Dylan cast her a disapproving look. "Don't be a misogynist. I can open the door for you. It's my bar. I can do what I want." Seth gave her a quick peck on her lips. Admittedly, their familiarity with each other had grown since she had been staying at his apartment.

Seth clapped a hand on Dylan's back and pushed him to enter first. "Age before beauty."

Kat laughed at his nonsensical phrasing. Seth was three years older than Dylan. And as for looks, they were on equal footing.

"Congratulations!" cheered a crowd of fifty of Dylan's friends from high school and law school. Kat and Seth stepped off to the side as Dylan got pulled into a swarm of people congratulating him.

His grandmother came over and hugged her. "Thank you so much for helping me organize this. By the look on his face, it was clear that he was truly surprised."

"You're so welcome. But Seth took care of all the invitations and guest arrangements." Kat clapped Seth on the shoulder.

"Well, I owe you then. You even managed to get my son and his wife to attend. That is a miracle." She took Seth's hand between her two shaking ones.

"It's the least I could do after you and your husband were so kind to help me find a new job." Seth kissed her on the cheek. “Thank you again.”

“It was nothing. You are a fine man. Terrible thing your parents did. You’ll be joining us for Thanksgiving tomorrow?” Kat breathed easier when Dylan’s grandma changed topics.

Seth covered his scowl. “I wouldn’t miss it. Dylan raves about your turkey.”

Dylan came over and kissed his grandmother. “Nana, this was so nice of you to arrange this party.”

“Oh no, dear. Your two friends deserve all the thanks.” She pointed to Seth and Kat. “I simply wrote a check. They did the actual work.” Dylan gave Seth a friendly kiss on the mouth and then he kissed Kat in the same way.

Kat froze in reaction to the public embrace. Seth elbowed her in the side. *What the hell?* She spun toward him. While he smiled, his eyes spoke with disapproval. *Shit.* She attempted to smooth out her facial expression and appear unphased and more normal.

Nevertheless, the kiss didn’t seem to bother Dylan’s grandmother in the least. “Dylan, you should count yourself very lucky to have such good friends. It’s the most important thing in life. Trust me, I’m old.” The kind elderly lady hugged her grandson. Her pleasant demeanor made her easy to be around. Kat wondered if her dad would one day turn into a content man rather than a bitter one.

The senator stopped by and kissed his mother on the cheek. Dylan introduced Kat, “Dad, you remember Seth, and this is my friend Kat.”

The senator extended a hand to greet both Kat and Seth. “Seth, I hear my father helped you land a job. How is it working out for you?” He sounded like a mobster whom you owed a favor.

"Great."

"Wonderful. Get experience and then when Dylan finishes up his clerkship, you both can join the campaign." He faced Kat. "And I understand you are in criminal law. I hope I don't find myself in a situation where I need your assistance someday, but I'm sure I'll cross paths with many who might." He laughed as if he was deserving of a comedy special.

"Thanks for flying out here for my party. Is Mom here?" Dylan managed to get a word in.

"I'm right here, Dylan. For goodness's sake, can't a woman take a minute to freshen up? Let's all get a photo together. Seth, would you mind snapping a family photograph? We don't have a professional photographer here." Did she have photogs around her all the time? Seth took several photos of Dylan with his parents and grandparents, but his mother insisted on even more after she didn't approve of the first round.

"I apologize for our quick departure, but we need to leave and catch a flight back. Dylan, congratulations, I'm proud of you." His dad patted him on the back.

"Good to see you, Mom." The senator gave his mother a gentle hug.

"Pleasure to meet you, Kat, and it was great to catch up with you, Seth."

"You, too. Safe travels back to California."

Dylan's parents breezed out of there.

Mr. Lawson stepped into the make-shift group and clapped Dylan on the back. "Can you come over here a minute?"

Kat gently nudged Dylan's grandmother to follow her dad. "It's time for cake. You don't want to miss out on getting a piece."

Mr. Lawson stepped up to make a speech. "I'm thrilled to congratulate Dylan on passing not just any bar, but the California bar. We all knew you would pass. Everyone, if you will, let's all raise a glass to Dylan."

He hoisted his glass of water. "Congrats, Dylan!" A collective call rang out. One of the waitresses began cutting the cake.

Dylan spent much of his time conversing with friends other than Kat and Seth. But over time, the crowd thinned. At the end of the evening, Seth, Kat, Dylan, and Cole were the last ones remaining. "I'm leaving for New York. It might be quite a while until we see each other."

Kat gave Cole a big hug. "Good luck. Promise me you won't start putting ketchup on your hot dogs."

"I swear."

Seth kissed Cole on the cheek. "A farewell kiss."

"I'm going to miss you, Seth. I doubt anyone in New York will be as friendly as you. And Dylan, don't go changing."

Cole accepted a hug from Dylan. "Thank you again for all your help. I know I'll be 3000 miles away, but if there is anything I can ever do for you, don't hesitate to call."

Her dad stepped out from behind the bar. "Good luck Cole. Don't be shy when you're in town."

"Thanks, Mr. Lawson." And with a final wave, Cole took off.

All the guests had departed. Her dad asked the trio, "One more old-fashioned tonight?"

Kat passed on the drink. "I'm going to help clean up."

"You two will join me, won't you?" her dad asked

Seth and Dylan.

They sat down, turning their attention to her dad, who set the drinks in front of them. Kat listened in as she cleared tables. "Kat's mom and I were never able to have a second child, but I feel like both of you have become my kids over the past three years. In the spirit of the Thanksgiving holiday, I wanted to let you know how grateful I am Kat has such remarkable friends. She's lucky."

She scanned the bar one more time and then joined Dylan, Seth, and her dad.

"Place looks spotless. Thanks for helping. I'll see you tomorrow at your aunt's house for brunch." Her dad hugged her.

They finished their cocktails.

"Goodnight, Dad."

On the car ride back to Seth's apartment with Kat sandwiched between them, Dylan and Seth's clasped hands rested in Kat's lap. "I can't believe what you did for me tonight. The party was amazing. I don't know how you tracked down all my friends from high school. And I hope neither of you had to donate a liver to get my mom and dad to attend. And having my grandparents there was the cherry on top."

"I owed you, Dylan, for all your help with my parents. It was the least I could do to repay you."

Kat's fingers darted out and gave Seth a quick, subtle pinch before turning to Dylan. "You mean a lot to both of us. That's what we do. We look out for each other. We help each other. And, we support each other. Distance hasn't changed everything."

Dylan said, "I think your father may have an idea about our relationship. He may know we are all more than friends." Kat's eyes went wide.

"What makes you say that?" She looked back and forth between the men on either side.

"I believe Dylan's right."

"No." Kat's throat tightened.

"He commented on how we're lucky and we should look after one another."

Kat didn't connect the comment to the acknowledgment of a more than friendly relationship.

Seth murmured, "Mr. Lawson is a wise man." He kissed Kat.

As they climbed the stairs up to Seth's apartment, Seth reminded them he needed to get up early to run in the yearly Chicago Thanksgiving run.

"Ugh. I can't imagine waking at the crack of dawn and racing." Kat looked forward to sleeping late.

"It's not just any race. There's hot chocolate at the end, and I have collected t-shirts from each previous year," said Seth.

"This has been a long ass day. I can't wait to sleep in." Dylan yawned.

"I'm bushed as well," Kat added.

They entered the apartment, washed up, piled in bed, and fell asleep.

The next morning, after brunch with her extended family, Kat held down the bar with her dad, giving the rest of the staff a day off. Very few customers dropped by, but her dad insisted on opening. He claimed the holidays were when people most needed a place to get away and relax with a cocktail. Kat and her dad chatted as they awaited strays in need of alcohol and peace.

"I know you aren't supposed to drink, but it's a holiday. Can I make you an old-fashioned?"

He nodded.

Her dad took a sip. "I think the student is now ready to become the teacher."

"Thanks, Dad. You know, I used to look forward to leaving my apron behind and working at a law firm. But now that I'm gone, I miss it sometimes. You created a great bar here." Her dad's satisfied smile spoke volumes. She hugged him when they closed up for the night.

The morning after, Kat, Seth, and Dylan woke up and had mind-blowing sex. Afterward, Kat called dibs on showering first. She turned off the water, grabbed her towel, and stepped out of the shower. Both Seth and Dylan stood before her. Dylan looked ill and Seth had tears on his face. The smile on her face fell immediately. "What happened?"

Seth stepped closer to her. "Your cousin just phoned. She went to open the bar this morning. Your dad wasn't in his office so she checked on him in the apartment." More tears fell from Seth's eyes. A sick feeling gutted her. "Your father was lying in bed. She dialed 911."

No. No. No. No. No. Don't say it. Don't. Tears streamed down her face.

"Your dad apparently passed away in his sleep."

Chapter 11

Seth

He lunged for Kat and caught her as she collapsed to the floor. She clutched her knees and rocked back and forth. She wailed over and over again. “No. No. No.” The pain in her voice rattled Seth.

Feeling close to his breaking point, the tightness in Seth’s chest made it difficult to breathe. He held onto Kat for her benefit as well as his own. His body shook. At first, he thought it was Kat’s movement. But then an uncontrollable tremble racked his entire body.

Dylan kneeled beside them. Dylan’s powerful arm wrapped around his shoulders; it was the only thing keeping him from shattering.

He hurt for Kat. Her dad’s passing after losing her mother at a young age was tragic. But Mr. Lawson had substituted as his parent for the past month. Seth clung to their relationship, knowing someone was looking out for him. With Mr. Lawson’s passing, Seth became orphaned all over again. Too many people had been ripped from his life.

While remaining on the floor, he convinced himself perhaps it hadn’t happened. Maybe somehow there had been a mistake. He hadn’t seen any proof.

“Kat, we need to head over to the bar.” Dylan’s voice sounded distant. “Sweetheart, let’s get dressed.”

Dylan lifted Kat. “Seth, I could use a hand here.”

Dylan’s request cut through the fog in Seth’s head. It was imperative that he directed his focus on Kat. He needed to help her. Seth pushed his own feelings aside by focusing on the immediate task.

Dylan helped Kat finish drying off while Seth picked out some clothes. Her screams silenced into a deadly quiet. She moved like a rag doll as Seth attempted to dress her lifeless body.

Dylan assisted Kat getting into the back of Seth’s car. He continued to hold the door open for Seth. “Sit with Kat. You’re in no condition to drive,” Dylan said. Seth didn’t argue. Kat rested her head on his shoulder.

While Dylan drove, Seth called her aunt and uncle and let them know they were on their way.

The glow of spinning red and blue lights emanated from the bar as they neared. Dylan parked behind the ambulance.

Seth and Dylan pried her from the car as she resisted going inside. Each held of one her hands as she stumbled through the door, sobbing. Kat’s aunt and uncle rushed to her and enveloped her in a hug. Loud sobs erupted once again. With each cry, the pain in Seth’s chest intensified.

“Where’s my father? I want to see my dad.”

A police officer approached, confirming their identities. “I’m sorry the EMTs are still in the apartment with him. Go take a seat while they finish. Do you know what medications he was taking?”

“I can help you find them in his bathroom.” Dylan escorted the cop upstairs.

Seth remained with Kat and held her hand.

Josie, the bartender, placed a glass of water in front

of Kat. "Thank you," said Seth as he slid the drink closer to Kat, hoping she would at least take a sip or two. She fluctuated back and forth between crying outbursts and silence.

The squeak of wheels rolling over a worn, uneven wooden floor made them all turn their heads. The black bag lay on the moving gurney. Kat jumped out of her chair and ran to her father's side. She flung her body on top of the figure and hugged her father for the last time. "No. No. No. No."

After several minutes passed, the EMT said, "Miss. I'm sorry, but we need to take your father now."

"Please. No."

Dylan grasped Kat by her shoulders, prying her away from the gurney and clutching her in his embrace. He held her as the EMTs wheeled her dad out the entrance. The front door of the bar clanged closed behind the last cop exiting. Tears spilled down Seth's cheeks as they lifted Mr. Lawson into the emergency vehicle. He shuddered when the back of the ambulance slammed shut.

"Oh God." Kat bolted out of Dylan's arms. Seth ran after her. The stall door slammed against the wall and Kat bent over the toilet. Seth rubbed her shoulders as she dry heaved.

She labored to stand up. Dylan handed her a moistened paper towel. "Here. Wipe your face. The cool water will help." She complied and they returned to the table with her aunt and uncle.

As Kat approached, she panned her head around the room and sniffled several times, resulting in her choking. "We need to get ready and open." Her voice shook.

Dylan lovingly placed his arms on hers and looked

her in the eyes. "Not today. It's okay." Someone had already hung a sign on the door explaining that the pub was closed for the day.

"No!" she shouted and pulled away. "Dad even opened on Thanksgiving. He said some people need to come here. I must open." Her head swiveled in every direction. She looked lost.

Dylan kissed Kat's forehead. "It's already past lunchtime." He led her back to the table.

"Oh."

"I've contacted the rest of the staff." Josie filled her aunt and uncle's coffee cups. "We all loved your dad." She leaned over, positioning the carafe by Kat, but Seth signaled her away with a discreet hand motion.

Once her burst of anger subsided, she slouched in the chair.

Her aunt cleared her throat. "Kat, dear, we need to handle arrangements."

"Can't you take care of that stuff?" She wiped her nose with a tissue.

Seth reached for Kat's hand. "Kat, your father would want—"

"Stop! How would you know what my father would want? *I* don't even know, and he was *my* dad." She yanked her hand away. Her face turned red. Her breaths came out in angry huffs as she glared at Seth.

He didn't argue, but stood up and walked away from the table. "Your dad wrote up a list of instructions for this scenario. I'll go get it from his office."

Upon returning, he gave the document to Kat. When she crossed her arms, refusing to look at the paperwork, Seth asked, "Would you prefer your aunt review it?"

Kat nodded, and more tears fell. Dylan handed her

another tissue and put his arm around her shoulders.

Her aunt flipped through the papers. “Your dad stated he wanted an event on a Sunday, the slowest day at the pub.”

“What about a wake?” her uncle asked.

“He specified paying respects at a brief church service, followed by the burial—” Her aunt choked up. “Next to your mother.”

Kat’s head dropped into her hands and sobbed.

Josie said, “If you all want to host something afterward at the bar, I can take care of everything.”

“That would be very helpful.” Kat’s aunt’s eyes went wide. “Kat, is it okay with you?”

She nodded once.

“Josie, I can help with the planning,” said her aunt. She focused on the paperwork again. Her head popped up. “He requested Kat, Seth, Dylan, Alex, and our two girls serve as pallbearers.”

“Girls can’t carry the coffin,” said her uncle.

“Bollocks. My brother can specify whoever he wants. Men or women.”

Dylan peered at Seth with questioning eyes. Dylan opened his mouth but then closed it as if he had changed his mind about voicing his thoughts. Seth understood. While he knew about Mr. Lawson’s plans, it must have been unexpected to Dylan.

“Oh shit.” All eyes spun to Kat. “I need to tell Alex.”

“Do you want to call her?” Seth extended his phone to Kat. In the rush of walking out the door, she had forgotten hers.

“I can’t call her. I need to tell her in person.”

Kat used Seth’s phone and texted Smirnova. After a few pinging messages back and forth, Kat said, “I have to head over to her apartment."

"Seth and I can take you." Dylan got up from the table.

After another round of tears while saying goodbye to her aunt and uncle, Seth drove with Dylan and Kat to Smirnova's apartment. Smirnova crumbled to the ground when Kat shared the news. When she eventually calmed her tears and regained the ability to speak coherently, she requested Kat spend the night.

Seth wanted to protest. He wanted Kat and Dylan with him for himself alone. And he worried if Kat would be okay without him and Dylan by her side.

When she embraced Seth, she whispered, "I can't leave Alex by herself."

Dylan hugged her goodbye too. "Call us in the morning as soon as you wake up. Please."

Those were the last words out of Dylan's mouth until they returned to Seth's apartment. Before removing their jackets, Dylan enveloped Seth in a silent, endless hug. They clung to each other for fear of falling apart.

"Shit." Dylan released Seth before he was ready. "I need a drink."

Seth grabbed a couple of beers from the refrigerator and joined Dylan on the couch. They ended up dozing to sleep there while watching TV together.

The next day they spent with Kat, but she stayed overnight once again at Smirnova's. Seth hoped the pattern didn't continue.

Sunday, the morning of the funeral, he dressed himself in a dark navy suit and paired it with a conservative plain white shirt and a matching tie with a monochromatic stripe. Dylan held up a black tie and a gray tie against the charcoal gray suit he had on.

"Which?"

Seth pointed to the one on the left. "Go with the black."

Dylan tied the knot, straightened his tie, and took a deep breath. "We're picking up Kat?"

"Not sure. I'll text her."

Seth—*Heading out. U and Smirnova ready?—*

Kat—*Already at the bar—*

Seth—*See you soon (red heart)—*

"Dammit." He had a bad feeling in his gut.

"What?"

"I'm worried about Kat." A suspicious warning nagged at him.

"We'll all get through this together." Dylan patted him on the back and they walked out the door. Seth hoped Dylan was right.

He kept his thoughts to himself throughout the funeral. In fact, little if any conversation occurred. Only a murmur of hushed conversations hummed in the church and at the graveside. The Canadian geese squawked louder than the mourners.

During the limo ride back from the cemetery, the melancholy began easing.

"I told you." Kat's uncle crossed his arms and pouted.

"What are you talking about?" Her aunt shook her head at her husband.

"Everyone was objecting to the choice of pallbearers."

"Oh please." She rolled her eyes at him.

Were there complaints about Seth and Dylan holding the casket? Was it the fact they were Jewish? Not Family? Seth shot Dylan a questioning look. Dylan shrugged and shook his head.

Smirnova fidgeted with her fingers. "Were people upset with me?"

"It doesn't take much to get these people's Irish up. Don't fuss over it. A few pitchers at the bar and they won't even remember."

Fortunately, for Kat's sake, nobody mentioned anything about her relationship with Seth and Dylan. She didn't need any extra issues on her plate.

However, the other whispers at the church would not be brushed aside with some alcohol. Seth wavered whether he should acknowledge the most difficult question on hand. He preferred planning an answer like in law school. Preparation for all potential objections made for stronger arguments. "Sweetheart, your family has been whispering about the fate of the bar."

Kat's jaw dropped open, but then she straightened her back and with her own Irish fury, said, "I don't know."

"It's fine. Don't worry about it now." He didn't want her to think he was putting pressure on her. "I only mention it so you can prepare."

Her aunt and everyone else in the limo turned their attention to him. "Aren't you the executor of the will? Didn't he specify who is going to run the bar?"

"No ma'am. The property and business rights were designated to Kat. He left the decision up to her on how she would prefer to proceed."

"You better not sell the family business." Her abrasive uncle acted like an ass.

"I would never," she murmured.

Seth glared at her uncle. He wanted to rip into the man, but didn't want to upset Kat more.

"You do not have to figure it out this minute." Dylan offered her a comforting one-armed hug.

"I don't know how to run a bar," she said. Seth intertwined his fingers with hers. He squeezed her sweaty palms, offering her his silent reassurance.

"Neither did your grandpa or your dad when they first started out. You're smart, you can figure anything out. You got through law school, for goodness' sake," said her aunt.

And there it was. The big question. Would she quit her law job to manage Lawson's Bar? Or hire someone else to run it for her and keep working as a lawyer?

Seth and Dylan knew how hard she worked to graduate from law school and how much her dad wanted her to become an attorney. She had done it *and* she passed the bar exam. No one could ever take that away from her. Her dad had been so proud.

It was a monumental decision. Even with his accounting background, Seth recognized it wasn't merely a financial choice. The bar represented family and a place for the community. It was Mr. Lawson's life.

Dylan kissed the top of her head. "We're behind you, no matter what you choose to do."

"Thank you."

"And we'll help you dodge questions you don't feel comfortable answering," Seth added, giving Dylan a knuckle-bump.

They acted as her bodyguards the entire afternoon. The repeated concerns confirmed the importance of the bar to the Lawson family.

Not long after dinner, those who stopped by and paid their condolences left. Even Kat's aunt and uncle said goodnight.

All the hugs and offers of thoughts and prayers drained every ounce of Seth's energy. The only thing keeping him going was anticipating lying in bed with Kat and Dylan. He missed Kat the previous two nights, yearning for her touch and reassurance.

Seth approached Kat, who was speaking with Smirnova. "Hey, are you ready to get out of here?" He didn't specify the location to keep their secret from Smirnova.

"I think I want to stay in my dad's apartment tonight."

Dammit. Seth wanted the privacy and comfort of being at his place as opposed to a room haunted by the ghost of her father.

"You sure you want to stay here by yourself?" Dylan slyly asked for an invitation.

"Don't worry about Kat. I'm staying with her," said Smirnova.

Fuck. For the third night in a row, Kat chose not to be with her men.

"Is there anything else we can do for you tonight?" Dylan remained politically correct, whereas Seth wanted to argue.

"Thanks, Dylan." Kat hugged him.

Seth wrapped his arms around Kat, squeezing her and not wanting to let go. "You sure?" he whispered in her ear.

"Goodnight, Seth." Her eyes appeared vacant.

She retreated into herself. His heart sank. And once again, he had lost her.

Seth and Dylan entered his apartment and Seth slammed the door shut. "Do you feel better?" Dylan asked, shaking his head and glaring at him in a disapproving manner. "Want to smash some plates too? Maybe throw a glass at the wall?"

No. He wanted control. Lately, too many things were out of his control and he couldn't stand it. His parents. Kat's dad. And once again, Kat pulled away from him after they had been sharing a bed together for weeks.

Seth stared at Dylan. He too, was going to leave. Seth would be left with nothing. *Fuck.*

He gazed at Dylan in his charcoal suit. His dark brown hair gelled into place. And, the face of a celebrity with a high-end derma regimen. Seth needed to get underneath his skin.

With determined strides, he closed in on Dylan. He stood a few inches shorter than Dylan, but his resolution inflated his confidence to dominate the other man. Dylan's typical confident look slipped. Seth possessively entwined his fingers in Dylan's hair, not giving a fuck about its pristine style. Seth preferred him a little less than perfect. He liked him naked and dirty.

Seth gripped Dylan's strands, twisting them in his clenched fist. Dylan's eyes filled with arousal. "Seth?" he asked.

Seth held firm until Dylan's chiseled face softened. He had never submitted. They had never discussed it. Seth waited for Dylan's consent.

"Seth, I need you."

"Need what?" Seth asked for consent, but Dylan only begged with his eyes.

Testing Dylan's willingness, Seth kissed him deeply, plunging his tongue inside and controlling all the movement between them. Dylan relaxed into his arms. The switch in control excited Seth. He backed Dylan into the wall and the back of Dylan's skull thudded against the plasterboard. Dylan sighed and opened his eyes. Relief swirled in his brown eyes. "Seth?" Seth pressed his lips against Dylan's neck and pinned him in place.

The evidence of Dylan's arousal grew thick and hard against Seth's abs. He hadn't expected Dylan's enthusiasm, but was enraptured by his response. Sweat dripped down Seth's back. A primal urge roared inside. He craved the shift in dynamics. He needed it.

Seth avoided a slip, causing a return to the status quo in their power exchange. Rather than pushing Dylan for verbal consent, Seth directed Dylan, while ensuring he always had the opportunity to refuse. Seth would never force him into something he didn't desire.

"Go to the bedroom." Seth set his gaze on Dylan's ass as the other man followed his instruction and entered the gateway to a new level of pleasure.

Wearing a three-thousand-dollar suit, Seth wasn't about to disrespect Dylan's fine clothing by tossing it aside. "Get undressed and get on the bed." Dylan hung up his suit jacket and removed his tie. He placed the cufflinks on the dresser. After undoing a few buttons, he pulled the shirt over his head, throwing it to the side. Damn, his chest was beautiful. He was broad and toned. Seth began unloosening his tie.

Dylan stood naked before Seth. *Gorgeous*. "Hop up on the bed. On your back." Dylan complied. Seth made Dylan wait while he shed his clothes. All the while Seth delighted in watching Dylan stroke his length. Seth savored the show.

He leaned over Dylan's body and planted kisses along his rugged jaw. Each kiss primed every muscle in Seth's body for more. "Grab the lube." Dylan handed it to Seth. “You good?” Dylan nodded.

“Keep stroking your cock while I prepare you.” Dylan’s eyes rolled back in his head as Seth massaged Dylan’s prostate. Dylan stroked himself with determination. Seth ceased. “Don’t even think about coming yet.”

He liberally applied the lotion on his shaft and crown. He prodded at Dylan’s entrance, giving Dylan plenty of time to change his mind. Seth eased inside and paused until Dylan relaxed and accommodated Seth’s intimate connection.

Dylan’s eyes drifted shut. “Oh god, yes.”

The need to claim Dylan thoroughly possessed Seth. His cock grew harder than imaginable as he pressed in deeper. Dylan stroked along with him. They were on the verge of exploding.

Seth came on a grunted cry of triumph at the same time Dylan released between them. The tension in Seth’s body subsided and his muscles became languid, collapsing on top of Dylan.

Beneath Seth, Dylan’s chest convulsed. A quiet sob followed. “Seth,” Dylan choked and gasped for air. Seth peppered light kisses on his head. He continued to hold Dylan and let him cry. He comforted his friend and lover while he unleashed his feelings.

Finally…

“That was unexpected.” Dylan blushed.

“You, okay?”

“I’m scared.” Dylan’s bold admission stunned Seth as it reflected his own fears about what came next. “I’m scared we won’t get her back.”

“Time will tell.” Seth summoned all his positivity and kissed Dylan’s jaw.

"But I won't be here." Dylan's chest caved inward as he exhaled his last breath.

"I will be." Seth brushed his fingertips along Dylan's arm.

"It scares me too. It seemed as if you two became more like an exclusive couple while I was gone over the past month."

"Yes. We grew close. But we always wanted you with us."

Until Mr. Lawson's untimely passing, Seth felt optimistic about getting everything he desired. But then life took an unexpected turn. Again. "I don't know how she is going to come around and through this."

"Seth?" Dylan paused. "Thank you."

Seth turned on his side, facing Dylan. Those two words required further explanation. "For what?"

"For making me feel comfortable enough to let go with you, where I didn't need to be in control. It's exhausting always being responsible."

"I only want the real you. I don't expect you to be anything in particular. Just you."

"This was my first time bottoming. For anyone. Ever." Dylan and he hadn't gone through every detail of their sexual past.

"You took it like a champ." They both laughed before falling back into a silence.

"I have to return to California this week," Dylan said. "My parents have several Christmas parties I must attend over the coming weeks."

"I can't imagine the holidays without the cold and the snow."

"If you ever need to defrost your nuts, you could come visit."

"Is Asa going to dress me up again? The tux he chose was amazing and I looked incredible."

"I will be the one undressing you." Dylan smiled.

"Very tempting." Seth winked.

"Can we plan a date now?" Dylan's thoroughness and pushing made him a great attorney.

"I need to focus on Kat." Seth sighed, wishing he could help both Kat and Dylan.

"Of course. It would be amazing if you both could come out and visit."

"Nothing would make me happier than if the three of us could be together," said Seth.

"I know."

Chapter 12

Kat

She and Alex cried together late into the night. The next morning, her head throbbed. Her sinuses were sore and swollen with congestion.

She turned over in the bed and discovered a cold, empty jumble of covers where Alex had slept. Kat grabbed her phone and found a message.

Alex—*Must get into the office early. I will come by after work. Call or message if you need anything. (heart)—*

Kat considered burrowing under her blankets and hiding from life in the comfort of a bed. She faced a difficult task. Her family's persistent nagging hadn't helped. She listened to all her friends' and relatives' opinions and had almost reached her decision.

To clear her head, she got in the shower. The steam relieved the pain in her sinuses, allowing her to think. Clarity replaced the convoluted mess, which had been whirling in her thoughts since her dad's death.

With the warm water rinsing out the conditioner in her hair, she plotted out what to include in a memo to her law firm. *Due to unforeseen circumstances, I am submitting my letter of resignation…With my father's passing; I have come to inherit my family's bar… difficult decision as both my career in law and the success of the bar were both visions of my father... Blah blah blah. Thank you, thank you, thank you.*

She stepped out of the shower, breathing much easier. Her nasal congestion been alleviated, and she felt like a huge weight had been lifted off her shoulders. Despite her improved mental state, the image in the mirror looked terrible. Her eyes were puffy and her nose was red and raw. She did her best to cover it with foundation, but frowned at the results.

"Fuck it." She moved on.

After throwing on some jeans and a T-shirt, she searched in her refrigerator for something to eat. Casseroles and whatnot filled the freezer to the brim. Her stomach perked up at the sight of a dish of macaroni and cheese. It wasn't the ideal breakfast, but she deserved some comfort food. She heated a bowl-full in the microwave until an echoing beep rang out; the timer on the microwave and her phone pinged at the same time.

Grabbing the warm dish, she sat at the table with a fork and her cell. She stuffed the cheesy pasta in her mouth and opened her messages.

Dylan—*I planned to come over this morning and help with anything you need. Can I pick up breakfast?*—

Kat rolled her eyes. *More food?*

Kat—*I'm good*—

Dylan—*?? on food or you don't want to see me?*—

Kat—*Sorry, I don't need any more food*—

Dylan—*Can I stop by?*—

Kat—*(heart)*—

She set aside her food. Instead, she emailed her law firm before Dylan arrived. She didn't want him trying to get her to change her mind. Once she came to a decision, she refused to engage in any further debate. She was done.

After she hit send, she received another message.

Seth—*I wish I could drop in this morning. As a new employee, I can't take off again (broken heart)—*

Kat—*No worries—*

Seth—*I will swing by after work—*

Kat replied with a thumbs-up reaction. It wasn't the most grateful response, but after exhausting her emotional energy bank over the weekend, she planned to meter her strength for the day.

She descended the steps from the apartment to the bar. She entered the main seating area, her heart trying to burst free. Light streamed in the front windows of the bar in a heavenly manner, enveloping her in her father's blessing. She didn't stand alone in the pub, although the staff had yet to arrive. Her dad's vision showed in every piece of furniture. The place exuded warmth and practicality. He arranged tables efficiently for both the customers and waitresses. He put a lot of thought into all aspects of the bar.

Her phone vibrated in her back pocket. Knowing Dylan was on his way, she checked her messages.

Dylan—*Here (smiley face)—*

She unlocked and opened the front door. She threw herself into Dylan's arms. The hug conveyed a welcoming greeting and a deep sense of comfort. His embrace communicated more than any words.

"I'm here. How can I help?" Wearing casual khakis and a stylish pullover shirt, he looked stunning and dressed suitably for lugging kegs or doing office work.

She knew the perfect job to put his talents to use. "Can you help get me out of my apartment contract? There's no need for it." She sighed. Every decision she made required a deep, cleansing breath. And Kat aimed to endure the day, moment by moment.

"Sure."

She sent him an electronic copy of her lease. "Thank you." Kat diverted her gaze, hiding from him.

Dylan cupped his palm on her cheek and steered her attention back to him. "Where are you moving to?"

"The apartment here. It made sense for my dad. It's free."

"You don't want to move in with Seth?"

Kat stepped backward and crossed her arms over her chest. "Why would I do that? Seth and I aren't dating."

"Up until Thanksgiving, you had spent every night at his place." Dylan raised an eyebrow.

"And, what?" She placed her hands on her hips.

He narrowed his eyes at her. "You seemed like you were entangled when I arrived."

"Well, we're not. I was just helping him get through a difficult time. He doesn't need me anymore."

"What about you? Might this be easier for you, having him support you?" Dylan pulled a chair from a nearby table. He sat down and gestured with his hand at the open chair.

Kat lowered herself onto the seat, her eyes wary.

"We both want to help you any way we can. I need to head back west in a couple of days. I feel bad I can't be by your side."

"Thank you. I appreciate it. But to be honest, I can't handle a relationship. I have too much on my plate."

"Seth could be there for you. I know he wants to be," he said.

"Seth wants a lot. He wants us to be a threesome. But that's not happening. Like you said, you're leaving.

I don't blame you. You are about to start an amazing job. I said the same thing when you got on the plane back in May—"

"But—" Dylan interrupted. Kat fired up her hand to stop him.

"Please. I just can't, Dylan. Anyway, Seth's situation was totally different. His parents hurt him. He needed me. I would have done anything to alleviate his pain. I lost my mom and dad too, but I'm left with plenty of wonderful memories. They didn't hurt me. They were taken away too soon."

Dylan slumped in his chair and chewed on his lip. He didn't hold back his thoughts. Kat checked the time on her phone and stood up. "I need to get ready here. If you can take care of the lease issue, it would be great." She went into the kitchen, leaving Dylan at the table.

Fortunately, the staff arrived on time. Each person greeted Kat with a reassuring hug. She stiffened her back and hastened each contact. After days of hearing "I'm so sorry for your loss," she reached her fill.

Kat addressed the entire team. "I have an announcement. From now on, I will be here permanently, attempting to assume the role of my father. I need everyone's help to get up to speed, so whatever you can share would be greatly appreciated. We all miss my dad, but the best way to honor him is for all of us to continue to serve everyone who comes through these front doors."

She stayed clear of the staff in the kitchen and took stock of alcohol, snacks, glasses, and other essentials.

"You aren't keeping your job as an attorney?" Kat's head popped up surprised to see Dylan sitting across the bar from her.

"Shit, Dylan. You scared the fuck out of me."

He didn't apologize.

"That's a huge decision."

"It's what I need to do. I know it in my heart."

"Are you good with it?" he asked.

Kat nodded.

"If you're good, all is good. By the way, I reviewed the lease. It was written by an idiot who left a few holes for you to get out of it. I'll take care of it."

"Thank you." She added it to her growing list of IOUs and gratitude notes.

"I can also help move your stuff out of your apartment."

"Oh yeah. I didn't consider that."

"Like you said, you have a lot on your plate." Dylan reached out an open palm and Kat handed over the keys to her current studio and the ones to the outside entrance of the apartment over the bar.

Promptly at 11:00 a.m., she unlocked the front door and turned on all of the lights. She checked on the ice. "I'll be right back. I'm going to grab some more."

Kat took one step, but the bartender placed a hand on her shoulder, stopping her. "That's not your job anymore, Kat. I'll go get it."

She knew how to bartend, how to waitress, and even how to cook in the kitchen. She wasn't sure how to *run* the business. Her staff cleaned and prepped. She didn't know what she was supposed to be doing.

The bartender started sanitizing the surfaces and wiping down the barware. "I've got this covered out here. If you need to double-check on deliveries, the crowd won't start rolling in for another half hour." Kat felt stupid because it was one more thing she was unaware she needed to take care of. She appreciated the bartender's polite suggestion.

Kat strode into her dad's office—*her office*. She started looking through his files. Luckily, her dad's old-school approach, of using paper records, made things easy to thumb through. She opened up his computer to see if there was anything pertinent on it. Among the few, the one marked "porn" stood out. She laughed at the fact not only did he not have a password on his computer, but he didn't bother disguising the name. She skipped *that* file.

When she got up, a dizzy sensation hit her. Feeling light-headed, she sunk back down into the chair. Her breathing hastened. A wave of unease washed over her until a knock on the door broke her spiral into despair. Josie peeked her head inside. "Sorry to bother you, Kat, but we are getting slammed out here and could use another hand."

Kat jumped up, but then slumped into the seat again.

"You okay?"

"Yeah, I'm good. I forgot to eat breakfast," she lied.

"Make sure you take care of yourself. Grab a bite from the kitchen."

Kat stood again, bracing herself. "See, all better. Maybe I got up too quickly."

The size of the lunch crowd didn't exceed the usual number, but many of the customers inquired about her dad, which slowed down the waitresses. Kat took it upon herself to greet all the regulars whom she had gotten to know over the summer. Her father was well-liked by all. After explaining that he had died of a stroke during his sleep a few dozen times, Kat felt more at ease. Being around the those who knew her dad and had stories or a funny tale to tell filled the emptiness inside her.

During the downtime between lunch and dinner, Kat reviewed some files while sitting at the bar top. She buried her head in paperwork.

"Good afternoon, Mrs. Casey. The usual?" Josie greeted.

"Yes, please."

Kat found her aunt seated beside her.

"Coming right up." Josie stepped into the kitchen and came back with a cup for her aunt. "Kat, would you like a cup of coffee too?"

"I'm good."

"Kat, stop and have a drink with me." The look in her aunt's eyes let Kat know better than to refuse.

Her aunt took a sip. The bartender also slid a sandwich in front of her aunt. "Thanks, Josie."

"The usual?" she asked. Kat spied the pastrami sandwich and fresh, sliced potato chips.

"I used come by the first Monday of every month to see your dad."

"I didn't know." Kat sipped the coffee.

"I swung by this afternoon because I wanted to thank you. Dylan called to let me know you intend to run the bar. I'm touched and grateful the place is going to stay in the family. I know by taking this on, you're sacrificing your law job and all the effort it took to get it. It means a lot to all of us. Your grandfather started this and then passed it on to your dad."

"Why didn't it go to you *and* dad?"

"Let's say your grandfather wasn't as broad-minded about the capabilities of women as your dad. It was a different time back then. Today, women have more choices. You can create your own paths in both your professional and personal life."

Kat half-smiled. Given Seth's situation with his parents, she knew many men and women still faced difficult constraints on their private lives. "Hey, I have a question for you. I was going through some paperwork and found a bunch of things with the name Loughlin on it."

"I would love to see those. Back when my grandfather came here from Ireland, his surname was originally Loughlin. As the story goes, when he migrated here, his thick accent caused a misunderstanding at immigration, where his last name got mistaken for Lawson, not Loughlin."

"I never heard that before." Knowing the history heightened her connection to the bar. Maintaining control of Lawson's served a purpose, different from defending criminals, but important.

Kat's aunt placed her napkin on top of her empty plate and Josie bussed it away. "I'm going to take off before things get crazy in here. Call if you need anything, Kat."

The break with her aunt reassured her about her decision.

She stepped into the office after the dinner rush to check on things to make sure everything was in order for the next day. Kat spun in circles, surrounded by the clutter.

The door opened, and her eyes darted in that direction. Dressed in a gray suit and a blue shirt, Seth apologized for startling her with a kiss on the cheek. "I would've been here sooner, but I had to work late. How are things going?"

"This is a mess." She shook her head back and forth,

disgusted by the lack of organization.

"I can help. I'm good with messy." Seth winked flirtatiously.

Kat laughed. "Only you could make a double entendre about paperwork."

Dylan walked in behind Seth and handed Kat the keys to her apartment above the bar. "Mission accomplished."

"What mission?" Seth looked between them.

"Kat is free and clear from her old lease and completely moved into the apartment upstairs."

"How the hell did you manage to get everything done in one day? You're incredible." Kat fawned, but then realized she was going to owe him big time for such an effort, and it made her feel uncomfortable.

"Amazing man, fucking amazing cock." Seth smirked. Dylan quirked a smile. "We should christen the place."

"Raincheck? Alex asked if she could spend the night again. With me." Kat fudged a little on the facts. Alex had offered to stay with her, not asked.

"You would prefer to be with Alex than us?" Seth sat on the desktop with his hands over his chest.

"I won't tell her no. You know, she was really close to my dad too." The fib grew.

"You know…" Seth started, but then Dylan put his arm around Seth's shoulders in a dominating manner.

Dylan interrupted, "You know, I'm starving. Think I can get some food and a beer?"

Relief washed over Kat. Again, Dylan lessened her stress. He had been a rock for her. "Absolutely. How about you, Seth, you hungry?"

Shit. She had accidentally set Seth up for a sexual

comeback. Dylan answered for Seth. "Food would be great. Thanks, Kat." He steered Seth out of the office.

Kat put in an order in the kitchen. While she was there, she shot off a text asking Alex if she could spend the night again.

She returned with two burgers. Setting it down, she poured a beer for each.

"Thanks, Kat." Dylan dove into the burger.

"Sorry we don't serve avocado on our burgers here." She caught Dylan with a mouthful, so he couldn't protest.

"Have you taken the time to eat?" asked Seth.

She was planning on sitting down with them, but all the deception spoiled her appetite. "I ate earlier." Kat scratched at her neck. The stress of lying made her skin itch.

Dylan swallowed and took a slug of his drink. "Taking care of yourself is important."

"I think I'm going to let the staff close up tonight and get some rest."

"Excellent idea."

Dylan and Seth headed out together after they ate.

Kat informed the staff she was going up for the night and climbed the stairs to the apartment. She knew she had options. She could be marching up the stairs at Seth's along with Dylan. His staircase case wrapped around the corners with an open column in the center. The view of the steel railings from the third floor made it a photographer's dream. However, it was also a death trap if one were to fall over the railing. Whereas here, the narrow stairway to the apartment above the bar was closed off and secure.

She unlocked the door to the apartment. She

expected the familiar scent of her dad. Instead, she detected a faint waft of his odor, but the aroma had changed. Adding all her belongings in the apartment masked the previous smell.

All her father's things sat stacked off to the side. The living room was overcrowded but organized. Dylan had accomplished a huge amount of work for Kat. *And how did she repay his thoughtful and amazing gesture?* She lied to him and blew him off.

"Knock-knock." She twisted and faced the door. Alex took a step inside. "Can I come in?"

"Perfect timing. I just walked in."

"The bartender told me." Alex looked around. Her eyes went wide. "Are these your things from your apartment?"

"Yeah. I think so." Kat worried for a moment if any of her stuff got lost during the move. She took a deep breath and reminded herself Dylan only did things to perfection. He wouldn't forget or lose anything in the process of moving.

"How did you get this all done in a single day?"

"Dylan did it all. He even got me out of my lease."

"Seriously, the man is unbelievable. He can do anything. I could totally see him being president one day." Alex put down her briefcase and opened the fridge. "Holy crap, your refrigerator is packed with food. Mind if I grab a beer?"

Kat stared at the bottle in Alex's hand and a tear rolled down her face.

"Shit. Was this your father's?" Alex placed the beer back inside.

"No, it's okay. I'll join you."

Alex grabbed two, popped the tops, and handed a

bottle to Kat. "To your dad and my pseudo-dad. He may not be drinking with us tonight, but his love will always remain."

"Cheers." Tears spilled down Kat's and Alex's cheeks.

"This must be hard on Seth too. He and your dad were close. And I heard his parents fired him and are suing him. I don't know the details, but that has to be difficult for him." Alex took a gulp.

Shit. Kat hadn't considered Seth's perspective. *She was the shittiest friend ever.* Kat put down her beer, no longer thirsty.

"You, okay?"

"I'm tired," Kat mumbled, speaking another half-truth.

"It's late. I need some sleep. These long days at work are kicking my ass." Alex finished her beer.

Chapter 13

Seth

A couple of mornings later, he returned from his run to find Dylan neatly rolling his clothes and placing the items in his suitcase. Seth stopped short in the doorway of his bedroom. “Why are you packing? You aren’t flying out for two days?”

“My mom texted and said I need to return today for an event.” Dylan continued folding.

Seth leaned against the wall, thankful the drywall held him up and didn’t let him down like everyone else in his life. He stared at his bed and envisioned lying in it alone. No Dylan. No Kat. Seth’s legs trembled.

“Did you shower while I was running?” He considered Dylan’s urgency to depart.

“Hoping for a round of wet and wild sex before I head for the airport?” Dylan shot him a sexy ass grin.

Damn him and his glorious, perfect smile. Seth was too angry to be taken in by Dylan’s good looks. He wanted to tell him to fuck off. On the other hand, although Seth was offended by the demeaning offer, he struggled because he also wished to seize the opportunity.

Dylan stopped packing and confronted Seth. He placed a hand on Seth’s shoulder. “Don’t pout. We’re all being pulled in different directions. I have family commitments. Kat is trying to adapt. And you've got a shit ton going on in your life too." As if Seth weren't aware of all the damn things that were pulling Kat and Dylan away from him.

"I hate I have no other choice than to leave Kat in this situation." Dylan threw a pair of socks into the suitcase and it ricocheted out onto the floor.

"I'll be there for Kat." Seth picked up the discarded sock roll and tossed it into Dylan's open luggage. "All I want to do is to be there for her."

"You need to be there in the ways that cater to her needs. Not yours. Everyone grieves in their own way."

"It's tough when she keeps lying about shit."

"I know. Don't take it personally. She isn't herself right now. It is important to support her where she doesn't feel compelled to lie." Dylan kissed Seth but kept his distance from his sweat-soaked clothes.

"I think she is going to require a lot of patience," said Dylan.

"Since when did you start understanding females so well, considering she is the first you dated?"

"Hah. We never went on a date." Dylan chuckled.

"We weren't just hooking up," Seth whispered. He hated the insinuation their relationship was anything less than significant.

"No, it wasn't a hook-up." Dylan closed his suitcase and pulled out his phone. "My ride will be here in seven minutes. Can you walk me out?"

Standing on the sidewalk, Seth suppressed his tears and fought to speak around the lump in his throat. "Sorry I can't drive you to the airport."

"I understand you need to go to work." The car pulled up and Dylan placed his suitcase in the trunk.

Opening the back door, he turned towards Seth. Dylan gripped Seth's hair and held him tightly as he pressed their lips together. Seth held on, refusing to let go as if his entire existence depended on it. Perhaps not his life, but his heart.

Dylan broke the kiss and got into the car. Emptiness consumed Seth as his love drove away.

He retreated to his apartment. His new job remained the only positive thing in his reality. He couldn't jeopardize it by being late. He forced himself into the shower and threw on work clothes. With no improvement in his mood, he prayed that inhaling fresh brisk air while walking to the office cleared his head.

He stopped upon entering his workplace. Christmas and Hanukkah decorations filled the lobby. *Oh my god.* With all the crap going on in his life, he had forgotten about the holidays.

Ornaments with every employee's name hung on the enormous tree. A menorah and a kinara rested in a prominent location. All the tasteful decorations impressed Seth, which included representation of all the cultural celebrations. The receptionist reached into a basket filled with small bags and handed one to Seth.

The gold bag reminded him of Hanukkah gelt. A sense of unease hit Seth. He hurried to his office, sat down, and pulled up photos on his phone from previous holidays at his parents' accounting firm. His parents limited the colors to blue and white with a small touch of silver. The decorations were aligned with Hanukkah, not Christmas or Kwanza. He composed a list of how Mr. and Mrs. Soloman disrespected people of other faiths, which amounted to a pattern of harassment. He forwarded the additional facts to his attorney.

Seth opened the snack-sized gift bag resting on his desk and pulled out a frosting-coated sugar cookie with a red stocking design. The treat sweetened his mood and gave him an idea.

Seth—*I've never decorated a Christmas tree. Can I help you decorate the bar?*—

Kat—*Sure. I could use a hand*—

Seth—*Can we turn it into a decorating party? I'm so excited. I'll come by after work to discuss all the details (dancing guy and Christmas tree)*—

Kat—*(crying laughing face)*—

Her use of emoji pleased Seth. Getting her to smile was a step in the right direction. He needed the holiday cheer too as an alternative to looking at all the serious issues around him and his friends.

During lunch, Seth searched the internet for decorating ideas. Instead of relying on Mr. Lawson's decorations, Seth stopped off at a big box store after work. Hoping Kat would approve, he purchased a couple dozen boxes of lights in a variety of styles. He wanted to have fun with Kat, not a headache.

Excited to show Kat his purchases, he bounced into Lawson's Bar. He glanced around, searching for her red lips. Seth found her talking to a customer in the corner. Her cheerful expression was a welcome sight. He placed keeping a smile on her face at the top of his priority list. A few ideas came to mind. He fantasized about making her scream and forget all her concerns.

Her jeans accentuated her petite hips and beckoned his attention. He wanted his hand there, fingers digging into her sides, tugging on her, over and over again.

She turned in his direction and he buried his naughty imagination. Despite the extraordinary effort, he reminded himself he needed to support Kat in her grieving process. Even if hers differed than his.

"Whatcha got in the bag?" She peeked her head inside.

"I brought some extra lights if you need or want them."

"I think all the Christmas decorations are stored in my dad's office. Care to help me search?" Seth wondered how long she would refer to her office as her *dad's*.

"That's why I'm here. You lead, I'll follow." *And I'll get a superb view of your ass.*

Kat opened the unlocked door. He had spent countless hours in the office with her dad, but he viewed it with a critical eye for the first time. Why did a bar need numerous filing cabinets? Several unlabeled boxes rested in corners and on shelves. And the computer on the desk looked like something belonging in a history museum. The general disarray irritated all his sensibilities.

"Wow! The lack of organization is unbelievable." His eyes wandered around. *How had he not noticed when he helped Mr. Lawson?*

"I know." Kat pulled a box down from above her head. It toppled over and the contents spilled all over the floor. She laughed. "I found some of the Christmas ornaments!"

Seth bent over and picked up the assortment of gold and silver tinsel and red stockings. "This might go easier if we organize a bit first." He tried not to distort his face in disgust over the mess.

"I think I inherited my father's lack of organization skills. I don't know where to begin." Kat worried her lip.

"Lucky for you, I follow experts on the internet." He

placed his index finger in front of his lips. "Shhh. I have a secret organizational fetish."

Kat laughed out loud. "Speaking of kink."

"Oooo. My favorite topic." Seth waggled his eyebrows.

She laughed again. "I was going through my dad's computer and found a file labeled porn." Kat made a face like she had eaten something distasteful.

Seth made a beeline for the office chair. "Let's fire up this old fart and check out your dad's porn folder."

"Ew. Seth, no." Kat swiped at his hand to stop him.

"It's not like your dad is going to be in the videos." Seth flipped it on and listened to the dinosaur roar to life.

"Dylan left just a few hours ago and you already need porn?" She continued her half-hearted attempt at physically restraining Seth's hands.

Her insensitive comment stung, but he gave Kat a pass. He reminded himself of the importance of offering her a wide latitude in her grieving process.

"Kat, let me give you a lesson. You can never have enough porn." Seth drummed his fingers and stretched his neck while the computer whirred and beeped until the screen flickered to life.

"Okay, so where did he hide this file?" He looked at Kat.

She rolled her eyes. "He didn't."

"Oh my God! It's labeled porn!" He burst into laughter.

"I know." Kat buried her face in her hands.

He opened the folder, and Kat moved to the other side of the office. "I can't look."

Seth clicked on the most recent item he had downloaded on Thanksgiving morning. Cheesy music began. Kat clapped her palms over her ears. "I don't want to listen either."

The video continued to play. Kat asked, "What is it?"

Seth cocked his head at an angle and looked at her. "Do you remember when Dylan said he thought your dad had figured out something was going on between the three of us?" He settled into the chair.

Seth could see the moment on Kat's face when realization sunk in. Her father definitely knew. "Nooooo." She wore a weary expression.

"Your dad wasn't a man to hold back. If he were upset or didn't approve, he would have spoken up."

Kat bit at her cuticles. The only other time she had done something similar was during the bar exam. Seth got up and hugged her.

"How bad is it?" She tucked her face into his shoulder.

"It was more lame than bad. Soft-core *porn-ish*."

She pulled back from the hug and looked to the heavens. "Thank goodness."

"Were you worried about him imagining you with us?" Kat blushed. "Like I said, if he was upset, he would have said something."

"Probably." Kat picked up another carton.

With the idea of sex fresh on his mind, Seth blurted out, "I topped Dylan the other night."

The box in Kat's hands crashed to the floor. "What the hell? When? How? What?" She bombarded him.

Seth sat on the corner of the desk, uncertain how much information to share.

Kat claimed the single chair in the office. "I'm sitting. Now explain."

"I guess things just aligned in a way, which shifted things between us." He looked at the ground, trying to make sense of the situation as he spoke.

Leaning forward in the chair, Kat lowered her voice. "Was this the first time?" Seth appreciated her soft-spoken tactfulness.

"It was my first time with Dylan." He weighed whether he should share about Dylan's past. They never held secrets. "It was Dylan's first-time bottoming, ever."

"Woah, that's huge." Her mouth dropped open.

"You should know." Seth smirked.

She smacked him on his leg. "You know what I mean. How was it?"

"For me, it's always about the connection, not the specific acts. Although, I have to admit, taking control felt pretty good. His trust and openness meant a lot to me."

"What about Dylan?" Kat narrowed her eyes.

Seth felt uncomfortable speaking about someone else's feelings. "You would need to ask him."

"Do you think it was a onetime thing?"

"He's back in California, with no plans of returning soon." Seth tucked away his emotions about Dylan because he didn't want to burden her with his troubles.

"I don't think Dylan is shutting either of us out on purpose. I get the sense his family is seriously controlling. He takes a lot on the chin, but I don't think it is easy for him." Kat looked down.

"I saw that when I was out there over Labor Day," Seth added.

"I know how much relatives can influence your career choices." Kat raised her eyes.

Seth felt two inches tall. He dropped his head,

shying away from looking her in the eye. "I know. I'm sorry. You were in a terrible predicament."

She placed a consoling hand on his leg. "I didn't say it to make you feel bad for me. I was referring to you. Your family fucked you, but now you are on a great career path."

Seth admired her ability to remain strong and level-headed in the middle of all her grief.

"We're all in a period of transition. Not just the three of us, but all our friends who graduated. I look at Alex. She's working insane hours and under a crazy amount of stress and I see that and suddenly I don't feel like running the bar is such a sacrifice. We're lucky we have choices." She impressed Seth with her positivity.

"Enough with career plans. Let's talk tinsel." His abrupt change of topics wasn't smooth, but effective.

"Fuck this stringy crap. All I need is a piece falling into someone's food or drink. The stuff must have been collecting dust for years. There has to be some health code against it." She lowered another box from the shelves.

"Good call. Let's toss the tinsel. Should we check out those strands of lights?"

Kat lifted a knotted ball of twisted-up lights. She plugged the mess into an outlet and a sporadic number of bulbs illuminated. "Fuck this mess."

"I bought plenty of lights. Don't worry about it. Are there any other boxes?" Seth looked around, but the clutter distracted him.

Kat pointed to a box way up high on a shelf, which had a piece of garland sticking out. "Great, more tinsel," she muttered, sliding the chair over, but she still couldn't reach it.

Seth knew he couldn't grasp it either, even standing on the chair. "Where's a ladder? I'll go get it."

"Screw it. Give me a boost." Kat stepped up on the desk and then kneeled on top of Seth's shoulders. She wobbled as she stretched for the box. Seth secured his grip.

"You know, if you wanted my head between your legs, all you had to do was ask."

Kat snickered. "Ha Ha." He offered her a hand to jump down.

She looked inside the box and her smile vanished. Her bottom lip slid between her teeth and her chin quivered.

Seth rubbed his hand in calming circles on her back as she carefully extracted a small felt Santa Claus holding a bell. She turned the little, metal key crank and set the toy on the desk. It rocked back and forth while ringing the little bell.

Tears trickled down her face. "My mother used to put this in my bedroom every year. I haven't seen it since she passed away." Seth kissed the side of her head as she fixed her stare on Santa until he stopped moving.

Seth whispered, "They are both still with you. Their memories will never disappear." He rested his hands on her shoulders, massaging away her stress.

"I know. I'm lucky to be blessed with so many good ones." Her mouth was so close to his.

He wanted to kiss them. "Maybe it's time Santa resumed its rightful place in your bedroom."

"Yeah." While cradling Santa in her arm, Kat reached for the door with her free hand. "Did you want to come upstairs? I have too much food for any one human to consume."

There was no chance he'd decline an invitation back to her place. "Great. I'm starved."

She walked in front as they stepped up the stairs. Her ass shifted from side to side with each step, teasing him. The view caused a tight situation in his pants. He almost bumped into her backside when she stopped to unlock the door.

Kat entered the apartment and held the door open for him. "Are you panting from walking up a single flight of stairs? I thought you were a fit runner."

He harrumphed. He needed to readjust himself.

Having her belongings settled throughout the room served as evidence of how her life had drastically changed. Much more so than his own, even though they both lost their parents. She uprooted herself to an apartment with a constant reminder of her loss. And, while he switched jobs, she altered her entire career. He agreed with Dylan. She deserved space to grieve in her own manner.

Kat returned from the bedroom with a fresh wet stain down her cheek. He respected her strength in facing all the adversity thrown on her. Like the Santa in her bedroom, he planned to stand by her and be the emotional base she needed.

Seth pulled a chair from the table. "Take a seat. Let me get you something to eat." She dropped into the chair.

He looked into the fridge. "Let's see what we got here. A yellowish casserole thing and a more orange-looking one." Seth pulled his head out and glanced over at her. "I think you oversold me on the food offering." She smiled.

"You're trapped now. You have to join me for dinner."

Being trapped with Kat felt like a dream, not a burden.

Seth returned to his hunt. "Wait, this looks like an edible chicken dish." He opened the lid for confirmation. "Bingo. We have real chicken."

"The mac and cheese is good."

He found the dish and took it out along with the chicken. He fixed a couple of plates, warmed them in the microwave, and sat down at the table with Kat.

Seth pointed with his fork at the boxes along the side wall. "Do those contain all of your dad's things?" Kat looked down into her food and poked at it. "Do you need help with those as well?" He wanted to kick himself for phrasing it poorly. "Now that you know my secret organizing fetish, you're not intending to deprive me, are you?"

Her upturned lips got to him every time. He would do anything to keep her smiling.

Seth swallowed the last bite of macaroni on his plate. "You were right. This is good. It bugs me when there's a crust on top. It's confusing. Is the dish supposed to be creamy or crunchy? It's not like a crumb topping on an apple pie, which is soft."

Kat's eyes brightened. "I think there is some apple pie in the fridge too."

"Hell yes. I love pie." He winked at her. Her return smile thrilled him.

They both picked around the overly dry, flavorless chicken. "I'll wash the dishes if you heat up dessert," said Seth.

"Deal."

Kat placed an extra-large piece on the table with two forks. "We're sharing this. Be warned, if you go beyond your half, I'm armed with a four-pronged spear." Seth raised his hands, feigning fear.

After taking one bite, he started laughing. "Did Alex eat your pie?" Kat laughed hard and started choking. He handed her a glass of water. Following a couple more coughs, she settled down again.

His cell phone rang.

"Is that Dylan?" she asked.

Seth answered and put it on speaker, placing the phone between them. "I'm on my way home from the airport. What's up there?"

"I'm eating Kat's pie." Seth bit the side of his cheek to keep from laughing.

"Seriously?"

Kat moaned. "Oh god, this is so good."

Dylan redialed via video call. They both answered and made sure Dylan could see them both taking a bite of pie.

"You two suck." Seth and Kat convulsed in hysterics. Kat laughed hard until she stopped breathing. "You done yet?" Dylan complained.

"A few more bites to go." She stuck another one in her mouth, dramatically moaning.

"You're killing me here, Kat." Dylan smiled with a sarcastic glint. "It is great to see you smiling. What else have you guys been up to?"

"Watching porn on her dad's computer." Seth plastered on an enigmatic smile.

"What the hell?"

"We were not!"

"Okay, *I* was watching porn while Kat covered her eyes and ears." She smacked Seth on the arm.

"I'm scared to ask more." Dylan squinted his eyes

and scrunched his face.

Seth cut to the chase and explained the situation. Dylan looked all too proud of himself. “I told you I could read people well.”

“Thanks again for everything you did with the apartment and moving.” Kat pivoted the discussion. Seth realized any time the talk neared the topic of the three of them, Kat diverted the conversation.

Seth chose not to back her into a corner. “Kat is going to let me help decorate the bar for Christmas and let me organize all the boxes.”

“Kat, you realize you are feeding right into his fetishes. Careful, he may explode all over the floor.” She laughed. Seth didn’t care if he was the butt of the joke if it caused her to laugh. Every giggle was like collecting coins in a video game. The more he collected, the more it strengthened his life.

Dylan disappeared from the screen and the sound went mute. Seth recognized the entrance to Dylan’s home in the background. He returned in view. “I must get going. I miss you both. Kat, if you need anything, call me any time. Seth, be good to our girl.” Dylan ended the phone call. Seth called it a night with Kat before things got awkward.

Chapter 14

Dylan

He stepped out of the car his parents had sent to pick him up. More specifically, one of their assistants arranged. Sprinkles of rain and the cool breeze dampened his cheery mood from chatting with Kat and Seth. The dreary weather matched his welcome home. He crossed the threshold of his California house and a chill went down his spine.

Abigail, Dylan's least favorite of all his father's aids, greeted him at the door, wearing an ingratiating smile. Dylan didn't trust her. In political life, a grin wasn't just a simple facial expression and words rarely meant what they appeared on the surface.

"Great to see you, Dylan." Abigail extended a helpful hand. "Let me grab it for you."

"I've got it, thank you." His mother would annihilate him if she caught him allowing a woman to carry one of his bags.

Abigail strode up the stairs and Dylan followed in step. He knew better than to dawdle. "Thank you for returning today. The senator had a last-minute change in his schedule and he wanted you to join him at a holiday event this evening."

"Is my mother attending too?"

"No, she is going to a gathering hosted by a

women's volunteer group. It's a divide-and-conquer night."

Abigail did not explain why it was necessary for Dylan to drop everything and return home? "Who is hosting tonight's party?"

"The mayor."

The curt answer raised another red flag. His father's assistant's deflection seemed suspicious.

"My father and the mayor go way back. Why did my dad insist I attend?"

"The senator didn't say. He told me he wanted you to be present. I texted you immediately to give you as much notice as possible. I understand modifying plans is inconvenient. I set up all the transportation. Your clothes are waiting for you in your room. Asa chose the outfit. The limo will leave in forty-five minutes. There is sufficient time for you to shower and change. Can I get you a snack to eat before you head out? You had a long day of travel." Finally, she stopped prattling.

The only thing more conspicuous than a short answer was an excessively lengthy one. He was certain that she was hiding something.

Instead of being a jerk, Dylan refrained from putting the woman in an uncomfortable position. She wasn't more than a glorified intern. No matter the intended usefulness of Dylan's appearance, it didn't alter his plans for the evening.

He followed directions and suited up. He checked his watch, and with a few minutes to spare, he headed down to the car. Dylan stumbled when he saw his father smiling at him. He wasn't on the phone or conversing with anyone. Was he waiting for him? Dylan slowed his pace.

His father approached him, a near-mirror image of himself with an added bit of salt in the hair. “It’s good to have you home, Dylan.”

“Thanks.” Dylan plastered on his political smile, still apprehensive about his father’s motivations.

Abigail stood a step behind them. “Sir, you need to get in the limo now in order to stay on schedule.”

Dylan’s dad put a hand on his shoulder. “We have plenty of time to grab a drink in the limo.” His dad gestured for Dylan to enter the car. As a senator and highest-ranking person, he usually entered the vehicle first. His dad’s affectionate gesture, similar to the role of a parent took aback Dylan.

His dad handed him a snifter of bourbon. Dylan brought the glass to his mouth, taking in the aroma. His father drank nothing less than the best. While the expensive liquor smoothly slid over his tongue, he longed for one of Kat’s old-fashioneds.

“I’m glad you could make it back in time. I apologize for tearing you away from your friends. How are they?” His dad took another sip of his drink and looked at Dylan expectantly, as if he didn’t expect the question to be rhetorical.

He doubted his father wanted a full breakdown. “Seth’s job seems to be going well, and Kat’s attitude will help her get through this transition.” Dylan sighed and stared at the floor. He worried immensely about his Kat and Seth. His concerns preoccupied his thoughts.

“The party Seth and Kat threw for you was exceptionally considerate. They obviously care about you a lot.” Dylan’s dad refilled Dylan’s glass. “The three of you are close.”

Dylan’s head popped up, and he locked eyes with

his dad. Mr. Lawson had seen something between the three of them. Had his father too? Dylan refused to admit his actual feelings and downplayed their relationship. "Three years of law school and rigorous studying together strengthens friendships. Like an army unit fighting as a team."

"When the war is over, it is every man for themselves." Dylan clenched his jaw and steeled himself for the next words out of his father's mouth. His dad finished his drink and set it down. "I think it is great how you have helped your friends. Being a politician means looking out for others and you have tremendous instincts for it. You have a brilliant future ahead of you. Like the clerkship. It's also time for you to get involved in the community here."

His father's intent became clear. The night was about introducing Dylan into society. What surprised him was the fact his father abstained from saying something to denigrate the relationship between Seth and Kat. Maybe he didn't grasp the depth of his connection with them.

"I believe the mayor intends to ask you to spearhead a new group to focus on assisting LGBTQ teens who are in dire situations." His father cocked his head to the side and looked at Dylan as if he were reading, unlike his mother who shot daggers at him to behave and answer properly. His dad offered him the opportunity to respond.

"A worthy cause." Dylan hesitated. His father didn't understand the demands of being a law clerk for a judge. "But it would demand a great deal of time."

"It would look great on your resume, and I doubt it would require much effort." His father steepled his fingers together. "I see judges frequently at events. I don't think their jobs consume excessive amounts of time like all the attorneys I know."

Dylan chortled. "That's because their law clerks are stuck in an office researching and typing away. Although, technically, the clerks draft judges' opinions as opposed to *writing* the responses." Dylan mimicked air quotes with his fingers.

His father's eyes furrowed. "Hmmm."

"Why is the mayor considering me for the position?" Dylan knew it couldn't be just because he was gay. The city had numerous open LGBTQ people to choose from. Many of whom had a lot of experience in this particular area.

"Honest?" His father dropped his hands unceremoniously into his lap. Dylan's ears perked up. "He's doing me a favor by giving you a steppingstone and a professional boost."

"So, you will owe him something in return?"

"No. I have been supporting the gay community since beginning my career, even before you were born. And helping support his initiatives has helped him."

"I hadn't realized you had thrown your weight into those issues for such a long time." Dylan considered how well his parents had accepted the fact he was gay when he came out to them. "Thank you," he mumbled.

"For what?"

"For never acting like me being gay was an inconvenience or worse." He looked at the floor, feeling guilty about how much better off he was than Seth.

"It was never a problem for your mom or me." Dylan raised an eyebrow. "Dylan, your mother doesn't have concerns about you being gay. However, she can be particular about other matters."

"Like everything?"

"She cares about how you present yourself. Don't take it personally. She does the same thing to me." They both laughed. "Let's enjoy tonight without her watchful eye." His father refilled both of their glasses.

While walking into the event, Dylan's dad threw his arm around his shoulders as they posed for a photo together. Dylan gleamed, knowing his mother would not approve of such a pose. She frowned upon it because it pushed the shoulder of a suit jacket out of place, which she included on her long list of cardinal sins.

Artificial snowflakes fell on their faces as they entered the great hall, which served as a sparkling transition to the expansive winter wonderland inside where an impressive-string orchestra played.

He and his dad snagged a glass of wine. His father took a single sip and placed his full glass on a nearby table. Despite Dylan's instruction in developing a discerning wine palette, he didn't care about consuming less expensive vintages. Like the lack of finish in the wine, his relationship with Seth and Kat hung in a delicate balance. Even though they parted from his sight, they remained on his mind. But he pushed the thoughts aside and focused on his duties at the event.

His father introduced him to everyone, always mentioning his upcoming clerkship. If he hadn't caught the reflection of himself in a tuxedo in the gigantic ice sculpture, he would have thought he was wearing a cotillion dress. His dad paraded him around like it was his coming-out party. The repeated conversations became monotonous and tedious.

His head whirled to the blond in his peripheral vision. He recognized the face.

"Asher, right?" Dylan offered his hand. Seeing him close up again, he noticed all the differences between the man and Seth. While very good looking, he didn't compare to his Seth.

"Yes. You clean up well." Asher eyed him up and down.

"Likewise."

"Looks like you are the bell of the ball." Asher snickered. "I didn't realize I had crossed paths with royalty during my run last summer.

"Heh." Dylan clenched his jaw, keeping his smile in place. Dylan flipped the conversation around. "What brings you here tonight?"

"Drumming up promotion for the university and donations of course."

A massive group, comprising of nearly fifty people, began singing a Christmas song. Asher leaned in. "And I am close friends with a few people in the choir." He didn't say whom.

When the song ended, the mayor picked up the microphone. "Let's give a hand to the San Francisco LGBTQ Choir."

The singers proceeded into the next song, and Asher turned his focus on the chorus. The quality of the choir was impressive. A couple of the soloists stood out as exceptionally talented.

A pat on the shoulder pulled his attention away. "Mr. Mayor, I would like to introduce you to my son, Dylan." Dylan promptly threw on his political smile and greeted the mayor appropriately, the way his mother had beaten into him.

"The pleasure is all mine." The mayor shook Dylan's hand. "Your dad has been telling me all about your great return to beautiful northern California. I understand you have a prestigious clerkship you are about to begin."

"I'm looking forward to working under the justice."

"The judge and I belong to the same golf club. I spoke to him about you and he had wonderful things to say. Apparently, not only is your father impressed by your accomplishments."

"Thank you. I put my all behind worthwhile causes and arguments." Dylan learned to accept praise from his mom but found being worthy of it more important.

"Everyone seems to think the world of your abilities. I was hoping you would want to join the board of our LGBTQ Committee. What do you say?"

Dylan's dad's expression mimicked his mother's, indicating only one correct answer.

"I would be honored, Mr. Mayor. Thank you so much the opportunity."

"With you involved, I'm sure we will see great things happen." The mayor strained his neck, scanning the crowd. "Have you met my son? He is close to your age. He can help introduce you to some of the other people involved in the organization."

His assistant fetched the wanted man. "Asher, this is Dylan Levine. He's going to be on the board. I was hoping you could point out some the prominent people tonight."

"Sure thing. We go way back. Let's leave the old men to their devices." Asher turned and walked off. Dylan followed, as expected.

When the two men had put some distance between themselves and their fathers, Dylan confronted Asher. "And you refer to me as royalty? You're the mayor's son! I think you out rank me, Your Highness."

"Okay, so we are both the next-gen leaders. Do you know what that means? We need to enjoy today." Asher introduced Dylan to many people. Asher effortlessly eased introductions while upholding respect. Dylan admired his style, and for a change, enjoyed the event.

The mayor reclaimed the microphone when the choir finished singing. "Let's hear it one more time for these wonderful singers." He waited until the applause died down. "Shall we ask for an encore?" A huge, bellowing hooray roared from the crowd. "Hit it!"

Asher handed Dylan a glass from a wandering waiter and then claimed two more. His mother would never approve of being caught double-fisting.

When the choir finished, Asher maneuvered through the mass, kissed the soloist on the mouth, and handed him the extra champagne flute. Curious, Dylan followed. "Dylan, I would like you to meet my boyfriend, Grayson."

"You've got an amazing voice."

"Yes, he does." Asher placed a loving hand on Grayson's shoulder.

"Thank you, sweetie." Grayson gave Asher a warm, affectionate smile. "Dylan, are you joining us?"

"We are heading to another party, where the average age is much lower. You should come." Asher finished his drink.

"Maybe some other time. I flew in from Chicago this morning. I think I'm going to call it a night. But, thanks."

"You ready? Or do you need to do one of your never-ending goodbyes?" Grayson rolled his eyes.

"I'm good. Let's go. Great to see you again, Dylan."

"Yeah, and nice to meet you, Grayson." Grayson didn't reply in kind, which unsettled Dylan. Basic niceties were like breathing at these events. The absence struck him as peculiar.

He found his dad once again, as they had kept in separate social circles for the later part of the night. His father said, "I'm ready to leave. You?" Dylan confirmed with a small nod.

Sitting in the privacy of the limo, his dad smacked his open palm on top of Dylan's bent knee. "I'm glad you accepted the position."

"I hope I didn't bite off more than I can chew." Dylan's head began to ache.

"You'll do great. I know it. You always do."

He refused to accept the compliment. His father had no idea how much effort it took to be at his best all the time.

"I saw you hanging around Asher and his friends. Keep in mind he doesn't hold the keys to the city, his father does."

"Do you have a problem with Asher?"

"He has a reputation." Dylan's shoulders tensed. The phrasing rubbed him the wrong way.

"You know what they say about making assumptions." Dylan preferred to make his own assessment of people.

"Where there is smoke, there's fire. You don't want to get burned."

After a long and trying day, Dylan didn't have the energy to decipher his father's words. If the problem with Asher was substantial, Dylan would discover it on his own.

After arriving home, he climbed into bed. He fell

backward and his head flopped into the pillow. His exhausted body sunk into his mattress. Air rushed from his chest. Taking slow breaths He breathed slowly in and out, his political mask melted away.

He shuffled his legs under the cold and uninviting sheets. He fussed with his pillows. The second pillow put a kink in his neck. He tossed it to the side, but then reclaimed it, hugging it close. The emptiness hit. It had been weeks since he had last slept alone.

He pried one eye open and peered over the crest of his pillow. His phone sat within an arm's reach. He doubted any message might make him feel better at the moment. Closing his eyes, he clutched his pillow tighter. He took five deep breaths and prayed sleep found him quickly.

The next morning, Dylan wrestled in the covers, seeking the perfect temperature. The Italian-made linen coddled him as he lingered in the bed. He reveled in the fact his alarm didn't jar him awake. With nothing on his docket for the day, he dozed for another hour until his body woke, fully rested. He enjoyed the moment of calm.

Propping himself up against the headboard, he grabbed his phone. He had messages from Kat, Seth, his mother, and Asher. Out of sheer curiosity, he opened Asher's message first.

—*(photo of Asher and Grayson naked at a club)*—

Dylan admired both good-looking men. Asher had a great ass. Maybe his dad was right about Asher's reputation. Dylan refrained from messaging back.

Kat—*Hope your party went well. And, thank you again for all your help getting me moved and dealing with the lease. If you can, send some of that nice ass weather this way. We are expecting our first Arctic freeze of the winter. You got out in the nick of time—*

He recalled how Kat's nipples hardened whenever it was cold, like when he and Seth pressed her up against the glass window in his condo. Her cheekiness reassured him she was rebounding.

Dylan—*I'll try and blow the warm weather your way—*

He hoped she was up for a little fun banter.

Seth—*Miss you. Sleeping without you beside me sucked—*

His moment of peace evaporated. The reminder ground on his nerves. Did Seth think calling attention to his needs would change anything? Dylan reached his limit with Seth's self-centeredness. He hadn't asked about how Dylan was doing. Was he blaming Dylan for leaving? It was enough. Dylan needed to focus on his issues, not Seth's.

Chapter 15

Kat

She plugged in an external flash drive into her laptop, intent on wiping it clean of all her law school materials. She no longer needed her notes, briefs, outlines, and bar review aids. By placing the materials on a hard drive, she preserved access to the files if she practiced law in the future. Pressing the return key, all her data vanished almost as quickly as her career. The ping of completion signified another step in moving on with her life. She ejected the flash drive and stashed it in the drawer for safekeeping. She closed the drawer, shut her eyes, and said a quiet goodbye to all the hours of time and stress.

A knock on the door, followed by an immediate creak of the ancient hinges, announced his arrival. Her employees knocked and didn't barge in. Instead, a blond in a navy winter pea coat and blue plaid scarf strutted in and kissed her on the cheek.

"Hey, you got rid of the old dinosaur of the computer."

"Yup."

"Did you save the porn file?"

"Ew."

"It's looking a hell of a lot more modern in here."

"Thanks to the help of a hot guy with an

organization fetish."

"That sexy man also has quite an appetite." Seth's normally sexy blue eyes looked boyish and needy.

"Can I feed you?" Kat stood, prepared to put in an order for Seth.

"Yes, please."

"Burger?" She didn't wait for an answer. He always ordered one.

"I think I'll go with a salad."

Her rubber-soled shoes screeched against the flooring. "Whoooоah. What the fuck?"

"Yeah. Yeah. Yeah. People don't stop bringing in damn desserts at the office. I need a salad to compensate."

She laughed along with Seth. "Can't you run off the calories?"

"It's fucking cold outside. I could lose my nose." Seth theatrically mimed with his hands his face was a protected treasure. His vanity knew no bounds.

"I meant on a treadmill, dumbass."

"Ugh. I hate running inside. Looking at my surroundings while running helps my mind not to wander."

Kat regretted bringing up the topic. She was worried about broaching subjects he was intentionally avoiding and threatened to derail him. "Do you care what type of salad?"

"The low-calorie kind."

"Not the taco salad?"

"Uh, no." Seth followed her. "Have you ever laughed in someone's face when they ordered that? I mean, if you want tacos, order tacos. No offense to your bar, but there are a ton of good taco places close by. Why order a taco salad? You're not really getting a salad or a decent taco." He followed her all the way to the door to the kitchen.

She turned back to face him. With an outstretched arm, she halted him with her hand on his chest. "Hold up right there. You aren't following me into Chef's sanctuary. Go sit it at the bar or I'm bringing you a damn taco salad."

Kat pushed her way through the swinging door. If Seth didn't move quickly, he risked getting walloped in the face when it swung backward. She put in an order for a chicken Caesar salad.

She paused before exiting the kitchen. Chef barked, "Can I get you something, Kat?" Kat cowered. Chef's fiery and forceful way of speaking still intimidated Kat. Even after Kat finally learned her first name while signing her paycheck, Kat continued to refer to her as Chef rather than Dierdre.

"When is the last time someone ordered the taco salad?"

"It's still on the menu?" Chef looked repulsed.

"Never mind." She scurried out of the kitchen.

Kat placed a sparkling water in front of Seth, who was sitting in his usual seat. "Your chicken Caesar salad will be up soon. Apparently, we don't serve taco salads anymore." He reached for the glass. "Want a beer?"

"Nah." Seth gulped the drink.

A girl with long, dark brown, curly locks sat herself down next to Seth. Resting her elbow on the bar, she flicked her hand in Kat's direction. "Excuse me."

Kat finished wiping her hands. "Hi. What can I get you?"

"Can I get a margarita?"

"Sure. Any specific kind?"

"Can you make it a blue margarita?"

"No problem. I hope you aren't feeling in a blue mood today." Kat employed her typical behind-the-bar banter.

"No. It's the first night of Hanukkah."

"Well, happy Hanukkah. One blue margarita coming up." She glanced at Seth, but he looked away.

Eager to get back to Seth, Kat threw together the drink. She served it up in one hand and carried over two shot glasses and a bottle of tequila in the other.

She banged the shot glasses against the wooden bar top with a loud clang. Seth's head popped up. "What's this?"

"A deconstructed blue margarita to celebrate the first night of Hanukkah." The woman in the seat next to Seth leaned in.

"AKA a tequila shot?"

"Okay, killjoy."

Kat raised her tequila shot in the air. "Happy Hanukkah." She threw back the tequila. The brunette watched as Seth downed the shot. Kat addressed the brunette. "Can you keep an eye on my friend Seth while I go get his salad?"

Seth's normal flirty smile resumed its proper place on his pretty face. "So, you're celebrating today too?" She left them to chat.

Dawdling, Kat retrieved the salad but held off serving it, giving Seth time for some flirtatious fun. She took a moment to text Dylan.

Kat—*Happy Hanukkah to my "Jew-ish" friend*—

Dylan—*Thanks. How's my Chicago girl? Staying warm?*—

Kat—*Liquor keeps everyone toasty. Sales are up. People procrastinate leaving and order extra rounds—*

Dylan—*(laughing smiley face)—*

Kat—*I need to go serve Seth his salad (smooch lips)—*

Dylan—*WTF (open-mouthed face)—*

With Seth's dinner in hand and an over-done smile, Kat snuck around the other waitresses. The other bartenders hustling around and mixing drinks blocked her view of him. When she made her way to the end of the bar, the brunette was gone.

Seth glared at her. "Really Kat. Branching out as a matchmaker, now?"

Unabashed, she placed the salad in front of him. "Where's blue margarita?" He shrugged and stabbed a piece of chicken with his fork. "Did you get her phone number?" Seth kept chewing and half nodded yes. He stuffed another bite into his mouth.

"See, I am a good matchmaker." She folded her arms over each other, very proud of herself.

"Kat, I wasn't going to be rude and tell her no when she offered me her number." He opened up his contacts and faced his screen toward Kat, giving her a full view of him deleting the woman's information.

"Why would you do that? She was pretty." She put her hands on her hips and waited for an explanation.

"Because I'm not looking to bring home a cute, little, Jewish girl to my mother."

"Fuck." Kat's mouth opened wide enough to cram her entire foot into it. She really fucked up. First, she had forgotten about Hanukkah, which was probably a trigger for Seth. The fact he had eaten too many Christmas cookies at work made more sense. Was he emotionally eating? He never mentioned his parents or the lawsuit, but the stress of it had to be gnawing away at him. She had been a shitty friend by not checking in on him lately.

She grabbed the bottle of tequila and poured two more shots. "More tequila? It should go well with the salt I threw on the wound. I'm really sorry. I wasn't thinking."

Seth tossed back the shot. "This holiday season sucks."

Kat poured another round. She raised her glass. "To a shitty holiday season."

"'Tis the season to get shit-faced drunk." They clanged their shot glasses together and swallowed the tequila.

Three shots later, Seth said, "I sent a message to my parents this evening wishing them a Happy Hanukkah."

Kat gripped the bar, fighting the urge to yell at him. It was a stupid move, legally and emotionally. She wanted to scold him for reaching out in the middle of a lawsuit without the advice of his attorney. On the other hand, she wanted to hug him and ease his pain.

She started wiping down the bar, allowing him the opportunity to rant, but he remained silent.

Kat held her tongue as long as possible, but then blurted, "Did they respond?"

"Nope." He closed his eyes and rubbed at his temple with his left hand.

She ached for Seth. She owed him more. He deserved better from her. Kat picked up the dirty shot glasses. "Let's go upstairs where we can talk." Seth nodded. She disposed of the glasses and Seth's empty salad plate.

Inside her apartment, Seth dropped his jacket,

walked across the living room, and fell onto the couch. Not sure how to best help Seth. "Can I get you anything? Something to eat? More tequila?"

"Can we just watch TV together?"

Kat grabbed a couple of glasses of water and sat down on the end of the couch. Seth laid his head on her lap. She turned on the TV and handed the remote to him. "You pick."

She ran her fingers through Seth's ridiculously soft blond hair. Most women dreamed of having hair as nice as his.

Seth flipped through the channels, speeding past a rom-com. "No fucking fake happily-ever-afters." He eventually landed on some action flick.

He snuggled in closer to Kat. She grabbed the nearby blanket and threw it over Seth's legs. "Mmm."

The gravel in his grunt sent tingling sparks to her lady parts. She hadn't felt anything like it in weeks. She hadn't purposely avoided having fun, but responsibilities had overtaken her life. Until now.

Seth's smooth hair brushed along her fingers. It shouldn't have felt erotic, but it did. The glide of his blond locks brought back memories of Seth sliding in and out of her.

Her mind wandered to the first time she, Dylan, and Seth ended up in bed together. New Year's Eve, three years ago. They had all survived their first semester of law school.

After finals and after Christmas, classmates set aside most animosity and competition for the night. A sizeable crowd gathered for drinking at Lawson's. When the bar neared closing time, a bunch of their friends reconvened at Seth's place.

Despite no one under the age of twenty-three, they acted like junior-high students. Someone grabbed an empty bottle and started a game of spin-the-bottle. Seth probably instigated it, but Kat wasn't certain.

****

She joined the game and sat beside Seth. He leaned over and whispered in her ear, "I hope when I spin the bottle it faces you." A drunken Kat laughed louder than normal. She thought Seth was gay and assumed he was joking.

As it happened, his first spin landed on Carter. Carter pecked Seth on the lips and made quite a show of taking a long pull on his beer to cleanse himself of Seth's cooties. Carter spun the bottle next and his eyes lit up when it pointed to Kellie. His kiss with Kellie turned into a full-on lip lock.

As Kellie had been sitting next to Kat, she placed a hand on Kat's shoulder. "You can take my turn. I think I'm going to take off now."

Kellie stared at Carter until he stood up. "Oh, I think I'm going to head out too."

"Way to catch on quick, Carter." Seth laughed.

Kat took the next turn. The bottle spun around and around before slowing down near Alex. Alex squirmed. Ultimately, it landed on Dylan.

Alex blew out a deep breath. "Phew! I love you like a sister, Kat, but I don't want to play tonsil hockey with you. No offense."

"No worries."

"Kiss. Kiss. Kiss," Cole chanted.

Dylan leaned over the table where the bottle rested. Kat met him and his mouth halfway. She lost her balance and caught herself with her hand on the back of Dylan's neck. He reciprocated the action, holding her close.

She didn't want to let go. She grabbed Dylan's hair. He moaned and deepened the kiss.

Someone cleared their throat loudly. "I'm going to go before the two of you set Seth's place on fire," said Cole.

Dylan and Kat separated, breathing hard. Kat looked Dylan in the eyes and saw a surprised expression on his face.

He sat back down. His dark eyes fixated on Kat. She fidgeted with her fingers. Upon sitting, she realized she and Dylan were the only ones remaining. The game had ended.

A few friends lingered in the foyer. Seth hugged them goodbye and shut the door behind them.

He returned to the table and picked up the bottle. "Well, we can't very well play spin the bottle with just the three of us."

Kat looked at Dylan, biting her lip and wanting to protest.

"But I have a better idea." Seth grabbed a rectangular box with a bunch of small rectangular blocks.

"Well, this should be interesting, considering how much we have all had to drink," said Dylan.

Seth said, "Yes, it will because this isn't the normal boring version. This is the *naughty* version." Seth dumped the blocks on the table.

Kat picked up one block and read the words inscribed on the block. "Kiss the person to your left." She looked at Dylan. "I think you were right; this is about to get interesting." Then she gazed at Seth.

The three of them built the tower of blocks in layers

of three where each layer rested perpendicular to the one below. All the questions faced downward, hidden in the stack. "Who goes first?"

"Ladies, always go first," said Seth.

Kat chortled. "As if this is a lady-like game."

"Okay, Dylan, you start us off."

Dylan pulled a block from the middle of the stack with ease. "Kiss the person to your right." Dylan turned toward Seth, who cocked an eyebrow and smiled devilishly. Kat watched with wide eyes. She had just kissed Dylan moments earlier and thought there was a connection, but the view before her made her second-guess herself. The intensity of the kiss between the men wasn't something she had ever witnessed.

Seth pulled away from the kiss. "You've got excellent lips." He focused on the tower of blocks and clapped his hands. "My turn." He slid out a block. "Kiss the neck of the person to your right.

He looked at Kat. "You good, sweetheart?"

Kat tilted her head to the side, exposing as much skin as possible. She strummed her finger, motioning him to approach. She wanted his lips on her flesh.

Seth began near her collar bone with a soft graze of his lips upon her skin. His breathing echoed in her ear, which turned into a deep, satisfying rumble. Heat pooled between Kat's legs.

She fell backward on the couch with Seth on top of her. He ran his tongue up her neck. She became distracted by the feel of his hard cock pressing against her. She wanted to grind herself against him, but he pulled away. Seth adjusted his pants before he resumed his seat.

Because her head was spinning, she sat up slowly. It

took a minute to regain her awareness. She drew in a deep breath. "Okay, my turn." She tested a bunch of blocks until she found a loose one in the lower half of the tower.

"That's cheating. You can't fuck with the blocks before taking one." Dylan scoffed.

"She can fuck with whatever wood she wants." Seth winked and patted Dylan's leg, half in a chastising manner but quite close to Dylan's upper inner thigh. "Go ahead, sweetheart."

Kat pulled a block out, weakening the entire structure. "Give the tallest person a thirty-second lap dance."

Dylan had a few inches on Seth. Kat stood, but hesitated.

Seth cranked up a song on his phone. "Here, this should help inspire you." The deep, pulsing beats made Kat think of a grinding motion with her hips. She straddled Dylan's legs and rocked her hips along his body. Her hands waved above her head as her chest moved in front of his face. She stepped away, but Dylan grabbed her hips. His dark eyes bore right through her, but yet, he didn't pull her in closer.

"Hands off the dancer, dude." Seth barked like a bouncer at a strip club and then laughed. Kat laughed so hard she fell onto Dylan's lap.

She maneuvered herself out of Dylan's way. "Go ahead, it's your turn."

He tested the blocks, as Kat had done, and took one near the bottom. The tower wobbled precariously but didn't fall. He read the instructions. "Lick the nipple of one of the other players." Dylan first looked at Kat, but a look of fear passed over his face. He turned to Seth.

"Lose the shirt." Seth tore at his shirt and whipped it off.

Dylan bent over and dragged his tongue over Seth's nipple. Seth moaned loudly. Dylan didn't cease. He dragged his tongue back down and continued toward Seth's belt. "Oh god."

"Hey, that's not what the block said," Kat complained.

Dylan argued, "So I embellished a little. Sue me."

"Fuck me," Seth mumbled.

Then he stood to take another block. Kat questioned, "What happens when the tower falls?"

Seth continued without answering her and read his piece. "Strip down to your underwear." He reached for his belt and undid it. He kicked off his shoes and then dragged his pants down his lean, muscular legs. His black cotton boxers stretched over his erection. Kat stared lasciviously. Dylan pinched his tight ass, causing Seth to jolt. "Hey you almost made me tip the tower."

Kat took her turn and removed one block from the very top of the tower. "What a boring safe choice," said Seth.

Kat blushed as she read the words on her block. Her heart raced. "What's it say?" asked Dylan.

"Engage two players in a three-way kiss."

"Oh, hell yes." Seth stood first. Kat concentrated on Seth's face and mustered some courage.

Dylan rose slowly.

This wasn't the first time Kat had thought about kissing Seth. She had often considered it. He was gorgeous, and his flirty personality made her think there may have been a spark between the two of them. For her, the prospect always remained a mere curiosity, not worthy of risking a friendship. But now, in the moment, the standard rules didn't exist. The nature of the game turned all the normal rules upside down.

Kat leaned toward Seth with butterflies in her stomach. He crushed his lips on hers. A burning sensation engulfed her entire body the instant Seth's tongue invaded her mouth. He didn't just go through the motions of kissing her for the sake of the game. He went all in.

His hands pulled her close. She explored his shirtless torso. Her hands landed on his hips. Her thumbs stroked along his happy trail. His cock grew beyond the confines of his underwear and knocked against her hand, demanding attention.

Kat expected Seth to push her to reach out and stroke his length. Instead, Seth stepped back from the kiss and left Kat gasping. "She can't follow through with the directions when you're so far away."

The game? Dylan? Kat's surroundings returned to her consciousness. She looked at Dylan. His eyes stood wide until Seth kissed him and Dylan's eyelids drifted closed. Seth placed his palm on Kat's cheek. "Your turn, sweetheart." Seth directed her toward Dylan. Kat needed the nudge, as their kissing had distracted her in a delicious way. She leaned into the experience.

Kat kissed Dylan. Unlike their previous kiss, Dylan let her lead. His reservations teased her. She bit at his lip, prodding him for more.

As she kissed Dylan, Seth teased his teeth along her ear. Their three bodies were pinned together closely. Her fingers itched to wander all over them. She wished Dylan was undressed, like Seth.

Seth moved his hand under her shirt and bra and thumbed her nipple. He adeptly switched from kissing her ear to kissing Dylan's jaw. Dylan's head tilted backward. Seth and she simultaneously kissed down Dylan's throat. His Adam's apple bobbed beneath their lips. "Ohhh." Dylan released a drawn-out moan.

Dylan's fingers brushed against Kat's waist. She lurched forward at the unexpected touch. The crash of blocks thudded beneath her. "Oops." Kat laughed.

"We win," Seth cheered.

"Dylan pushed me into the tower. I refuse to take the L."

"Fine, I'll take half the blame? What happens now?"

"Those who knock it down must strip out of their clothes," Seth said. Kat's mouth popped open. Dylan reached for his shirt buttons.

Seth whispered in her ear. "Are you willing to play, sweetheart?"

The throb between her legs drove her to say yes. "Is this still a game?"

"Are you having fun?" He didn't answer her questions, but she didn't want to stop.

"Let's take this game to the bedroom. Dylan?" Seth bit his lip as he waited for an answer.

Referring to the situation as a game, removed the taboo. Nothing was forbidden. No guilt. She treated it like an innocent game. As long as it remained a mere game, there were no stakes and no potential harm to anyone.

"Count me in." Dylan unbuttoned his cuffs while standing in the living room. "Kat?"

"Fuck it. Why the hell not?" *Gotta live-a-little.* She wanted both Dylan and Seth. She dismissed everything, causing her to question her decision. Declining the opportunity meant possible regret in the future.

"You read my mind." Seth smiled saucily. "Let's take this to my bedroom." He ran his finger down the front of Dylan's button-down shirt. "I know how expensive that shirt is. Take it off before the buttons go flying." Kat laughed, wondering about the actual cost. His family came from money and Seth knew clothes.

As Dylan undid each button, he exposed more of his naked chest. Her interest in the cotton garment vanished.

Seth led the way to his bedroom and Dylan followed on his heels. Kat appreciated the view from behind. Seth's tight ass looked scrumptious. She wanted to take a bite. And Dylan's back revealed all those delicious muscles maintaining his perfect posture. She swallowed the saliva in her mouth. The men in front of her were delectable.

By the time they reached the bedroom, Dylan's shirt lay on the ground and his pants were undone. They stood beside the bed. Dylan slipped his shoes off and pushed off his slacks.

The two men, wearing only their underwear, stared at her. Seth raised an eyebrow at her. "What are you waiting for, sweetheart?"

The hunger in their eyes emboldened her. She recognized the opportunity in front of her. Two gorgeous men, nearly naked, stood before her. The luck of the Irish presented her with a chance of a lifetime. "Your attention."

She pulled her shirt from her jeans. "Sweetheart, need a hand with the clothes?"

"Am I not going quickly enough for you, Seth?"

"The show is sensational, but I need to touch you." The intensity of his gaze felt like a physical touch. She eagerly awaited their strong hands on her body.

"Then give me a hand. Better yet, all four hands." Seth twisted her body, placing her between him and facing Dylan.

Dylan inched her shirt upward. "You all good with this?"

"Oh yeah." Kat kissed Dylan like a signature on a contract. Her head sprung from the removal of her t-shirt and her eyes popped open. Uncertain about the look in Dylan's eyes, she placed a gentle hand on his face. "Are *you* all in Dylan?"

"Of course he is." Seth answered for Dylan as he unhooked her bra. The straps of her bra grazed her skin as the fabric slid down her arms. Sparks zinged like static electricity.

Dylan got down on his knees and slid Kat's jeans down her legs. His fingers gently caressed her hamstrings. Her need for closer intimacy waxed and her patience waned.

Seth pulled Kat away from Dylan's clutches and helped her onto the edge of the bed. "You smell so good. I need to taste you."

Unlike Seth's directness and eagerness to push things to start, Dylan looked a little lost. His touch seemed tentative. His mannerisms felt restrained. Kat reached out for Dylan's hand. She repeated his words. "You want this, Dylan?"

His shoulders rose as his chest expanded and he inhaled deeply. Dylan placed his hand in hers. His moist fingers exposed his trepidation.

Seth hadn't yet touched her as he said, "Do you want to pleasure Dylan?"

"Yes."

Dylan inched closer until his knees touched the side

of the bed. Kat tugged on his boxer brief without exposing his manhood. "Dylan?"

He slowly lowered his briefs. His cock was at half-mast. He stroked himself a few times. "Let me." She replaced his hand with her own, stroking until he fully hardened.

He closed the gap. Kat turned her head to face Dylan at the side of the bed as she lie on her back. She reached out with her tongue and licked the tip of his cock. Dylan leaned in closer. She opened wide and allowed him to make the final move. Slowly, his cock filled her mouth. She wrapped her lips firmly around him and licked the head round and round.

Dylan's head fell backward. "Oh god."

"That is sexy as fuck."

With Kat's legs hanging over the end of the bed, Seth roughly yanked off her thong. He pushed at her knees, exposing her core. His warm breath erased the cool bereft sensation. Kat twitched with each passage of Seth's tongue. She struggled to focus on pleasuring Dylan. She fought to maintain the connection, but when Seth fingered her opening her back arched away from Dylan. "Oh fuck!"

Dylan's breath came in frustrated pulses.

Seth laughed arrogantly. "Excellent idea. Are you down for DP?"

Kat almost orgasmed again at the thought. "Hell yes."

Seth grabbed a couple of condoms and a container of lube from his nightstand. He behaved like a choreographer of a musical and directed Dylan and Kat into place. Kat straddled Dylan, who lay on his back. His eyes drifted shut as she eased her slick pussy down his thick shaft. She bent over and kissed Dylan while Seth lubricated her backside. The fullness of Dylan inside her and Seth's teasing drove her crazy. Her body naturally rocked her hips but Seth held her in place.

When Seth finally slid his cock inside, Dylan cried out. "Oh my god."

"Dylan, hold still," Seth ordered.

"I can't. I'm so fucking close."

In and out. Push and pull. Moans and groans.

The tightness and fullness made Kat feel complete. But the push against her clit on Dylan's pubic bone torqued her arousal to a level she never imagined. Their groans mingled together as they all orgasmed.

"Holy fuck."

"That was incredible."

"Unbelievable."

"Let's wash up and go again." Seth offered a hand to both her and Dylan who continued to lie in astonishment.

"You really are filled with the best ideas." Kat stood and kissed him.

"I'll second that." Dylan kissed Seth too.

****

An ugly choking snore dragged Kat from her fond memories. Seth shifted his position and his breathing resumed a quiet lull. He remained out cold, snoring with his head on her lap.

Sweat beaded on her back. *Was the heat on too high? Maybe Seth's head created the problem. Doubtful.* She burned for a repeat of the amazing sex she shared with Seth and Dylan.

She whispered to her sleeping friend, "I think you may have been right. The three of us were perfect."

Unfortunately, it didn't change the fact Dylan was starting a job in California, 2000 miles away from Chicago. His career was on a coastal path, which didn't facilitate a relationship.

Kat sighed and switched the channel on the TV.

Chapter 16

Seth

A few weeks later, he perched himself on his favorite bar stool at Lawson's. Sipping his old-fashioned, his body thawed from the inside out. Another artic freeze blew into the area, which caused the temperature to drop to negative fifteen degrees Fahrenheit. January in Chicago sucked.

Seth envied that Dylan escaped to warmer temperatures. He should have stowed away in Dylan's luggage when he flew back to California, after celebrating the new year together. With Dylan on his mind, Seth texted him while Kat attended to other patrons.

—Have a great first day at the clerkship tomorrow—

Dylan unexpectedly responded.

—Thanks man—

When Dylan first left for the west coast six months earlier, Seth resented the distance. His bitterness lessened as Dylan maintained their relationship. More so, Dylan had supported Seth as he dealt with the pain of being separated from his parents. And he had helped Kat through her struggle. Dylan deserved a supportive friend.

Seth—*You are going to be amazing. I'm really proud of you—*

Dylan—*Thanks*—

He grew concerned with Dylan's terse responses. *Was Dylan nervous?* Texting masked emotion. He needed to see Dylan's face and hear his voice.

Seth—*Got time for a video call?*—

Dylan—*Yeah, give me a minute to head up to my room*—

The boisterous people around Seth made his location less than ideal for talking. He found Kat roaming among the tables. "Mind if I use your office?"

"No. Go ahead." She continued chatting with her customers.

"Thanks Kat."

Seth opened the unlocked door. Kat's laptop, with all her financial records, lay on her desk. Even if she trusted her employees, any customer could sneak in and steal it.

He sat himself in her desk chair. Seth propped up his size ten oxfords on her desktop and leaned backward. He launched the app on his phone, but Dylan beat him to the punch. He answered, "Hey there handsome."

Dylan's lips turned up in a grin, but the smile didn't reach his eyes. "Hi."

"Show me what you are wearing on your first day." Dylan always dressed to perfection. Seth didn't need to double-check his wardrobe choice, but he wanted a detailed image of Dylan on his first day.

The background behind Dylan shifted, the images sparked Seth's memory of naked times in Dylan's bedroom. His chiseled jaw disappeared from Seth's screen and focused on a dark suit and necktie.

Seth scrunched up his face. "I thought California was supposed to be liberal."

"The state is, but not a federal courtroom." Dylan went quiet and zoomed in on the tie. Seth loved the shade of blue he had chosen. In fact, he had many ties in the identical hue to match his own eyes. He narrowed his focus. The tie looked familiar. "Is that mine?"

Dylan switched the camera back to himself. "Guilty as charged." The brazen look on Dylan's face was sexy as all hell. The fact he wanted a piece of Seth wrapped around his neck on the first day warmed his heart. The combination made him hard. He wanted to wrap his lips around Dylan's cock.

Seth swallowed, torn between asking for phone sex and offering a supportive shoulder. "I wish I was with you to help distract you."

A glint of mischief flashed in Dylan's eyes, and then the image blurred for a second. He must have propped up his phone on something because both of Dylan's hands reached for the buttons on his shirt. Slowly, he undid each. His shirt fell open, revealing the sculpted muscular definition of his chest. *Damn, he was beautiful.*

"Dylan," Seth murmured.

Dylan unbuckled his pants. Seth gaped as Dylan's thick length appeared on the screen. Seth followed Dylan's lead and started undressing.

The background behind Dylan shifted again until his pillows framed his face. His dark brown eyes commanded attention, but Seth wanted to see more. As if Dylan read Seth's mind, Dylan readjusted the phone, and Seth got a good view of his chest, abs, and his fucking amazing cock. Seth itched to reach out and…Dylan began stroking himself. "Come on Seth."

Seth wanted him. If this was the only way, he would take what he could get. He finished removing the rest of his clothes. He mimicked Dylan's hand motion, caressing himself in just the right manner. The sight of Dylan spurred his movements. Dylan moaned and the angst of an impending orgasm surged.

"Yes, Seth." Dylan breathed and released a low guttural moan. Seth's eyes drifted closed. The two-thousand-mile difference between him and Dylan faded. Memories of Dylan filled in all the sensory blanks. The strength of Dylan's touch was palpable. Seth sighed, recalling the stretch when Dylan entered him. The sensation was as real as if he were beside Dylan.

"Adjust your camera. I need to see you." Seth's eyes popped open and redirected his phone. The action didn't break the sexual connection. It was no different from shifting to better accommodate a lover in real life.

"Seth…yes…Seth," Dylan moaned. The gravelly roughness in his voice affected Seth deep in his core. Not merely in an erogenous manner, but his heart swelled as well. The miles between them had not broken their bond.

"Fuck yes." Seth stroked himself more quickly. The stirrings of an orgasm built. "Dylan…"

"Seth."

"Oh god yes," Seth hissed between clenched teeth. His impending release came in like a rushing storm on the horizon.

"Come with me." Streams of cum shot out on Dylan's chest. The sight made Seth lose control and his orgasm ripped through his body.

As his warm cum cooled, the reality of Seth's surroundings pierced the bubble of his rapture. He grabbed tissues from Kat's desk and cleaned up efficiently. Needing both hands, he sat the phone down and zipped up his pants.

Continuing to get dressed, he slipped his shirt on. "What's the hurry?"

While buttoning, Kat entered her office. She cocked her head and glared at him. "What the fuck Seth?" She slammed the door behind her.

Dylan's voice cut the tension. "Hi Kitty-Kat." Kat didn't laugh.

Seth tucked his shirt into his pants and buckled his belt.

Kat grabbed Seth's phone. Her eyes lit up, but her facial expression morphed into a scowl. "Seriously, I can't fucking believe the two of you. This is my place of business. You understand the potential sexual harassment case if any of my employees saw it. Do you have no respect?"

"Sorry, Kat. I assumed Seth locked the door."

"I wasn't thinking." Seth knew the difficulty of being in the middle of a lawsuit and a sex scandal. He didn't wish anything as unpleasant on anyone.

"Not with your brain." Kat didn't laugh at her joke.

"Give him a break, Kat." Dylan's weak defense didn't move her temper needle.

She usually fired back with a smartass quip, but she didn't respond. The tension in her jaw made her look like she was grinding her teeth. Her normally pale skin flamed with an angry red.

"Despite the immediate *dumbassery*, I'm glad I can wish you good luck for beginning your job tomorrow. You are gonna kick ass."

"Thanks, Kat."

"Let me know how it goes. I can't wait to hear all about it."

"Sure thing. And Kat, go easy on him."

Seth reached for the phone from Kat.

She didn't hand it over. "Hanging up. Bye." Kat ended the call. She didn't give Seth a chance to say goodbye.

"Well, you're dressed now and I have a business to run, so why don't you head on out."

"Jesus, Kat. I know it was dumb not to lock the door, but no one other than you ever comes in here." She didn't smile. She always smiled at a good double entendre. "All your employees saw you working out there. There wasn't any reason for them to enter your office. They never do."

She started breathing harder, her shoulders lifting with each breath. *Why couldn't she see the humor in the situation?*

"It was just our Dylan."

"There is no *our*." Seth's heart clenched. He had been grasping at pieces between Dylan and Kat.

"Really? We have been there for each other. Don't give me crap about geography. How many times has he flown here? How many nights have we been together? You can't deny we have continued our relationship since graduation." *Try and argue against my reasoning.*

"Dylan is starting his clerkship tomorrow. He will not be bopping back and forth between Cali and here anymore." Her coldness hurt.

"Don't close the door on the three of us. We have something incredibly special." Seth needed her to understand.

"Maybe you have time to take off and visit him, but I don't. The two of you can make the distance work." Kat raised an eyebrow at him and nodded toward the desk chair.

“Are you actually pissed off about what happened in here?”

“Seth, I’m all about having fun, but not here. Not when you could jeopardize my business. Not when—” Kat closed her eyes.

“When what?” He insisted she finish her thought. Leaving things unsaid usually went sideways.

“There is no more three of us.” Her icy eyes were colder than the frosty January air whipping through the streets of Chicago. She continued to hammer the nail in the coffin. “It’s a new year. It’s time to move on.”

He knew she was wrong. Rather than argue with her, he retreated. “Sorry, Kat.”

Her eyes remained directed at the desk chair. She kept her gaze fixated even when Seth kissed her on her cheek. “I’m sorry again. I’m going to get out of here.” She nodded but didn’t reply. She crossed her arms across her chest and didn’t follow him out of the office.

He walked out, hoping she would forgive him soon.

He shot Dylan a text while walking out of Lawson’s.

—Woah, she’s crazy pissed—

Dylan—*Why? Nothing happened—*

He was correct. She shouldn’t be hurt.

Dylan—*You should know better than me. You’ve been with more girls.—*

Kat never behaved like the typical girl, but maybe Dylan was onto something. Just because she rarely acted like one didn’t mean she wasn’t capable of the same feelings. Since they hadn’t gotten caught, there wasn’t an actual problem. If not the location, then what caused her reaction—the who or the how?

Seth—*IDK Never seen that expression—*

Dylan—*She’s texting me now—*

He stopped walking, worrying about why Kat would text Dylan over him. This was a first for Seth. He never gave a second thought to Dylan and Kat communicating.

Seth—*So?*—

Dylan—*She just wished me a good day for tomorrow*—

She had already wished Dylan good luck. She didn't need to repeat it in a text.

Seth—*She say anything about walking in on us?*—

Dylan—*Nope*—

He hoped he would get a text from Kat as well.

Nothing.

Dylan—*Gonna workout before I go to bed*—

Seth—*(Thumbs up) Good luck tomorrow*—

He shook his head. Kat's behavior bewildered him. Perhaps he needed a bit more patience. She had a bar to run. His day started much earlier than Kat's. He fell asleep that night before hearing anything from her.

The next morning, he grabbed his phone, shut off his alarm, and checked his messages. Nothing. "What the hell?" He threw his phone on the bed and it almost bounced off. He snagged it before falling on the floor and shot off one more text to Dylan.

—Don't be too cocky on your first day. Although you have every reason to be (eggplant)—

Kat didn't seem to be as angry at Dylan. Seth refused to be the first one to extend an olive branch. He had apologized several times. He didn't know what he should apologize for.

For the next five days, things remained radio silent.

Friday night, Seth considered stopping by Lawson's on his way home from work. Not wanting to disturb Kat, he skipped the detour. Instead, he picked up some spicy shrimp soup from the Thai restaurant a couple of blocks from his apartment.

Upon entering his frigid apartment, he hit the lights, unzipped his jacket, kicked off his shoes, and set the food on his kitchen counter. Crystalline ice patterns trimmed the edges of his windows. He cranked up the temperature on the thermostat.

Sitting at the kitchen island, he took the soup out of the thin plastic bag and removed the lid, hoping the warm food would soothe the chilly emptiness inside. The container was lukewarm. He got up and reheated his dinner in the microwave. While the bowl circled round and round, Seth texted Dylan.

—How was your first week?—

Dylan*—(thumbs up) going for drinks with the judge—*

His lips curled up at the image of Dylan schmoozing. Dylan was destined to do great at his clerkship. Seth wanted all the best for him. However, Seth wished he would have worked for a judge in the Chicago area instead. All three had reached a point where their careers were on a promising trajectory.

Grabbing the hot container from the microwave, it warmed Seth's fingers as he placed it back on the kitchen island. He sat and stirred the food, wishing he could fix Kat's icy mood as easily as the soup. *What was her problem?*

Was he approaching this issue the wrong way? He reached for a nearby yellow-papered legal pad. If Seth could get a perfect score on the logical reasoning section of the LSAT then he should be able to figure out what the hell was going on with Kat. Being an accountant, he thought all problems could be logically resolved. He sketched out various charts with boxes and arrows, the same tricks used on the law entrance exam. Of course, his method failed. Matters of the heart defied logic.

The spicy seasoning in the soup tantalized his tastebuds. The burn on his tongue escalated spoonful by spoonful. Drops of perspiration beaded on his brow. He wiped the sweat away and remembered how she mocked him because it was silly to eat food if it created such a reaction. He zoned out, thinking of Kat.

Suddenly, he started coughing uncontrollably, spitting a mouthful onto the kitchen counter. His tearful eyes went wide. He had bitten into Tien Tsing pepper with a spice rating of about 60,000 Scoville heat units. The fire roared in his mouth. Guzzling water didn't help. He needed relief. Ripping the door open on his refrigerator, he scanned his barren appliance. No milk. No cheese. One lone blueberry yogurt, which he purchased weeks ago. He peeled back the aluminum foil lid and shoved several spoonsful in his mouth without checking the date on the carton. Ah, relief! The dairy dampened the pain. Unfortunately, the expiration date threatened future discomfort.

"Shit."

He figured it out. In Kat's eyes, he had proven her fear valid. Back in June, she stated she didn't want to date him without Dylan, because she was afraid he would always need a man too. In her mind, the incident in her office proved her theory correct.

But why would she be upset if she had already concluded she didn't want to date Seth? *Thou protest too much. She wanted him. At least part of her did.*

Kat had endured the pain of losing two parents and had been raised to suppress sadness and focus on only good memories. In other words, she pushed down her emotions. She probably wasn't even cognizant of her feelings for Seth or Dylan. *There was hope.*

Smiling, Seth placed the remaining soup in the refrigerator and slipped on his shoes and jacket. The silence with Kat needed to be put to rest.

He sauntered into Lawson's with a glint in his eye, confident Kat still cared for him.

He found Smirnova sitting at an odd angle at the bar. She had several half-empty glasses lined up in front of her. He kissed Smirnova on the cheek, who lost her balance in the act. "Whoa there, sweetheart." Seth grabbed her shoulders and steadied her on the stool.

"You are such a gentleman." Smirnova's breath smelled of alcohol.

"Oh sure, he's a model citizen." Kat's bright eyes dimmed.

Her sarcastic remark did not surprise Seth, but he refused to take the bait. Debating with Kat wasn't the way to win. And he desperately wanted back into her good graces. Preferably into her body as well. "What have you two gorgeous women been up to?"

Smirnova gestured with her hand to the glasses in front of her. "I've been testing out drinks. Kat's a great bartender."

"Yeah, she is." Seth honed in on Kat's eyes. "What do you have going on here?"

"I'm trying out some cocktails for a special Valentine's Day menu."

"Cool. Can I be a taste tester too?" He tilted his head toward Smirnova. "She may not be the most discerning of testers at the moment."

"Have you forgotten she is the queen of shooting

vodka?"

"I'll drink to that." He looked in front of him for a glass to toast with. He plastered on his most charming smile. "Can I please get a drink?"

Kat returned his grin.

Smirnova put a hand on his arm and shook her head at him. "I bet you can get whatever you want with that smile of yours."

"Sadly, not always." He pretended to watch Kat mix the cocktail, but he narrowed his focus on her eyes. Her gaze met his and he grinned.

Smirnova slurred her words. "Surely, you have a date for Valentine's Day."

"I do. With this bar stool here." He patted the side of the stool.

"Oh, come on. You're too good-looking to not have someone to go out with." With a crinkled mouth, Smirnova shook her head in disbelief.

"Nope. I'm flying solo." He caught Kat paying attention to his answer while appearing to keep herself busy mixing another drink. Her masquerade of disinterest failed.

"How am I expected to find a man, if you can't? You're like perfect." Seth laughed at Smirnova's over-exaggeration. He was far from perfect.

"Thanks for the ego boost, but I'm picky about the men and women I choose to date." He hoped Kat didn't miss the comment.

However, Smirnova must have been processing slower due to the alcohol. She didn't react at all. But then she froze. She quirked her head to the side like a dog trying to process information. "Wait, what?" She looked at Seth with uncertainty.

He raised an eyebrow and smirked. Kat mouthed. "You sure?" He nodded back again.

"What?" he continued teasing Smirnova. Her brows furrowed together.

Kat stepped closer and placed a drink in front of him. "Seth's bisexual."

"Really?" Seth waited for Smirnova's reaction. "You get to pick from men and women and you still don't have a date. That doesn't make any sense."

"Life doesn't always make sense." He took a large gulp of his drink, relieved by Smirnova's nonconfrontational response. She didn't seem to care one way or another about his orientation. Maybe one day, Kat could share with Smirnova about her dating both him and Dylan.

"This is fantastic, Kat."

"I agree. Can I get one more?"

"Hang on, I've got a different drink I want you to try tonight." Kat strode away and reached for a green bottle and a pitcher of juice.

Seth finished the concoction in front of him.

Kat set a pink-colored drink in front of Smirnova and Seth. "This is gin-based."

While Alex swigged, Seth asked, "How many drinks are you planning on offering?" Seth ran the financial numbers through his head.

"This one is good too. I love all your drinks." Smirnova placed her glass down on the bar.

"Which are your favorites?"

Smirnova pointed to three glasses. Kat had labeled the napkins underneath each. She wasn't randomly mixing drinks. She had planned everything, including keeping the glasses in front of Smirnova for reference's sake.

"Of course, you would choose all the vodka-based ones." She laughed and turned to Seth. "How about you?"

He held up a finger, signaling for her to wait, and took a sip from his glass. "This is really good." He took another pull from it. "I hope it makes the cut."

"Cool. I think I'm going to go with three. The gin one." Kat pointed to the pink drink in Seth's hand. Then she pointed to the empty glass in front of Smirnova. "The vodka martini. For a third, I'll do a champagne and strawberry thing."

"Like an English tennis grand slam tradition?" Seth mimicked volleying a tennis ball with his hand.

"Aww, champagne is romantic for Valentine's Day," mumbled Smirnova.

Kat pointed toward Smirnova with an outstretched finger. "Bingo."

"Have you thought about doing anything special on the menu?" said Smirnova.

"I can't force the people in the kitchen to come up with something so soon." Kat started clearing away the glasses.

"What about maybe just purchasing dessert from a bakery and selling it?" Seth suggested. Kat looked at him with consideration in her eyes.

"Yes! Chocolate is even better than champagne. You must have chocolate lava cake," said Smirnova.

"What is the deal with women and chocolate for Valentine's Day?" The notion dumbfounded Seth. After the chocolate cake on his bedroom floor from when Mrs. Soloman had walked in on them, he never wanted chocolate cake ever again.

"Chocolate is foreplay for our vibrators." Kat's posture relaxed. Smirnova blushed.

He beamed. His smart-ass Kat was back. Had she forgiven Seth?

"Who says vibrators are just for when you are alone?" He almost considered saying vibrators weren't exclusively for women, but he didn't want to scandalize Smirnova or make her choke on embarrassment.

"Touché." Kat smiled devilishly.

"If you two keep this up, my cheeks are going to be redder than the vodka martini." Smirnova hid her face in her hands.

"Can I get you another drink to match your pink cheeks?"

"No, I think I'm past my limit tonight. I'm going to head out." Smirnova reached for her wallet and placed cash on the bar top. "Bye." She dashed out of the bar, although she wobbled a little.

Seth watched Smirnova scurry out before turning back to Kat. "Did I say something wrong to make her leave so quickly?"

"No, she and I sometimes get into an argument over whether she should pay for drinks when she plays the role of guinea pig for me."

"She wants to cover the expenses and you don't want her to?" Seth tried to understand.

"It's like the opposite of dine and ditch."

Seth laughed but thought Kat didn't comprehend the necessity of separating friendship, business, and money. He kept his opinion to himself. He was trying to dig his way out of the doghouse with Kat.

She wiped the bar clean where Smirnova had been sitting, not rushing to get away from Seth.

He entangled Kat in conversation. “I’m surprised she doesn’t have a date for Valentine’s.”

“Yeah. She doesn’t make a lot of time for fun.” Kat shrugged.

Most of their attorney friends were tight on time. The thought of spending energy looking for someone new horrified Seth. Not because of the effort, but because he refused to admit he didn’t have even the slightest shot of being with Kat and Dylan.

“Are you making time for fun?” *Shit.* His stomach plummeted. What if Kat was dating other people? It had only been a week, but the possibility existed.

“Like you in *my* office?”

“Again, I’m sorry.” *Think. Think. Think.* He needed to fix it. “We should have waited for you to join.”

“Would it be fun for Dylan or a cruel tease?” She removed the rest of the glasses and avoided listening to Seth’s response.

He finished his drink while considering whether Kat had any fun in her life. When she returned, he asked, “Have you thought ahead to St. Patrick’s Day? It lands on a Friday this year.”

“My dad always served green beer on the day of the parade.”

“The Loop will be jammed when the city dyes the river green. And big business for you. Ever consider throwing a party here? Maybe incorporate special drinks and food similar to what you are doing for Valentine’s.”

Kat’s mouth went crooked and she remained quiet. “I wonder why my dad never made a big deal about the holiday. Maybe he tried and it wasn’t a good idea?”

“You could ask your aunt or uncle. They might know.”

"What if they don't like me changing how things are done?"

"They might not, but it's your bar, not theirs."

"What if I screw things up by making changes?"

"What if you make things awesome? What if you have fun in the process? You don't have to reinvent the wheel. Make a few minor changes. Tweak things here and there. Dip your toe in the green river."

Kat smiled. "I'll give it some thought."

A smile spread across his face as they engaged in conversation. Her grin was the perfect end to his week. Unfortunately, upon returning home, the expired yogurt took revenge on his insides.

Chapter 17

Dylan

The sunshine streamed through his window, landing on his face. He dared not open his eyelids to confirm the sensation. He moaned as he placed a protective forearm across his eyes. His head ached. His stomach threatened repulsion. He breathed through his nose, hoping to quiet the nausea. The high thread count of his sheets and pillowcase were his only comforts.

The wrapping of knuckles against his solid wood bedroom door sounded like a drumbeat echoing in a cavern. "Oh god." He prayed the evil noise would cease, but it continued. Over and over again. Whoever was banging needed to go away. "Fucking stop."

The clink of the latch inside the handle didn't give him sufficient warning. As the door swung open, so did the dam holding in the contents of his stomach. His eyes popped open. He slammed his hand over his lips. *No. No. No. No.* He rolled off the bed and stumbled to the bathroom. He lifted the lid of the toilet just in the nick of time.

After he flushed away the last remnants in his stomach, he forced himself to rise from his kneeling position. He leaned on the counter and rinsed out his mouth. He needed to lie back down.

In the bathroom doorway stood his mother's

assistant, Craig, handing him a robe. Dylan covered his naked body, but showed no concern about how his state of undress might affect the man. He stood to his full six-foot-three-inch height and peered down at Craig.

"I need to see your phone."

Uncertain about Craig's intentions, Dylan refused to hand over the device, storing several compromising images of himself with Seth and Kat. "I don't think so."

"Listen, your mother is quite upset about the photos you have been posting on social media. I'm here to wipe your accounts clean."

"Not happening." Dylan glared at Craig, who blocked the doorway.

"She plans to curate your online presence. You know Mrs. Levine is going to get what she wants one way or another, so let's just sit down and get this over with. Listen, you can watch everything I do, so you know I'm not intruding on your privacy."

"You don't think wiping out my social media is violating my privacy?" Dylan pushed past Craig and sat on the side of the bed, within reach of his phone.

"No, Dylan. Your outward presence is public and reflects on the senator." Craig extended an open palm.

Dylan didn't appreciate being treated like a disobedient teenager. He handed his phone over to Craig. "Can you please unlock it?" the other man asked. Dylan falsely assumed Craig had already mined his passcode.

Craig opened up an app and deleted the shot from last night. He and Asher had attended the same St. Patrick's Day-themed party, which Dylan had organized for the LGBTQ coalition. "My father wanted me to be involved in the group. What's wrong with the photo?"

"This is the third one of you and Asher together."

"He's the mayor's son! He's dressed in an expensive suit. What could be the problem?"

"If you're seen with the same man three times, people will assume you're a couple." Craig's fingers continued destroying Dylan's accounts.

"You mean a gay couple?" Dylan cracked his knuckles and watched Craig in action as another piece of him was taken away by the family's commitment to the senator's career. When push came to shove, his dad's role in politics always pulled rank over being a father.

"No, I'm referring to the fact that it appears you are no longer single. Being unattached at your age is more advantageous for the senator. He cannot have someone else's views casting a shadow on his own."

Craig handed the phone back to Dylan. "I downloaded all of your photos for you to keep for your personal storage. Just so you know. Mrs. Levine doesn't have issues about you being gay. I'm gay. She has never shown me a hint of homophobia. On the contrary, she's been pretty cool."

What the hell? His mom was never open with him. Why was she kinder to strangers than her own son?

"Do you want me to set up new anonymous accounts for you? Then, you can keep in touch with close friends or randomly scroll."

Dylan's phone rang.

"I can do it, thanks." He sneered at Craig, not grateful in the slightest. Dylan answered the video call. Craig waved goodbye as he exited Dylan's bedroom, closing the door behind him.

Seth and Kat spoke in unison. "Hey, Dylan!" Their cackling hurt his head. Dylan would have laughed at their ridiculous over-the-top emerald-colored outfits, but laughing threatened to worsen his headache. In the background, the Chicago River had been dyed a bright shade of green. Seth and Kat embraced, swaying to the music. Their noses and cheeks were rosy. "Been drinking already?"

"Seth helped me dye the beer green this morning. We sampled a lot along the way." Seth held up his stained fingers into the screen as proof. They looked like they were having a great time.

Something inside felt off. Dylan first worried he was going to puke again. He stared at their smiles. Consumed by envy, he couldn't help but feel a burning resentment. He missed his friends and the whole Chicago St. Patrick's Day experience. Kat had dragged him to the parade for the past three years. "I wish I could be there with you guys."

"Me too. I'm hosting a huge party at the bar. Alex and Seth helped me come up with a bunch of ideas and drinks."

Kat's smile didn't seem as big as usual. This was her favorite holiday… It was also Kat's first St. Patty's Day without her dad. He hoped the party filled a bit of the void he was sure she was feeling.

"I saw the photos you posted. You looked wasted. Hungover this morning?"

Dylan couldn't recall the specifics of what he uploaded the previous night, other than Craig mentioning that it included Asher.

"Rough start to the day."

Seth raised his voice. "Hey, I went to check out the photos, but *everything's* gone!"

"Shit, were you hacked?" Kat bit at her finger.

"Calm down. My mom's assistant deleted the shit."

"What the fuck?" Either Seth was offended by the motherly interference or he was overreacting because he was drunk.

"It doesn't matter. I'm hungover. Don't have the energy to be upset about it. I'll set up other accounts later."

"Damn. I missed the photos." Kat stuck out her lower lip and pouted. Dylan wanted to bite her lip. Unlike Kat, Dylan had been forbidden to pout.

"Wasn't he the same guy in several of your photos? What's the deal with him?" Seth wore a pinched expression. "You too looked cozy together." Seth's normally beautiful smile vanished.

"Asher is the mayor's son."

"Hey, I want to see. Send me the photos," Kat demanded.

Dylan texted her two.

"He's cute." She nodded approvingly. Seth scowled at her.

Ah, Seth was jealous. Funny how jealousy could run in both directions. "He's just a friend. He's dating some thespian singer." Seth's expression only softened slightly.

"Time to head back to the bar. Just remember, hair of the dog is the best cure for a hangover." Kat laughed.

"You two have fun." The word *two* didn't sit right with Dylan.

"Feel better, Dylan," said Seth.

The call ended and he fell back into his bed. Kat usually had great ideas, but more drinking to fix his headache was not one of them. Dylan needed sleep. In his dreams, he wouldn't agonize about the party he was missing. Hopefully, the pounding in his head would cease too. He closed his eyes and drifted off.

A few hours later, he awoke more refreshed. This time, he got up on the correct side of the bed, ready to face the day. His headache dimmed. As he walked into the bathroom, the scent of cleaning solvent pleasantly surprised him. It beat the stench of a night of over-indulging in alcohol.

He went to the kitchen as his appetite returned. The personal chef bustled between the stove and the work island. “Are you already starting on dinner?”

“No, I’m prepping some meals for the next couple of days. I can make you something. Breakfast food often settles well on an agitated stomach.” Having an ensuite bathroom hadn’t kept all matters private.

“Please. Thank you.”

Dylan sat at the table and started setting up new social media accounts when his mother entered. “Good afternoon, Dylan.”

“Hello, Mother, you look beautiful.” Compliments paved his way to his mother’s chest cavity. The jury was out on whether a heart filled the space under her ribs.

“Thank you. I’m glad I found you. Here’s a printout of the schedule for the next quarter, including all the events you are expected to attend. Please take a look at it and inform Craig if you have any conflicts with work.”

Dylan glanced at the list before looking up. “We’re doing a Passover seder?”

“Of course, your father is Jewish.”

“But we have never celebrated.” He narrowed his focus.

“We used to celebrate with your grandparents when you were little and we lived in Chicago."

“That was over twenty years ago. Why now?”

"Really Dylan, does it matter?" His mom sighed. Did her facial injections prevent her from showing emotion or did she not have any? At least she didn't chastise him.

He examined the schedule more closely. "Why is the dinner scheduled for seven hours?"

"We have invited a conservative rabbi to the meal and I was told a full service takes a very long time." His mother followed directions, just like him.

"Excuse me, Mrs. Levine, when would you like to discuss the menu?" The chef approached the table where Dylan sat, ready with a pen and pad of paper.

"We don't need to bother. Per instructions, I hired an expert for the event who knows how to prepare all the customary dishes and brings in a set of cookware and place settings dedicated for the holiday."

"Oh, okay. Will you be keeping to dietary traditions for the whole week?" The chef jotted down a note.

"And eat matzah for seven whole days? No. I'll pass on all the non-digestible carbs." His mom rolled her eyes. If Dylan did such a thing, she would scold him.

"You know, I'm sure I could come up with several recipes which adhere to the rules but are more according to your typical tastes."

"Excellent. Don't want the senator getting caught eating a California Club on sough dough during Passover. Can you imagine the PR nightmare?" No one laughed at his mother's joke.

Did his mother roll her eyes again? Dylan was almost certain. *Huh.* She found creating the perfect look to be a chore. His dad was right. It wasn't something she directed only toward him. Every time he disappointed her, it meant more work for her. It wasn't personal.

Dylan skimmed over the schedule one more time. "I don't have any conflicts with these dates." He held up the paper as a reference. "But if some big important case comes into the judge's chambers, I may need to put in more hours."

"I'm sure you can work around it." His mother turned on her heels and vacated the kitchen.

The chef placed a bacon, egg, and cheese croissant and a large coffee on the table in front of Dylan. "Here you go. The best cure for a hangover." Dylan smiled. The sandwich smelled wonderful. "Did you want something else?"

"No. This is perfect. My friend had suggested more alcohol." He smiled because Kat often thought liquor was the answer.

"I could make you a bloody Mary."

"No, thank you. This is great. Really." He bit into the sandwich. The chef was right. He started feeling much better after taking a few bites.

As he ate, he scrolled through posts on his new social media account. He came across a video of Lawson's Bar. If it weren't for the caption and username, he hardly recognized it. The entire ceiling had green, white, and orange balloons with ribbons cascading below, out of reach of people to disrupt. Pitchers of green beer rested on most of the tables.

The video ended with Kat giving a shout-out to attract more customers to the bar. Her call to action made his chest tighten. He wished he was with them.

Fortunately, he didn't have commitments with his family for the night. While his hangover had subsided, conforming to his mother's exacting standards was exhausting. Instead, he became engrossed in a marathon of vintage psychological thriller movies.

That following morning, he woke up feeling great. Despite having yet another luncheon and staged media event with his father, his newfound perspective about his mother pacified his misgivings. In fact, with his new attitude, he skated through the next month of holidays and events.

But then, Mother's Day approached. A little over a week before the fateful Sunday, Kat reached out to Dylan.

—*Have you talked to Seth about Mother's Day?*—

Dylan—*No. He hasn't mentioned anything about it*—

Kat—*I invited him to a brunch at my aunt's*—

Dylan—*Good. He shouldn't be alone*—

Kat—*I haven't heard back. It's weird*—

Dylan—*That's not like him (thinking face)*—

A good deal of time had passed since Dylan had last spoken to Seth. Tax season in March and April kept him very busy. They had exchanged a few text messages but hadn't actually talked to one another. *Damn.* Dylan's stomach turned. They hadn't spoken since the St. Patrick's Day parade. It had been weeks. Dylan had thought about Seth many times. It wasn't an out-of-sight, out-of-mind scenario. Of course, he mostly fantasized about Seth at night. The lack of communication made him a terrible friend.

Dylan—*I'll call Seth*—

Kat—*(thumbs up) Update me after?*—

Dylan—*ofc*—

Kat—*(puckered mouth face)*—

Had she downgraded Dylan? She used to send a kissing face with heart eyes. Now, she signed off with no red lips and no hearts. Dylan felt untethered to Chicago like he was floating out in the middle of Lake Michigan without land in sight. He didn't like it. It knocked down his confidence.

He called Seth. The phone rang, the call went to voicemail. Uncertain why he didn't answer, Dylan assumed the worst. Was Seth pulling away from him, like Kat? Was he blocking his call? Rationally, he knew there could be one of several good reasons, but that didn't appease his concern.

After pacing back and forth in his bedroom, Dylan went to the gym. Better to burn off nervous energy than drive himself mad in his bedroom. Running on the treadmill didn't quell his anxiety. His mind ran faster than his feet. He opted instead for lifting weights. Despite adding several plates to the bench press bar, he kept the weight low enough to pump out numerous reps, rather than seeking a maximum lift. After feeling a good pain in his pecs, he continued with chest flies and push-ups. He scanned his work out room, picked up the medicine ball, and placed it on his yoga mat. On his fortieth fitness ball pushup, he felt the burn in his arms. He powered through and started doing pull-ups. Then, he hit the dip bar. His heart rate increased, not bothering to take a break between sets. Pausing afforded him time to think. Concentrating on Seth and Kat stressed him out.

In the middle of reaching upward with a dumbbell in his hand, Dylan's phone rang. He completed the snatch in perfect form before setting down the weight. It was Seth.

"Hey. Sorry it took me a while to get back to you. I was out for a run."

Dylan sat on the bench, happy to hear Seth's voice.

He suppressed an accusatory response. “I thought talking while running was supposed to be a good thing?”

“I’m training for a marathon with a run club.” In other words, Seth was speaking to other people and disregarded Dylan’s call.

“Is this your first?”

“Yeah, I kind of needed something else to focus on.”

Was he trying to avoid Kat and him? Probably not, considering Seth returned the call. The uncertainty disturbed Dylan. Their closeness had slipped away.

“Anything I can do to help?”

Seth laughed. Dylan pictured Seth’s glorious smile in his mind. “Like when we got caught in Kat’s office?” He chuckled again, which made Dylan think things weren’t too bad. “I’m in the park, stretching. I’m not interested in getting arrested today.”

It was Dylan’s turn to laugh. Although, being alone in the gym with all the endorphins running through his veins, the other option would have been hot. “You caught me downstairs in the weight room.”

“Hope you aren’t skipping leg day again.”

Dylan leered at the squat rack, then cast his eyes back at the mirror. Guilt was visible on his face. *How did Seth know?* “Whatever.”

“No seriously. I want you to run with me.”

“Run a marathon? Are you fucking kidding?”

“I signed up for the San Francisco marathon, which is on a Sunday. We could jog the 5K on the day before.”

Participating in the race would be an excellent political move and a fun experience with Seth. Uncertain which ranked higher in importance unnerved Dylan. Since when had his political aspirations started steering his decisions? “I’m in!”

"Great. We'll have a blast. I promise."

Dylan never considered jogging fun. It was something he forced himself to do to stay fit. But the thought of seeing Seth cheered him up and gave him something to look forward to.

Good friends never avoided difficult topics. Tension built up in Dylan's body as he feared how Seth would respond. "I didn't want to bother you during tax season, but do you have any updates on your case?"

"My father reached out to me the other day. He said with Mother's Day coming up, it would be great if we could drop all the issues."

Dylan bit his lip. Fury burned for the disdain toward Seth's parents. "Did you contact Cole's dad?"

"He thinks they are feeling the pressure of the counterclaims. He wants to leverage LGBTQ month and make this a bigger issue."

"Is that what you want?" Dylan worried about the stress this was causing Seth. Maybe it was best if it ended. "Is this why you training for a marathon?" *Was Seth running from his problems? Why wasn't he running to him or Kat?*

"I don't know." Dylan hated hearing Seth sound sullen. He had a lot of heavy shit on his mind. He was beautiful when he was beaming bright. Dylan loathed Seth's parents for trying to dim his light.

"I want to help." He wanted to fix everything for Seth.

"I have an attorney to deal with my parents." Seth's words were laden with acid.

Sure, his attorneys were top-notch, but they only helped with the logistics. Mr. Kensington's job didn't include emotionally supporting Seth throughout the process. Why wasn't Seth reaching out to Dylan or Kat anymore?

"I'm here for you, anyway I can help." He hoped the reminder didn't fall on deaf ears.

"Thanks."

After the call, he texted Kat about Seth's lawsuit. Seth and Kat remained radio silent for the rest of the week.

Around 9:00 a.m. on Mother's Day, Dylan was putting on the outfit Asa had set out for him. He received a text message but ignored it and continued getting dressed. Another followed soon thereafter. And another. And another. Unable to ignore the beeping, he checked the phone. All the messages were from Seth.

Seth—*HELP! Kat is catatonic*—

Seth—*Where are you?*—

Seth—*Found her at her mother and father's gravesite sitting by herself, rocking back and forth*—

Seth—*She won't speak*—

Seth—*Where the fuck are you?*—

Seth—*She won't look at me*—

Three moving dots indicated he was typing another message. This was insanity. Frustrated, Dylan called Seth, but his phone went instantly to voice mail. *What the hell?*

Seth—*Can't talk. I'm sitting with Kat right now*—

Annoyed by the inconvenience of texting, Dylan's thumbs flew over the keyboard.

Dylan—*Start from the beginning*—

Seth—*When I showed up at her aunt's to celebrate Mother's Day, Kat wasn't there. I called her to see if she was running late, but she didn't answer. I tried calling again a few minutes later, thinking maybe I caught her in the shower. Nothing. That's when her aunt remembered her father used to go to her mother's gravesite every Mother's Day to say thank you for giving him the blessing of Kat. Kat's aunt drove me to the cemetery. We found her and brought her back to her apartment. I've been holding her ever since.—*

Dylan—*Answer the damn phone—*

He rang Seth again. This time, he picked up. "Put me on speakerphone." Dylan paused for a second. "Kat, can you hear me?"

"Yes," Seth answered.

"Hey Kitty-Kat. I know this is a very hard day for you. You've got us both now. Seth and I are here for you. We can't replace either of your parents, but I promise you will never need to visit the cemetery by yourself ever again. Right now, I'm going to ask you to do something, which may be hard. Seth, are you still holding Kat?"

Dylan had seen when she got the news about her dad's passing. She fought to keep her feelings inside. The veins on the side of her neck bulged.

"Yes, I've got her."

"Good. Now, Kat, I want you to swallow the lump in your throat. The one I know you are holding onto for dear life. It's okay to let go. Seth is there for you."

"She's shaking her head back and forth. And tears are running down her face." At least she released some of the tension.

Dylan calmly coaxed her. "That's good. Kat, you can do this."

"She looks like she's going to be sick." Feeling her pain, Dylan thought he might too.

"You can do it. Swallow the knot. You don't need to hold back your feelings anymore. We are here for you.

Seth, hold her *securely*."

A blood-curdling scream roared through the phone. It was deep and guttural, as if Kat was physically being ripped apart. She wailed. She cried out again and again until her cries faded to sobbing.

"I've got you. I've got you, sweetheart," said Seth.

"We've got you, Kitty-Kat. Seth and I got you."

She hiccupped back her sobs and gasped for air. More than a half hour passed before she quieted.

"Let me go grab you some more tissues. I'll be right back."

"You're doing great, Kitty-Kat. It's good to let it out. You're very brave."

She remained speechless. Dylan pieced together the situation based on the information Kat had shared in years past. Her father had protected her from the pain of Mother's Day by turning it into a day of gratitude. Standing by her parents' graves must have proved too much for her…

His chest stayed tight even as Kat's hysteria subsided. He prided himself as someone good at predicting potential problems. The skill helped make him a great lawyer. The fact he didn't know about her yearly cemetery visit wasn't an excuse; he should have anticipated Kat's meltdown. He regretted not asking the right questions and gaining a better grasp of the situation. A more considerate friend would have known. He had failed Kat.

Her breathing eventually evened out.

"She's asleep. How did you know what to say?"

Dylan sighed as the painful memory washed over him. "During my summer clerkship, the Chicago judge I worked for had set up several field trips. He said being a judge required appreciating everyone's perspective. To teach me, he made me attend the funeral of a murdered child. I watched as the mother tried to stand strong as she held the hands of her two remaining young children. She remained after everyone departed the ceremony. The funeral director put an arm around her shoulders, and she collapsed."

"Jesus…I'm so glad you knew what to say."

"The fact you are there holding her right now is the only thing keeping me from losing my mind." Dylan wiped at the tears on his cheek. "Will you be able to stay with her?"

"Of course. I feel awful that I wasn't aware of her tradition with her dad. I would have gone with her."

"You and me both." Dylan bit his lip, regretting he needed to end the call. "Listen, I need to go do a photo-op for my family. Can you please text me when she wakes up and let me know how she's doing?"

"Sure thing." Seth hung up.

Chapter 18

Seth

He breathed in through his nose and out his mouth just like when he ran long distances. Seth worked on maintaining control, but his heart raced. He tried calming his nerves, but his legs bounced despite his efforts of restraint as he sat in the reception area of Kensington's law firm. He had received a message from the office; his parents had sent in a settlement offer. The assistant did not indicate the quality. However, if it was a terrible proposal, Seth suspected Mr. Kensington would not waste either of their time with a face-to-face.

Anticipation prodded at him. Not a day had gone by over the past seven months when the issue hadn't weighed on him like an anvil on his shoulders.

Unfortunately, Cole was busy working in New York and wasn't available to talk while Seth waited for his meeting with Mr. Kensington.

He worried his hands together, twisting and turning. If Kat had been by his side, she would have laced her fingers with his own. He didn't deserve to be comforted. His counterclaims were harsh and held the possibility of crushing his parents' firm. They had raised him. He enjoyed a solid relationship with his father. What type of resolution did he expect from Mr. Kensington? Better yet, what did he want to hear?

Kat and Dylan had different opinions of the type of outcome they hoped Seth would eventually get. Her anger drove her to seek monetary compensation. Whereas Dylan's desires focused on embarrassing the company publicly. Even with Kat and Dylan's best intentions, Seth needed to make this final decision on his own. If not, he might blame them in the future.

The receptionist tapped at the headset resting on her ear and rose from her chair. "Mr. Kensington is ready to see you." Seth's heart beat like it was race day. He swallowed to clear the knot forming in his throat. Nothing worked.

Mr. Kensington stood and greeted him with a firm handshake and a hand on his shoulder. While the gesture of support may have been intended as comforting, the extra effort worried Seth as if to prepare him for the bad news. "Why don't you take a seat, Seth." Seth slowly lowered himself into a chair at the conference table. He stared at the papers like they were a poisonous creature.

Sitting at the head of the table, Mr. Kensington took a deep breath. *Shit. This can't be good.* He patted his hand on the documents. "I have the term sheet for the settlement here. I think you will find it to be an excellent offer. However…"

Seth's heart felt as if it was going to jump out of his chest. Like when he sprinted, he drew in air through his nose and nodded.

"I have contacted several LGBTQ organizations in the area to consult with them about this matter. As you stated, it was important to you to ensure the settlement made a positive mark in this area of law. As you know, I cannot accept the offer on your behalf without your approval."

Seth glared at the paper as Mr. Kensington slid it closer for him to view. There were more figures on the papers than he had expected. Despite years of working as an accountant, the digits overwhelmed him. Looking at other people's financial figures didn't stir an emotional reaction. He steadied his hands on the table as a dizzy spell hit him. This was why intelligent lawyers didn't represent themselves.

He gazed at the numbers, which went in and out of view as tears welled in his eyes. He remained silent.

"As you can see, the final amount far exceeds your actual damages. As you were able to find a job quickly, you didn't endure a substantial quantity of lost wages."

"I don't have to pay back the cost of law school?"

"No. That claim on their lawsuit was ridiculous."

Seth couldn't take his eyes off the large seven-figure dollar amount at the bottom of the statement.

"How did you get them to agree to such a high settlement?" Seth's stomach felt queasy. His gain would mean his parents' loss.

"By leveraging support from LGBTQ groups. The fear of pride month starting in a few days pushed them. Things could get brutally ugly for them if they didn't settle now."

"It's a lot of money." Seth continued to focus on his breathing.

"Yes. You don't sound pleased."

"This is going to bankrupt my parents' firm, which will personally bankrupt them."

"I anticipated this may be of a concern to you. I have a letter from your father." Mr. Kensington handed it to Seth. His eyes widened, but then he lowered his head, conceding the necessity of reviewing it.

The letter read…

To my loving son, Seth.

I cannot say in words how sorry I am for what has happened between you and your mother and me. I'm aware of all the settlement terms which are being presented to you. While I cannot tell you to accept the offer, I do not want you to refuse to accept it based on concern for the business, your mother, or myself. We always intended the business to become yours. The money specified in the settlement is simply fast-forwarding your entitlement as our son. I hope one day we can rectify our relationship.

Seth took a deep breath. "Why didn't he just reach out to me?"

"I can't say for certain."

Lawyers always knew more than they said. "What do you know?"

"I believe the business is being dissolved." Mr. Kensington looked like there was something he was holding back.

"And?"

"As I understand it, your parents are getting divorced. Your father filed immediately following the incident."

"Why wouldn't he tell me?"

"That answer I am unaware."

"Do you think I should accept?"

"Read through all the non-monetary specifications. I believe all of your expectations for admission, apology, and prevention are met."

Seth nodded along as he examined the document.

"I assure you the complete settlement will have all the i's dotted and t's crossed. It will be fully binding and free of any loopholes for the defendants to avoid repercussions." Mr. Kensington emphasized the adversarial circumstance by avoiding using the familial relationship.

"If you don't want to accept, I am behind you and am willing to take them to court. Based on the valuation of your parents' firm, I'm sure we can get more."

Tears streamed down Seth's cheeks. His legs began shaking and the vibrations moved up his frame. He couldn't keep his fingers still. A bottle of water and a box of tissues appeared before him. Mr. Kensington placed a steady hand on his back.

"Part of me wants this all over with, but I also hate the concept of settling." Seth clenched his hand in a fist, hoping to stop the trembling.

"The law has limits on what it can offer. Your acceptance does not condone the party's behavior. You are merely approving of the punishment for such a crime. Her actions should be considered assault. Unfortunately, nothing is going to take away the pain of your mother's words." He patted Seth's back until he calmed. "This has been overwhelming. It's okay."

Finally, with a thready voice, Seth said, "Let's accept the offer." The finality felt heavy. It wasn't a relief. He expected to feel unburdened, but it was the opposite.

"We should have the final paperwork complete with all the details negotiated within a few days, including a schedule for the payout."

"Thank you, Mr. Kensington. I appreciate everything you have done."

After leaving Mr. Kensington's firm, Seth took his time returning to his office. His head throbbed and he was uncertain if he had it in him to concentrate at work.

As soon as he saw the sign for his favorite hot dog restaurant, his mouth watered. Regardless of whether or not hot dogs qualified as healthy sustenance for training for the marathon, he didn't care. He desperately needed some comfort food, substituting some emotional eating for the absence of his friends' support.

He stood at the diner window, beside the one-foot-deep table affixed to the entire length of the wall. Seth took a monster-sized bite and waited for the mouth-watering satisfaction. He chewed and chewed, but no gratification came. He barely choked down a mouthful. It tasted vile. He tossed the rest in a trash can.

He continued on his way to work. Sadness engulfed him as he imagined sitting at the baseball stadium, eating a hotdog, without his father.

Before entering his building, he swiped his fingers across his cheeks. The wind dried up most of his tears. He walked like a zombie through the office to his cubicle, not stopping to say hello to anyone. His lips remained pressed together, forming a straight line, betraying any hint of his usual smile.

He worked impassively at his desk until his boss messaged him and requested he stop by. His boss offered him a gracious smile. Seth forced himself to return the affable greeting, but the act felt very uncomfortable as it wasn't genuine.

His boss gestured for Seth to sit. "Thanks for stopping by." The words of gratitude sounded odd. As an employee, did Seth have an option of not complying with his boss's request? "Listen, I don't mean to poke my nose into your personal business, but I am aware of the change in the status of your legal issues."

Seth narrowed his eyes. "How do you know?"

"Some of your parents' clients have contacted the firm here to open new accounts. Several in fact."

Seth swallowed. He laced his fingers in a praying position, his knuckles turned white from gripping tightly. He bit the inside of his lip. Seth refused to allow himself to cry in front of his boss.

"Listen, I can't imagine how difficult this has been for you. I don't expect you to share if you aren't comfortable, but I want you to know my door is always open. You have been an amazing addition to the firm. You do fantastic work on your own, but you are also a great team player. We appreciate it."

Seth tried to say thanks but it came out more like a croak.

His boss took a deep breath. Seth noticed the compassion in his eyes. "Why don't you take the rest of the day off? Maybe go for a run. I heard you placed in the St. Patrick's Day race. Very impressive."

The tension in his body uncoiled. "Thank you."

His boss didn't push him out the door, but engaged in friendly banter. "How's your training for the San Francisco marathon going?"

Seth grinned as he welcomed the change of topic. Anything to distract his mind. "I'm keeping on track. Pun intended."

"Better you than me. I can't imagine running that far. The only thing I like to run for is a yellow ball on a tennis court."

"Ever play pickleball?" Seth's enthusiasm for conversation returned.

His boss smirked. "I've dabbled. But, seriously, what a dumb name for a sport." Seth laughed at the expression on the other man's face.

His boss's phone rang. "I need to answer this call. Go home. Take the day. I'll see you tomorrow."

Seth waved as he got up and exited his boss's office. Taking the suggestion to heart, he left work early, went to his apartment, and laced up his long distance shoes.

Taking advantage of the extra daylight hours, he set out on a longer run. He readjusted his marathon training schedule in his app, which coordinated a mix of lengthier, shorter, speed, progressive, interval, and recovery runs. His preparation required more than just running a ton of miles. Upon returning home, he logged his mileage and times.

He showered, but while he cleaned his body, mixed emotions about the settlement flooded Seth's mind. He threw on some boxers. He towel-dried his hair but didn't bother applying any gel or mousse. With a deep sigh, he muttered, "Fuck."

Opening the refrigerator, nothing looked appetizing. A knock on the door surprised him. He checked the peephole. A rush of warmth washed over him and the corners of his mouth turned upward. Kat stood on the other side.

He unlocked and opened the door. He reached for Kat in an awkward hug, as the plastic bag she was holding obstructed him. Despite the hindrance, Seth clung to Kat. He let the weight of his head settle into the crook of her neck. "Thank you."

"Let's get inside before your neighbors see you." Kat pushed her way past him.

"As if I care if they see me in my boxers." Seth rolled his eyes and closed the door behind her.

"No, I meant with your hair looking like crap." Seth

laughed as she placed the flimsy bags on his kitchen counter.

Her slapstick comment eased the tension. He took in the aroma from the bags. The nondescript white plastic didn't reveal the contents. He stepped over and peeked inside. Hopeful, he grabbed the cylindrical carton out of the bag and opened it up. "You brought my favorite Thai soup?"

"I thought you might be hungry. You never have anything decent in your fridge." She downplayed the gesture. Seth watched as she took out a container of plain noodles for herself. Unlike her usual commentary on the plagues of spicy food, she picked up a fork without complaint, swirled the sauceless pad Thai around the utensil, and ate it. The simple selfless act touched Seth.

He put down his spoon. "I assume you know. But how?"

"Cole texted me." She stuffed another bite of food in her mouth, keeping any excess comments to herself.

Seth was at first pissed Cole broke confidentiality, but then remembered Kat and Dylan signed an agreement back in the beginning.

"Did I not order the right soup?" she asked.

Seth looked down at the full paper carton. "Sorry, my mind was elsewhere." He spooned several bites into his mouth. The heat of the spice cleared his head as a sheen of perspiration formed on his face. "It's perfect."

"Good."

Still, she remained tight-lipped. Kat didn't pester him for details or even press him about how he felt. Why had he assumed she would have pushed her opinions on him during the meeting with Kensington? They continued to eat in companionable silence.

Halfway through his soup, he took a deep breath. “Thank you.” She grinned knowingly. He could have easily ordered delivery for himself. In reality, he appreciated the gesture and her presence. She had his back even when he didn’t ask.

“Dylan asked me to tell you to call him when you are ready to talk.”

Seth nodded.

“We are both here for you. This has been months of agony. Just because the legal battle has been put to rest doesn’t mean the emotional fallout will clear quickly.” Her eyes welled with tears.

After losing both of her mom and dad, she spoke out of empathy. Whereas his parents kicked him to the curb in a spectacular public display of hatred.

He shut his eyelids, holding in the building moisture. “I’m so tired.”

“Are you finished eating?”

Seth glanced down at his nearly empty container. “Yeah.”

Kat cleaned up the kitchen in an almost motherly fashion. Maybe it was a habit from running the bar. He felt his chest constrict with gratitude for her considerate affection. More tears threatened to spill.

Her arms wrapped around him. He leaned into her slight frame. “I’m here for you, Seth.” With that, the dam broke open. Like a thunderstorm, the droplets ran down his cheeks. His body convulsed as he sobbed. Kat continued to hold him and repeatedly told him it was okay. She didn’t offer false hope that the situation would be fine, but she made him feel safe in allowing his feelings out.

His crying ebbed and flowed as he considered all he

had lost. His mother. His father. His work family. He finally ceased blubbering. “Do you have time to sit? Watch something?”

“Sure. I gave Josie a promotion to assistant manager. She closes up once a week.”

“Good.” Seth tossed Kat the remote control. “Find something while I go throw on some sweats.” He padded off to the bedroom.

When he returned, Kat sat curled up in the corner. Seth sat beside her and laid his head in her lap and wrapped a blanket over his body. He checked out the show on the TV set and became engrossed. “You hate this movie,” he commented.

Kat ran her fingers through his hair. “It’s your favorite.”

Seth smiled. It was nice to be spoiled on such a horrible day. The monetary compensation provided a remarkable nest egg, but what Kat had given him tonight was worth much more to him. “Kat—”

She cut him off. “Quiet, I don’t want to miss any of these awful cheesy lines.”

She knew him all too well and prevented him from professing anything too serious. She continued to run her fingers through his hair as if the issue had been abandoned.

When the movie concluded, he was tired and wanted to call it a night. He had no desire to continue sitting in front of the screen. He rose from the couch and offered Kat a hand. They stood sandwiched between the coffee table and couch. Momentarily pinned within inches of one another. He looked deep into her eyes… “Please stay.”

She didn’t look upset by the request. “I need you,

Kat. I understand if you prefer to go home, but I want you."

She leaned in and softly placed her lips on top of his. Rather than pulling away, she closed the space between them until her chest brushed up against his own. "Seth, I want you."

Those three words meant everything. More than saying "I love you." Someone could love you and still push you away. Kat wanted him and Seth needed to feel wanted.

Earlier, he had appreciated being cared for like a child. But now, he needed to feel like a grown-ass man, capable of standing on his own.

He took her face between both of his hands and kissed her, relishing the firm press of his lips on hers. Without feeling a sense of urgency or pressure, he didn't rush things between them. He enjoyed every second of her body against his own. There was comfort and safety in her arms.

Kat denied him the opportunity to make a proclamation earlier. But he knew it with one hundred percent certainty. He loved Kat.

Seth took a break from kissing her. "Bedroom?"

"Yeah." She caught her breath. Seth could see a fresh look in her eye. He recognized her lustful gaze, but this was something different. Desire?

He led her to his room.

"Seth?"

He turned to answer her. She opened her mouth, but nothing came out. She was on the same page as him. He tenderly kissed her.

Seth continued in to the room. As they positioned themselves beside the bed, he slowly dragged Kat's shirt up and off. He peppered kisses along her shoulder and up her neck. She helped remove his t-shirt. She placed her palm on his heart. Their pulses beat in sync. She removed her hand and pressed a tender kiss where her touch had previously rested. Then Kat began peeling off the rest of her clothes, as did he. They continued until both stood naked.

Unlike their normal bedroom escapades, the pace lacked speed. However, the intensity topped the charts.

Kat lie in the center of the bed and Seth crawled over her, drawn to the look in her eyes. “Kat?”

“Kiss me.” She cut off the conversation.

Their kiss carried-on as she eased a condom down his length. *Damn.* Her fingers sent shivers through his body. Aligning their bodies, he entered her. Her core gripped him securely, and the warmth melted a piece of his heart. They moved together as their kiss continued. Never once did their lips part. Neither could speak as long as their mouths tantalized each other. A delicious burning ignited in the base of his cock and intensified until the flames burst as he and Kat orgasmed together. A heat consumed his entire being. With oxytocin racing through his veins and fatigue in every other part of his body, Seth relaxed into slumber.

Chapter 19

Kat

She stared at the Fourth of July decorations strewn about the bar. She had a great time decorating. But removing the festive crap sucked. She didn't want to deal with the burden of taking it down. At least with Christmas ornaments, the enjoyment lasted weeks. The bar would look ridiculous if she kept the red, white, and blue stuff up past July fifth.

She planned on trashing the streamers and balloons after closing time on the fourth, hoping her best friend would have entertained her, but Alex left the bar early with some tall, handsome guy. Then Kat and Josie enjoyed a few of her red, white, and blue lemonade slushies. Feeling buzzed didn't combine well with standing on a ladder. She enjoyed red and white fireworks, but she didn't need to see those colors flashing on top of an ambulance if she fell in a drunken mess.

Continuing her procrastination, Kat shot a text to her best friend.

—I want all the details from last night! (smiling devil)—

She lost interest in her post-holiday cleanup and obsessed over what she envisioned happened after Alex left the bar. The man, in some ways, reminded her of Dylan. Both men were clean cut and exuded confidence.

Although, Dylan's extroverted charisma dominated his persona and attracted Kat to him. Alex's hookup was more reserved.

Unlike Alex, her sex life had become non-existent. She only had memories of Dylan and Seth to satisfy her lustful cravings. She and Seth had only hooked up once since the night of his settlement offer. His work had gotten substantially busier after many clients moved from his parents' firm to his current firm. And his training for the marathon had ramped up, which left him physically exhausted. All this combined with Kat's late-night lifestyle didn't leave time for screwing.

A ping on her phone brought her back to reality.

Alex—*at work, details tonight, bring the whole bottle of vodka!*—

Maybe she needed the alcohol to loosen up her mouth? Alex wasn't much of a talker when it came to sex.

Kat—*super hot sex?*—

Alex—*(fire)*—

Kat—*going for seconds?*—

Alex—*NO!!! (red face with &$!#%)*—

Oh yeah, Alex had a serious story to share, but Kat appreciated the fact Alex needed to focus on her work.

Kat—*I'll save a barstool for you. (hand sign for peace)*—

She slid her phone into her pocket, looking forward to catching up with Alex. She climbed back up the ladder. Reaching for the streamer attached to the ceiling, a knock outside the entrance interrupted her. Her cousin stood outside Lawson's front. Kat climbed down and plodded toward the door while reaching for her key to unlock it. She pushed it open and her cousin stepped aside, avoiding getting smashed in the nose.

"Hey, Lauren. Come on in." She locked up behind her. "What are you doing here on a Sunday morning?"

Her cousin glared at her.

Something must have happened to put such an unusual, surly look on her face. "Someone piss in your cereal?"

"You could say that. My dad."

This wasn't going to be a quick visit. "Want to sit down and tell me about it? The kitchen isn't up and running yet. Want a drink?"

"Sure, thanks." Lauren followed Kat over to the bar and planted herself on a stool. "Can I get a bloody Mary?"

Kat raised an eyebrow at her. "Coffee?" she offered instead, grabbing two mugs and poured the black fuel. "Cream or sugar?" Lauren shook her head back and forth. Kat placed the mug on a saucer in front of her crabby cousin and assumed the position of combined bartender and therapist.

She wiped at the bar, waiting for Lauren to speak. Lauren took a few sips of coffee. "My dad is ticked off I haven't found a job yet." She crossed her arms across her chest. "I just graduated a month ago." She leaned over and rested her forearms on the wooden bar top. "I mean, what's the big deal? Most of my friends haven't found a job. Their parents aren't freaking out."

Kat remained silent as Lauren played with a napkin. "Some of my friends are spending the entire summer traveling." She looked down into the half-full mug and mumbled, "I wish I had parents like them."

Kat sipped her coffee. The conversation required an extra shot of caffeine and patience. She reminded herself she was just as immature as her cousin at twenty-two. Kat's dad cured her by putting her to work at the bar—"Your dad sent you here to ask for a job?"

"Yeah, kind of." Lauren scrunched up her face.

Kat concealed her all-knowing smile behind a strategically positioned hand. She liked Lauren and avoided sounding condescending. "Do you want to work here?"

"Seems like it could be fun. You always look happy here when I stop by."

Kat froze for a second. *Was she happy?* For months, she had struggled with learning all the tricks of running the bar. Somewhere in the transition, she had gotten the hang of things and started enjoying it.

"It can be fun, but work is work. It isn't like working at a bar on a reality show." Kat smiled, thinking about her favorite guilty pleasure on TV, which led to thoughts of California and Dylan. She refocused on her cousin.

"I know. Hey, my friends say I make great drinks." Lauren smiled cheekily.

Kat rolled her eyes. "This isn't a frat party with beer pong either."

"Yeah, I get it," Lauren whined.

Kat teased out Lauren's level of commitment. "Didn't you major in finance in school?"

"I switched to communications in my sophomore year." Lauren cast her stare downward. "My dad found out at graduation. Oops."

"Did you try getting a regular full-time job?"

"Yeah. I sent out like a bazillion resumes. I couldn't get anything. Same answer every time. *Need more experience.* It wasn't like I haven't been trying."

Kat nodded with understanding. "Okay. How does

working part-time sound? Then you can continue your job search?"

"Cool. I can't wait to get behind the bar." Lauren downed the coffee and hopped off the bar stool.

"Calm down. You don't have any experience working at a bar."

"Great! You too?"

"Because you are family, I will give you a chance and teach you."

"Okay." Lauren rolled her head.

"You can start by taking down all the holiday decorations."

"Okay." She looked around, clueless.

Kat pointed to the ladder and the trash can. "Hurry up, I need the ladder gone before we open." Then she walked away and texted her uncle, updating him on Lauren.

Uncle—*Knew you had a heart as big as your dad. Thank you.—*

She grinned as her eyes welled up with tears. As the afternoon progressed and Kat gave Lauren simple tasks, loving memories of her dad warming her heart.

The time flew by. She sent her cousin home around 4:00 p.m. Lauren looked tired, but Kat didn't fault her. The first day at any job can be draining.

Later, the dinner crowd on Sunday was lighter than usual, and Kat managed to keep an eye on everything. In walked Alex who strutted toward her favorite seat. Kat made a beeline for the end of the bar, grabbing a bottle of vodka on the way. She poured as Alex situated herself on the stool, placing her purse on a hook under the bar.

"You're the best." Alex tossed back the shot.

"On a scale of one to ten, how was the sex?" Kat

rhythmically tapped her hand on her leg, waiting for Alex to spill all the details.

"Fifteen!" Alex grabbed the vodka and filled her glass. Kat possessively reached for the bottle, torn between irritation with Alex and embarrassment for getting distracted and not pouring the drink herself.

"Oh, hell yeah. He looked like he'd be good in bed."

Alex took another shot. Damn. She outpaced Kat with vodka. *Those Russian genes.*

"Why the fuck are you here and not going for a repeat?" *Why did she ever let him leave her bed?*

"We work at the same firm." Alex's shoulders raised as she inhaled deeply.

"It's a huge firm. Who gives a shit?"

"He does!" Alex put back another shot. "No ifs, ands, or buts."

"Oh, come on. That's absurd." Kat threw her hands in the air, gesticulating in a grandiose manner.

"Yup."

"That really sucks!" She poured Alex another one.

"I think he ruined me for all other men."

Kat raised a glass. "To mechanical devices that lack emotional complications and always deliver." She projected her frustration onto her friend.

Alex clung her glass with Kat's and both women drank. "That's depressing."

Imagine trying to replace two men. That's impossible.

"I think I need to find other ways to cope and fill the void."

"Seth started training for a marathon," Kat said.

"To cope with sexual frustration? How can a man that beautiful lack sex?" Alex whistled a catcall.

Kat laughed. "Ha! I think it had to do with his lawsuit. He's running in the San Francisco marathon later this month."

"Good for him. He didn't deserve that shit. But, I'm not a runner."

"What about reading or meditation?" Kat picked up those tips from eavesdropping on patrons.

Alex rolled her eyes.

"Yeah, those are crap ideas. Sorry. You already do too much reading and thinking." Kat tapped her fingers on the bar top as she brainstormed. "What about art? Maybe take a class."

"Not a bad idea…"

"I heard about a new hot art teacher at a nearby college. Next time I see my friend who teaches over there, I'll get the information."

"Cool. You should take the class with me! It will be like we are back in school together."

"Nah. I don't have the time to get away from here."

"You need to work on getting a break for yourself. It isn't healthy." Alex stopped shy of stating the obvious, but Kat understood. The fact her dad never took any time off probably contributed to his premature death.

"I have been jogging occasionally. And as for art, I've been delving into learning the art of mixology."

"I love being your taste tester! But for now, I think I could use a large glass of water."

"Want something to eat too?" Kat grabbed a tall glass, shoveled in a scoop of ice, filled it, and handed it to Alex.

After several refills of water and an appetizer, Alex took off.

Back at home, Kat lie in her bed. A message from

Dylan came in. The two-hour time difference worked in favor of their relationship. Respectfully, he avoided messaging during work hours. The notification was a welcome sight after a long day at the bar.

—Seth tells me you aren't coming out for the marathon with him (crying eyes)—

Kat's excitement about getting the text plummeted. She shifted into defensive mode.

—I can't leave Lawson's for an entire weekend (raised eyebrow with a scowling face)—

She resented the necessity of restating the obvious multiple times.

Dylan—*I understand—*

Kat—*Do you? I feel like I keep repeating myself—*

Dylan—*Would you prefer we don't keep asking? And then you think we don't desperately want you there because we didn't ask?—*

He made an excellent point. Fighting with attorneys sometimes sucked.

Dylan—*I want to see you—*

He hadn't visited Chicago since January. Kat assumed he wasn't interested.

Dylan—*I would come to visit but I can't work remotely for the judge during the week and my dad has me running around making personal appearances on the weekend—*

Had he read her mind?

Kat—*I know you would if you could—*

At least she hoped he would. A bit of doubt rattled her nerves.

Kat—*I miss you—*

Dylan—*It's nice to know—*

Kat—*Of course I miss you (three red hearts)—*

Did Dylan not understand how she felt? Had her feelings been lost in the 2000-mile gap between them?

Dylan—*You hadn't stated it in so many words*—

Kat—*I never wanted you to feel guilty about going to California. Seth slathered it on thick enough for the both of us (eye roll)*—

Dylan—*Does Seth speak for you?*—

Kat—*No*—

Her cheeks heated with embarrassment. In trying to shield Dylan's feelings, she denied him the chance of knowing *her* sentiments.

Dylan—*Seth has been more tight-lipped about his emotions lately (big red question mark)*—

If neither she nor Seth were communicating with Dylan, how was he to know he hadn't been forgotten? Kat felt like shit.

Dylan—*I know both of you have been dealing with a lot of serious shit over the past year*—

Fuck. She was a crappy friend.

Kat—*I'm sorry Dylan*—

Dylan—*I should have said something earlier*—

Kat—*I really do miss you in every way. I'm so sorry (praying hands)*—

Dylan—*Call me, this is a pain in the ass texting*—

She dialed.

"No video call?" *Was that disappointment in his voice?*

"I'm in bed. The lights are out."

"I miss being in bed with you."

Did he mean with her and Seth? She assumed so. Kat had never been alone with Dylan. It was an unconscious decision. Their schedules aligned, allowing for frequent sexual activities. Why would they ever kick someone out of bed? They were happy being a threesome.

That was then. What about now?

"Kat? You there?"

Kat whittled at her lip. "Yeah." She choked on the words.

"Cat got your tongue, Kitty-Kat?"

She took a deep breath. "Have you been dating anyone?" Kat sat up in bed, not wanting to hear bad news while lying down.

"No, not really."

She pounced on Dylan's word choice. "Not really? As in if you were too drunk to remember it doesn't count?"

"There's my favorite quick-tongued girl." Dylan chuckled. "I didn't want to risk you hanging up on me if I referenced the infamous video-call sex incident."

Kat relaxed and even giggled. "In my defense, it was my office!"

Dylan cleared his throat. "Kitty-Kat, you went nuts over it."

"Let me skip the apology part and I won't hang up."

"Fair enough."

"Why the hell aren't you dating anyone? Mommy and daddy getting in the way?"

"No, I don't allow their politics to control every aspect of my life."

"You're in San Francisco, for fuck's sake. Why? Men are probably throwing themselves at you, given your good looks. Have you considered your standards might be too high?"

"I've considered it."

Of course he had. He grew up entitled. Kat cringed

at her assumption. He had never acted like this around her. "And?"

"I realized nobody could ever compare to you and Seth?"

Without being able to read Dylan's face, Kat assumed he was exaggerating and responded in kind. "I agree. Seth is something pretty special. And well, I am one of a kind."

"Seriously, Kat. I miss you." His deep voice woke up her girly parts.

"I miss you too." She realized the genuine truth of her words after she said them.

"I miss everything. I miss us. I miss being with you." The conversation turned intense.

"I miss you too." She repeated with sincerity.

"Do you? Seth told me about the two of you last month. It's not like you are alone. You have Seth. I told you when I left you two should date."

Whoa! The shock of Dylan's words paralyzed her. She needed to respond appropriately. No glib or contrite answer would suffice.

"Dylan." She cleared her throat to offer herself an extra moment to compose her thoughts.

"First, I'm attracted to you both." Kat caught herself before she let the L word slip from her mouth. "I like each of you, separately and together."

"And second?"

"Sorry, I don't have a well-prepared speech. I just miss you, Dylan."

"But have you decided Seth is everything you need?"

"My heart is big enough to have feelings for both of you." She smiled at herself for side-stepping the L word once again. "And I still doubt I'm enough for Seth."

"So you just miss that I fill the male role on Seth's dance card?"

His defensiveness started irritating her. She was out of practice at arguing. It no longer spurred a fun mental challenge. "No, Dylan. Stop acting like a dumbass. My concerns about Seth have nothing to do with you. I miss *you*. Y. O. U."

"I miss you too." He let out a long breath. Kat was relieved to put the issue behind them too. "What were you doing before I messaged?"

"I told you I was in bed. You know the place where people typically sleep." Her hand bumped into the dildo resting beside her leg.

"I'm familiar with the concept. Thank you for the explanation." Dylan grunted. "Were you scrolling, reading, or what?"

Well, she wasn't on her phone. Nor reading. Her face heated. "What?"

"What were you doing?"

"I told you." She laughed.

Dylan lowered his voice. "What were you up to, Kitty-Kat? Did it involve batteries?"

"Don't be absurd. Everyone knows electrically operated devices are much more powerful."

"Well, don't let me get in your way. Turn it on."

Did he mean it?

"Come on Kitty-Kat."

What the hell. She flicked the switch and the device came to life.

"That is one intense buzz. Now where were you? Before I called?"

Kat placed the vibrating bulbous end near the apex

of her thighs. Nothing about the placement hit her in the right place.

"You sure you are doing it correctly? By your breathing, it doesn't sound like it."

Shit. How did he know? She adjusted the vibrator so it rested at the junction of her legs. Her breath hitched.

"That's my Kitty-Kat." His deep voice and praise sent shivers through her.

She didn't need his help to find her pleasure. She had become proficient over the previous months. Not only did it heighten the experience, but she also sought to hear his voice as well.

"What kind of vibrator are you using?"

She moved the shuddering end closer to her pleasure center. The tingling intensified and a hum coursed through her body.

"Is it inside of you?"

"No." She exhaled.

"Good, because I want to be there. Sliding in and out of you."

"Dylan are you…?"

"Feeling your lush channel constrict along my cock? Yes! You feel perfect."

"Oh, God." The memory of their time together felt real. His scent permeated her senses as if he were lying next to her.

His wide shoulders hovered over her and covered her like a blanket. Protected from everything in the outside world, allowing her to focus.

She fell deeper into the moment and mewled in pleasure.

"That's it, Kitty-Kat." Dylan's breaths came in rhythmic moans.

"Dylan."

"Kat."

"I miss you."

She applied a bit more pressure in the precise direction until she gasped for air.

"Yes. Kat. Come with me."

"Yes. Yes. Oh, God, Dylan!" The words roared from her mouth as forcefully as the orgasm ripped through her body.

Wow. That was intense. So much better with Dylan on the phone than taking care of business by herself.

"You sound like you're struggling for breath. Are the smoke-filled skies in California giving you breathing problems, or was it as good for you as me?" she asked.

"I told you I missed you."

She believed him. More importantly, she didn't think she was just something in bed he did to satisfy Seth. Maybe she was more to him than a task to ingratiate himself with Seth. Because God knew Seth was worth it.

But still, phone sex was not the same as being together, in person, without Seth. Would it be too much for Dylan to handle? Would he ever be interested in it?

"I miss you too, Dylan. I'm sorry I didn't make it clearer to you sooner."

"Hopefully, I can see you soon."

She yawned. "Sorry. I hope so too."

"No sorries. It's late and you had a long day."

She yawned again. Kat was tired and content.

"I'll let you get some sleep. Goodnight."

"Goodnight, Dylan. And thank you."

"For phone sex?"

"Hah!" She chortled. For his friendship? For his forgiveness? Dylan's question was a fair one, but Kat didn't have an answer.

Dylan let her off the hook and didn't press. "Goodnight Kat." Maybe his political background strengthened his ability to read the room. He knew when and when not to push her.

Chapter 20

Dylan

A few weeks later, he called Kat again. He insisted on a video call. Dylan aimed his phone camera down the length of the bathtub.

She answered, “Hey sexy, you did it!”

“I did.” Seth grimaced while soaking his marathon-battered body in the tub.

“What an impressive result. You were like a machine out there!”

Dylan turned the focus back on himself. “Aren’t you going to commend me on my fabulous 5k?”

“Nice job, Dylan. What was your time? Thirty or thirty-five minutes.” Kat shook her head in a disapproving manner.

“Not fair. I had to keep pace with my dad. You know. Can’t make the senator appear unflattering.” Dylan scowled at Kat.

“Excuses. Excuses.” Seth flicked some water at Dylan.

“Behave there or I won’t give you a thorough massage after you finish soaking.” Dylan tried to appear fierce, but Seth’s damaged body broke his dramatic reaction. Seth looked too cute and helpless in the tub, like a puppy in need of help.

“Wish you were here too, Kat.” Seth raised his

voice, beckoning attention. "Better yet, you should have been here last night when I had a lot more energy."

"I owe you a massage when you get back as a reward for your amazing finishing time, especially in the San Francisco marathon. How hard were all the hills?" Dylan angled his phone so Seth could see Kat talking.

"Brutal. My quads are killing me."

Dylan respected the hell out of Seth for running twenty-six point two miles, but the attention from Kat nagged at him. He faced the camera on him. "Can I get a massage too when I come to town?"

"Absolutely." Kat turned her head and held up a finger to someone off screen. "Listen, I gotta go help one of my servers. Feel better Seth. And congrats to you both."

Seth blew a kiss into the phone.

Dylan set his cell down. "Ready to get out of the tub and get something to eat?" He reached for a towel and extended his hand toward Seth. As Seth emerged from the suds, his bloody nipples had stopped bleeding, but remained painful-looking. Dylan wished Seth had listened to him about better preparation and using tape over his sensitive nips.

Seth eased out of the tub like a senior citizen. He clung to Dylan's arm for support. Water droplets cascaded to the ground, landing on Seth's poor toes. He lost four of his nails. The marathon had taken a cruel toll on his body.

Seth placed a hand on the counter, standing at a precarious angle, further than the Leaning Tower of Pisa. "You okay to stand?" Dylan wrapped the plush towel around Seth's waist. He avoided the open sores on his chest and blotted gingerly at the droplets on Seth's back.

Standing in front of Seth, Dylan searched for reassurance in Seth's normally smiling blue eyes. Instead of smiling, tears streamed down his cheeks.

"Shit. Are you in pain?" Dylan scanned for injury. He looked for signs of severe cramping in his muscles. Nothing.

Seth reached out to Dylan. With arms strewn over Dylan's shoulders, Seth planted his face against Dylan's chest. A spine-chilling wail erupted from Seth. Dylan held him like a man-size rag doll. The cries carried on and on.

He crouched to the ground while assisting Seth to a sitting position on the floor.

"What is it? What hurts?" Should he call a doctor? Take him to an emergency room?

The shrieking morphed into sobbing and Seth hiccupped as he gasped for air. Dylan continued to hold him without causing Seth any extra discomfort.

His lack of speaking became quite worrisome. "Seth, it's okay." Dylan hoped his calm tone would soothe whatever was upsetting him.

Was he having a panic attack? Dylan purposefully over-emphasized his breathing, taking exaggerated breaths in and out. He had seen a video on social media suggesting it was a good way to settle someone. Dylan hoped Seth mimicked the rhythm.

Between gasps for air, Seth choked. "It didn't work."

What didn't work?

Dylan finger-combed Seth's wet blond hair, waiting for further explanation.

"Oh god, it hurts."

"What hurts Seth?" Dylan stood. He had reached his

limit. "Let me take you to the emergency room."

Seth shook his head back and forth. "Oh god, it hurts." Dylan wanted more details. He needed more information to assess Seth's situation. He scanned the other man's body once again. Seth sat on the floor, propped up against the side of the bathtub. He didn't reach out in a protective or soothing manner toward any specific area. *What was causing his pain?*

"I thought I could run from it, but it didn't work." Seth curled into a ball and clutched his knees to his chest.

Understanding crashed into Dylan. The source of Seth's agony wasn't physical, but emotional. Not any less painful, of course. Dylan kissed Seth's head and wrapped his long arms around Seth's frame. "I've got you."

He spoke softly into Seth's ear, "You can't run away from grief. As much as you may wish, it wasn't possible. It will chase you and beat you down when you are most vulnerable."

"Dylan."

"You're exhausted from the race. You can't be expected to fend off your parents' wretchedness. Grief has a way of showing up and catching you by surprise. Even if you think you were already past it." Seth nodded in agreement.

He continued to hold Seth, kissing his head. Seth didn't speak. What was there to say? What his mom and dad had done was beyond horrible. He needed to cry it out. Dylan had heard countless familiar stories from individuals in the LGBTQ community in San Francisco. Each story upset him, but Seth's pain broke his heart.

The clenching sensation grew in Dylan's chest. Three little words almost bubbled out of his mouth.

Dylan wanted to tell Seth he loved him. The realization triggered a strong urge to declare it to him. As badly as Dylan desired to share his revelation with Seth, it wasn't the right time.

He hoped Seth knew he wasn't alone. He wanted to reassure Seth that he was loved. But Dylan's love wouldn't replace the loss of his parents' affection.

As much as Dylan wished he could eradicate Seth's pain, he needed to wait. This was Seth's time. He needed to feel the pain and allow it to seep through him. Sorrow needed to be experienced from beginning to end. Hiding from it, like he had been doing with running only delayed the inevitable.

He held Seth on the floor of the bathroom for about an hour. Discomfort gradually set in. "Seth, sitting here is shit for a sore body. How about I give you a body massage?" Once again, he offered Seth a hand to help him stand. Unlike his normal smooth jaguar-like motion, Seth's rickety movements worried him.

He helped Seth walk to the bed. Seth winced.

"Where does it hurt?" Dylan asked.

"Everywhere."

"No really, where?"

"My feet. My calves. My hamstrings. Dude, everywhere."

"Is it getting worse?"

Seth nodded.

Dylan ensured Seth lie safely on the mattress. "I'll be right back."

Seth moaned. The anguish in his voice worried Dylan. He darted down to the kitchen, reached into the refrigerator, and hurried upstairs. With care, he helped Seth into a sitting position. He removed the lid and handed the cold jar to Seth. "Drink this."

Seth scrunched his nose in protest. "What the fuck? Pickle juice?"

"Drink it. NOW. Before the rest of your body starts to seize."

Seth brought the rim to his lips and sipped the tangy liquid. He managed to swallow about a third of the jar. Thank goodness for his affection for pickle relish on his hot dogs. The grimace on his face relaxed.

Dylan took the jar, screwed on the lid, and set it on the nightstand. "Good. Do your legs feel any better?"

"Yeah. They still hurt, but the charley horse sensation is gone."

"Great."

"How did you know to do that?"

"I once cramped up at a tennis tournament and my coach made me drink the same thing. He always carried it in his cooler, just in case."

Seth laid back and shut his eyes. "Can I get the massage now?"

"Sure." Dylan leaned over and placed his lips gently on Seth's. Seth's sexy smile broke free. "You taste like Chicago. I'm Jonesing for a hot dog." He craved a lot of things about Chicago.

"Let's not discuss food at the moment? The pickle juice still needs to settle."

Dylan laughed and focused on his massaging duties. He skipped rubbing Seth's feet as much of the bottoms were in varying degrees of blooming blisters. Instead, he began above Seth's ankle.

Seth moaned and groaned as Dylan continued to provide a deep tissue massage. He adjusted his ministrations. As his hands crept up Seth's quads, naughty thoughts popped into his head. Dylan logically knew Seth was in no physical shape for getting down and dirty, but some parts of his anatomy failed to understand.

He spent over an hour working on all of Seth's muscles, both front and back. He had worked up quite the appetite. "Ready to get something to eat?"

"Yes, but do I have to move?" Seth wore his sexy ass grin.

Damn. His smile got Dylan every time. "Of course not. How about pizza? Something convenient for eating in bed."

"Anything sounds good right now. Especially the not moving part."

While waiting for delivery, Seth dozed off.

Dylan woke his sleeping beau with a kiss. "Pizza's here. Want to eat or go back to sleep?"

Seth sat upright against the headboard. "It smells good."

Dylan threw down a picnic blanket on top of the duvet, then flipped open the top of the box. As Dylan sat beside him, Seth grabbed a slice. Dylan anxiously waited for his culinary critique, worried he might snub the pizza.

"Not bad for west coast pie." Seth took another large bite. He continued as he chewed, "Thank you for the pizza."

"Of course. This kind of reminds me of those times when we ordered pizza while studying during law school." Dylan took another bite.

"You mean because Kat and I were on a tight budget and could only afford cheap, shitty pizza?" Seth cocked his head and glanced upward at Dylan. His smiling eyes got him once again.

"Ha. Ha. I meant the comfort of the food and

company." Dylan nudged Seth's shoulder.

"Too bad Kat couldn't be here too."

Dylan agreed. Thoughts of Kat crossed his mind frequently since their intimate phone call.

"Did Kat mention our conversation a few weeks back?" Dylan's stomach twisted. *What if she said something negative?*

"No man. To be honest, she and I haven't talked much. We have been like two ships passing in the night. Now that the race is over, I'm hoping to spend more quality time with her."

Moments without Dylan. "Mmm hmm." The idea didn't settle well with him.

"Why?"

"We kind of ended up having phone sex."

Seth shrugged. "So? I mean phone sex is fun, but did you expect her to brag about it?"

"No, but it was a first for us."

Seth continued to focus on the pizza. He wasn't understanding Dylan. Dylan needed to stop speaking in a code and expecting Seth to read between the lines.

He faced his embarrassment. "It was the first time we had any kind of sex without you." Dylan held his breath.

Seth's head swiveled and his baby blues gleamed with realization. "Oh." He paused and looked away. "I'm a little stunned. I assumed you and Kat shared time alone together, just as you and I have done."

"No."

"Do you mean after you moved to California?" Seth narrowed his eyes.

Dylan took a deep breath and laid it out there. "Nothing before or after I moved."

Seth's jaw dropped open. "Oh."

"Yeah, oh." Dylan nodded and drew his lips in a straight line. He fought against hiding his face in his hands and looked away from Seth's look of surprise.

Seth guided Dylan's face, urging him to make eye contact. Can I ask why?"

Dylan rolled his eyes, searching for an answer. Uncertainty flooded his mind. He never refrained from any particular opportunity, but he never sought a specific time with Kat without Seth. "I'm not sure."

"Are you attracted to Kat?"

He glared at Seth as if he were a complete idiot. How could Seth ask such a stupid question after the three of them had engaged in an amazing amount of earth-shattering sex together? It wasn't like Dylan hadn't participated fully and willingly.

"Okay. Okay." Seth rolled his eyes and held up his hands in surrender. "Sorry. I get that is rather redundant. Did something change, encouraging you both to take the leap together?"

"I don't know." Neediness. Loneliness. How could he be certain? Dylan looked at Seth and realized it was Seth's absence from Dylan and Kat's life. While he had been absorbed in his marathon training, he wasn't missing, but less available. Maybe he and Kat had relied on Seth as the connecting link in the past. But when the link was withdrawn, the connection between Dylan and Kat appeared like magic.

"So?" Seth's enlarged eyes pled for more details.

"So what?"

"How do you feel about the situation now? How do you feel about her?"

Dylan couldn't tell Seth he thought he was in love

with Kat. He hadn't said the words to Seth yet. He had thought about it on several occasions, but the words never fell off his tongue. *Shit.* He couldn't say the words to one and not the other. Could he? Was it an all-or-nothing situation?

Dylan knew Seth wanted to hear those three words. A throbbing headache pulsed behind Dylan's eyes.

"Dylan?"

He rubbed soothing circles on his temples.

Seth took one of Dylan's hands and sandwiched it in between his own. "Let's start easy. Did you have fun the other night?"

Why did he bring this up with Seth? He preferred to drop the matter. The discomfort bothered him. "You need to rest. We don't have to delve into this." He considered excusing himself to take a shower. And claim some privacy in his own head.

Seth's firm grip acknowledged the gravity of the situation. "No. This is more important. *You* are important." He tugged on Dylan's hand. "Answer the question. Did you have fun the other night?"

Dylan crooked his face. "Yeah. Of course. Kat is always cool."

"Absolutely. But would you want to be with her in real life?"

Seth went from a softball question to a ninety-mile-per-hour one. Every nerve-ending in Dylan's body lit up. Either it was nervousness or lustfulness.

"Your eyes look like thoughts are swimming around in your head. It's a pretty simple question. I'm guessing the answer is yes. What is holding you back from saying yes?"

"I'm not sure."

"It's okay. Do you think if the situation presented itself, you would say yes?"

"Yeah. But I don't see that happening soon, as she can't ever fly out here with her crazy work schedule."

"I guess you have time to figure out your feelings." Seth picked up a slice of pizza and fed it to Dylan.

Dylan smiled as he chewed, appreciating that Seth tried to look out for him in his own way.

After Seth finished the pizza, he dozed off. Dylan remained on his side of the bed. He avoided placing his arm near Seth's chaffed chest. But when he turned and nuzzled into Dylan, he wrapped his arm around the other man, feeling warmth and contentment spread through his body.

Once again, Dylan weighed his feelings for both Seth and Kat. For Seth, the lingering question existed. Was Seth still pushing for the three of them to be together for Seth's sake? Or were there other motivations involved? And as for Kat? Did she need or want him? Or was he in her life just to satisfy Seth?

These questions were impossible to answer while Dylan remained in California. He needed to find time and catch a flight to Chicago. Over the next couple of months, he made three attempts at scheduling flights, but on each occasion his father forced Dylan to cancel the plans.

But one person held power over the senator. Dylan leveraged his Nana's input and the Jewish holiday. Surprisingly, his father granted Dylan a reprieve from political duties. Dylan booked his tickets to Chicago before his father changed his mind.

On the gorgeous fall day, Dylan appreciated the array of vibrant hues of the foliage as he stood on his grandparents' stoop. Dressed in a pristine cooking apron, Nana greeted him at the door of their home in the suburbs. "*L'Shana Tova*."

Dylan kissed Nana on the cheek. "Happy New Year." The savory scent of dinner wafted into the foyer and his stomach growled.

"Oh good, you're hungry. Dinner is ready. Let's go sit."

He shuffled beside Nana toward the dining room and caught his grandpa dipping an apple slice in some honey.

"Sorry, I couldn't wait any longer."

Dylan smiled at his look of shamelessness and hugged his grandpa before sitting at the table. "This looks and smells amazing." He missed true home-cooked meals.

While his grandpa proceeded with the blessing over the bread and wine, he recognized the label. "Where did you get this wine?"

"Your father sent it a few weeks ago and said we should break the fast with a good bottle. Since you are here, I didn't want to wait until Yom Kippur to open it."

He took a sip, but the notes in the wine tasted off. He smelled a whiff of a plot between his grandparents and his father. Dylan eyed his grandparents skeptically.

After three matzah balls and several helpings of brisket, his satiated stomach overshadowed his previous suspicions. Dylan leaned back in the seat.

Nana brought out a cinnamon babka. "Always need something sweet to complete a meal."

Dylan's eyes widened as his full stomach objected. Choosing the path of least resistance, he avoided upsetting Nana and accepted the plateful of cake. "Looks delicious. Did you bake it?" He poked at the dessert and pretended to eat it.

"Oh dear no. I can't bake things like this anymore."

"My waistline is finally getting the break that it needed since she stopped tempting me with all her desserts." Nonetheless, his grandpa took an extra-large slice.

Dylan wiped his mouth and set his napkin on top of his plate, hiding the uneaten portion. "Nana, that was an amazing meal. Thank you."

"I'm delighted you could join us." She brought the coffee pot from the nearby buffet to the table. "It would be nice if we could see you more often."

Jewish guilt, combined with a food coma weighed on him. He needed a jolt of caffeine. "I would if I could. The senator keeps me very busy on the weekends and the judge has a full docket too."

His grandpa set down his dessert fork. "Your father mentioned your schedule when we spoke."

"I'm so glad he carved out the time so you could come in for the holiday." Nana's smile rounded out her heart-shaped face.

The conspiracy began to unfold. "And when did you both speak to the senator?"

"Like I said, a few weeks ago."

Dylan debated whether to ask his grandpa. "You said you talked about wine."

"Yes."

"And?" Dylan leveled him with a serious glare. Dylan turned toward the sound of a coffee cup clanging on a saucer.

"Oh, for heaven's sake. Enough of the tiptoeing. It's tiresome. Just tell him." Nana glared at his grandpa.

"Grandpa?"

"Okay. I had a long conversation with your father about your career. He feels your strengths lie in the law. Your heart is always in the right place, which makes it difficult for you to stomach the world of politics."

Dylan's lips curled upward. Had his father truly seen him this entire time?

"But not California government," said Nana.

They were both in on the act. Dylan narrowed his eyes. What were they up to? No one in his family acted or spoke without a full plan in place.

"We think you would make a wonderful judge."

Dylan cocked his head to the side as he considered the idea. "Hmmm." He nodded.

"Of course, you don't have the experience yet." His grandpa pushed his plate forward and leaned his elbows on the table.

"You have all the attributes. You are exceptionally bright and you are compassionate." Nana took another sip of her coffee. Her compliments warmed his heart, and a heated flush crept into Dylan's face. The compliment also made him uncomfortable.

"And you inherited my good looks and charisma." They all laughed at his grandpa.

Dylan hesitated in responding. The unexpected topic knocked him off balance. Their plan had merit, but the execution required a lot of time and planning.

Before Dylan protested with a lengthy list of qualifiers, his grandpa interjected, "We have already taken steps. You have an interview tomorrow in the prosecutor's office."

Whoa. The possibility of a career deviation flying at him at the speed of sound made his chest tighten.

“This is a lot to process. Why didn’t you mention this before I arrived?” Was he expected to behave like a puppet and act every time his family pulled the strings? The manipulation rubbed him the wrong way.

“Your father knows you have a great deal to focus on right now. He didn’t want this to distract you. With a clear schedule and mind, you can apply your attention to this opportunity.”

Dylan’s heart rate returned to a steady state as he contemplated the prospect of moving to Chicago.

“I’ll admit it. Selfishly, I would love to have you living back here.” Nana didn’t hide her coy smile.

His grandpa said, “I imagine both of your friends would like it too.” He raised an eyebrow at Dylan.

Crap. Did they know? Did his father know?

His heart pumped hard enough he could hear it in his ears. “Umm,” Dylan stuttered. His mouth went dry and his tongue failed to function.

His grandpa cleared his throat. “You must have been thinking about what you were going to do after your clerkship.”

“I just…” In all honesty, Dylan assumed he would work for his father. His entire life he worked and behaved for the benefit of his father’s career. He followed along with the plan set out for him. *Was that happening again?* Perspiration began beading on his neck.

Nana reached across the table and placed her caring hands on his own. “It’s high time you start thinking about your own life. I love my son and I know you love your father too. But this is *your* career. Your life.”

“Your grandma and I proposed this idea to your father.”

"But I persuaded him to focus on what would be in your best interest rather than his own." A glint of power flickered in her eye.

"Anyway, we all see an amazing amount of potential in you. A job in the state's attorney's office is the perfect stepping stone." His grandpa grabbed a folder from behind an oversized vase. "Here are the details about the interview. It's tomorrow at 9:00 a.m."

Dylan squirmed in his seat. He clasped his hands beneath the table as the idea swam in his head. *Oh fuck.* "The Illinois bar exam." He heaved a guttural groan and his head fell forward.

"You passed the California exam. Illinois will be a piece of cake." His grandpa smiled and emphatically swung a cake-filled fork in his mouth.

Dylan scowled. His family assumed everything came easy for him. No one understood the effort he expended. Well, except Kat and Seth.

"Any other big surprises you plan on springing on me tonight?" Dylan flinched and braced himself.

His grandpa held up a single finger. "One more thing. When you move here, we are giving you the condo on the lake."

Was that an inducement to get him to move? If so, at a value of well over one million dollars, it was a hell of a bribe. Then panic struck. "Are you both well? Is there something I should know? Why would you hand over such an enormous gift now?"

"Oh honey, don't worry. We may be slower but we are in fine health. But we can't keep up with city life anymore."

His grandpa added, "What difference does it make if we give it to you now or in our will?" Seth probably could discuss several tax implications…

"Thank you." Dylan got up and hugged both of his grandparents. "Thank you isn't sufficient."

"Well, you could offer to help clean up." Nana stood up and started clearing the table.

"Of course." Dylan grabbed the large serving pieces and made several trips to the kitchen. While he washed the dishes, Nana put away the food. His grandpa retired in front of the TV.

When he and Nana had finished, his grandpa walked him to the door. "Let me know how the interview goes. I look forward to hearing all about it."

"Sure thing." Dylan hugged his grandpa.

Nana handed him a full-size shopping bag filled with leftovers. "Please share with Seth and Kat. I feel terrible neither of them has their parents on Rosh Hashana." She was well-intentioned even if Kat was Catholic and didn't celebrate the holiday.

Dylan kissed Nana goodbye and climbed into the car waiting at the curb.

Anxiety about seeing Kat suddenly overshadowed the stress about the job interview. The app indicated he had thirty-four minutes to get his shit together before arriving at Lawson's. How would the sexy tension between them on the phone translate to being in person? Without Seth.

He popped a mint in his mouth before entering the bar.

Chapter 21

Kat

She grabbed the new smoke top, which had arrived in the mail earlier in the week. With a lighter crowd, she experimented with innovative cocktail ideas.

Her cousin Lauren snatched Kat's favorite bottle of bourbon. "Which flavor of wood chips are we trying tonight?"

Kat found apple detracted from the overall taste. "Let's try maple wood."

Lauren took a step backward. Kat slid the empty glass in her direction. "Go ahead, you mix the drink." Kat had mixed hundreds over the years. Her cousin needed the practice. Kat waited patiently as her father did when he taught her how to make an old-fashioned.

Lauren stared at Kat as she tested the cocktail. "It's getting better. A few hundred more and it will be perfect."

Her cousin sighed and slumped forward.

"Hey. This isn't little league. I'm not here to pass out participation trophies." Kat moved on, refusing to dwell. She placed the smoking device on top of the old-fashioned and filled the hole with a large pinch of the maple wood chips.

Her cousin held up the small torch like it was a gun. "Put your hands in the air. I'm armed and dangerous."

Her tough act came off as more comedic than threatening.

"Go ahead. Light it up." The smoke dispersed above the alcohol. When the density increased and appeared opaque, Kat said, "Okay, ease up pyro."

The smoke flowed as if it were a dancing fog over the side of the glass. Her cousin twisted the orange rind, swabbed the rim, and tossed it into the cocktail. With a flourish of her hands, her cousin presented the modernized old-fashioned to Kat.

Kat tried to remain open-minded as she tasted it. The aroma tantalized her senses. She shut her eyes and considered the fresh distinction of the smokey flavor. The drink lacked something. "Hmmm."

Lauren reached for the cocktail. "Can I try it?"

While Lauren took a sip, Kat said, "We should start testing it out and see how customers react. I'll offer it at the same price point, for now. If it becomes the preferred option, we can officially put it on the menu at a higher price." Kat enjoyed talking out bar ideas with Lauren.

"Good plan." Her cousin smiled. "Want to make another?"

"Hell yeah." Kat kept a less-than-close eye on her cousin and scanned the bar.

The door to the entrance opened and—he walked in. Her smile reached her eyes when she saw his broad shoulders and chiseled cheekbones. His wide grin showed off those perfect teeth, leaving her heart pounding. After months of separation, he stood before her. She wanted to vault over the wooden bar-top and hug him, but she froze.

"Hi." His deep voice sent a shiver down her spine.

Her nervous tension constricted her throat and she

muttered, "Hi."

"What are you making here?"

When Kat failed to respond, her cousin spoke up, "A smoky old-fashioned."

"Looks interesting." Dylan's eyes bore into her soul.

Damn, he looked good.

Her cousin slid the drink toward Dylan. "I made it. Try it." She blushed.

Oh hell no. He's mine! Kat wanted to claw her cousin's eyes out. She took a beat and reminded herself that her cousin had never met Dylan and knew nothing about Kat's history with him.

Dylan flashed his pearly whites. "Thank you, but I have more pressing needs." He held up a grocery bag. "My Nana sent a ton of leftovers. Can I put them in your refrigerator?"

"Of course." Kat moved toward the rear exit. She peeked backward, verifying Dylan followed. She found her cousin gawking at his ass. Kat had done it many times herself. The man had a great butt.

They ascended the stairs to her apartment above the bar. She felt his presence close behind her. The air around her heated. A coating of sweat beaded on her neck. She itched to kiss him, but waited. What if he wasn't thinking the same thing?

Upon reaching her door, she unlocked the deadbolt. Was it time to unlock the connection between the two of them?

Dylan stepped inside and dropped his duffle in the doorway. Her head snapped at the thud of the bag hitting the floor. *Get a grip woman.*

Dylan's typical self-confident look slipped. He looked awkward.

"Shit." She reached for the shopping tote in his arms. "All this needs to go in the fridge?"

"Yeah."

Pulling out container after container, Kat placed them into the refrigerator. "Was she expecting to feed an army?"

"She was sorry you and Seth couldn't make it to dinner."

Was Dylan missing Seth right now?

"This was really nice of her." She shut the door and stashed the empty bag under the sink. "Can I get you something to drink?" The question was less hospitable than a reflexive response of her day job.

"No thanks." He appeared to be staring at her lips. She mirrored the intensity of his gaze. Neither leaned in toward one another.

Kat worried her hands together and sought a dish rag. She grabbed the dishcloth hanging on the oven door and wiped down the perfectly clean table. She peered out of her peripheral vision and found Dylan gawking back at her. Her shirt clung to her moist skin. *Maybe I should turn on the air conditioner?* She stepped over to check the thermostat. It was a balmy sixty-three degrees Fahrenheit.

"Hey, do you mind if I hop in the shower? I feel gross from traveling." Dylan picked up his duffle.

"Sure." She shook her head. "No. I mean, it's fine." Kat wiped her sweaty palms on her jeans.

Dylan opened his bag outside her small bathroom and carried some clothes in with him. He didn't bother closing the door behind him. Did he intend it as an invitation?

Should she join him? She listened as the water came

alive. The glass door banged against the steel frame. The clang spurred her to move. She stripped and entered the bathroom. Steam billowed out, moistening her flushed cheeks. It wasn't the only place she was wet. Her desire grew as certainty rooted itself.

She slid the door open. *Oh my!* His backside looked delicious. "Can I join you?"

Dylan turned and faced her. His million-dollar smile shot a bolt of electricity through her. Her heart raced.

He extended a hand. "Get in here." He pulled her against him.

Crashing into his chest, his arousal prodded her abdomen. "Were you thinking about me?" *Or was he rubbing one out after a long day?*

"I was recalling all our dirty phone calls." He cupped her breast in his palm, toying with her nipple.

Her sex ached with need. "Anything in particular?" She stared at his lips, hoping his desire for her was more than a convenient lay.

Leaning down, Dylan pecked Kat's cheek, unlike how he kissed Seth, with a fierceness. *Was he nervous? Or was it because he felt the necessity to be more tender with her?*

Kat reached up, her fingers tunneling through his dark, wet hair. Holding him tightly against her, she pressed her lips more firmly against his. She wanted his acquiescence. She craved his passion.

Nothing. Was he not feeling it? His hard-on indicated the opposite.

Suddenly, he forced her back against the wall. His tongue dove into her mouth, claiming her. He growled.

Mmmm yes. Her tongue was otherwise engaged, preventing her from vocalizing. *Oh hell yes.*

He leaned against her. His weight and strength comforted her in a reassuring way. While their phone sex over the past few months was fun, flirty, and full of explosive endings, Dylan's touch made her heart flutter. Her fingers roamed over his chest.

She tried to stand taller to meet his kiss. She stood on her tip toes and he wrapped an arm around her waist.

"Ahhhhh!" Her foot slipped out from under her, but Dylan caught her like a superhero.

"We should get out of the shower before someone gets hurt." He stared down at her with fire in his eyes.

She smirked. "I suppose the height difference is a potential hazard. I know something else that is slippery and a whole lot more fun."

"*My* sexy Kitty-Kat." Dylan winked.

His emphasis on his special nickname made her heart melt.

They got out of the shower together, not bothering with towels. Dylan's broad shoulders blocked her exit. She looked up at his fully dilated eyes. "Come here." He picked her up underneath her arms and set her on the bathroom counter. The chill on her ass dissipated and her knees fell open. Dylan stepped into the space between them.

Her eyes were at the same height as his broad chest. His shoulders moved up and down while his breathing filled the silence.

His length neared her opening. She inched her sex closer to him. She wanted him in her.

"Do you have condoms in here?" He pulled a drawer open.

"No."

He pivoted toward the door. "I've got some in my

bag."

Kat grabbed his arm. He looked back with concern.

"I had to go on the pill months ago." He narrowed his eyes at her. "All the stress of taking over the bar really fucked up my cycle and my doctor recommended it." The corners of his lips turned down. "I haven't been with anyone."

His mouth drew into a devilish grin. "So, we are good without protection?"

She cocked an eyebrow and nodded.

"Oh fuck yes." He moaned.

Her pulse raced. The moment felt enormous.

He bent down and kissed her. His warm breath blew against her ear. "Let's take this to the bedroom."

She kissed him once again, nipping his lip. He lifted her into his arms. "Let's go then," she said. His smile got her every time.

He kissed her as he carried her and set her down at the foot of her bed. His kiss intensified, almost frantic. Her desire escalated. She was close to climaxing from his passionate kiss alone.

However, Dylan didn't make a move to take things further. *Was he nervous?* Dylan had never masterminded their sexual arrangements.

Kat crawled onto the bed. She coaxed her finger in a come-hither motion. "I need you, Dylan."

His eyes ogled her from her toes up to her face. "Fuck I want you."

Thank God. She released a breath she had been holding. He slinked like a cat until he hovered over her.

His hand brushed across her clit as he angled himself at her entrance. "You're so wet Kitty-Kat."

She smiled at their similar feline description. She

purred, “Now. Please.”

Dylan slowly pressed inside her. “Oh Jesus.” His eyes pinched tight. He continued to bury himself deeper and groaned when he was entirely in. His pelvis ground against her.

“Mmmmm.” A tingling sensation hummed throughout her body and her channel gripped his hard, masculine length.

“Fuck. If you do that again, I’m not going to last.”

Kat grinned devilishly, writhing and pushing him closer to the edge.

“I had no fucking idea it would feel this good without a condom.” He took a deep breath and moved more intently.

Memories of all their previous phone sex calls raced through her mind. At the time, the orgasms were great. Far better than taking care of business alone.

But now, with his weight above her and his cock inside her, she neared complete bliss. The pinnacle of which approached like water on the verge of boiling. A delicate heat grew from within.

Dylan moved quicker. “Oh God, Kat.”

“Dylan.”

He moaned.

She hung on to that last moment of pure ecstasy before succumbing to the orgasm. “Ahhhhh.” She panted as waves of pleasure rolled through her.

Dylan slammed his steely length deep inside. “Fuuuck.” His body convulsed in synch with her own.

Warmth spilled down her thigh, a mix of both his and her own.

He collapsed on top of her. At first, she enjoyed his muscular frame dwarfing her petite one. Then she pushed him off. "I can't breathe."

He rolled to his side and she snuggled into him. "Better?"

"Perfect." She stroked his arm as they lie in a close embrace. "How about you?"

He kissed her head. "Perfect."

Kat savored the moment, but Dylan would have to return to California in a couple of days. She exhaled. Should she tell him how she felt?

"Was that a contented sigh or the deep thought kind?"

"I'm physically sated if you're fishing for a compliment."

He cupped her face and looked into her eyes. "I appreciate the praise, but what's really on your mind?" He knew her well and didn't allow her to use her sarcasm as a defense mechanism.

She avoided mentioning she already missed him. "Have you thought about what you are going to do after your clerkship?"

It was his turn to take a deep breath.

Uh-oh.

"My grandparents made a surprising suggestion. I have an interview tomorrow morning in the state's attorney's office. They think I should work towards becoming a judge. Here. In Chicago." His eyes grew enormous.

The look bothered her. "Wow! What a great idea! You would make a phenomenal judge."

"Thank you. Can you not mention this to Seth?"

"The interview or the fact that we had sex?"

"I'm sure he wants all the details about the sex." They both laughed. "I meant the interview. At least for now. I don't want to get his expectations up."

"You know, secrets suck." Kat leveled Dylan with a condescending look.

"I know. I know. You don't need to keep it long. I will tell him after I find out if I land the job or not."

"As if they wouldn't want to hire you on the spot."

Dylan kissed her sweetly on the lips. Then, scooped her into his arms. "You are very good for my ego, but that isn't what makes me so damn attracted to you." He brushed his lips against hers and then kissed her chest above her heart. "It's what's in your head and heart."

"You're not attracted to my body?" She smirked.

Her joke fell flat. His lips formed a line and the light in his eyes dimmed. "You know I am. I can't explain it, as I'm still not attracted to any other women."

"Sorry. Bad joke."

"I've been attempting to figure it out lately. Unlike Seth, I don't identify as bi. Not even bi-curious."

"Do you need to wear a label like a nametag? Or are you trying to decide how you feel about you and me?" She avoided eyed contact.

"No. I figured it out months ago."

Kat's heart sank. He hadn't pronounced any feeling of love.

Maybe he's just not into you. He isn't espousing anything at the moment either. This is bad.

Nausea overwhelmed her. The urge to vomit nestled at the bottom of her throat.

Shit. This is about to end. Right after sex too. What a dick! Her bubbling rage tamped down her queasiness. She drove herself into a frenzy. She worked herself up to brace for the impending pain.

"I love you, Kat."

Her eyes flicked up toward him. She narrowed her eyes in confusion. “Huh?”

“I love you. I wanted to tell you many times, before and after having phone sex with you.”

“But you didn’t.”

“I didn’t want to say it until we had been alone together. I felt the need to confirm our connection like *that*, without Seth, before saying it.”

“And you believe it now?”

“No. I believed it before. I didn’t know how to admit to it.”

“Are you in love with Seth?”

“Yes, but I haven’t said it to him.”

“Why the hell not? You know he loves you.”

“I know he wants us to be the perfect threesome. Until we find a way to make it a reality, I don’t want to raise his expectations.”

“You don’t need to have all the answers. Life doesn’t always work out as you want or plan. It’s about living life as the punches come at you. Seth had to do it with his parents’ lawsuit. You helped me when my dad died. You should let him know about your feelings and intentions.”

“Is that all you have to say?”

“No.” Kat kissed Dylan soundly. “I love you.” The words fell naturally off her tongue. “But I think you are being completely stupid about not telling Seth.”

“Stupid? There’s a knock to my ego.” He threw himself backward back on the bed with such force he made the mattress bounce. “Hmm.”

“You are cute when you pout. I love you. And I trust you enough to call you out on your shit.”

“Okay, I’ll phone tomorrow. He needs his sleep for

his marathon. Speaking of which, when did he even plan to run this one? He didn't mention anything about it to me."

"Me neither." She scrunched her face. The suddenness of Seth's decision puzzled her. "Screw his sleep. Never put off telling someone you love them. You never know if it could be your last chance."

Dylan kissed her forehead. It wasn't sympathy in his eyes, but understanding. "Okay. You're right." He grabbed his phone and opened the video-call app.

Seth picked up on the first ring. "Hey." The light was on in the screen's background and Seth's eyes looked wide awake.

Dylan cocked his head to the side. "Hey, did we wake you?"

"No, I was up. You said we. Is Kat with you?"

Kat pushed into the screen view. "Yeah. Shouldn't you be getting rest for your race?"

"You two look comfy. And deliciously naked." Seth's eyes gleamed. "Why are you bothering to call me?"

Shit. Maybe we shouldn't have called. "Sorry. I know sleep is important before a race."

"No. Don't worry about it. Why are you naked and phoning me?" A devilish spark appeared in his eyes. "You both look disheveled. I want details!" He attempted to hide a sexy smirk with his fist, but his smile reached all the way to those blue wonders.

"Yes, alert the media. We had sex." Kat scoffed. She didn't see it as a big deal.

"You're too succinct. Dylan, share all the fun parts." Seth tilted his head to the side and batted his eyelashes. He looked like a cartoonish puppy dog with oversized, weeping eyes.

Dylan cleared his throat. "In a second. I wanted to tell you something first. Although, after having dialed you, I'm thinking maybe I should have waited until we were in person."

Kat shoved Dylan's shoulder. He turned toward her. She mouthed the words. "Tell him."

Dylan took a deep breath. "Since I moved to California, I have had time to get to know myself."

Kat broke in, "Besides his familiarity with his right hand."

Dylan rolled his eyes.

Seth impatiently prodded. "And?"

"We all have grown a lot this past year. I realize you and Kat have had to deal with plenty more than me. I don't mean to minimize those issues."

Kat grabbed Dylan's hand. "We understand."

Seth added, "You were with both of us through it all."

She kissed the side of Dylan's head. He smiled in return and sat up straighter.

"I have undergone significant personal growth in terms of understanding my sexuality over the past year. I think the distance has given me more time to get to know you and Kat separately as individuals. During law school, I used to just see us as a collective. Also, meeting more people out here in San Francisco who are much more open helped me internalize my own feelings."

Leave it to Dylan to express himself in a long-winded fashion of antiquated legal summaries. Kat massaged his shoulders, hoping to spur him along and get to the point.

"You have helped me to become more open-minded, and your strength in owning your own sexuality has been an inspiration to me. Correspondingly, Kat has brought out a different side in me. Somewhere along the line, I fell in love with both you and Kat. I love you, Seth." Dylan turned and kissed Kat. "I told Kat for the first time just a minute ago."

Seth opened his mouth to speak, but Dylan had a way of speaking and dodged interruption.

"I would have waited to tell you in person, but Kat pushed me to call you. I wish I could kiss you right now."

Tears slid down Seth's cheeks and his Adam's apple bobbed.

"And by a wonderful miracle, Kat admitted she loves me too." Kat leaned in and kissed his cheek.

"I love you." Seth's lips moved, but no sound emanated. He placed a hand over his mouth and the tears continued to flow.

"I should have said this in person, because I desperately want to hug and kiss you right now. And I'm sorry it took me so long to realize. You knew all along." Dylan shook his head. "I've said it several times. You guys are smarter than me."

Seth wiped at his eyes. "I love both of you. I can't wait to see you both." The love in those blue eyes shone brightly. "You, my friend, have always been the most gifted in law and logic. And Kat has an elevated positive way of looking at life."

"But you were the one who knew we were right for each other."

"It's only because I have a few more years on you two and experience in unconventional relationships…Speaking of sex."

"I thought we were talking about our relationship?"

"Yes, but I already switched to thinking about sex. So now we are talking about sex. I want to hear all about what you guys have been up to tonight. And no holding back details."

"Later. You need sleep. I don't want to screw up your energy for the race."

"Don't worry about it." Seth set off Kat's bullshit meter.

She leered at Seth. "Spill. Now. You're up to something."

"I'm not actually running a race."

"What the fuck? I fly into town. Finally. And you fucking leave town?"

"Yeah. I knew you two needed to be together. Alone. Without me. It was the lynch pin to getting us to move forward in the relationship together."

"You're fucking brilliant." Kat laughed. "I love you."

"I'm just glad it worked. Wait. What did you say?"

"I love you," Kat repeated. Dylan kissed her on the head.

"This is the greatest night ever," said Seth. "I love you both. I wish I was with you."

"Are you actually out of town? Where are you? When are you getting back?" Dylan rifled questions at Seth like a prosecutor.

"I'll be back Saturday evening before you have to go back to Cali. I'm out east like I said, but I'm here as race support for a colleague. If it wasn't a work friend, I would hop on a plane ASAP."

"Hopefully by then I might have some other good news to share with you."

"Cool, but I want to hear the sex details now." Seth's

arm traveled south down his chest before it disappeared off the screen.

Chapter 22

Seth

Despite the next few weeks of arguing between the two, Seth couldn't wait to see Dylan. He needed Dylan. Kat needed Dylan. They all needed each other's support to get through the one-year anniversary of Kat's dad's passing.

He arrived just after Dylan's flight landed. Even with Dylan's long strides, it would take at least ten minutes before he could walk from the gate to the exit of the massive international airport. Seth veered off to the right and slowed to a crawl along the arrival lane. With no cops in sight, he parked near the terminal's last vestibule. His phone rang.

"Hey handsome. I landed, but need to grab my luggage."

"Great. See you soon."

Seth calmed. Knowing Dylan was in town, not two thousand miles away, comforted him. He wished Dylan didn't have a return flight back to Cali booked already.

He snapped his head to the left upon hearing a whistle blare. The police officer outside his car signaled for Seth to move. *Dammit.*

Focusing on driving, he circled the airport. After proceeding around three times, his knuckles turned white as he clenched the steering wheel.

A half-hour later, his phone rang. "Sorry, it took so long. I'm heading out now."

Relief and irritation brewed in equal portions. "Meet you at the end of arrivals." Seth slowed, keeping an eye out for Dylan.

Dylan waved from the curb. He carried one designer duffle on his shoulder and wheeled a second piece beside him. The amount of luggage only accommodated enough clothes for an extended weekend. Seth scowled. He wished Dylan was returning for good.

He came to a stop, popped the trunk, and hopped out of the car. Dylan greeted him with a chaste kiss. He placed his baggage in the car and Seth slammed the trunk. Dylan caught his attention before entering the passenger seat. "I'm so sorry I'm late." They both sat and closed the doors. Dylan leaned over for a longer, but still modest kiss. "Where's Kat?"

"She ended up falling asleep early. I didn't have the heart to wake her." Seth swallowed the lump in his throat.

"Kat went to bed early? She never does that."

"The stress of the memorial service and the Thanksgiving holiday is getting to her."

"All those firsts after a death in the family are painfully difficult. I hope this coming year is better for her."

"I bet if you announced you are moving here, it would cheer her up."

"For fuck's sake, Seth. Did you have to go there before we even hit the highway? Can't you be happy we are together now?"

"It's hard to be happy at the moment. When we have all admitted we love each other, but you still won't commit to moving here." The well-lit highway and lack of traffic made driving easy for Seth, but he struggled to win the argument with Dylan.

"Well, I'm sorry the job at the state's attorney's office didn't work out," he said, his tone dripping with sarcasm.

"It's just stalled out," said Seth.

"They are holding the position for another guy," growled Dylan.

"He didn't pass the bar the first time. I doubt he will pass in February either. If his father didn't have so much political clout, they would have fired him immediately. When he shits the bed a second time, they will offer you the job for sure."

"But it isn't a sure thing."

"Life isn't a sure thing. Can you stop looking for every conflict?" Seth gripped the steering wheel tighter.

"It's what I do for a living," said Dylan.

"Me too, but life isn't a legal analysis," said Seth.

"Can we please table this for the weekend? Isn't it enough dealing with Mr. Lawson's death and Kat?"

"Okay. But I think we should create a plan to be together."

"Seth, *please* just let it go for now." Dylan reached for Seth's hand. "I love you."

"I love you." He burned with frustration. A year and a half post-graduation, and their chance at a threesome seemed tantalizingly close, but for Dylan's inactions. Dylan had his heart, and Seth wasn't going to give up. They remained silent for the rest of the car ride.

By the time they returned to the city, the lights were off inside Lawson's Bar. Seth parked in the delivery spot behind the bar. He and Dylan climbed up the metal stairway to the outside door of Kat's apartment. Seth used his spare key and entered slowly. His ears perked up for any sign Kat was awake. Nothing.

Dylan headed straight for the bedroom while Seth locked up. He did his best to minimize the noise of engaging the deadbolt. He followed Dylan, but stopped at the doorway. Kat was in bed, curled into the fetal position, holding the covers tight to her chest. Dylan bent over and kissed Kat on the side of her head.

She mumbled, "Don't leave me." She didn't turn toward Dylan. With a groan, she clutched a nearby pillow, and her breathing returned to normal.

Dylan looked at Seth with concern. He stepped closer, tugged on Seth's arm, and guided him into the hallway. "Did you hear her?"

Seth nodded and pulled his lip inside his mouth.

"Did she mean me?" His response was narcissistic, but at least there was consideration about the consequences of his actions.

"I don't know. Maybe her dad? Maybe her mom?" No way to determine for sure who she referred to in her sleep. With the stress of her dad's memorial, she could have been dreaming about him. Was she remembering losing her mother at such a young age? Or did she mean Dylan or Seth?

Dylan sighed. "I need to grab a shower. I'll be back in a few." He gave Seth a quick peck and padded toward the bathroom.

Seth shook his head at Dylan. The man had a brilliant mind for the law. He had a kind heart. He needed to figure out how to interweave the left and right sides of his brain.

The sound of water spraying in the bathroom

washed away some of Seth's frustrations. And thoughts of Dylan naked helped too. From the doorway, Seth gazed at Kat, cuddled into a child-like ball. He entered her bedroom, undressed, and climbed into bed. He curled himself around her petite frame. She gripped the covers tightly. He set his palm on top of her slim fingers. She let out a sigh and her hand relaxed. Seth wove his fingers between hers.

Seth's eyes drifted closed. The scent of fresh soap and shampoo brought to life his other senses. The blanket peeled away from his body and a cool draft blew against his backside. The mattress jostled and Dylan snuggled his damp body against him.

The last bit of tension in Seth's muscles eased. Bookended by Kat and Dylan, Seth counted his blessings.

"Goodnight." Dylan kissed the back of Seth's head.

"Love you."

****

The next morning, Kat's alarm blared at 7:00 a.m. Seth tried to hit the snooze button, but he couldn't because Kat and Dylan pinned his arms.

Dylan sat up first and leaned over Seth. The noise quieted. Dylan kissed the side of his and Kat's heads. "It's time."

Kat remained still. Seth pecked her forehead. "Come on, sweetheart."

"Unh-uh," she grumbled.

"We're here for you, Kat. You'll get through today." Dylan helped her to a sitting position.

"Good. Now do you have anything chosen to wear?" Seth opened her closet door and contemplated options.

When she didn't answer, he looked back at Kat. Her

lips formed a flat line and her eyes appeared vacant.

"I'll go make coffee." Dylan stepped out of the room.

Seth slid hangers in the closet from right to left. "It's chilly out. Something with long sleeves would be good." Her dresses were all sleeveless. A few business suits were crammed in the corner. He feared choosing an outfit which would call Kat's attention once again to how she gave up being an attorney to run the bar. It was much too short to wear to church, but he found a gunmetal-colored blazer Kat had once worn as a dress. A pair of onyx black leggings complemented the dark tones in the jacket. He held the two items up together as an ensemble. "How about this? It's conservative, but still comfortable?"

"Sure." Her lips turned up the slightest amount.

Seth took two steps over and kissed her on the lips. "You would look great in anything." He stared deep into her lifeless eyes. "Do you want to get in the shower?"

"Did it last night."

Even though Seth thought it might do her some good and help her mood, he didn't push. "Do you mind if I grab a quick one?"

She shrugged. Her blasé attitude concerned Seth.

"Okay. Be right back." He stepped out the door and finished up in the bathroom in record-breaking time.

When he returned to the room Kat and Dylan sat on the bed holding coffee mugs. Neither of them had bothered to get dressed.

"Oh, so you are capable of getting done quickly in the bathroom?" Dylan smirked.

Normally, Kat would be the one with a quick jab. At least she smiled at Dylan's mockery.

With only a towel wrapped around his waist, Seth asked, "Can I make you some breakfast?"

Kat shook her head back and forth. "I don't think I could keep anything down."

"Dylan?"

"I'll pass. I want to grab a shower." Dylan kissed Kat.

Seth gazed at Dylan's tight ass covered in boxer briefs as he walked out the door. He narrowed his eyes, remembering Dylan had just showered a few hours ago. *Was he taking matters into his own hand in the shower?* Seth suppressed the thought and willed away his thickening cock underneath the bath towel.

Kat's naked state was not helping him tamp down his arousal. He shifted his gaze and took a big swig of the coffee. "Ow!" He slapped his palm over his mouth. "Fuck…hot…too hot." He panted through the pain.

On the bright side, his burned tongue extinguished his inappropriately timed sexual desire.

Kat chortled behind him. He turned around and her smile eased his pain. "So glad my suffering can make you laugh."

She stood up and kissed his tender lips. "Better now?"

"Yes. Thank you."

The time posted on Kat's smart home speaker glowed like a warning sign. "We should get moving, so we arrive at the church promptly."

Dylan strutted into the room looking gorgeous as ever in his towel and had a suspicious smile on his face.

Kat got up and started putting on her leggings. "My aunt texted me last night. She is picking me up in a limo."

Seth clearly heard the word *me.* Not *us.*

"Would you prefer to go with your family?" Dylan placed his large hands on her slender shoulders.

"I don't want to upset anyone or argue with my family."

"We're here for you. No need to worry about us. We can drive to the church ourselves and meet you there." Dylan kissed the top of her head. He stared at Seth whose mouth was agape and held up his hand, gesturing in a tamping-down motion.

Seth bit his tongue. It pained him to be separated from Kat. Losing Mr. Lawson had gutted him. He needed Kat and Dylan.

He turned away and faced the mirror as he slid on his navy-blue suit pants and jammed each plastic circle through the stitched holes. One button nearly popped off his white dress shirt. Seth balanced the length of his solid-colored tie around his neck.

Dylan's large hand came down on his shoulder. "Nice tie." Dylan mouthed the words, "You, okay?"

Seth's upper eyelids spread his bubbling tears as he opened his eyes. Thank goodness he skipped breakfast because his stomach felt uneasy.

Dylan's hands took over and finished knotting it. "Looks good." He leaned in and whispered in Seth's ear. "Keep it together." Dylan sounded as cold as his mom.

Seth narrowed his eyes at Dylan. *What the fuck dude?*

Kat bumped into Seth as he buttoned his suit jacket. "Sorry."

She was dressed, boots and all. "No worries. You look amazing."

"Thanks. I'll go do my hair." She headed toward the bathroom.

Dylan sat on the bed, tying the laces on his expensive black dress shoes.

Seth asked, “What’s your problem?”

Dylan looked up from his loafers. “We need to be her support today and not add to her stress.” He rose from the bed and lowered his voice. “I love you. We’re going to get through today.”

With pleading eyes, Seth gazed at him

Dylan kissed him. “I know you can get through this.”

Finishing up last, Seth locked the apartment before heading downstairs to the bar. The staff had already started preparing for the brunch scheduled for after mass. He counted all the members of Kat’s family standing in the bar. The limo arrived out front.

Kat’s uncle wrapped an arm around her. “Time to go.”

She turned back to Seth, standing beside Dylan, and mouthed. “Love you.”

Seth did the same. She smiled and continued to walk to the vehicle. The rest of the family crammed themselves into the standard-sized limo. Clearly, the limo wasn’t large enough to accommodate two more people.

When Seth saw how packed it was, it eased his irritation about driving without Kat. He turned to Dylan. “Ready to go?”

After Seth pulled out of the parking lot, Dylan reached for Seth’s hand. “Now that we are alone, what’s going on?”

“Really? It’s like funeral two point O?”

“But it’s not. We all miss Mr. Lawson. And Kat’s doing well now.” Dylan gave his hand a supportive squeeze. "Come on Seth, what's going on?"

Seth bit his lip and gritted his teeth. His chin quivered.

"Seth?"

He fought not to lose control.

"Is it about your dad?"

Seth nodded.

Dylan rubbed his shoulder. The pain in his chest eased, and he took a deep breath. "I feel like it's the funeral I never had for him." The tears fell from his eyes.

"I know it hurts. And it's going to hurt for a long time. But your father isn't dead. He may come around and make amends."

I'm not holding my breath.

Seth swallowed the knot in his throat. "It's not just that. Mr. Lawson stepped in after the whole thing went down with my parents." He sighed and his body sank behind the steering wheel. "I miss him."

"I'm sorry." Dylan held Seth's hand.

He parked in the church lot. Before getting out of the car, he opened the mirror on the sun visor. His hair looked decent, but his eyes appeared bloodshot. Nothing could be done to fix it.

Dylan grabbed a few tissues from the stash in the car and handed them to Seth.

"Thanks."

Dylan placed his arm around Seth's shoulders as they walked toward the entrance. Like a gentleman, Dylan opened the door of the church and allowed Seth to step inside first, but kept his limbs by his sides. Dylan followed behind as they maneuvered between people in search of Kat. An emptiness replaced the security of being tucked into Dylan's possessive hold.

In front of the first pew, Kat's aunt and uncle stood glued to her sides as they spoke to the priest. Seth didn't interrupt but sidestepped the priest in an attempt to put him in Kat's line of sight.

As soon as she turned her head and saw him, she threw herself into Seth's embrace. Her breaths came in heaving gasps. Seth wrapped his arms around her, trying to anchor her to him amidst a storm of emotions, filling his need for her too.

Biting his lip, Seth drew blood, fighting not to lose it along with Kat.

Dylan stepped between them, claiming her attention. He kissed her cheek. "No matter what the priest says today, he cannot come close to honoring your dad the way you have done the past year. I'm sure he's looking down on you every day as proud as can be."

Kat took a deep breath. "I think so. Hopefully, he turns a blind eye sometimes." Her lips drew into a straight line.

A pipe organ playing a classic piece filled the sanctuary. "Sit right behind me." She pointed to the center of the second row. Seth kissed her on the cheek before assuming his position.

Through glassy eyes, Seth searched the other pews. He didn't see any of their other friends from law school. He scanned the entrance near the back and caught Smirnova straggling in at the last minute. The men on each of her sides were fucking hot. They walked with a hair's distance between them. And the smiles on the men's faces looked out of place at a memorial. *Lucky girl.*

Smirking, Seth faced forward. Out of his peripheral vision, he saw Smirnova sliding down the row. Seth and

Dylan stood and hugged her. Seth enjoyed the close-up view standing behind her. "And who are these two lovely lads?"

Smirnova froze, and her eyes widened.

Sidestepping her awkwardness, Seth extended his hand to greet them. *Ian and JD were delicious.*

The priest took his position at the pulpit and they all sat down. While leaning over to reach for a bible, Dylan elbowed Seth in his side. "Seriously? Flirting at a memorial?"

Seth smiled without feeling an ounce of remorse.

Dylan grinned back at him and leaned closer. Remembering his surroundings, Seth sat up and didn't kiss Dylan.

The lack of inspiration in the priest's sermon failed to keep Seth's attention. His mind wandered to the puzzle about Smirnova and her two hotties. He planned to piece the story together later and get all the dirty details about what was going on between those three. Thoughts of sex made the time at church fly.

After the religious service, Seth and Dylan joined Kat and her family back at Lawson's. Full pitchers of beer rested on every table alongside a bottle of whiskey. The atmosphere didn't resemble a memorial. The only similarity to any shiva Seth had attended was the immense quantity of food set out.

Kat's aunt intercepted Seth and Dylan as they stepped inside Lawson's. She hugged each of them. "Sorry about the limo."

Dylan laid a gentle hand on her arm. "You don't need to be sorry."

"No, I do. I left the order up to my husband. I swear the man is an *eejit.* I gave out to him." Her Irish accent thickened.

Kat's uncle stumbled over next to her aunt. "Christ almighty woman. Quit *yer gurning*." He slapped a hand on each of Dylan's and Seth's shoulders. "*Yer* both good fellas. Kat's lucky."

"Thank you," Seth said.

"She's a great friend," Dylan said.

"Do you think I came up the *Lagan* in a bubble?" Her uncle narrowed his eyes at Seth and Dylan.

Seth choked back a laugh.

"Sir?" Dylan looked like a kid getting caught with his hand in a cookie jar.

Her aunt said, "Don't be *scundered.* We know *yer courtin*." She smiled and hugged Dylan and then Seth.

Seth hung on for an extra moment. "Thank you." In a hushed voice, Seth said, "We love her."

"Very much." Dylan slung his arm around Seth's shoulders.

"What's the *craic*?" Kat's accent caught Seth off guard. He turned his head to see her holding a near-empty drink. She brought the bar's signature old-fashioned to her mouth and emptied the glass.

"*Yer* got two grand men," said her uncle.

Kat looked back and forth between her uncle and aunt. "*Yer* not *ragin*?"

"No dear," said her aunt.

"Grand. I'm going on the *lash*." Her uncle finished his stein of beer.

"I'll pour *ya* a pint of *gat*." Kat walked over to the nearest table, picked up the pitcher, and filled his glass with more stout.

Fortunately, her aunt and uncle stepped away, allowing Seth, Dylan, and Kat a moment of privacy.

"Your accent is fucking adorable. I can't believe you've been hiding it."

"Eh, whiskey in the limo."

"Your uncle hit it hard?"

"Just wait. We have the whole day ahead of us. Are you guys hungry?"

His stomach growled. "Yeah. I think I better." He needed to get some food if he wanted any chance of keeping up with the family's marathon of drinking.

Kat stood up from the table. "I'm craving a corn beef sandwich. You coming?" She looked down at Dylan who remained seated.

He pushed his chair back. "I'll catch up in a minute. I need to use the restroom." He walked out of earshot.

Kat faced Seth. "What's up with him? Doesn't he know the Irish leave the serious tone at the church?" Her smile brought relief to Seth. If she could grin through this day, Seth should be able to as well.

"Apparently." He appreciated the lighter attitude as compared to all the shivas he had attended. "He gave Smirnova and JD an earful about how he thinks threesomes can't work out."

"Shhhhh. You heard about Sasha, JD, and Ian?" Kat gestured with her hand to keep his voice down.

"As if they could hide it." Seth laughed. "Anyway, I'm concerned about Dylan."

"Yeah, I know."

"You're not?"

"No. He loves both of us. His issue with returning isn't about you or me. It's about learning to make a choice free from pleasing his parents. You were forced into the situation. You need to allow him to get there on his own." Kat grabbed a corned beef sandwich off the tray on the bar. She handed Seth an extra dish. “Now prepare a plate for Dylan and apologize for putting so much pressure on him to decide.”

Chapter 23

Dylan

Once again, the atmospheric river flooded the streets of San Francisco. While an umbrella protected his hair, the stench of feces in the city offended his sensibilities. He mourned the seasonal end of perfect weather.

Dylan pulled out his phone as he stood in the security line of the courthouse. While waiting his turn for the electronic scanner, he opened his social media. Seth's most recent post included a photo of him and Kat wearing Santa hats outside in a snowstorm with pristine white fluff all around them. He envied the happiness glowing in Seth's blue eyes.

He placed his phone and keys in a plastic bowl. Setting it on the conveyor, he cast aside thoughts of Chicago. After security inspected his briefcase, he ignored a couple of messages, stuffed his belongings into his pocket, and hopped on the elevator. The antiquated equipment moved at the pace of a turtle and blocked out all wireless service.

Upon exiting on his floor, his cell blew up with messages. The pinging noise turned into a continuous hum. He skimmed through the texts while walking to his office, passing the coat hook on the back of his door, and sitting down. He scrolled through message after message, then glanced up from his phone and found a newspaper on the center of his desk opened to the headline, “Senator Slams Gun Ban.” *Shit.*

The judge’s assistant stepped into the doorway with a serious look on her face. “The judge wants to see you. *Now.*”

Of course, he does.

Dylan didn’t hesitate, but she blocked his exit. “Remove your jacket. Dripping all over his office will not improve matters.”

She had a good point. He tossed his raincoat on the hook.

Dylan shrunk his shoulders forward and relaxed all the muscles in his face. He purposefully hid his normally confident appearance. His parents had trained him on how to project an apologetic expression. Funny how his father got him into this uncomfortable situation and may help him get out of it too.

Dylan stood in the doorframe of the judge’s chambers. “Good morning, Your Honor.”

“Sit down.” The overweight judge gestured to the chair. He seemed tense and was breathing like a bull gearing up to attack.

Dylan lowered his gaze, trying to appear ashamed.

“I assume you’ve seen the article in the paper?” He slapped the newspaper down on his desk. “Did you know this was going to be published?”

Dylan raised his head and looked him directly in the eyes. “No, Your Honor.”

His jowls wobbled as he shook his face from side to side. “I didn’t think so. Your work on the draft of the decision never wavered outside of my position.”

“I don’t agree with my father’s stance on guns.”

“I know, but sins of the father speak loudly.”

"Yes, Your Honor."

"Listen, I knew I might encounter this issue when I hired you. And you have proven to be an incredible clerk."

Shit. Am I getting fired? Beads of sweat formed on the back of Dylan's neck. His cheeks heated. *This is the greatest failure in my life. Fuck.*

"I'm not firing you. Contrary to that, I was hoping you would contemplate staying for an extra year. Your grasp of the law and ability to write makes you exceptional at your job. However, wanting to live up to my obligations as a legal mentor, I must suggest otherwise. This position may not be ideal for you."

"Thank you." He refrained from smiling by pressing his lips into a straight line.

"Listen, Christmas break begins in one week. Please consider your future and decide if staying another year is right for you, allowing me time to find a suitable replacement."

"Thank you, Your Honor."

"Dismissed." The judge redirected his attention toward his computer screen.

Upon returning to his office, Dylan removed his suit jacket. His dress shirt clung to his damp skin. He wasn't sure what was more terrifying, almost getting fired from his job or deciding about his future.

Instead of wallowing, he buried his head in drafting the judge's current opinion.

Dylan didn't bother stopping for lunch. By the time he got home after work, his stomach cried out for dinner. The aroma of Italian food wafted from the kitchen, smelling like heaven. Drool pooled in Dylan's mouth.

His feet followed his nose. "Oh my god, it smells

amazing." The source of the scent on the stove drew him closer. "Please tell me it's ready to eat."

"You're in luck. There's also chicken parmigiana in the warming drawer." The chef pulled out a plate and spooned a healthy-sized helping of spaghetti onto it.

"Mmmm. Yes." Dylan took the dish and sat down at the table. He stuffed a forkful of pasta in his mouth. "Thank you." The food hit the spot.

He paused with his fork halfway to his face when his father entered the kitchen. The senator sat at the opposite end as Dylan.

After setting dinner in front of him, the chef held up two bottles. "Wine?" The senator pointed to the one on the left and resumed eating.

It puzzled Dylan that his father didn't greet him.

With an open bottle in hand, the chef showed the label to Dylan. "Would you care for a glass?"

"Please."

She set a full goblet in front of his father and then Dylan.

Dylan looked her in the eyes. "Thank you."

His father's aloofness made Dylan's skin crawl. He itched to pounce at his dad and rebuke his lack of awareness for those around him. Dylan denied his father the pleasure of a fight.

His father kept his gaze on his food.

Look at me. Dylan curled his fingers into a fist below the table. And, for the first time, he appreciated the phrase hot under the collar. He fought the urge to tug his tie loose and unbutton the top of his shirt.

The senator continued looking down at his dish, refusing to offer Dylan the courtesy of eye contact. "Don't act like a child."

How dare he call me a child? Children throw temper tantrums. I have remained calm and haven't said a word.

The senator raised his eyes and glared at Dylan. "You have grown up with countless privileges and opportunities. I will not defend my political stances with you when you do not research all the issues that are considered in the decision-making process of my campaigns. You have choices. It's time for you to make them."

Shit. With one poignant arrow, his father disempowered Dylan's fury. Dylan shrank like an impaled balloon.

His father's stare bore through him. "I will always love you, whatever path you choose to take. If you want a position on my team, I will make it happen. If you want me to make Seth an offer he can't refuse to come out here and join the team too, I can make it happen. If you want to move to Chicago and start on the road to becoming a judge, I will support it too."

Dylan's jaw dropped open. "You spoke to Nana and Grandpa after my interview?"

"My mother never shies away from offering me her opinion." His father harumphed.

"The judge is giving me a week to decide about returning for a second year." Dylan waited for his father's suggestions. He finished off the glass of wine.

"Looks like it's time to make a choice." His father's overstatement of the obvious surprised Dylan.

"Well?" Dylan asked.

"Well, what? You're a grown man."

He expected his father's opinion. "You aren't going to offer me any advice?"

"Dylan, you can analyze the most complicated legal

issues."

Dylan grunted and stared at his empty wine glass.

His father sighed. "One thing I'll suggest is with life decisions you think with both your head and your heart." His father's vacant look made him wonder. *Did he have regrets?*

"Dad." Dylan reined in the formality to shift to a more personal conversation. "You mentioned offering Seth a job."

"Yes. He's bright and could do well out here. And he cares about you."

Dylan's chest ached and tears formed in his eyes. He mumbled, "Kat?"

"It's unlikely that there's anything I can use to tempt her away from Lawson's Bar and her family. I believe she cares about you very much as well."

"But?"

"Listen, I'm able to offer you opportunities. I can't tell you how to feel."

Dylan poked at the food remaining on his plate. He reached for the bottle of wine resting in the middle of the table and refilled his glass.

Deep in his thoughts, Dylan forgot his father was sitting with him. "Not easy to make choices, is it?" his father said. Dylan looked him in the eyes, pleading for advice.

Getting nothing in response, Dylan excused himself and brought his dish to the sink. He needed privacy, not more wine.

Up in his room, he scrolled through photos of himself with Kat and Seth. He loved them dearly, and their absence was unbearable.

He considered his future. With a law degree, a solid

resume, and family connections, he held the power to direct his future, but yet still felt insecure. The back of his neck prickled. He massaged it with his hand as he paced around his bedroom.

Should he ask Kat or Seth for help? Would he offend Seth by debating the pros and cons of him pursuing a career in Chicago? Decided, Dylan called Kat instead.

He strutted back and forth across his room as the phone rang.

"Hey man, I saw the news about your dad's gun issue." *Shit.* Kat didn't answer her cell.

"Hey, Seth. Are you with Kat?" Dylan knew it was a dumb question, but hoped he at least didn't sound disappointed.

"Yeah. I didn't run off with her phone."

"Right," Dylan mumbled. He had to reconsider his approach while being considerate of others' emotions. As if the situation wasn't difficult enough for Dylan. Walking on eggshells made it even more thorny.

"Are you alright? You sound off."

"Is Kat around? So, I can talk to you both?"

Seth spoke away from the phone microphone. "It's Dylan." He resumed speaking, "You're on speakerphone."

"What the hell happened, Dylan?" Kat jumped into the issue.

"You saw the article about my dad?"

"Yeah. How did the judge react?" asked Seth.

"Well, I didn't get fired."

"But?" Seth asked.

"He doesn't think it is in my best interest to continue working there." Dylan rubbed at his temples.

Kat asked, "Is that the polite way of forcing you to

resign?"

"No, but he said he wants to know if I plan to leave by next week."

"Is your dad urging you to join the campaign?" asked Seth.

"Not exactly." Dylan stretched his hand to rub both sides of his forehead.

"You're being evasive. What the hell is going on?" Kat's cut-to-the-chase forwardness made it difficult for Dylan to continue dancing around the topic.

"I need to make a decision about the next step in my career."

"What are you considering?" Dylan appreciated her genuine concern.

Shit. Dylan prepared himself for Seth's verbal assault. "You've got to be kidding me. You have the option of moving to Chicago and you're *still debating* the issue. Do you not love us?" Seth raised his voice.

"It's not like that. I do love you. And Kat."

"Is it that you don't love us enough? And don't give me the excuse again about not having a job lined up here. It's next to a done deal." Seth grunted. Dylan closed his eyes, hating himself for hurting Seth's feelings.

"I'm madly in love with both of you. It's just…"

"You're lucky to have options." Kat's reminder of Dylan's privilege stopped his pacing. He grimaced, sat down on the bed, and slumped over. "You're always great at weighing possibilities. Just like when you helped me after my dad passed. What's going on?"

"Kat's right. Is there something about us that's making you hesitate?" Seth's tone turned much calmer.

"We haven't discussed our relationship." Talking about uncomfortable subjects made his skin crawl.

"We built our connection organically over the past four years. I can't imagine a more solid and real attachment," said Seth.

"But it's all been private." Dylan needed help to open up about the issue.

"I'm not keeping us under wraps, if that's what you want. I did that with my parents and it nearly shattered me."

"I know. I would *never* ask you to do anything of the sort. I love you."

"I'm cool with being out and open." Kat added. "I think my dad knew. I think the fact he made you both pallbearers meant he approved."

Dylan heard a quick kiss between Seth and Kat. He appreciated Seth's gesture because it was exactly what he wanted to offer Kat.

"Your parents are two thousand miles away. They shouldn't be an issue," said Seth.

"Are you worried about friends? I mentioned to Alex that we had a threesome during school. Now, she's dating two men. And Cole knows. Honestly, I doubt it would shock anyone who knows us. There have been rumors."

"True," said Dylan.

"Is it your potential political career?" Seth should have known.

"My dad suggested I follow my heart and not my head."

"Your professional aspirations are a priority to him. Sounds like he's giving you the green light. You can't get a much better endorsement." That was a significant statement coming from a woman with no potential of receiving a parent's approval.

Dylan's face and neck started feeling hot. Looking in his bedroom mirror, his cheeks turned pink. He took a deep breath. *You can tell Seth and Kat anything.* "My grandparents. I'm afraid to come out to them. I care a lot about what they think."

"Oh." Kat and Seth went silent.

"We could announce it to them with you. When you are in town. Yeah?" Dylan appreciated Kat's support.

"What if they don't approve?" Dylan's stomach churned.

"Stop focusing on every catastrophic thing that could pull us apart. Can't we focus on how great it will be? We'll *finally* be together again after the last year and a half." Was Seth correct?

"I can't help it. I plan my arguments ahead of time." Dylan relied on these skills as a lawyer.

"Kat is quick with her words. She'll have your back. And your grandparents already love me. How can they object? With my smile, I'm able to coax anybody into anything. I got you to sleep with a woman for the first time." Seth made a good point. Connecting with Kat changed his life for the better.

"What about you, Kitty-Kat? Is this something you want?"

"I used to be content with decent things in the past. You know, don't tempt fate and push my luck. But now, I believe luck is something you create. We were lucky to have found each other, but we need to put in the effort to continue our luck. I think it would be foolish not to try."

"Perfect. We all agree; you are moving here," said Seth.

"I still have a little thing like my job to work out." Dylan had helped both Seth and Kat during their transitions. They should support him by helping in the decision-making process.

"Nonsense," said Seth.

Fuck off. Seth acted like an ungrateful asshole. Dylan and his grandparents were instrumental in redirecting Seth's career.

"It isn't nonsense to Dylan." Kat understood Dylan's insecurities better than Seth.

"I know. Your job isn't nonsense, but worrying is. You will be fine. Be optimistic." Dylan's anger waned.

He recalled the moment Seth's mom walked in on them and the resulting lawsuit. The image of Kat crumbling upon hearing about her father's death haunted him. Dylan internalized Kat and Seth's pain and the misery lingered. "Really? After all the disasters this past year, how can you be optimistic?"

"Because Kat was right. We are going to make our own luck. We deserve it." Dylan agreed that Kat and Seth deserved it, but remained uncertain about his worthiness.

"Speaking of getting lucky, when are you coming to town?"

Dylan started pacing again. The judge needed an answer. Kat and Seth wanted one too. He discarded his phone on his bed. He freed himself from his constricting shirt and threw the sweat-soaked item on the floor. Back and forth, he marched across his room once again.

"Dylan? You there?"

He picked up his phone off the bed. "Yeah." He rubbed at his temples.

"I know what it means to make a huge change in your career path. What can I do to help?"

How did Kat handle making such a massive decision

all on her own?

"You aren't alone, Dylan. Your parents, your grandparents, and even the judge have offered you their opinions about directing your future. All of which was separate from your relationship with us. They all trust you to choose the right choice." Kat managed the same thing. She listened to those around her, quit her law job, and took over the bar.

"Dylan, even if you don't choose to get a position in Chicago, we'll figure out a solution to make our relationship work. Long distance is tough, but we will find a way," said Seth.

Oh my god.

Tears welled in Dylan's eyes. Seth finally showed a willingness to compromise and accommodate others.

"I agree with Seth. We will make it work, Dylan." The kiss on the other end of the phone sent the tears spilling down his cheeks.

The weight on his shoulders lifted. Without the pressure of meeting other's expectations, clarity surfaced. "I'll fly in on Christmas."

"Really?" Kat's voice brightened.

"My last family obligation is at midnight mass on Christmas Eve. I'll catch the first flight out in the morning. The bar is closed. And we can pick up Chinese food and eat dinner at my grandparents' house."

"I love you." Seth sniffled. Dylan did as well as the joyous tears continued.

"I love both of you," Kat added.

"I love both of you. And Seth, thank you…" Dylan considered several items worthy of gratefulness.

While ordering his list in his head, Kat said, "For suggesting the wooden block stacking game?"

"Yes." They all laughed.

About a week later, Kat laughed so hard she cried as they all sang along with Christmas carols on the car radio, and Dylan and Seth botched the lyrics. Kat's teasing eased the tension as they pulled into his grandparents' driveway.

They locked up the car and paused on the walkway to the front door. Seth kissed Dylan and laced his fingers on his free hand with Dylan's. Kat took his other hand and he bent down to kiss her. Together, they inhaled when the door opened and presented themselves, all holding hands.

"Hi, Nana." Dylan kissed her cheek.

"I'm so glad you're here. Come in quick. It's cold." Nana stepped aside and all three entered.

Seth shut the door behind them, blocking the icy wind, which cut through Dylan's sweater. He packed his winter wool jacket in the shipping boxes, which were midway between California and Chicago.

Leaning down, Seth kissed Nana's cheek. "Where would you like me to put the food?" She pointed toward the dining room table. Seth winked at Kat as he reached for the bag in her arm. He excelled at sucking up.

Kat embraced Nana in a big hug, unlike her usual greeting. *Had the two of them choreographed the entrance?*

"Merry Christmas, Kat. I'm so happy you could join us tonight."

"It's great to be here. I spent the morning at my aunt and uncle's house with my extended family, including many wee ones hopped up on sugar cookies." Dylan reached for Kat's hand and squeezed it reassuringly. While it wasn't her first Christmas without her dad, she missed him.

"After all the chaos, care for a glass of wine?"

"Yes, please."

"Dylan, could you go grab a couple of bottles from the cellar?"

When Dylan returned, everyone was seated in the dining room, including his grandpa. He displayed the label for his grandpa. "Is this okay?"

"That will do. Would you mind opening both before you sit?" Dylan found a bottle opener on the nearby server and placed the bottles in the center of the table.

Nana spooned a helping of sweet and sour chicken from one of the takeout containers. "Dylan, how long are you in town? I hope we can plan another dinner before you go back."

Seth took Dylan's hand, hidden from his grandparents' view. Dylan inhaled. He prepped for this moment. "We will have plenty of time. I'm moving here."

His grandpa put down his fork. "Did the job in the prosecutor's office get confirmed?"

"No, but hopefully after I take the Illinois bar in February, I'll secure one." Dylan put his chopsticks across his plate. Without waiting, he poured wine into his glass, neglecting the appropriate breathing time.

"I have no doubt he will find something." Kat smiled at him from across the table.

Sitting beside Kat, Nana patted Kat's hand. "I agree, dear." Nana peered at Dylan.

He shrunk in his seat and took a large swallow from his wine glass.

"I know that look. I raised your father. Dylan?"

He swallowed around the lump in his throat. He

remained silent. Seth brought their clasped hands from underneath to resting on the table.

Nana noticed the movement. "Is there something you want to say? Is that why you invited both of your friends here tonight?"

Dylan begged Kat with his eyes. She got up from her seat and stepped behind Dylan, placing her delicate hands on his shoulders. "I have something I need to tell you." His mouth went dry. He turned and faced Seth and mouthed the word, "Help."

Seth plastered on his most sensational smile. "We all wanted to share some fantastic news with you. Dylan, Kat, and I are dating." Dylan's stomach plummeted.

"You don't have a health concern?" Nana asked.

"No." Dylan shook his head.

"Are you pregnant?" asked his grandpa.

Kat gasped. "No."

His grandpa finished his glass of water. "You aren't withholding catastrophic news?"

"No, not at all." Sweat trickled down the back of Dylan's neck.

"You sure? Because you don't look well." Nana poured herself a glass of wine.

"He was nervous to tell you." Seth placed his hand on top of Kat's hand on Dylan's shoulder. They were out. Dylan awaited his grandparents' response.

"Your father had the same look when he told us he got engaged to your mother." Nana looked at his grandpa. "That was a heated conversation."

Kat tapped Dylan on the shoulder. "I don't get it."

Seth whispered back at Kat. "Because Dylan's mom isn't Jewish."

"We never expected Dylan to marry a nice Jewish

girl after he came out. And, now, we have a better chance at grandkids." Nana's comment caused Seth to choke on his water.

Jesus. Dylan didn't see *that* one coming. He laughed.

His grandparents' reaction made his head spin. "You aren't upset the three of us are dating?"

"I would rather you date two great people who love you and respect you, than one man or woman who we despise." His grandpa nodded at his wife.

"Cheers to that." Seth raised his glass.

Dylan didn't join the toast. "What about a potential career in politics? It's hard enough for a gay person, but someone in a polyamorous relationship?"

His grandpa shrugged. "It just takes money to work around sexual scandals in politics. Besides, your relationship is more of a controversial concern than an unsavory issue. And, you only intend to run for a judgeship. It's different from a seat in the Senate."

****

The next few months flew by while Dylan spent his days cramming for the Illinois Bar Exam. While much of the material was the same as the California test, he needed to refresh his memory on some issues and gain an accurate understanding of the differences. Despite Seth and Kat's enthusiasm for throwing parties, Dylan refused to celebrate after taking the exam, wanting to wait until he got his results. How could he rejoice with such a high level of uncertainty?

Seth filled a stein with green beer and placed it in front of Dylan. "Drink up."

Dylan looked at his watch. "Seth, it's 8:00 a.m."

"Then drink fast. We need to leave for the parade

soon." Seth's prompting lacked force as he wore a ridiculous crazy green wig, orange shirt, and green suspenders. Nonetheless, Dylan drank along with Seth.

They spun around on the stools and watched Lauren and Kat finish decorating the bar. Kat's other cousin came out of the kitchen with a small tray full of corned beef sandwiches, speared with flags of Ireland. "Here. You all need to eat something before a day of nonstop drinking."

"Thanks, Riley." Kat hugged her cousin. "Firing the old chef and hiring you was one of my best decisions this year." The smile on Kat's face made it worth Dylan's embarrassment of wearing a two-foot-tall leprechaun hat on his head.

While they ate the sandwiches, Kat hopped behind the bar and prepared nine green tea shots. She placed three in front of Dylan and three in front of Seth. "Let's drink to lucky number three." She tossed back her shot first. "One." She motioned for Dylan and Seth to drink. She took the second shot. "Two." The men followed along. She held up the third in the air, and they all drank together. "Three. Lucky me." She leaned over the bar and kissed both Seth and Dylan.

Seth kissed Dylan. "Let's get going. I want to get a good view when they dye the river green.

The threesome set out toward the riverfront. As they neared the bend, Irish bagpipes rang out louder and the streets grew more crowded. Dylan's cell phone vibrated in his pocket. He put his phone to one ear and covered his other ear with his fingers. "Hello." He stopped walking. "I'm sorry, can you repeat that? It's really loud on my end."

The prosecutor from the state's attorney's office

raised his voice. "Our office received advanced notice about the bar results. You passed! I hear Irish music. Are you at the Chicago parade? If so, it's perfect that you are in town because we would appreciate it if you could begin on Monday. I'll email you the full offer. Come in on Monday and we can finalize a position for you here."

His smile burst open and he vibrated with energy. "That's great news. Thank you. I'll see you on Monday."

He hung up and grabbed both Seth and Kat in a three-way hug and kissed each of his partners repeatedly. "I passed and *got the job*!"

"This is a very lucky day!" Kat kissed Dylan. "Not that you getting the job was lucky, you earned it. But now, we have even more reason to celebrate."

"Congrats, Dylan." Seth kissed him then tugged one of Dylan's and Kat's hands. "Let's hurry and get a good spot."

Their luck continued. They arrived just as a crew poured the powder into the river and the two speed boats maneuvered around and around churning the dye until the river turned bright green. Seth ordered Dylan and Kat to pose for a photo with the iconic tradition in the background. "This is a much better shot than last year because we are all together. I have to admit I was jealous when I saw the photo you took with that California guy."

"You never had reason to be jealous. It's always been the two of you for me."

Kat lowered Seth's arm to her eye level and checked out the image on his phone. "Lucky us."

"I have a better plan about getting lucky." Seth hurried them back to Kat's apartment. They used the outside entrance, bypassing Kat's cousins.

Seth slammed the door closed and winced. "I think

I blew our covert mission."

Kat shrugged. "Who cares? But that gives me an idea." She winked and started peeling off her clothes.

"Hell yes." Dylan flung his ridiculous hat to the side.

Seth howled. "Oh my god."

Dylan followed Seth's line of sight. Kat had a temporary tattoo on her mons, reading "Kiss Me I'm Irish."

"Love to." Seth bent and kissed the design.

"Me too." Dylan carried a naked Kat to the bed. He took his turn and Seth joined him. Seth tongued her clit while Dylan fingered her. The scent of sex made his cock harden. Her moans filled the room. Seth and Dylan's combined effort had her screaming in minutes.

Dylan kissed Seth. The flavor of Kat's release on Seth's tongue inspired Dylan. "Kat, don't move. Seth don't leave Kat empty." Dylan directed Seth and went to grab the lube from the nightstand.

Seth accepted Dylan's direction. He slid his gorgeous cock into Kat's delicious wet channel, producing a bewitching noise.

Dylan hurried as he prepped Seth, who readily acclimated for Dylan's entrance.

He pressed into Seth's opening. His chest clung to Seth's damp back. He growled possessively in Seth's ear. "I'm never leaving." Dylan sped up his motion and Seth followed in sync.

"Yes. Yes. Yes," Kat chanted.

All their moans melded together in one collective sigh of relief.

Dylan gasped for air. "Holy shit, that was fucking good."

"I am a fucking lucky man," Seth said as he kissed

Kat, then Dylan.

“The three of us are fucking lucky.”

A word about the author...

Liz Ellyn, an award-winning erotic romance author with degrees in both engineering and law, blends skillfully crafted erotic scenes with heart-wrenching romance. Indulge in life's guilty pleasures on her website at https://lizellyn.com

Thank you for purchasing
this publication of The Wild Rose Press, Inc.

For questions or more information
contact us at
info@thewildrosepress.com.

The Wild Rose Press, Inc.
www.thewildrosepress.com

www.ingramcontent.com/pod-product-compliance
Lightning Source LLC
Chambersburg PA
CBHW072310020726
47501CB00002B/465